GODLY
HEATHENS

GODLY HEATHENS

A Novel

H.E. EDGMON

WEDNESDAY BOOKS
NEW YORK

First published in the United States by Wednesday Books,
an imprint of St. Martin's Publishing Group

www.wednesdaybooks.com

Map Design by Westley Vega

The Library of Congress Cataloging-in-Publication Data is available upon request.

ISBN 978-1-250-85361-5 (hardcover)
ISBN 978-1-250-32443-6 (international, sold outside the U.S.,
subject to rights availability)
ISBN 978-1-250-85362-2 (ebook)

Our books may be purchased in bulk for promotional,
educational, or business use. Please contact your
local bookseller or the Macmillan Corporate and Premium Sales
Department at 1-800-221-7945, extension 5442, or
by email at MacmillanSpecialMarkets@macmillan.com.

First Edition: 2023

10 9 8 7 6 5 4 3 2 1

For anyone worried you might be the villain in your own story. Maybe you are.

I think you deserve a happy ending anyway.

CONTENT WARNING

This story features a candid depiction of mental illness that, although based on my lived experiences, may make some readers uncomfortable. The main character grapples with managing their symptoms, accepting their own and a family member's illness, some internalized ableism, and some ableism from others. There are references to self-harm and suicide.

Other potentially upsetting content includes:

- Graphic gore and body horror.
- Violence, including murder and torture.
- Off-page sexual violence, including experiences that involve children.
- Abuse, including child abuse and off-page domestic violence.
- Mentions of transphobia and racism, including references to slavery and genocide.
- Animal death.

GRACIE, GEORGIA

UNCEDED MVSKOKE TERRITORY
20 MINUTES FROM THE FLORIDA-GEORGIA LINE

APPROX. 96 CHURCHES AND 69 PEOPLE
(AND SOME OLD GODS, APPARENTLY)

1

YOU CAN NEVER COME BACK
FROM THIS

So, I'm standing there, trapped in one of my favorite nightmares, discussing gender euphoria with the demon who lives rent-free in my head.

"None of them know what to think when they look at me. They can't decide if I'm their god or their monster."

Well, maybe not *everyone's* idea of gender euphoria, but certainly *mine*. Boy? Girl? Unspeakable horror.

I call this place the Garden of Death, a field of dry brown grass and wilted flowers, with massive trees scorched and twisted as if struck by lightning one by one. There's a pond at the field's center, its surface as black and still as spilled ink, interrupted only by the glow of the red moon overhead and the occasional scaled creature flicking its tail up from the water. The garden is beautiful and horrifying and I'm never afraid here, though I suspect I should be.

Maybe my unwarranted bravery is because I'm not *only* here. I can see the garden, the forest, the world I've dreamt for myself, but I can see my bedroom, too. The black sheets on my twin-size bed rucked around my knees. My clear plastic backpack tossed by the door, unzipped and overflowing with loose, half-torn papers. Hank, the decrepit dog I've had since kindergarten, sleeping next to me.

The garden is an illusion—a good one. But if I focus, I can see past the smoke screen. It isn't real.

It never feels entirely unreal, though.

The demon's profile is facing me, his head tilted up to consider the navy sky through the lifeless tree limbs. There's nothing about him that immediately indicates anything *demonic*. In fact, I think he's the most beautiful dream-man I've created. Mahogany curls frame the sharp angles of his face. Full, dark pink lips perpetually smirk beneath the straight bridge of his nose.

It's only when he turns his head toward me that I'm struck by the abyss of his perfectly pitch eyes. No whites, no irises, just a cavernous black stretched across their surface, uncannily similar to the pond in his rotting garden.

And only when he speaks do I catch a hint of a forked tongue flicking against razor-sharp teeth.

"You enjoy making them uncomfortable." This would be an accusation from anyone else, but the demon isn't scolding. If anything, he's amused. "We have that in common."

"I enjoy making them uncomfortable," I agree. The tips of my fingers brush dead stalks of grass as I move through them, making a wide circle around my demon. "But let's not overstate our similarities. I've built my dominion on wonder and yearning. You are the king of cacoëthes. Your kingdom knows only bloodshed and damnation."

I literally do not even know what cacoëthes is. Dream-me is *so* big-brained and sexy.

"Bloodshed and damnation. Such a macabre image." Though I'm almost positive I meant to insult him, the demon looks unbothered. When he tilts his head at me, a curl falls across those fathomless eyes. "Are you implying I'm a sadist?"

"I am implying nothing." I shrug. "I am merely pointing out that your people need never debate the monstrousness of *their* god."

"And yet, here you are." His smirk becomes as sharp as a blade.

From my safe distance on the other side of his garden, I curl my fingers into my palm, nails biting into tender flesh. "And yet, here I am."

Of course, there really isn't such a thing as a safe distance, not from my demon.

After all, entire realities divide us, real-me and this thing I stitched together in my nightmare world, and he still won't leave me alone.

He moves to stand in front of me, grasping my chin between his knuckle and thumbclaw, gazing down at me with a look that says he would suck the marrow from my bones if given a flicker of opportunity.

"I could argue monstrosity is in my very design. I am naught without it." His breath ghosts against my mouth.

Dream-me grits my teeth instead of parting my lips. Big-brained but so *stupid*.

The demon leans in closer. He smells like old paper and warped wood and still air; like dust and decay and things long forgotten that are better left that way. "But what might it say about you, creature, that you *choose* to crawl into a monster's nest?"

I want to kiss him, even if it would bleed my mouth. I've done it before—maybe. In all the years since I started dreaming of the demon and this whole unreal world, I've never really managed to follow the plot. Scenes happen out of order. Characters die and reappear. Kisses are given and taken away.

But right now, he's looking at me like he knows what it's like to kiss me. And like *he* wants to do it again, too.

Instead of letting him, I jerk free from his grip to ask, "Did you invite me here to flirt? I was under the impression something important awaited."

"Flirting with you is always important, Magician," he chides with another laugh. "Unfortunately, it isn't why I summoned you." He curls two fingers toward his palm, gesturing away from the clearing. "Come."

We leave the garden behind, disappearing together like two shadows past the tree line.

As we walk, I'm too aware I'm not walking at all. I *feel* my dream body as it moves through the woods, as vividly as I feel my real body, trapped in bed. And I can't seem to control either. Dream-me is puppeteered by someone else's whims. Real-me can never be woken until it's time, and I never know when that is until it's over.

I hate this feeling, always have.

I also hate knowing where the demon is leading me, because I'd rather not venture there. We're moving in the direction of his . . . home? Palace? Evil lair? In any case, I've been many times before, chronologically or not. It's creepier than the Garden of Death, and not nearly as enchanting.

The mouth of the cave is a hollow opening carved into rock, jagged teeth at the base and top that remind me of the demon's own. It's dark here. I snap my fingers, the nails on one hand clicking together and sparking a bright, white light in my palm. It illuminates a long, wet hallway stretching up into the underbelly of a mountain at the edge of the woods we've just left behind. I know, at the end of the hall, we'll reach a rock slab of a door, and beyond that we'll be deposited directly into the demon's bedroom.

We don't make it there, though. As we creep farther along, the darkness begins to dissipate. Another light emerges at the end of the tunnel, different from the light in my hand. This one is closer to golden, a subdued yellow glow pulsing in and out. With trepidation, I clench my fist to extinguish my own light when I realize this fluttering pulse matches the beat of my heart.

There is never light in the lair, not any other time he's brought me here, and there never will be again.

"Are you redecorating?" I tease, even as unease makes my tongue thick. Something is wrong, and I know it.

He turns his head toward me and smiles. Every smile the demon has ever given me has been awful, but there is a hidden message in this one that is particularly vile.

Dream-me swallows. Real-me tries to focus on the pop punk poster behind his head, back in my bedroom in Georgia, barely visible through the illusion.

The light is a girl.

She's beautiful, exceptionally so, and impossibly dainty. Her eyes take up an incredible amount of her face, the widest, bluest things I've ever seen. Her orange curls are as long as the rest of her body, bundles tucked back with intricate golden clips and strands of gemstones. If I tried, I think I could make out every fragile bone in her body past the paper-thin layer of her porcelain skin.

The light is coming from that skin. It radiates off her to illuminate the rock dust in the air around us.

Those beautiful eyes are swollen and red, with tear tracks hanging like lanterns from the corners. Her tears aren't like any I've ever seen. These are made of gold, glittering lines trailing over her round cheeks.

She's on the ground, her hands and feet bound in black ties, another between her lips. My demon's captive.

I've never seen this girl in any nightmare before, but I have the sense dream-me knows exactly who she is.

As carefully as building a bomb, I bite out, "At last, you have gone too far. You must know you can never come back from this."

"Is that true?" Even now, the demon seems mildly amused. He corners me until my back presses against the cave wall, uneven stones digging into the notches of my spine. His hand curls around my waist. Disgust and excitement both feel like nausea. "Do you believe the others ever worried they had gone too far? As they toiled for epochs trying to bury me?"

His mouth brushes against my ear. Maybe it's my imagination, but I swear I can feel the whisper of fangs. "Do you think the *Sun* worried she'd gone too far as your scales tipped further and further out of balance?"

For a moment, the only sounds in the cave are our breathing—his too even, mine too frantic—and the mewling of the poor girl in the dirt at our feet and a dull echo replaying it all back to us.

At length, I raise my hand and press my nails to his chest, shoving him away from me. Five minuscule tears flare in the silken black of his shirt. The demon doesn't stumble, only leans irritatingly against the opposite wall. I flick my gaze to the girl and back to him. "And what is your inspired plan, monster? To take the day for yourself?"

"The day, the night, the land and sea, and all things in between." His smile has yet to soften. "But you think me far more selfish than I am. We will share dominion over this world, creature. Our empire will soon be beyond compare."

The girl—the Sun?—gives a scream around the rope against her tongue.

I meet her eyes. Though she cannot speak, her golden tears say enough. Silently, she pleads with me to ease her fear. To sway her jailer. To save her.

"Why would I continue to aid you?" I demand of the demon, though I do not look away from the Sun. "Already I court the wrath of the others. I took pity on you when you came to me, whimpering like a kicked dog about their abuse, but why would I risk *everything* just to sate your hunger?"

"*My hunger,*" he seethes. "As if your black heart does not ache for every wicked gift our alliance has brought you. As if you do not hide behind my monstrousness so you might deny your own."

The Sun's eyes widen. I look away from her, facing him again. His smile has finally vanished, replaced entirely by teeth.

"The balance is my gift and my burden. I keep the scales. That is all I do. And *this* is not balance."

"Neither is allowing them to keep me leashed!" His hand flies out, grabbing a fist of the Sun's curls. He yanks her backward, dragging her across the dirt to press her against his legs, forcing her throat back. Over her muffled wails, he continues, "And I am not the only one they've kept on a chain, creature. They would suppress us for another eternity before bowing to the true magnitude of our power. But follow me down this path, and there is no force in this world that could stop us."

Dream-me looks down at the Sun, considering the pitiful icon.

Real-me focuses on the slow-spinning ceiling fan overhead, the dirty, dog-fur-covered blades barely visible in the moon-light through my window. Real-me doesn't want to look at the Sun. Real-me doesn't want to be here anymore.

These dreams are rarely *good*. But this one is ratcheting into the worst of them.

Dream-me asks, "How will we do it?"

The demon laughs as the Sun screams.

"You know how." He eyes me expectantly, but I say nothing. With a hint of irritation, he presses, "If we do this, we must abandon the secrets between us. Let us abandon pretext—I know of the blade."

My heart loses its footing. "How?"

"You are not the only scheming creature to whisper in my ear, Magician. But that is a story for another night. We have little time to spare." A spark of light ignites behind those black eyes. "Are you saying yes?"

I tilt my head to glance down the hall from where we came. Too far away to see this world's moonlight through the cave's opening. "The Moon will come for us."

This time, when the Sun screams, the demon takes her jaw between his hands and twists until the bones shatter. She goes as limp and silent as a doll. "As I said—we have little time to spare. Do you have the knife?"

Dream-me looks at the Sun's broken body.

Real-me wonders: If I throw up while I'm sleeping, will I choke to death?

From inside the soft lapel of my robe, I pull free a delicate dagger. It is perfectly weighted to the palm of my hand, fine silver with black gems along the handle. They catch the now-fading light from the Sun's skin, glittering shadows erupting along the cave walls. Wrapped around the blade is the engraving of a snake, curled upon itself and swallowing its own tail.

The demon looks as if he might start to salivate. His forked tongue rolls against his perfect mouth. With effort, he drags his eyes from the dagger to meet my stare. "They wonder if you are their god or their monster. Let us show them you have always been both. It is time this world finally looked upon its reckoning."

A terrible thrill curls up my belly.

With wicked magic and a sharp knife, I carve the power from the dying Sun's body and offer it to my demonic god.

And real-me is forced to watch the whole thing, every laceration, all night long.

2

IT COULD BE WORSE

I barely wake up with enough time to hightail it to the bathroom before I upchuck last night's chalupa combo.

In the aftermath, I drop my head against the toilet rim and groan while saliva dribbles from my mouth. My brain is wading through mud. I'm awake, I know I am, but I can't seem to *wake up*. The only thing tethering me to my body is the sickly weight lodged in my stomach, keeping me curled up on the bathroom floor.

Somehow, Hank has lifted his aching, geriatric body to hobble down the hall after me. He huffs, collapsing in the doorway, eyeing me with those comically droopy eyes. His presence helps a little.

But I can't get the dream to fade.

I've always known I'm not entirely *okay*. That may be putting it mildly. The dreams started when I was little, barely old enough to remember a time when my fantasy world didn't exist. They've always been too vivid, too real, too detailed to be comfortable. They've never felt like other dreams, normal dreams about losing all my teeth or showing up to class naked.

But they've never been *that* bad before. That girl, filleted like a fish in my hands . . .

Fuck this. There's no way I'm going to class today, naked or otherwise.

With maximum effort, I manage to shove my hands against the tile floor and hoist myself up. I stumble, jelly-kneed, nearly falling over Hank, but a hand on the wall keeps me from ending up on the ground again. I weave my way back toward my bedroom as my dog growls, angry with me for making him come all the way out just to turn around and go back where we came from.

Sorry, old man.

My alarm's going off when I drop back into bed. I snatch my phone off the bedside table, shutting off the blaring, and pull up my texts to send a message to my mom. Gotta let her know I'm sick, not just ditching.

There are already seven texts waiting for me. The number elicits a mixed-bag response. On the one hand, I *do* love to be perceived, and I *will* die if I am not the center of constant attention. On the other hand, it is *six o'clock in the morning.*

Five are from different potentials at school, townies I'll swap DNA with at some point but haven't found the time to yet. One is from Mom, reminding me she took the car for an early shift and I'll have to make the trek down to the bus stop. (No, very much I will not.) The last is from Enzo, sent at three in the morning. It's the only one I care about.

Little Dumbass

Good morning, Gem, my darling, my love, my capricious little tornado locked in a cage of human flesh. It is not exactly morning as I type this, but I suspect it will be by the time it finds

your eyes. Please remember to eat a real breakfast and take your
medication before heading off to English class today, else your
brain will short circuit and you'll fail your very important exam.
Such a thing would be rather unfortunate, especially as I would
have no choice but to mercilessly mock you afterward. ☺

Enzo Truly is my best friend in the world, a flamboyant
Native trans boy in Brooklyn I'd give an organ just to hug one
time. And I *hate* him.

I hate him in the way that I've never seen another person so
clearly before, in the way that I'm so close to him it's more like
I'm inside of him, in the way that everyone is kind of disgusting
when they're peeled back all the way.

And anyway, Enzo borders on being incapable of acting human. No one texts like this. *He* doesn't even text like this when
he's not making an effort to be the most theatrical person alive.
He says he's adhering to queer culture by being ostentatious. *I*
think he's uncomfortable being genuine without a performative
element.

I punch off a reply, still waking up, trusting autocorrect to
catch any typos.

you?? telling me to take care of myself while sending your
poor body into another episode of sleep deprivation?? get
off my ass and go the duck to sleep, please.

I hope he doesn't respond because he's sleeping. And also, I
hope he *does* respond because I always want to be talking to him.

As much as I hate Enzo, I love him more than I ever knew I
could love another person. I don't even like people. I don't even

know that I like *him*. But I love him so much it scares the shit out of me.

And he's right. I really *can't* skip class today. I have my English midterm, worth an outrageous portion of my grade, and Ms. VanHoos has a tree-sized stick up her ass when it comes to makeup tests.

Flunking out of my junior year would be an option if I planned to rot away in Gracie, Georgia, the rest of my life. Which I don't. I need my GPA as sparkly as possible when I start working on applications this summer. I have to *somehow* be more impressive than the Manhattanite brats whose parents can buy their way in, and *also* convince one of these colleges to give me all their money so I can afford to go there at all. And that means actually caring about my education, at least for the next few months.

Resigned, I drag myself back out of bed, just in time for Hank to reappear in the doorway and stare at me in wounded disbelief.

Gracie is a town split in two. There's the country—backwoods littered with farmhouses built before the Civil War; plantations tucked behind iron fences like keeping others away will hide the shame of what happened there; cotton fields and gator-infested swamp water nestled up together. And then there's downtown—mom-and-pop shops selling whatever the hell artisanal soap is; public housing for the 40 percent of its citizens living below the poverty line; cookie-cutter apartments built in the last ten years in a last-ditch effort to save this place from extinction.

This town'll be dead before too long, and we'll all be better off for it. Gracie's the sort of place people stay when there's no other option, and it sure as hell isn't somewhere people *choose*.

Except my mother. She grew up here, but she got out; went to college, became a nurse, started a perfect white-picket-fence life in the suburbs of Atlanta. I'd be there now, if she hadn't moved us back here four years ago. Now we're *country people*, living out in the boonies in the ancient two-bedroom she grew up in, handed over from her parents when they retired down to Tampa. She swears she'll finish fixing it up someday. I think they told her the same thing when she was a kid.

Then, my mother isn't exactly most people, not where the demographics of Gracie are concerned. This town is built on the bones of Mvskoke people. Her own ancestral lands—*our* ancestral lands, Seminole territory—are less than a two-hour drive from here. When we left Atlanta, when she said she needed to crawl back to the safety of her roots, I know she didn't just mean the little town where she went to high school. She meant something buried deeper.

And I get it. The language spoken on these lands all those years ago is the same one that belonged to our people; it's the same language I feel sometimes on the tip of my tongue, unable to speak it because it's been robbed from me, but still living inside me like a muscle memory I can't actually remember. I don't know many people who would understand me if I said this out loud, but I swear the land *itself* in Gracie speaks that language.

Sometimes, it talks to me. And I get the feeling, as clumsy as my mouth is, it understands me when I talk back.

But this whole country is built on bones. I still have to survive in it. And Gracie wasn't designed for me to survive in.

So—New York. Enzo gets it. He's only been back to his

ancestral land twice in his whole life, all because someone put an imaginary border between where he was born and where he comes from. But he's happy in Brooklyn. He has friends, and he actually likes the adults in his life, and he . . . *does things.* Maybe that doesn't sound like much. But compared to Gracie, it's everything. I gotta get out of here.

It's not even my mom's fault, I guess. It's my dad's. If he hadn't been crazy, if his crazy hadn't ruined their marriage, if the divorce hadn't snapped something inside my mom so hard she crawled back home licking her wounds . . .

But I don't think about my dad.

Outside, the hot morning air is damp and thick. The sky is still dark, black only just beginning to lighten into purple, the silvery glow of the moon peeking over the tops of oak trees. Frogs croak obnoxiously from out of sight while little flying terrors zoom in the air overhead. The motion-sensing light struggles to flicker on when I step onto the porch.

The South isn't as bad as people who've never lived here like to say it is.

Look, I'm pretty sure there are Confederate-flag-humping neo-Nazi transphobes up north, they're just a little quieter and a lot richer than the ones here. I've yet to get hate-crimed in the school cafeteria—more often than not, people just aren't sure what to do with me. Which is fine—more often than not, I'm not sure what to do with them, either.

But the food here is god-tier. Country music is so much better than most people are willing to admit. And there are few things more fun than getting in a big truck and driving too fast down a mud-soaked back road.

Doesn't mean I want to die here. Just means it could be worse.

The mile to the bus stop is all dirt. While the sun creeps up, the air goes gray and foggy, everything hanging in that unreal space between night and day. It reminds me of my dreams. The fog is thick enough I can just barely make out what's ahead of me, like looking at my bedroom while I'm asleep. I think of the demon, and the hair on the nape of my neck bristles. I think of the beautiful girl with glowing skin that went dark, the Sun bound in black rope, and if I'd actually eaten breakfast, I'd probably lose it.

Terrible things have happened in my dreams before. I've done awful things. I've had awful things done to me. But last night felt like a tipping point. A therapist might ask why my subconscious mind is so committed to this fantasy about blood and gore and magic and sex demons. But first I'd have to find a new therapist, and then actually tell them about the dreams at all.

I've never told anyone about them. I'm not *that* stupid.

There aren't a lot of neighbors out here in the middle of nowhere, but down at the almost-end of the dirt road, facing each other from opposite sides of the street, are the Gracie Church of God and the Wheeler place.

Strange family. There's a brood of kids, maybe a dozen of them, all homeschooled so they can run the farm. The house is tucked back far enough into the fog that I can only just make out its fuzzy outline. Out front, the field is filled with cows, dotted black and white and brown. I stop a couple feet short of the metal fence to try to get a look at them.

Living out in the country might not be my endgame. But I don't think I'll ever get past the point where I pass a field of cows and think "Look! Cow!"

It's hard to see most of them through the haze, but one stands close enough to the road to make out. She's beautiful, tan hide and a beige chest, a brown mouth, and a white almost-heart on the center of her forehead. Big black eyes stare back at me when I cluck my tongue in her direction. I grin, raising my hand to wiggle my fingers at her, and—

Well, she's not actually looking at me, but beyond me. Her tail flicks, a nervous warning. I let my arm fall to my side and twist my head.

The only thing behind me is the church. The parking lot is empty, still too early in the morning for even the most dedicated parishioners. The building itself is right at the edge of the road. It's ancient and falling apart, but then, that's not exactly uncommon in Gracie. And it's small, little more than an outhouse and just as impressive, with white paint chipping away on all sides to reveal the rotting wood underneath. Maybe it's nicer inside. I wouldn't know. I've never actually set foot in *any* church.

It's not that I hate their god. It's more like he's a neighbor who's never introduced himself to me. I see him around all the time, sometimes his dogs shit in my yard or I smell whatever he's grilling on his back porch—but neither of us has ever tried to be friends. It's not a big deal. You don't *have* to be friends with your neighbors.

There's a cross out front draped in fog, and a letterboard sign next to it. I assume the words are from a Bible verse.

So we fix our eyes not on what is seen, but on what is unseen, since what is seen is temporary, but what is unseen is eternal.

I look back at the Wheeler field and the damn cow who's still staring right past me. Unblinking, unmoving except for that twitching tail.

That weight in my stomach hasn't eased since I woke up.

I turn toward the church again. Nothing. Not as far as I can see, anyway. The farther I look, the foggier things get, and the more difficult it becomes to make out any shapes. Past the empty parking lot and flimsy old building is the tiny little cemetery. From here, I can only barely make out a hint of headstones. Other than that, it's just fog, and fog, and fog, and the shadow darting through the graveyard.

Wait.

Shadow?

Vaguely person-shaped but moving too quickly to actually *be* a person, a shadow darts between the tombs. My mouth goes dry. My palms tingle all the way to my fingertips.

Behind me, the cow gives a long, low cry, and the shadow begins jolting toward the road.

"Mornin', Echols."

The thick country twang interrupts my thoughts, slamming the brakes on my terror.

And the shadow is gone. Actually, not just the shadow. I blink once and the fog has cleared up. The graveyard is empty, but the parking lot isn't. When did a car get there?

When I turn around, a few more cows have huddled in front of the gate. And Buck Wheeler is with them.

Buck's the oldest of the Wheeler kids, maybe a year younger than me. He's small for his age, built like a baby bird, with gaunt cheeks under his too-big hazel eyes. Every visible inch of his tan white skin—and there's a lot of visible inches, since the kid is wearing nothing but flannel pajama bottoms—is dusted with freckles. He rubs his buzzed head against the side of one cow's face and smiles at me with prominently crooked teeth, a gap between the front two.

"Morning."

He's a nice enough kid, but as weird as the rest of his family. Even if most people are trying to claw their way out of Gracie, I'm pretty sure the Wheelers are gonna be here generation after generation. Where else would people like them go?

"Should hurry up and get to your stop. Bus is gonna be here any minute." He giggles, like he's told a funny joke, though I couldn't guess what the punch line is.

There's no way I'm actually going to be late, though. I left with plenty of time. I glance down at my phone to double-check and—wait, *how*? It's been half an hour since I left home. How's that possible? How long was I standing here staring at nothing?

"Later, Buck!" I book it down the road, kicking up dust as I go. I think I can still hear him giggling behind me.

> pretty sure i bombed the english test.
>
> so glad i dragged my ass out of bed for this.

I text Enzo at lunchtime, choking back on anger that would like me to throw a tantrum. VanHoos can *eat me*.

The GHS cafeteria is half inside, half out. No one sits inside unless it's raining, so the courtyard is packed. I still have my table of one. A few people acknowledge my existence when they pass. No one tries to join me.

For the first time all day, I remember to check my unread texts. Most are awkward "hey" or "you up?" messages I wouldn't have responded to even if I were awake when they came through. I need everyone to like me, but I have no energy to make conversation when the bare minimum is all they're offering. I should be pursued passionately, with vigor, so I can just be hot and funny and throw in a wink every now and then.

There's *one* from Indigo Ramirez that's interesting. Indy is one of those kids who sits in the back of class with hood up and headphones in, drawing eyeballs or anime characters. Weird—but interesting. And beautiful.

The text is nothing but a selfie. In it, he's lying stomach-down in bed, facing a full-length mirror on the nearest wall. He's holding the phone lazily, his pose designed to look as not-posed as possible. (A goal that's embarrassingly familiar to me.) The bare curve of his spine dips down toward the hem of his boxers, his backside arched *juuuust* enough to be on the wrong side of safe-for-work. Or the right side, depending on the judge.

I came out in the sixth grade. And even though Atlanta isn't some LGBT haven or anything, I at least knew other people—kids and adults—who were *like me.* When we up and moved to Gracie, I was terrified of having that taken away from me. I didn't want to be alone.

And don't get me wrong, I'm lonely as shit. But not in the way I was expecting. The percentage of queer kids isn't actually any smaller in a town like this. It's just that less of them can talk about it in public. A lot of them don't even talk about it in private—until they meet me.

I've been responsible for *many* first times since I got here. My sacred duty to the agenda, or whatever.

Indy's yet another possibility to consider. Without thinking too hard about it, I shoot back a selfie of my own.

It's from a week ago. I'm sitting on the bathroom sink at home, wearing nothing but denim cutoffs and a black binder. My hair, thick and long and hickory brown, is braided to show off the shaved sides. I've got my cheek resting on my knee, chin tilted to show off my jewelry—six piercings in each ear, a bridge, hoops in my nostril and septum, a labret, all yellow gold against my copper-tinted complexion—and the line of skin that stretches from my binder to jeans, belly and waist and hips.

I'm good at selfies. It's hard not to be when I take a hundred at a time and delete all but one, analyzing the most infinitesimal changes.

Still. I'm hot. The students at Gracie should be grateful they get to look at me, much less anything more.

More being limited to usually decent sex. Not anything as scandalous as going on a date or hanging out in public. It's one thing to use me to figure out their own shit, but another thing entirely for anyone to admit they might *like* me.

In New York, Enzo's got all these other trans friends. They spend time at each other's houses and casually kiss on the mouth and hang out at *gay bookstores,* because that's a thing that exists there. He says they already like me.

Ugh. Whatever.

"Gem, my deity." Ezekiel "Zeke" King suddenly appears, dropping down onto the bench across from me. His size makes the table feel tiny, when a moment ago, when I was alone, it was huge. Though my patience for cis men is thin, Zeke is one of the kindest boys I've ever known. He does not have a single thought in his head.

Sleeping with him would be like sleeping with a golden retriever. I can't believe I trained him to call me a deity.

"Zeke, my boy." I lock my phone and set it down so I can aim finger guns at his chest. "What can I do for you?"

"I been thinkin'. You're on testosterone, right?"

"No." The possibility of taking T isn't off the table. Maybe it's something I'll pursue later, when my real life has started.

Still, I cannot wait to see where Zeke is going with this.

"Oh." He frowns, rubbing a hand over the back of his neck, shifting his giant body slightly. "But some of y'all—people, you know, they take testosterone, right?"

"Yes. Some people do."

"Yeah! So, didya know you can't take testosterone and play football?" His entire face screws up in thought, bushy blond eyebrows meeting over the bridge of his nose, pink lips forming a circle. He raises his hands, motioning like he's juggling something. "Like, it's a *steroid*. You're on *steroids*, you know?"

"*I'm* not," I remind him. "And I think the stuff they give trans people is different than what athletes take to cheat at sports."

Maybe. Actually, I don't know. Knowing that would require me knowing anything about sports in the first place.

"Huh. But they're both called testosterone. . . ." He nods very, very slowly. "I don't really know what that means. But I think I'm onto something."

What he's probably onto is the first connection his brain has ever tried to make.

"You know what, bud, keep thinking on it. You'll get there."

He smiles so big my own cheeks get sympathy pains. "You sure are crazy, Gem."

"That's what they tell me." I shake my head with a smirk as Zeke throws himself onto his feet and trots away, very possibly on his way to solve the issue of trans athletes being banned from sports.

I adore him. That was exactly what I needed to not think about that English test. Maybe the day can still turn around.

Someone slides in front of me, blocking my view of Zeke's retreating back. I tilt my head up to her face just as she's dropping into the seat he vacated.

Suddenly, my lungs aren't big enough to take a deep breath. She's the most breathtaking girl I've ever seen.

"Finally." She reaches across the table to place her hand over mine. "Sorry I'm late."

Unfortunately for us both, I've never seen her before in my life.

3

GENUINELY CANNOT DO THIS ANYMORE, BESTIE

The girl being a stranger is only notable since Gracie is the size of a thumbtack. I would've remembered seeing her before.

She's *unreal*. Pretty, yes, with sharp cheekbones and round lips. Her skin, a gold that reminds me of candlelight, is perfect in way that would be annoying if she weren't so hot. And I'd be a liar if I pretended not to notice her . . . impressive chest.

But "pretty" isn't the right word.

I'm tall (by transmasc standards), but she's got a few inches on me, clearing six feet. The rest of her matches her height—broad shoulders and a round belly, thick arms and wide hands. One of her muscular biceps is *tattooed*, the head of a bear surrounded by pink and purple flowers. She's got giant mismatched earrings—a Ouija board in the left lobe, a sword in the right. Her eyes are mismatched, too. They're both brown, tinged with enough cherry they could almost be red, but one of them is splotched with sage green like spilled paint across the iris. Her black curls are pulled into a half-assed bun, wild and thick enough they look likely to pop her hair tie.

The bear isn't the only tattoo she has. Three lines run from her russet-red lower lip to the bottom of her dimpled chin. I recognize them as tribal markings, though I couldn't name the Nation they're from. Even if it were possible I didn't remember her for any other reason, I would have remembered a Native student with traditional tattoos.

She's still touching my hand. I feel like I should apologize. Or pay her.

"I was born in *Alaska*," the girl continues, seemingly oblivious to my gay turmoil *and* the fact that we do not know each other. "It's a long story. We give our families everything they need, and they still find ways to screw it up. You know what I'm talking about."

I absolutely do not know what she's talking about.

"Anyway." She blows out a hard breath, sending a curl flying toward her forehead. It falls right back in her eyes again. "Do you have the knife?"

And just like that, I'm back in my nightmare.

"As I said—we have little time to spare. Do you have the knife?"

All morning, I've tried to fight my way back to normal, but I haven't been able to shake the feeling of *wrongness*. I've just been stumbling around in a fog, like I've got one hand in this reality, and the other trapped beyond a door I can't actually see. Now this?

My fingers tremble beneath hers. The girl's bushy eyebrows crease, concern decorating her face.

She brushes her thumb against my knuckles and my breath catches its sleeve on my teeth.

Somehow, I manage to choke out an eloquent "Huh?" and

yank my hand away. It's clammy and cold and boring on its own.

A beat passes, this girl staring at me like a puzzle, until she finally mutters a curse, then, "You don't have any idea who I am, do you?"

"Well . . . I didn't wanna say anything." Somehow, mouth on autopilot, I string the words together while my head explodes. "But I'm pretty sure I'd remember you if we'd met before."

I'm a lot more than pretty sure. Everything about this girl demands my attention. I wouldn't be able to forget her. Not unless there was something seriously, seriously wrong with me.

Which is a whole other thing we don't have time to unpack.

"Well, you wouldn't, because you don't." She rubs the tips of her fingers into her eyelids, taking a deep breath. "Okay. It's fine. Death and battle aren't here yet. We have time to fix this."

I think she's talking to herself, not me. Still. "Who and what, now?"

My dad, the last time I saw him, was making about as much sense as this girl. I was twelve at the time, and didn't really have the *emotional maturity* to grasp what was happening, still blaming myself and my coming out for the way my family fell apart. I'd tried making sense of his rambling, tried to under-stand what he wanted, and felt guilty when my mom finally took me away from him.

"Look, normally, I'd give you more time to process, but we don't *have* time. I have no idea where the knife ended up, and if one of them finds it before we do, it's game over. I need your help. And that means you have to remember. Have you at least been having the dreams?"

The dreams.

The world seems to crawl in slow motion, background noise

falling away until it's just the two of us here in the courtyard. I can see my classmates, but only through a filter, like a photograph where they've all been blurred out and this girl, this weird, cryptic girl, is the only thing with any sharpness left.

Saliva bursts along my tongue, nausea rolling through my gut and creeping up my throat. Goose bumps collect along my arms. Tremors burst under the surface of my skin.

"I have no idea what you're talking about." This is a lie, of course. But what else am I supposed to say?

"The dreams, Gem." How does she know my name? "The ones of the Ether. The ones that feel like you're still awake."

The Ether bounces around in my head like the screensaver on an old DVD player, changing color every time it hits the side of my skull. It's completely unfamiliar . . . but it isn't, maybe . . . but I can't remember where I might know it from.

I realize, discomfort bubbling in my gut, that talking to her—or being talked *at* by her—makes me feel the same way I do when I'm dreaming. Like everything is happening in a fog I can't quite pick my way through. Like the moment is happening *to* me. The sinking feeling of unreality gets comfortable in my chest, stretches out into my limbs and makes me heavy.

I think about the shadow moving in the graveyard this morning, the one that disappeared in an instant along with the fog.

What if my dreams really are starting to bleed into my waking life?

What if I plucked this girl right out of my head?

Bile claws at the back of my mouth, and I grit my teeth. No. I don't accept that. I *won't*. I force myself to blink through the filter, to look at the people around us.

A group of girls at a nearby table nods in our direction, likely making commentary about her appearance. A boy in a letterman jacket hovering by the trash cans stares at her with his mouth partway open.

Other people can see her. She isn't a dream. I'm not hallucinating. I'm fine.

Well, no. Something is still very wrong. But I'm not as bad off as I could be.

"I. Do not know. What you're talking about." It tastes like a lie, and I don't understand.

Something softens in her expression. She frowns, barely shaking her head. "I'm sorry. I know this sucks. You deserve a gentler introduction. And I hope one day soon you'll realize that I'm only doing this because I love you." She takes a deep breath. "So. My name is Willa Mae Hardy. And everything else aside, honey, it's really good to see you again."

My panic nausea makes room for a small rush of sapphic nausea at her words.

Anyway.

Nothing about the name Willa Mae Hardy rings a bell, not even in the same weird, detached way the Ether did. I *know* I've never met her.

So, how does she know me? How does she so *clearly* know me?

As if she hadn't proven that already, her next question is "So, what the hell happened to your dad?"

It isn't even just the question that takes me off guard. It does, and I hate it, but more than that, it's the way she *asks* the question. Completely unbothered, no hesitation, like we're best friends catching up on school gossip. Not at all like she's a complete stranger who just asked to unlock some of my level-ten trauma.

But how does she know *anything* happened to my dad?

I dunno, Gem, maybe the same way she knows about the dreams?

No. She *can't* know anything about me. She's crazy, and rambling, and my brain is leaping to make connections. I've never heard of the Ether, and she has no idea about my night-mares.

Not even Enzo knows. How would I go about explaining to anyone that I spend my nights trapped between two worlds? Watching visions bleed into reality? Considering my family history, I know exactly how that conversation would go.

"I don't know what you're talking about." I sound like a parrot.

"Well, it's just you and your mom, right? But your dad's not dead, and he's the one with the Campbell blood. If you don't have your memories, and the knife's lost, he must've been cut out of the loop. What happened to *his* parents?"

My eyes rise to her face. She's watching me with a soft ex-pression, genuinely curious instead of critical.

Campbell blood.

I never met my dad's parents. They died young, leaving him and his little brother orphans when they were still in elemen-tary school. I've heard plenty about them, though. His mother was Diana Echols—maiden name Campbell.

That can't be a coincidence. At a loss, I answer honestly. "Freak accident. He was just a kid."

"*Oh.*" She nods, clucking her tongue. "Yeah. Record keep-ing's not a perfect system. Families fall apart, things go missing. *I* almost got lost. If my grandfather hadn't found me . . ." Her voice trails off and she shakes her head. "Anyway, that sucks. I'm sorry."

Is she offering her condolences for my dead grandparents? Like, thanks, but it's not as if I had the chance to miss them.

I think their deaths did a number on my dad, though.

"It's . . . fine?"

"Well, no, it isn't. If they'd lived, you'd know who I am instead of sitting there having this little crisis. Now we have to play catch-up. And I don't think you're going to like it." She sighs, making a fist and propping her chin up on her knuckles. "But it will *be* fine. Once we have the knife back. Once we get away from Poppy and Marian. Things will be okay then. We'll be all right."

She sounds like she's trying to give me a pep talk, or maybe convince herself of whatever it is she's saying, but . . . okay.

"Who are Poppy and Marian?" I don't want to feed into the delusion, but I don't actually know what else to do.

"The worst. Both of them." Willa Mae rolls her eyes. "Hey, I don't suppose I could convince you to come to my place after school today, huh?"

I.

What?

"Um." My head pounds. "I . . . would rather not."

"Yeah. That's what I figured. Unfortunately, we're crunched for time, so getting you to believe me might require some trauma." It would sound like a threat—it definitely *should* sound like a threat, she's planning to traumatize me—except she sounds genuinely upset. "If there were any other way . . . but we *have* to find the Ouroboros."

Ouroboros. She says the word and my heart beats like it's trying to run away. Why does that sound familiar?

Willa Mae's still talking. "It's not like anyone eased *me* into anything. At least *I'm* not strapping *you* down in a torture chamber."

"I'm sorry, what? Did that happen to *you?*"

She shrugs, tucking a loose curl behind her ear. Maybe she would answer me, but the bell blares at the same moment, cutting off whatever was coming.

Around us, the rest of the student body starts to head to class. I can't move.

Willa Mae stands and tightens a hand around the black strap over her shoulder. The look she gives me is long-suffering, even though it has no right to be. "Just be careful. Try not to run into death before I find a way to bring you back, Magician."

And then she's gone, disappearing into the throng of people, nothing but a few inches of her head visible until even that vanishes inside.

I'm alone when I finally sputter, "*Magician?*"

I've been called that many times before. Just never while I was awake.

"*You are not the only scheming creature to whisper in my ear, Magician.*"

Fuck. This.

I can't do today. I gave it my best shot, dragging my ass to school to take the English test I probably failed anyway, and now . . . now what? I don't know. Whatever is going on, I'm not going to figure it out while my brain tries to ooze out of my ears. What I need, and all I *want,* is to go home, crawl into bed, and force Hank to take a nap with me. A real nap, uninterrupted by sharp teeth or golden blood or beautiful and unhinged people.

I text Enzo again.

genuinely cannot do this anymore, bestie.

i'm leaving for the rest of the day. call me when you get

home from clown college.

Always best to end any messages about my questionable grasp on sanity with a joke, so he knows everything's totally fine. *Clown college* means the performing arts high school where Enzo's a senior.

If anyone spots me slinking from the courtyard toward the parking lot, they don't say anything. I don't have the car today, so I can't *actually* go home. But right next door is the Piggly Wiggly, where I *can* drown my sorrows in Flamin' Hot Munchies until a twelfth grader with a half day wanders over and I convince them to give me a ride.

Mom's home by now. I *could* call her and tell her I'm sick, ask her to come get me.

I'd rather loiter at the grocery store.

Halfway across the parking lot, a breeze kicks up, sending hair across my face. I snatch the elastic band off my wrist and tug it into a ponytail.

The breeze brings with it a nasty burst of cold, too. *Cold.* It's March in the Deep South. It doesn't dip below the sixties, and it was hot as hell when I left my house this morning. So, explain why my nipples are stabbing through my sports bra right now.

At the edge of the lot, where I can start to make out the faded Piggly Wiggly sign through the trees surrounding the campus, asphalt morphs into dirt. It always smells like a dispensary out here, the spot where stoners hang out when skipping class. Not that *I'd* have firsthand knowledge of that.

As soon as my shoes hit dirt, my stomach churns again. Saliva threatens to gag me. The wind carries an awful smell right to me, and I dry-heave under the assault.

Where the hell is it coming from? I look back toward the school, searching the parking lot for anything out of the ordinary. Nothing. But I swear I've smelled something like this before, when field mice get in our house and die in traps in the pantry, and . . .

Death. It smells like death.

As soon as the thought occurs to me, the smell is gone. I blink into the glaring sun, watching the doors of the school through half-open eyes. My stomach settles. It even seems a little warmer.

Huh. Weird.

I turn back around, and there's a girl standing so close I could reach out and touch her.

She looks ill. That's the first thing I think. She's the palest girl I've ever seen, with translucent skin the color of bone. I can make out the blue and purple veins in her arms. Her lips are gray and chapped, limp blond hair hanging to her chin, ice-blue eyes sunken into her face.

Her outfit doesn't match her at all. White tights with plastic purple and yellow daisies sewn onto them. A striped crochet dress in varying shades of pink, reminiscent of the lesbian flag if you squint. *Blue hearts* painted around her eyes.

Neither of us moves. Me, because I'm trying to coax my heart to crawl out of my ass. Her, because she might actually be a limited-edition life-size Corpse Barbie.

Finally, I say, "Um . . . hi."

When the girl smiles, her dry lips crack until they bleed.

She takes a step toward me. I'm surprised by how gracefully she moves, considering she looks like the wind might knock her over.

"How did you pick the name Gem?" Her voice doesn't match her face, either. It's deep and lyrical, surprisingly beautiful to listen to. Her accent isn't Southern. I wonder where she's from. "See, the poppy flower, it's been used to represent death for a long time. That's how I picked mine. But *Gem*. Gem, Gem, Gem. It isn't your legal name, is it?"

It isn't.

My mom isn't perfect, but she could be a lot worse. She never misgenders me, has never tried to force me to be less of myself. When I came out and extended family had issues, she went to bat for me, always made it clear she'd pick me over them.

But. Of course, there's a but. Anything legal or medical, like changing my name or going on hormones, she's making me wait for. In case I change my mind. In case, after enough meds and therapy, I wake up one day and I'm not *me* anymore.

She's not transphobic. She just thinks *I'm* only trans because I'm sick in the head.

Whatever. My mommy issues aren't the point right now.

"Excuse me?"

"You know what it makes me think of?" She takes another step. I step back, trying to keep space between us. "Gemstones. You know, like crystals? Some humans think those little rocks can do magic. Do you believe that, Gem?"

"Uh . . . I don't know."

Am I cursed? First the girl in the courtyard, now this. Did I sleep with an evil witch's boyfriend?

She tilts her head, and I swear those too-blue eyes glaze

over. "I totally don't. Like, how could a stupid rock be more powerful than *me*, you know?"

"Um . . ." My throat is so tight I can barely speak. Adrenaline thrums through my muscles, urging me to *run*.

This isn't right. I don't know what *this* is, but I need to get away. "Who are you?"

"Oh, there are so many ways I could answer that. Like, my name is Poppy White, and I'm a sophomore who just moved here from Nebraska."

So much for Gracie not being the sort of town people choose. That's two new girls in the same day.

Wait. *Poppy*. Willa Mae mentioned a Poppy.

It was a warning.

I don't have time to dwell on the girl's identity. She moves toward me again, so quickly this time that I don't have the chance to back away. She's faster than she looks—and *stronger*, I realize, as she fists my shirt and yanks me closer. I wrap my hand over hers, trying to push her away, but I can't.

"And," she drawls, voice suddenly louder, suddenly deeper and more powerful than it was seconds ago. "I am the avenging angel sent to read the record of your sin. I am this story's inescapable epilogue. I am the god of death and I have not forgiven you."

Oh.

It's . . . spooky. She's super creepy, which I'm pretty sure is what she's going for.

But I don't know what I'm supposed to say to all of *that*. And as intimidating as she's trying to be, I'm more weirded out than afraid. I raise my free hand and wiggle my fingers in her face. "*Ooooooh.*"

"You're . . . mocking me." Poppy blinks. And then, unexpectedly, she laughs. "You always have a sense of humor. It's one of your many charms."

"I— Thank you?"

"Now, Magician." She sighs, tilting her head back. She's so thin I think for a minute it might just snap right off her neck and go rolling around the parking lot. "Where's the Ouroboros?"

Magician. Ouroboros.

Now I'm more worried *my* head might go spinning off.

"I don't know what you're talking about." How many times can I say that today?

She tilts her head in the other direction, thin hair falling over her face, narrowing her eyes. After a beat, she asks, "Pinky swear?"

This girl is a freak. I stick out my pinky out.

"Pity." Poppy clicks her front teeth and does *not* twist our fingers together. "Marian's going to be so upset."

"Who?"

The question has barely left my mouth before I stop breathing.

Just stop. I can't suck in air, and I don't know why. It's like someone's flipped a switch and my lungs don't know *how* to inflate anymore. I try to breathe, and my body doesn't respond, like that part of me is just . . . off.

Poppy's hand glides from my chest to curl around my throat. "In this lifetime, battle follows death. She'll just *hate* me going off-script like this. She's so excited to carve your nasty little heart out. But it's fine. We'll find the knife after we've buried you. Oooh, then we'll make an *event* out of playing with your corpse."

My *nasty little heart* feels like someone's standing on it, and it doesn't take long before I can't keep myself upright anymore. My knees go out, and Poppy's hand tightens around my throat as she guides me, too gently, to the pavement. She's so much stronger than she looks. Black spots pop into my vision. I think about trying to push her away again but can't seem to move at *all* anymore.

"If we had more time, I'd give you a proper send-off." She sighs, nearly dreamy, and moves one hand from my throat to brush her knuckles against my cheek. "You don't deserve a quick death. But there's so much I need to do, and your guard dog's already on my ass."

I don't have it in me to wonder what she's talking about. I'm about to die. I'm going to suffocate here in the school parking lot, all because I decided to skip class. My eyes close once the black spots are all I can see anyway. What a dramatic after-school special.

Except I don't die. Not yet.

In a painful rush, air refills my lungs. The only sound I can make is a choking scream as my chest threatens to crack open at the pressure. Poppy's still kneeling over me, but she isn't looking at me anymore. Her head is tilted toward the sky, where a flock of birds are now circling overhead.

"Vultures, Mountain? *Really?*" She growls, grinding her teeth and whipping her head in the direction of the school again. "*So* dramatic, and for what?"

"You hardly have room to talk."

Blinking away tears, I twist my head in the direction of the voice. Willa Mae is standing a few feet from us, broad shoulders tensed, staring at Poppy with a mix of revulsion and rage.

"What are you *wearing?*"

Not the question I was expecting, but a fair one.

Poppy gasps, looking down at her outfit before shooting Willa Mae a glower. "It's camp!"

"Mmm. Are you sure?"

I'm still trapped underneath the girl who is actively attempting to murder me.

Poppy leaps to her feet with shocking agility, and I roll away as quickly as I can, shuffling on my knees toward the nearest car. Hiding behind the oversized tire of a lifted Ford, I weigh my options. Run for the school? Run for the Piggy Wiggly? Which one's more likely to get me killed? I don't know, can't make up my mind, and indecision keeps me frozen.

Willa Mae's voice cuts through the panic. "Gem. Do you see the white Jeep five spots down?"

Huh?

I peer around the truck's tailgate, blink down the row of cars. My teeth chatter when I force out, "Y-yes."

"That's mine. It's unlocked. You're going to get in it and go home. I left a spare key in the center console for you."

That doesn't—that doesn't make any sense. Why would she have done that? How could she have known to?

But it makes as much sense as anything else. I force myself to move, to scramble toward the Jeep.

"You always have been an obedient bitch," Poppy chides. "How long's it gonna take you to realize they only keep you around to save their hide? Another hundred years? Another thousand?"

"Speaking of bitches, where's your girlfriend?"

"On her way. I was planning to give her the Magician's spine as a welcome-home present."

"Romantic."

Poppy giggles the most disturbing little giggle I've ever heard, like some kind of haunted baby doll.

My fingers curl around the driver's-side handle of Willa Mae's car. Before I can wrench the door open, ice-cold fingers curl around the back of my neck. Poppy tosses me, as if I don't weigh over two hundred pounds, back to the ground.

Looking up at her sickly frame illuminated by the sun, I watch as the flock of vultures descend. They swarm her, sharp beaks striking out in precise attacks, ripping at her paper-thin flesh. It's too much for my brain to process, the way they tear the skin off her bones in effortless strips, the way they bloody her in their choreographed attack.

And it happens so *quickly*. I can't get myself to move, can only stare on in disbelief. Everything about this moment feels unreal. Am I dreaming? I can feel the ground beneath me, can move my body of my own accord, but I don't feel like I'm awake.

These things can't actually happen while I'm awake.

Somehow, worse than what's being done to her body is her reaction to it. Poppy doesn't seem to register the pain. Instead, with that inhuman speed, she snatches the birds from midair, hands tightening around their throats until they deflate. They don't fly away, don't try to save themselves, and keep going in for meat even as she picks them off, one by one. Within moments, she has a pile of dead vultures at her feet.

With blood dripping from an open gash on her forehead, painting the blue hearts around her eye a violent purple, she laughs again. "You're going to have to do better than that."

Willa Mae's hands slide underneath my armpits and she puts me on my feet. "Get out of here. Now."

Yes, ma'am. I clamber inside her car, slamming the door behind me. The spare key is exactly where she said it'd be, waiting in the center console. I slam it into the ignition, then jerk into reverse and stomp the gas. I need as much distance between me and these girls as possible, and I almost hit every other car in the lot to get it.

Just before pulling onto the main road, I glance in the rear-view mirror for one last look at them. What I see doesn't make any sense. It can't be real. But then, neither can any of this.

One of the trees has moved. Its branches have stretched out from the tree line and into the parking lot. Their sharp ends are skewered through Poppy's shoulders, wrists, and calves, lifting her off her feet, exposing bone and muscle around the wood. She's suspended, a spread eagle, twenty feet off the ground, her streaming blood horribly red against her ghostly skin.

She's still laughing.

4

TO SEE YOU WAS TO ABHOR YOU

You ever get behind the wheel of a car, and suddenly you're somewhere else? You've driven several miles, but you don't have any memory of the drive, and you're not sure how you got there, and it's terrifying because, holy shit, you were just behind the wheel, you could have killed someone?

I remember leaving the school parking lot, seeing Poppy's body dangling in the tree behind me, and then . . . nothing. Nothing, until I'm pulling up to my house.

Poppy's body.

There's no way I actually saw that, right? None of what happened today is possible. And if it's impossible, that means it all happened inside my head.

I press my fingertips against my throat, remembering the girl's corpse-like hand. I couldn't breathe while she was touching me, and I can't breathe now. My mind races from one thought to another, flashing among gruesome images. Poppy, and Willa Mae, and the birds, and the blood.

There's a ringing in my ears that doesn't stop, that gets louder and louder until it drowns out even the sound of my struggle to breathe. Maybe it isn't ringing at all. Maybe it's screaming. Or worse—maybe it's laughter.

I *fall* out of the car more than anything else. I can't seem to see straight, like the world has gone tipped on its side, gone fuzzy at the edges, like I'm looking at everything through bad reception. After a few tries, I manage to stumble my way toward the house. I don't make it inside, though. I collapse on the porch steps, slumping into a ball near the dirt, and press my face into my knees.

For years, I've worried there's something really wrong with me. Only "worried" isn't the right word. I've *known* there's something wrong with me. Something in me is too broken, too ugly, too *wrong*. And I've tried to ignore it. I've sucked it up and done my best impersonation of Normal, always watching the people around me to figure out how to fool everyone into thinking I was one of them. But deep down I knew it was pointless. This day was inevitable. My human mask was always going to slip. I was always going to lose my grip on reality completely.

Just like my dad did.

I don't hear the front door open, but I know it must have when Hank bumps up against my side, knocking his big-ass head into mine. He licks my cheek and it's enough to drag me back into my body. I suck in a deep breath, lower lip trembling, and shove my shaking fingers into the thick, dirty white fur around his neck.

From behind us, my mother speaks. "The hell is going on? Whose car is that?"

"A friend's." Sure, let's go with that. "I got sick. She let me take it."

I nuzzle my face into Hank's throat and my mom pauses for way too long before asking, "What kinda sick?"

Really not sure how to answer that one. I brush my thumb against Hank's fuzzy ear and don't say anything.

She clears her throat. "Seriously, Gem, you havin' some kinda episode?"

That gets me to look at her.

My mother looks a lot like me, in all the ways that don't matter. We share the same dark hair and rosy-brown skin, the same honeycomb eyes, the same high cheekbones and pointy noses and rectangular bodies.

In all the ways that *do* matter, we couldn't be more different. She's the kind of woman who strives to be perfectly put together. A ten-step skin-care routine, a box of dye to touch up her roots anytime gray starts to peek through, outfits put together with the sole intention of being forgettably pretty. She hates attention in the same way I need it to survive.

We both care too much about what other people think. I don't know how we can wear it in the exact opposite ways.

She's looking at me critically. One hand fiddles with the plain silver necklace she's always wearing.

"I'm not having an episode," I mumble. "I'm fine."

I am probably having an episode. I am not fine.

"Mhm." She raises one of her overplucked eyebrows. "You been takin' your meds?"

When Enzo asks if I've taken my meds, it feels like someone tugging a blanket over me when I'm tired. I know he asks because he loves me, because he wants to make sure I'm taking care of myself. Because he wants me safe, and comfortable, and if he isn't around to see to that himself, he needs to know I'm doing what I can on my own.

When Mom asks if I've taken my meds, it feels like sitting trial. She's accusing me of a crime, and she is my judge, jury, and executioner.

She was the one who demanded I start seeing professionals last year, when things started to get . . . bad. She'd caught me with stolen pregnancy tests and Plan B more than once, I almost had to repeat sophomore year because I was sleeping all day instead of going to school, and when she locked away the razors to keep new scars from appearing on my skin, I started using needles to poke holes in my face instead.

So, okay. Maybe help was warranted.

But I refused to keep seeing the first therapist after our third session, when she let it slip how she thought trans people were a sign of Armageddon. My mother yanked me out of the care of the second, once she started to suspect I was *too* interested in our appointments—and she doesn't even know I have pictures of his dick on my phone, or that our first session ended with his hand up my skirt.

When we couldn't find anyone else, she sent me to a psychiatrist, hoping meds could fix me. He agreed I was depressed, conceded maybe I could have ADHD, but refused to slap a more *aggressive* label on me. Despite my family history and my mother's insistence, the kind of diagnosis she thinks I need is usually reserved for people older and worse off. Or at least not as good at masking.

To hear her tell it, she's advocating for her kid, trying to take care of me when she knows something is wrong, and no one is listening to her. *I'm* pretty sure she just wants to prove I'm like my dad so she can get rid of me the way she did him.

Still, the meds have helped. I haven't cut myself in seven

months, and I've been doing *so good* at getting up and getting my ass to school. And the compulsion to get validation by sleeping with anyone who looks at me . . . has lessened, a little.

But pills can't fix what's really wrong. My mother's right. And I really hate that she's going to get what she wants.

"For fuck's sake." I roll my eyes, indignation hot enough to stop my hands from shaking. "Yes, I've been taking my meds. Even crazy people get stomach bugs sometimes."

She narrows her eyes. She doesn't like me cursing in front of her. It offends her deep-rooted Southern sensibilities. But of all the hills to die on, that one's really not worth it. "Sure was nice of your *friend* to let you *borrow* her car."

Huh? *Oh.*

Oh my god. My mother thinks I stole the car.

I cannot do this right now.

She sighs as I move past her and into the house, careful to twist my shoulder so it doesn't touch hers, like physical contact might burn us both.

Hank shuffles into my bedroom just before I slam the door closed. I flick the lock, too, though it's only symbolic. My mother has taken a screwdriver to my doorknob more than once, and she'd have no problem doing it again. The stubborn illusion of privacy is better than nothing.

My head hits the pillow, my eyes on the ceiling fan whirring quietly overhead.

Okay.

All right.

There are two options here.

One—I have finally, and undeniably, lost my shit. I have tumbled so far over the deep end that there is no getting my feet back on land, not on my own. My weird-ass dreams have now spiraled into full-blown hallucinations, and either I invented Willa Mae and Poppy entirely, or I invented our encounters. Either way, I'm now *officially* a danger to myself and others. There's no more avoiding telling people about my psychosis. I have to tell someone because I have to get help. And maybe, with a different kind of medication, or more treatment, I'll get my head on straight.

Two—I haven't invented anyone at all. Willa Mae is a real person who really came to Gracie looking for me. She knows me, somehow, from something I don't remember. And she knew Poppy was going to show up.

Oh, and there's something important about a lost knife. Maybe even the same one I used to kill the *Sun* in my dream last night. Which maybe wasn't a dream at all.

There is no best-case scenario. There is only one terrible possibility and another.

The fan continues to spin. Warm air wafts against my face, making strands of hair tickle my cheeks. I don't know how long I lie still.

At some point, my phone is vibrating in my hand. Enzo's face on the screen tells me I have an incoming FaceTime call.

Shit. I forgot I asked him to call me.

Obviously, I shouldn't answer. There's more than too much going on. I don't have the time or the spoons to have a conversation with Enzo today.

I sit up, struggling to find the best angle that doesn't read *I'm in the middle of a breakdown,* as the call starts.

"Well, hello, darling. It's nice to see you're still breathing. Your last message was awfully desolate."

As soon as he speaks—even if he has no idea how bad the timing on that joke is—I can't help but smile.

I *really* like looking at Enzo. Sharp-jawed and soft-mouthed, with cool beige skin and eyes that could be made of fallen autumn leaves. That swoopy hair always falling across the lenses of his glasses, this week dyed a deep storm-cloud gray. His button nose, slightly upturned. The way he dresses like a character in a children's book, all bright colors and flashy accessories and a hint of glitter. He's a lot to look at. And it's nice.

Today, he's got beaded earrings in, probably handmade by his mom. She came to the U.S. from Brazil long before he was born, and his dad grew up on a farm in Canada. How they all ended up where they are, I don't know.

They're really incredible people, though. Supportive and kind and I've never actually known anyone but Enzo who seriously likes their parents.

It's nice. He deserves that. Of all people, he deserves it.

"Aw, babe, I didn't know you cared so much." I compartmentalize because I have to. I shove Poppy and Willa Mae and knives and vultures and glowing skin out of my head. I fix my human mask in place.

I've gotten so good at pretending to be someone else, it's easier than being me. I just hate when I have to perform for Enzo.

"Oh, shut up." He laughs sharply and rolls his eyes. From the picture on the screen, I know he's in his room. His bed's in the background, tucked under the window overlooking Prospect Park, beneath his shelf covered in pictures of his family and friends and the little knickknacks he's acquired like the goblin king he is. In the foreground, he leans against his desk and grins. "You know how much I love you."

And I do, is the thing. I know how much he loves me. More than anyone else ever has.

But could he love the me I am when I stop pretending? Could *anyone*?

"Yeah, yeah" is all I offer him in response.

A long pause follows, where Enzo and I just stare at each other. I'm not sure what he's seeing. Doesn't matter. I could look at him forever.

Finally, he tugs one hand through his hair. I follow his manicured nails, the gaudy rings on each finger, the way the silver shifts over his skin.

When he clears his throat, I meet his eyes again. He hedges slowly, "You wanna talk about what happened?"

Without my permission, my eyes burn. Yes. I want to talk about what happened—I *need* to. And I *can't*. It's time to tell someone, I know it is. But that someone can't be Enzo. That . . . I just . . .

I just need him to keep loving me as long as possible. And that means I have to keep up the ruse that I deserve him.

Instead of telling the truth, I opt for being honest. It's different. "Someone was asking me about my dad. Just—it was already a long morning. It was one more thing I couldn't deal with."

"Oh." That one word weighs a thousand pounds. I don't talk about my father unless I'm already spiraling and decide things can't get much worse. Enzo knows this. "Ah. What someone?"

"This girl—I don't know. Her name's Willa Mae, she's new at Gracie. I—I don't know." There is so much left to say and nothing I can tell him. "I don't actually, uh, wanna talk about what happened. If that's okay."

"Of course that's okay." Enzo bites his lower lip. My eyes follow the line of his teeth, and his mouth, and the curve of new, one-year-on-T stubble on his chin. "Can you just tell me where it hurts?"

And everything in me comes slamming down.

The horrific nightmare of the demon and the Sun. Whatever I witnessed at school, whether it was real—impossible—or all in my head—as bad as impossible, if not worse. The building tension between me and my mom, living every moment knowing she's watching me, waiting for me to screw up again.

Everything is too heavy. Everything is always heavy, but these last few days, these last few hours, it's worse.

Everything hurts. I don't know how to live like this.

"No." He is so kind and so good and someday he's going to realize I've tricked him into loving me, tricked him by pretending to be normal and *right*, and I'm going to have to look into his beautiful face and see how badly I've hurt him. But it can't be today. Because I am selfish and ugly and everything he isn't. Because if I were the kind of person who could let him go, I might actually be the kind of person who deserved him. But I'm not.

I can't tell him what happened today. But I also can't tell him I've spent my entire life looking at myself through fog, pretending to be alive and hoping that one day I'd actually start to feel like I was, and now I'm terrified there's no hope left.

"Okay. That's okay. Hey, we don't have to talk about it."

He takes all of me in stride, because of course he does. My stomach aches.

"I picked up some new poetry books from that secondhand store with all the adoptable cats. God, Gem, once you're here, I gotta take you there. How do you think Hank would feel if we adopted a cat?" His voice trembles slightly, but I know he's doing his best not to let me hear it. The lopsided smile he gives me would be contagious if I weren't so deeply broken.

Usually, fantasizing about my future with Enzo is the one thing that can bring me back. Today, it's not enough.

Do I have a future at all?

What am I?

"Anyway." He shuffles out of bed, moving over to the bookshelf on the other side of his room, and rifles through his things. "Let's crack one open. Maybe there's something good in here."

I don't answer, but I know he's not really looking for me to.

Enzo is an artist at heart. He likes color, and poetry, and he wants every moment to feel like a scene in a play. He thrives on finding the beauty in everything he does, even if he's the only one who can see it.

He's also planning to go premed after clown college, because, as he's explained to me, "capitalism." But I have a feeling he sees the beauty in saving people, too.

I lie down, putting my phone on my bedside table, propped up against a glass of ancient, stale water. Hank groans, hoisting himself up into the bed and settling against me. I thread my fingers into his fur.

"Okay, here we go." Enzo picks one of the books, then settles back down in his own bed. He spares another grin for Hank before his dark eyes meet mine through the screen. He only holds them there for a moment before looking down at the page.

Something buried deep inside me screams to be let out. I don't say anything.

"'Because your eyes were two flames, and your brooch wasn't pinned right, I thought you had spent the night in playing forbidden games.'"

He knows how to put on a show, even when it's just his mouth at work. Words drip off his tongue like molten sugar and wisps of smoke. I could listen to him talk forever. As much as I like looking at him, I close my eyes to savor the sound.

"'Because you were vile and devious, such deadly hatred I bore you. To see you was to abhor you, so lovely and yet so villainous.'"

The pain in my stomach begins to lessen. My breathing slows.

"'Because a note now came to light, I know now where you had been, and what you had done, unseen—cried for me all the long night.'"

At some point, Enzo watches me fall asleep.

5

ACCEPT THE IMPOSSIBLE

When I come to, I'm starving, it's dark, and Willa Mae is pulling back the screen on my window to force her way into my room.

I remember coming home, remember crawling into bed and disappearing into the sheets, crashing hard as soon as the adrenaline rush faded. I must have depression-napped through the rest of the afternoon, missing lunch and dinner, and—

As the girl lurches past the threshold and nearly falls face-first on my floor, I jerk upright. The memory of what happened today slams into my ribs so hard I worry they'll shatter.

Hank, the lump who thinks he's a guard dog, who barks anytime a possum skitters too close to the house, is staring at Willa Mae while she jumps back to her feet. Tongue hanging out, panting happily, just watching her.

Thanks, bud. I feel so safe.

"Glad to see you got some rest," Willa Mae huffs before inviting herself into my bed, dropping onto the foot and throwing her legs up alongside mine. "Was worried you might have a meltdown."

Falling asleep and having a meltdown are, I think, not mutually exclusive. If anything, my brain melted so hard that the only option left was to turn itself off for a while.

Hank scoots on his belly down to the end of the bed and plops his head into Willa Mae's lap. She reaches down and scrubs him behind the ears with her short fingernails.

"Tried to come and talk to you sooner, but your mom wouldn't let me in. Told me to take my car and go. Had to park down the street and wait till her light went out." Willa Mae's wide nose crinkles like she's tasted something bad, and she shakes her head. "No offense, but she's *very* unpleasant."

None taken. Still, there's an embarrassing part of me that feels like I should say something to defend my mother. I don't. She doesn't deserve it, and, anyway, Willa Mae and I have more important things to talk about.

"What the fuck happened?" As soon as I ask the question, there are a hundred more racing to the finish line of my tongue. "Who are you? How do you know about my dreams? Who the hell is Poppy? *What* is she? What are *you*?"

"What are *you*, you mean?" She looks up from where her fingers are sliding in and out of the fur on Hank's head, gaze sharp as it cuts across my face. "That's what you really want to know, isn't it?"

Well.

Even if I had the thought in the middle of a breakdown, the fact that nothing about my life feels real is still *true*. As far back as I remember being a person at all, I've felt disconnected from the people around me. It's like everyone else has some kind of handbook, that they've all been present for a class where they learned how to be human, and I overslept and missed that day. Like everyone else is in on something I'm standing on the edge of.

Only they don't *know* I don't know, so I have to keep my ignorance a secret. I've studied them, cataloged the way they behave, tried to mold myself into the kind of person normal people want. Mysterious, and charming, and witty; attractive enough in all the right ways to get people to accept my lie. But never, ever enough that they might actually get close to me. 'Cause if they got close, they might be able to see past the act, to realize I've been faking it this whole time.

The dreams make it worse, another layer of separation between *me* and *them*. But even without the dreams, I've always known I don't belong.

I lean back against my pillows, tucking the edges of my blanket around my hips, watching this strange, hot girl in my bed, petting my dog, like she owns the place.

Finally, I ask, "What am I?"

The answer, when it comes, should sound more unbelievable than it does.

"You're a god, Gem."

Around us, the quiet seems heavier in the aftermath of her sentence. The air-conditioning is on, a gentle hum that fills our old house, which creaks every now and then as it settles. The tags on Hank's collar jingle when the old boy shifts. Outside, bugs and nocturnal critters yip and chirp in symphony. Willa Mae breathes soft but jagged as she waits for my answer.

I'm suddenly very aware I fell asleep in my clothes. I've got on sneakers under my blanket, and it feels wrong. They hug my toes, rubber soles pressing against cotton sheets, and it makes my teeth hurt like a fork scraping a dinner plate.

"You're crazy." It's weak, and we both know it. I don't even think I mean it. There's no heat behind the words.

"Maybe." She shrugs. "But I can be crazy and right. You're a god. And I'm a god. Poppy, too."

"I am the avenging angel sent to read the record of your sin. I am this story's inescapable epilogue. I am the god of death and I have not forgiven you."

I swallow.

Willa Mae continues, "For whatever it's worth, I didn't *want* to tell you like this. If your family's records hadn't been lost, you would have known about everything a long time ago. You were supposed to grow up with the truth. Even if you didn't, I was supposed to find you a lot sooner. I'm sorry I didn't."

Her apology sounds unnervingly sincere. For reasons I don't know yet, it makes my throat hurt, closing tight like there's a lump of hot glass shoved in my windpipe.

Obviously, this answer only creates about a million more questions. But my mind is still running circles around itself, unable to sit too long with the weight of what she's saying. I toss the blanket back and throw my legs over the edge of the bed, kick off my shoes like that'll help me focus.

She's still going. "At least you have the dreams. Some of this should already *feel* familiar. And they'll only get stronger now that we're together."

Right. I glance to the side to look at her again. God, she's pretty.

God. Ha.

Hank, the dumbass, is flopped on his back with his tongue hanging out. She rakes her knuckles over his chest.

"How do you know about the dreams?"

Willa Mae frowns, then rolls her fingertips in little circles over her eyelids like she's trying to get rid of a migraine.

Like, *my bad,* sorry the scariest and biggest thing to ever happen to me might require *you* to take an ibuprofen.

"Okay. Uh, let me just—I'm gonna start at the beginning, yeah?"

I blink. "Okay."

When she speaks again, I get the feeling this is a speech she's given before, the words practiced, studied. It reminds me of Enzo reading lines. "Think of the universe as you know it like a trench coat. And inside the coat, there are dozens, hundreds, maybe thousands of hidden pockets. And sometimes, inside those pockets, there are even smaller pockets, with zippers on them. Earth is one of the pockets in the coat. And the Ether is one of the smaller pockets inside that one. That's where we come from. The Ether. A world that runs alongside Earth, that follows a lot of the same rules, even shares some of its history, but is kept completely separate because of the zipper."

"What do you mean, shares some of its history?"

She shrugs one shoulder. "In some ways, the Ether is like an alternate version of Earth. I'm not sure when *exactly* it branched off. But some things are the same—languages, and food, even some people appear in both."

"Huh." That's too much for my brain to conceptualize. "Wait, so, the zipper is just a metaphor?"

"For f— Yes. Yes, the zipper is a metaphor." She rolls her eyes. "In the Ether, we were gods. It was *our* world. But you and I weren't alone. There were seventeen of us in the pantheon. We each had our own realm, with congregants who worshipped us. We took care of that world, and our people, and things were *good.* For the most part." She sniffs and flexes her hand against Hank's chest. "But one of the gods was not like the others. He held the power to taint our kingdoms, turning our people into shells of their former selves. We pushed back, tried to keep him away—but he was greedy. He didn't just want our people; he wanted our *power*. He murdered four of us, stealing their gifts and their lands."

"So, a colonizer."

She makes finger guns at me in agreement before continuing, "The rest of us had no choice but to run, or we would be next. And so, we came here. We left our world behind for this one, lifetimes ago. Literal lifetimes. Every few generations, we reincarnate into the same bloodlines."

It's a ridiculous story. No, more than that, it's an *impossible* story. And I don't have any reason to believe her. I don't even know this girl.

Except the line between possible and impossible has always felt blurry, and it's only getting worse now. And, if I'm being honest, there's something deeply appealing about being told I'm not losing my mind. About just accepting that I'm actually a *reincarnated god*.

Hell, I've been known to walk a thin line between self-loathing and a debilitating god complex, but this is a new low—or high?

"So, let's say we were gods."

"Well, we were, so, yeah, let's say that."

"What did we *do*?"

She smiles. It looks out of place in this conversation—too happy. "God of the land. Plants, animals, any living thing that made up our people's world. That was my domain."

The vultures and the trees and my stupid dog rolling around in her lap like they're old friends.

Okay. Sure.

"They called me the Mountain."

The Mountain.

Something hits me square in the chest, so hard I have to gasp to keep from choking. Sense memories assault me—wet grass under my bare feet and rough tree bark digging into my back; laughter so loud it makes me smile in response; warm liquid dripping from my fingers like honey.

What the hell?

"And . . . me?"

Something in her smile sharpens like the tip of a knife. She leans forward, a wicked gleam in her eyes, and I think, for a second, she's going to put her hands on me again. That maybe she's going to touch me like she did at lunch, stroking my knuckles with her warm fingers.

She doesn't. My heart still punches into my throat.

"You are the god of magic. And your power is unfathomable."

Real or unreal, impossible or not, I don't know if my ego can take hearing that.

"It was because of you that we were able to get out of the Ether. None of the others could have dreamed of doing what you did. *You* opened the zipper and *you* made sure we could keep this slice of immortality. A taste of the power we once had." She swallows before her pink tongue shoots out to wet her lower lip. My eyes follow it the whole way across. "We owe you everything."

Well.

Hm.

"So . . . if you *owe me everything* . . . why doesn't the god of death seem very grateful?"

I'm not sure if I'm asking in a serious way, or just entertaining what is probably a shared delusion.

It's impossible. I know it's impossible. But if my options are believing in something impossible or believing I've lost all touch with reality, I guess this is what I'm going with.

Willa Mae opens her mouth and closes it. Opens it again. Sighs. Bites that damp lower lip.

I don't need her to answer, though. There's a part of me that already knows the story. It's the same part of me that didn't flinch when she told me we were gods; the part of me that's just waiting to hear it out loud. Maybe I already know everything I need to.

All I have to do is accept the impossible.

"We will share dominion over this world, creature. Our empire will soon be beyond compare."

My fingers twist, knuckles turning white over my thighs.

"They would suppress us for another eternity before bowing to the true magnitude of our power. But follow me down this path, and there is no force in this world that could stop us."

My stomach roils. I'd lose my dinner if I'd actually eaten it.

"They wonder if you are their god or their monster. Let us show them you have always been both. It is time this world finally looked upon its reckoning."

My mouth goes dry.

I'm not looking at Willa Mae when I say, "Tell me about the other god. The one we had to run from."

She's quiet at first. I can feel the way she shifts on the foot of the bed, but I still don't turn my head toward her. At length, she explains, voice gone slow like she's stretching taffy off her tongue. "We called him the Shade; a thing of the shadows. He held sway over things that were never meant for the light.

He uncovered secrets bound for the tomb and gave them new life. The god of things forbidden."

Shade. Magician.

My demon and me.

If I let myself think about it, I can still hear the Sun's wet screams as I sculpted her body into something terrible and new.

"I helped him." Empty stomach or not, I'm going to be sick. I have to stand up, rubbing my palms against my arms, trying to flatten the goose bumps. "You say I saved everyone, but I helped *him*. I've seen it. I've dreamed about it."

"Of course you have."

I don't understand the accusation in her mumbled words. Don't have the chance to ask, either.

Willa Mae stands, joining me in the center of my bedroom, finally reaching out and putting her hands on my shoulders. This close, she towers over me. I'm not used to feeling small, not physically, but there's no avoiding it now.

This close, I know what she smells like. It reminds me of haystacks and tilled soil and herb gardens and wildflowers, all earthy and untamed—but with something else beneath it, something smoky and sweet and wrong, like stolen cigarettes and overcooked stovetop caramel.

Our eyes lock. With her warm, capable hands keeping me steady, I couldn't look away if I wanted to.

"You made mistakes, but you fixed them. The Shade was a manipulative *monster*. He forced you to do things you never would have done without his influence. And as soon as you were outside that influence, you made sure he could never hurt us again. The others should try remembering that."

"How many others?"

Willa Mae's hands fall from my shoulders, and she leans back on her heels, shoving her hands in the pockets of her ripped-up jeans. "Ten of us are left on Earth."

"And they all . . . hate me."

Naturally.

"They don't *all* hate you," Willa Mae hedges. "They don't all remember you."

"Great." Very cool.

She huffs. "We all have the dreams. Not as intense as yours. You're so closely tied to the magic that keeps us coming back, yours have always been more vivid than anyone else's, but we *all* get glimpses of the past. For some of us, though, that's all it ever is. Glimpses. They write it off as weird dreams, and that's it. But we travel through family lines. And some of us plant seeds. We make sure records are kept, and passed down, so that when we come back, we have someone who can remind us who we are. And once we know, it's like a switch gets flipped. It triggers something in the magic. The memories start coming faster. We start to integrate with who we used to be."

"That was supposed to happen to me. On my dad's side."

"Right. It's an imperfect system. We're gone for generations between lives. Sometimes things get lost. Some of the others haven't come back to themselves in *several* lifetimes."

"But the ones who do remember . . ." I let myself trail off without finishing the thought out loud.

Willa Mae sighs. "Right now, there's only two we need to be worried about. Poppy White is the Reaper—the god of death. And with the Reaper here, it won't be long before we have to deal with the Lionheart, the god of battle."

That same sensation of *remembering* hits me when she

mentions those two, but it isn't nearly as intense this time. Or as pleasant. The idea of the Reaper and the Lionheart makes my skin crawl and my lungs ache—it feels like being buried alive.

Oblivious to my crisis, she continues, "Neither of them actually wanted to leave the Ether—because they're *unhinged*—and they aren't exactly grateful that you saved their asses. No good deed goes unpunished, you know?"

The way Willa Mae talks about these people, you'd think we were just shit-talking some other high schoolers.

And I guess, technically, we are.

"Death and battle go hand in hand, and they're both gunning for your ass."

"So . . . why don't *you* hate me?" I frown, narrowing my eyes in her direction. When she doesn't immediately answer, I wave my hand demonstratively at her body. "I mean, it sounds like past-me was kind of a . . . dick."

It sounds like past-me was a whole lot worse than a dick, but whatever.

Willa Mae takes a deep breath and leans against the edge of my desk. She considers me with her head tipped forward, through her eyelashes. "Like I said, you made a mistake. But you were coerced by a monster. And I forgave you for that a long time ago."

The thing about growing up feeling like you're on the outside, feeling like you have to study everyone's moves and take hints from the tiniest inflection in their tone, is that you get pretty good at noticing when something's off. And I know there's something else in the story that Willa Mae isn't telling me.

"Poppy called you my guard dog."

"You shouldn't trust anything that comes out of Poppy's mouth."

"Well sure, that's generally my rule of thumb when someone tries to murder me, but it's also not the point." I nip the inside of my cheek, glance up and down Willa Mae's body. Her shoulders are tense, jaw tight. I totally do not look at her boobs. "She asked me about a knife."

Willa Mae huffs, leaning back as far as she can against the edge of my desk, tilting her neck back so she can stare at the ceiling fan. *Whoosh.* "Right. The Ouroboros. It's a weapon you made, that you brought here from the Ether. As far as I know, it's the only thing that can *permanently* kill us. It stops the reincarnation cycle in its tracks. And more importantly, as far as Poppy and her girlfriend are concerned, it transfers our powers to the killer."

"Why would that be more important?"

"Because you're the only one who can open the door back. *Unless* they kill you with the Ouroboros and take your magic for themselves."

"Do you have the knife?"

It doesn't feel like a realization, but a *memory,* when I say, "It's how the Shade killed the other gods. *We* used the knife to harvest their powers. *I* created the weapon that ruined our world."

She sniffs and doesn't meet my stare. "You also hid it away from him and got all of us to safety."

"Those of you I *hadn't* murdered yet."

The Sun's screams echo in my head.

Willa Mae sighs. *"Anyway.* We've done a good job keeping the knife safe for generation after generation. But last time,

Reaper and Lionheart were closer than ever to finding it. Someone in your bloodline had taken it, and was supposed to be transporting it to a new hiding spot. I got my head bashed in before I learned if he succeeded. So this time, after my grandparents found me and made me remember, I went looking."

"*Made* you remember?"

She waves me off. "But it's not where we agreed to hide it. Which means, right now, *nobody* knows where the knife that kills gods is."

"That . . ." I don't have a word for what that is. I settle on "Blows."

"Sure does. So, I'm gonna need you to get caught up real quick. We've got to get our hands on that blade before the others do."

I plop down on my bed again. Considering her, I reach up and rub my thumb beneath my lower lip, fidgeting with the piercing there when I do. "If it's just me and the knife they want, why are you even here?"

"I mean, I don't exactly think it's a *good* idea for them to go flitting off back to the Ether. The place has been in shambles for forever by now; can't imagine what the people are like, after all that time alone with the Shade. I'm a good co-god, you know. I'm trying to look out for them. Protect them from themselves." She mumbles the words, just before scrubbing her palms over her round cheeks. Finally, she throws her arms out and huffs. The movement is enough to startle Hank, who'd fallen asleep at the foot of the bed. He shakes himself out and slides down to the floor, settling into a squishy ball at her feet.

Willa Mae gives him a long look before continuing. "And like. Okay. Here's the thing. You're gonna figure this out on your own soon. Now that we've met, the dreams are going to start getting bigger. They'll be more detailed, and won't just be about *him*." The way she says *him*, you'd think it was a slur. "They'll be about you, and the lives you've lived since you got here. A thousand years of them. And when that happens, you're going to start seeing more of me. And then you'll know that what I'm about to tell you is the truth. But until you know for sure, until you start to *feel it*, you're gonna think I'm nuts."

My demon—the Shade—isn't the only one I've ever dreamed of, in that other world. He's just been the star of more than his fair share.

And, until now, I didn't know there was a cast list I should've been keeping track of.

"I already think you're nuts."

I don't, actually. Somehow, I've decided she's telling the truth.

"Right. I just." She groans and rolls her eyes. "Okay. Look. The thing is—we're soulmates."

It's like I knew she was going to say it before she does. It isn't the first time someone's rambled their way toward a proclamation of *wanting me*. I still don't have any idea how to respond.

On the one hand: I think kissing her might be life-affirming. On the other hand: everything else.

What ends up coming out of my mouth is "You are a complete stranger."

Which is true, maybe, but doesn't seem to concern her. Willa Mae drops off the desk and moves toward me with purpose, shoulders rolling with a predatory intent that reminds me of the bear on her arm. When we're inches apart, she leans down until our noses nearly touch. "I am the god who has ruled alongside you since the dawn of another time. And I have known you and loved you in your every flawed iteration. Every name you have gone by, every face you have worn, I have been at your side. My soul knows yours, and yours knows mine, and if I have to wait a little while for you to remember, that's fine. I'm gonna keep saving your ass in the meantime."

I've always told myself being demiromantic *and* slutty means I don't lack much in the intimacy department. And I could almost believe that.

Except for one problem—there is little in life that I want more than to be loved in a way that is all-consuming. It's stupid, but I want an *epic* love. I want it so badly it scares the shit out of me—because there is nothing more terrifying than the idea of being *known,* and you can't be loved like that without being known. The idea that someone might look at me and really *see* me, that someone might understand me in my entirety, and instead of flinching away pull me closer, is . . .

Well, it's always seemed impossible. But possible, impossible, real, unreal, there don't seem to be any rules anymore.

This girl is terrifying.

"So, this is your plan. We find the knife. Hide it somewhere super secret where the others will never find it. And then live happily ever after, until our next trip around the sun?"

She shrugs and drops to the floor, cross-legged. Hank flops his head into her lap and she tugs at one of his ears. "Whatever, it sounds goofy when you put it that way, but yeah. I try to do as much good as I can for the land while I'm here, too. But that's gonna look *a lot* different this time around. Things have gone off the deep end since I was last here. You heard of climate change?"

"Oh. Yikes." What a shit time to be a god of the land.

"Mhm."

"Huh." I join her on the floor, enough space between us that there's no risk of touching, even if she stretches out her legs again. "Here's the thing, though. I sort of have a happily-ever-after planned out already." And it's one I've been waiting years for. A chance to finally become *me*, myself, Gem Echols. Not the different versions of me I've been forced to play to blend in with other people. Certainly not whoever the Magician is. As if I needed another identity crisis. "And that ending doesn't involve playing keep-away with vengeful gods from coat-pocket worlds or, uh, any of the rest of this."

Willa Mae blinks at me. "What about your human existence could possibly be more interesting than being a *god*?"

Summoned, Enzo's face appears in my mind. I can imagine him in this perfect future we're going to build together, an apartment covered in plants, with a spoiled ex–shelter cat, and Pride flags hanging off the fire escape.

He's not the whole reason, but he's a pretty big part. "Um, the everything? So far being a god means nightmares, identity issues—oh, I almost *died*. And you're telling me this is just getting started?"

"Well . . ." Willa Mae frowns. The tips of her ears heat to a dark red.

Eventually, when she says nothing else, I say, "Right. Where's the opt-out form?"

"Oh, fuck off. You're *going* to get your memories back. Your magic, too. And you're gonna have to find the Ouroboros, because—"

"Because if I don't, I'm dead. Perma-dead. Right." My stomach growls. I slide my fingers through my hair. "Is there a way to destroy the knife?"

She frowns. "Um. Yes, technically. You created it alongside a knife-chain. Supposedly, it could cancel out the magic of the Ouroboros."

An emergency self-destruct button. Perfect. "So, we find them both, and use the chain."

Willa Mae stares at me for a too-long moment. When she finally speaks, she sounds disappointed. "Why would we do that?"

"So I can go have the life I want"—*with whoever I want*—"without having to constantly worry about being gutted?"

"You *saw* Poppy. She's going to lose her shit *even more* when she finds out her one chance at getting back to the Ether is gone. Even if she can't perma-kill you, she can still string you up and torture you in her basement for the next eighty years. And in every lifetime after."

I consider that for a moment. Something nasty wriggles in my bones when I say, "So, maybe we also take care of Poppy."

"Take care of?"

I run my finger along my throat in a slashing motion, then cringe at my own behavior.

Willa Mae's disappointment grows thicker. She looks like she's considering taking care of *me*.

"Look, she started it." I actually don't know if that's true. Technically. "Just—like—if we get rid of the knife and she keeps coming . . . I mean, we can hit her with your car or something. But—she has to have something better to do, right?"

This is ridiculous. I am talking about another human being. Sort of?

Willa Mae shakes her head, more to herself than to me. "Right. Uh. I mean, no, we probably don't hit her with my car. And no, I'm not sure she does have anything better to do. But it could be done. A this-lifetime death, to get her off your back, and let you do . . . whatever it is you're planning to do."

"Oh." I hadn't actually expected her to agree. "And, um. How exactly can it be done?"

"She can die a human death. But she's smarter than you, and she's more prepared. The answer to killing Poppy is the same to finding the knife. You need to harness your magic. Once you learn how to wield it again, we can use it to get our hands on the Ouroboros *and* destroy it *and* deal with Poppy, when she inevitably goes nuclear. Marian, too. The Lionheart is already harboring a thousand-year-old grudge because she wanted to stay behind and go toe to toe with the Shade. If you kill her girlfriend? She's going to—I really don't even know—cannibalize you while you're still alive, maybe."

"Huh." I'm less and less excited to meet Marian. "Well, okay. How do I do that? Harness it?"

"I can help you." She shrugs one shoulder. "But let me be clear: this plan sucks. In the past, we've done whatever we could to *stay away* from the others. We kept the knife safe. We kept *each other* safe. But if all you want is to go about your life as Gem Echols, all of this is going to get *a lot* worse before it gets better."

"But it was gonna get worse before it got better anyway, right?"

Even her eyebrows look disappointed in me, somehow. "You're talking about facing an ancient war head-on, without a weapon. Right now, Poppy and Marian are a whole hell of a lot stronger than you. And that's *without* them tapping in the sleepers. If they trigger the other gods' memories, we might have to *take care* of more than just those two."

Murder. We're talking about murdering a bunch of other teenagers.

But then, maybe none of this is real. Maybe that's why I'm not panicking.

Willa Mae leans in again, frowning. "Are you really sure whatever human life you want is worth *all* of that?"

"You think I'll change my mind. When I start remembering more, you think I'll want something different."

She takes a deep breath and rises to her feet again. "Yes. Look, I understand how it feels to wish you were like everyone else. But you're not. You've always known you weren't, you just didn't know how much you weren't. *I* know. Right now, I know you better than you know you."

"You know the Magician. You don't know me."

Gem. I had to fight for that name. I've had to fight for every scrap of my identity that feels like me. I'm not even done fighting yet, but I can't stomach the idea of just giving up now and walking away. Of being told that the me I've worked so hard to be, the me I've imagined I could *become,* isn't real and never was.

I can't have fought this long and this hard to be human just to . . . not.

"Sure." She shrugs. "But *you* won't be this *you* for much longer. So, I'll help you with this plan. You might die anyway, but you definitely would without me. And when you decide you're ready to reevaluate, we will."

I hate being told I don't know myself. My mother likes to say that shit to me all the time.

Of course, I hate it extra because it's true. But that's not the point.

"Thanks" is all I say. At least she's agreeing to help me.

"Okay." Willa Mae nods and moves back toward the window. "You should eat something. I can hear your stomach from here."

"Oh. Okay."

"Good night, Echols. Tomorrow, shit gets real."

Long after she's gone, Hank watches the window like he's hoping she'll return.

6

YOU DESERVE SOMEONE NICE

Life is full of little surprises. Some days, you find out you're a reincarnated god embroiled in an ancient war that's maybe your fault. Others, you walk into homeroom at seven thirty in the morning and find the girl who tried to kill you flirting with your favorite football player.

I just about trip over my Doc Martens knockoffs, stumbling to a stop in the doorway, all but open-mouth gaping in Poppy's direction. No. No way, definitely not Poppy. Can't be. That's not *her* sitting at a desk in the front row, wearing a pink leather trench coat and go-go boots, with little yellow emoji stickers applied to the corners of her eyes. That's *another* corpse-bride look-alike with the fashion sense of a Care Bear on psychedelics.

She meets my eye and smiles, raising one hand to wiggle her bony fingers at me. Her short nails are painted alternating shades of neon, a nausea-inducing rainbow. Zeke glances in my direction, checking out who's stealing her attention—not that I'd *like* to be. He grins at me before she says something that pulls his eyes back.

No. Abso-fucking-lutely not. How is she here right now? No, 'cause like, *literally* how. I watched her get impaled. I knew she wasn't dead-dead, regrettably, but shouldn't she at least be . . . immobilized? Incapacitated? Enjoying a stint in the hospital? It hasn't even been twenty-four hours since her stint as a tree ornament.

"Watch it, Gem." Ms. Lachowski puts a hand on my shoulder, easing me into the room so she can close the door behind us. "Everyone, take your seats."

Poppy doesn't even look at me as I ease my way around the room, circling the long way to get to my desk rather than cut through anywhere near her. She doesn't look at me, but I can still *feel* her creepy little eyes following me somehow, like she's got another set hidden in that scraggly, too-white-to-be-natural hair.

I sink down in my seat, staring at the back of her head.

What am I supposed to do if she comes at me here? In the middle of the classroom? In front of a bunch of . . . not-gods?

On TV, when the main character finds out the new kid is a ghost, or a faery, or a zombie, or whatever, it's always imperative that The Humans never find out. Which has never made any sense. Like, hello, your boyfriend is a thousand-year-old immortal with an army of the undead out to get him? Maybe you should tell your parents.

Except I get it now. Because if *I* go and tell someone I'm afraid the new girl is out to *murder me,* I'm pretty sure we'll all get called in for a special session with the counselor, and my mother's gonna start shoveling stronger antipsychotics down my throat.

And that's *without* me mentioning we're all reincarnated gods.

What would it be like to have normal-people problems? Zeke drops into the desk directly ahead of me, blocking my view of Poppy. He twists his big body around to shoot another grin. "Dude. Two new girls in two days and you're already talking to *both* of 'em? You're a legend, my guy. Uh, person."

As with most conversations with Zeke, there is so much to unpack. But I focus on "I'm not *talking* to anyone."

"Oh, really?" He giggles. It is adorable and absurd. "'Cause I for sure saw you holding hands with that inked chick yesterday. Now Poppy says you and her had a *special moment* in the parking lot?"

He winks, all conspiratorially, like he thinks this special moment involved tongues.

Meanwhile, I still feel the phantom weight of her hand on my throat.

I play out what would happen if I told Zeke that—the way his grin would get worse, and he'd say "*Whoa, kinky.*" And I know that didn't actually happen, but I still glare at him.

The line between reality and the things I'm making up is a moving target at this point, anyway.

He shrugs, unbothered by my lack of enthusiasm. "Shit, I ain't ever seen anything like either of 'em before in my life. Get why they'd go for you, but . . . damn. Yo, did you hear the rumor Poppy's dad is some kinda arms dealer for a secret military? Is that true?"

"Uh. I have no idea." It would be the least interesting thing I've learned about Poppy. I lean forward, chest smashed against the desk, and clap his shoulder. "But, dude, I'm not talking to either of them. And you don't wanna go there, either. They're both freaks."

Zeke's eyes narrow, his thick eyebrows getting all puppy-dog-droopy on me. "That ain't very nice, Gem."

"Seriously—"

The intercom overhead hums to life, and—with a last too-judgmental look of hurt—Zeke turns his back on me to pay attention. Ms. Cannon, the front-desk secretary, starts rattling off the Friday announcements. I tune them out.

Instead, while everyone else stands for the pledge, I chance another look at Poppy.

She's the only other person still in her seat. As if she feels my stare—or maybe she's watching me with her hair eyes—she tucks her chin against her shoulder, glancing back at me. The glassy white-blue of her gaze reminds me of a dead fish. My whole body gets the ick.

And that's *before* she smiles. That horrible smile that stretches her gray skin in a way that doesn't look human. I imagine it peeling back from her gums, splitting her cheeks open until they're wide and bloody and raw. I imagine her unhinging her jaw so she can pry her mouth open until the apparently-all-seeing back of her head touches her shoulder blades.

I picture her crawling onto her desk and turning to face me, skeletal body crouched and twisted and wrong. I think of everyone else screaming and moving out of the way, and me, frozen in fear, unable to run, while she crawls toward me on all fours like an animal, scrambling over the desks between us until she can swallow me whole.

It's only a daydream. It's only in my head. Poppy is just sitting there, smiling, lazily kicking one foot back and forth while the rest of the class chants.

But she's getting . . . hazy?

The filmy layer that erupts behind my eyes reminds me of my dreams. The boundary between real and unreal, like a physical thing I can see and almost touch. Poppy, sitting at her desk at Gracie High School, becomes cloaked in fog. And something new, *somewhere* new, bursts to life.

Atlanta, Georgia, in the late 1920s; the heart of the Oakland Cemetery. The graves here are already growing close together, beginning to show the wear of time that'll only get worse over the next century. In this spot, beneath the fountain at the cemetery's center—where turning one way means grotesque Confederate memorials and turning the other reveals a line of tiny gravestones in the Black corner—there's a plot of greenery untouched by death. A massive flowering dogwood tree looms, branches in bloom.

We've gathered here to do something terrible.

Willa Mae did say the dreams would get more vivid—that they might even happen while I'm awake. But there's another difference between the dreams I've had before and this. Here, I'm not witnessing a scene I don't understand. Here, I'm *remembering*.

My name is Billie Campbell. I'm nineteen years old. By day, I build my father's banking empire. By night, I smuggle liquor into a speakeasy and perform in the underground drag scene. And at all moments in between, I manipulate the comings and goings of this city with my magic. Since I was barely old enough to read, I've used it to protect myself from being found by the Reaper and the Lionheart.

But nothing lasts forever—I know that better than most. And now they're here.

In this life, the Reaper is a drag queen interpretation of a Southern belle, with big hair and a bigger dress that would be more at home in the 1820s than now. She's still too close to decay to be considered pretty, though her hair is fuller and her skin warmer than that of her current incarnation. She goes by Wanda. And right now, she's on all fours in the dirt, dress in tatters, with the dogwood roots expelled from the ground to twist around her wrists and ankles. The sharp-edged limbs, like spiked serpents, lacerate her flesh wherever they touch, digging in until her blood pools freely around the wood. But they aren't holding her in place—they're trying to drag her back into the earth with them.

Her shoulder pops out of place as her arm is yanked elbow-deep into the soil, the disgusting sound making now-me queasy.

Yet this Reaper behaves as if she doesn't notice her now-useless limb, or the way her skin is shredded by rocks and twigs as the tree buries her alive. Instead, she tilts her head toward me and laughs.

My blood is already staining her teeth. It dribbles down her chin as she cackles. I remember the feeling of her canines in my throat, the sugary stink of her, the way she went after me like a rabid dog. Why was she so angry?

She doesn't seem angry anymore. "This is your plan? To *entomb* she who *begets eternity?*"

Then-me gnashes my teeth, furious at her taunting. Honestly, now-me feels kind of stupid and I didn't even do anything.

At my side, the Mountain—now Rosalie, the headstrong eldest daughter of a railroad tycoon—crouches down until her face is inches from the Reaper's. She's smaller here, where Wanda isn't as frail, but the size difference between them is still pronounced. When Rosalie raises a hand and strokes the other god's cheek, her palm nearly covers her whole face.

I note the gold band with a massive stone on her finger.

An engagement ring. Right. This Mountain and then-me are getting married soon.

She sighs. "We don't enjoy hurting you, Reaper."

"Save your sweet-tongued lies for the Magician. At least they pretend to believe you." Wanda-Poppy-Reaper smiles one of those terrible toothy smiles before she spits my own blood into my fiancé's eyes.

The school bell blares, and the cemetery disappears. When I blink, homeroom comes back into sharp focus. The morning announcements are over. Everyone's scrambling for the door.

And Poppy, still seated, is looking right at me. When we meet eyes, hers narrow. She tugs a bedazzled iPhone out of her pocket, frantically typing as she finally stands and rushes out.

Before Zeke can follow her, I lurch to grab his elbow. "Hey! Hey."

He frowns, looking down at my hand. "What's up, Gem?"

"I mean it about those girls, okay? Especially Poppy. She's not nice, Zeke." My hand slides down his arm, and I give his wrist a squeeze before letting go. "You deserve someone nice."

He doesn't look convinced, but, after a long moment, at least he nods. "All right. I hear ya."

And I believe him. Like a dumbass.

Today, when Willa Mae joins me at my lunch table in the cafeteria—too bleak and gray for the courtyard—I don't offer her a greeting. Instead, I throw my arm out in the direction of *Poppy's* table, the one where Zeke King and a gaggle of other too-nice-for-me-to-sleep-with Gracie residents have gathered, all of them staring at Poppy like whatever story she's telling is *so* interesting. Meanwhile, I've lived here for years and I eat alone, but whatever. "What are we gonna do about this?"

Honestly, I wasn't expecting "don't throw yourself at the feet of the girl who looks like she's being tethered to life with chewing gum and safety pins" to be that difficult a rule for Zeke to follow.

Willa Mae follows my hand, one eyebrow popping up as she assesses the group. She doesn't seem surprised, which is irritating.

"What?" She turns back with a shrug. "She stealing friends of yours?"

"I— Well, yes, actually, Zeke is my friend. And— Oh my god, look at what she's doing now!" In horror, I watch Poppy place one disgusting hand on Zeke's biceps, tilting her head to gaze into his eyes. I can only wildly speculate about what she says, but he smiles. "She's seducing him."

Willa Mae snorts. "Yeah, no. She isn't. And even if she were, that's not our problem."

It is so deeply transphobic, to me, because I am trans, that she won't get offended about this. My go-to for people willing to talk shit and be petty is Enzo—I can't exactly text him and tell him what's going on.

Well, I could. But I don't think it'd have the outcome I want.

"How is she not in the hospital? I *saw* what you did to her."

Willa Mae shrugs. "Death is fickle, so the Reaper's healing is advanced. It's just like her gross superspeed—death can arrive without warning."

Well, that's just *great.*

Forcing myself to look away from Poppy trying to have *eyeball sex* with *my* golden retriever, I look back to Willa Mae.

The Mountain. Rosalie.

Land goddess. Ex-fiancé. Shit, did we ever get married?

"So. I had a . . . flashback? This morning."

"Oh? Tell me about it." She pulls a canvas tote onto the table, pulling out plastic containers of food. My mouth salivates at what looks like roasted sweet potato wedges. My vending ma-chine lunch of salt-and-vinegar chips seems way less appealing at the sight of her spread.

"Um. We were in Atlanta. Oakland Cemetery."

"*Ooooh.* Yeah. Rose and Billie." She sighs, taking a bite of avocado toast before resting her temple on her fist. "Yeah, no. That night didn't end well for us."

That look she's giving me is . . . not okay. All fond and knowing and soft. Like she's thinking about those people, and what they used to be like together. The way they used to love each other.

Not me. She's not thinking about me, even if she's looking at me. I'm not *Billie.*

I wouldn't hate for someone to look like that while thinking about me, though.

God, for crying out loud, anyway, whatever.

"Rose and Billie and *Wanda,*" I remind her. "She's always been creepy, hasn't she? Although she looked *less* terrifying a hundred years ago."

"Yeah . . ." Willa Mae frowns, poking a fork at her sliced straw-berries. "She kind of gets worse, every time. I have a theory—well, someone shared a theory with me once. In the Ether, Poppy's shtick was helping souls cross over. She was kind of in charge of the whole . . . afterlife thing. And I think, maybe, because of that, she's not really . . . resting properly between go-arounds. Like she can't find peace in *this* afterlife, 'cause it isn't hers."

"You're telling me she's going to look worse than this when she comes back next time?"

Willa Mae shrugs.

Huh. So, I guess Poppy wasn't just the god of being dis-gusting and committing murder. She was in charge of the whole white-light-and-eternal-slumber thing. Like, instead of Thanatos she was Hades.

(I have this theory that every queer kid goes through either an intense anime or Greek mythology phase. Personally, I identified with Icarus to the point of deep concern.)

Anyway, that paints a very different picture. But even as I think about it, imagining this other version of her, it's like . . . yeah, of course this is true. It clicks together in perfect sync in my head. Like it's just one more thing some part of me already knew; like I was just waiting for someone to say it out loud.

"Okay, be straight with me." I totally do not think about how I don't want her to be straight with me, given the option. "Is defeating her even possible?"

I glance around the room to make sure no one might be listening to us. Willa Mae still attracts attention, but the sort that indicates the audience is going to keep their distance. Still, I lean in closer—and pretend I don't feel the warmth coming off her when I do. "You told me last night my magic was *unfathomable*. Well, Billie Campbell had been using magic since they were like, six, and they still just stood there and let Rosalie do all the heavy lifting. I don't know. I'm feeling pretty fathomable, I'm not gonna lie."

Willa Mae smirks. Smirks! "You're worried you're not strong enough?"

"Okay, no, I didn't say that, exactly. It's just: I've never tried the whole abracadabra thing. And, so far, I don't even have proof that I *can*."

She taps her fingertips against the tabletop, narrowing those weirdly mismatched eyes. Finally, she shrugs and stands, starting to push food back into her tote. "Well, let's get you some proof."

"Pardon?"

"Let's get out of here. We'll go back to my place. I'll show you the start of what you can do—if you'll let me."

"I . . ." Even before I say it, I know she's going to laugh at me, and I can't stop myself from saying it anyway. "I can't skip class again."

She doesn't laugh. Her eyebrows do shoot all the way up into her hairline, though. Willa Mae tosses her tote bag over her shoulder before crossing her arms at me. "You're joking. Why not?"

"Because I have to keep my GPA up. Because some of us actually care about going to college, and I'm pretty sure NYU isn't going to give me a scholarship if they think I don't care about school." If I'm gonna put all this effort into stopping Poppy just so I can have the human life I've planned out, I can't just let all those plans fall apart while I do it. "Besides, if the school calls my mom, she's gonna put a tracker up my ass or something."

Willa Mae doesn't look swayed. "Okay, well, there's not gonna be any college in your future if Poppy stabs you to death before graduation."

Noted, and fair, but not enough to change my mind. I cross my arms and tilt my chin up at her.

She leans a palm onto the table, tilting forward and cocking her head at me. A tangle of her dark, wild hair falls against her neck. I do *not* look at her cleavage.

"Besides, aren't you a little curious, Echols? Isn't there any part of you that's excited to get a taste of what you can do?"

Something horribly wicked lights up her eyes. My chest catches a chill, the fan blades of my heart spinning too fast.

And suddenly, through no fault of my own, I'm headed to her car.

Because I'm reckless but not naïve, I *do* pull out my phone to text Enzo.

> so. yesterday.
> you remember me mentioning a new girl at school?

His reply comes before I've even buckled my seat belt.

Little Dumbass
The one who dared beseech you to unpack your daddy issues?

> do they not teach comedic timing at that fancy acting
> school your parents are paying for?

> but yes.

> anyway, i'm headed to her place rn.

Little Dumbass
OH?

Forgive me, I was not aware impromptu peer counseling was one of your turn-ons.

> ugh. not like that. we're just gonna hang out.

Little Dumbass
Curiouser and curiouser, darling . . . You mean to tell me you intend to spend time with a Gracie resident in full dress? Not a single asscheek out?

i mean, i have no control over whether or not she decides
to show me her asscheeks. but that's not, idk, my PLAN.

and in my defense, she's only been a gracie resident for
like a day.

anyway, i just wanted someone to know where i was
going, in case i'm never seen again. her name is willa mae
hardy.

Little Dumbass
Every single thing you say about this girl makes me all the more
certain you should stay far away from her.
Have fun!

"Who's that?" Willa Mae scans my phone's screen with interest.

I shove it into the front pocket of my black shortalls. "A
friend. It's rude to eavesdrop, you know."

She scoffs, hands flexing around the steering wheel. "Oh,
okay. You're a paragon of manners in this lifetime, huh?"

"I'm a freaking *delight* in this lifetime."

"Mhm." She chuckles. "Lemme guess. You're texting this
friend to let them know where you're going in case I . . . lock
you in my basement? Keep you there so you can't break up
with me?"

"We—we aren't *dating*?!" Which is just as disturbing as her
knowing why I was texting Enzo in the first place.

"Whatever." She shrugs. "You seem to have a lot of friends
at Gracie. But also none. That's typical."

"Oh, okay." Whatever that means. "He doesn't even live in Gracie."

Something indecipherable settles on her face. Her hand tightens a little on the steering wheel. "New York?"

"Okay, stop, that's just weird. What, is one of your powers being psychic?"

"NYU," she offers without context.

"Oh." Right. I told her I wanted to go to NYU. I tap my fingers against my fishnet-covered thighs. "Uh. Brooklyn."

"But he's just a friend?"

"You know, I find the whole *just* part of that question borderline offensive. Also—we're not doing this. We're never doing this. And even if we were, it's way too early for it right now."

Willa Mae shrugs, not agreeing but not fighting me on it, and doesn't say anything else.

Enzo is absolutely right. I should stay far away from her.

Oh well.

7

VERY RATIONALLY AFRAID

We drive for less than five minutes in silence before I feel the need to peel my own skin off. Gracie's a spread-out town, with too many empty miles stretching between one side and the other. The school's right at the center of it, tucked alongside the downtown shopping and First Church of Gracie, our very own hub of corporate Evangelism. To the north are the *nice* rural houses—farmlands owned by families with generational wealth their ancestors didn't work for—and the suburbs—closer to downtown and filled with people who didn't want to live in the sticks but didn't want to live near poor people, either. To the east are the poor people in question—trailer parks and low-income housing, neither rural nor urban but some uncanny valley between the two, where everyone is either a hungry dog or trying not to get bit by one. The south is home to the *country* folk—that's where my mom and I live, a bunch of empty brown fields and dilapidated buildings with bones as old as the town itself, where only the coyotes can hear anyone scream.

Willa Mae is headed west. Western Gracie is much the same

as southern Gracie, with houses spread out miles and miles apart. But where my part of town is all dirt roads and dried-out crops, the west side is swamp country—gators and moss and mildew, with a single winding, narrow road cutting through the river.

For all I know, it could be another half hour before we get where we're going.

"So." I twist my shoulders toward the driver's seat to face her. "Couldn't help but notice we were very *white* a hundred years ago."

Willa Mae scowls. "*You* were very white a hundred years ago. Me? The god of land, a colonizer? That would make no sense."

"Aren't you kind of a colonizer now, though?"

I've never seen anyone look as offended as she does now. She almost veers off the road when her head jerks toward me.

I hold up my hands. "I just mean—aren't we all, kind of? We came here to . . . take over Earth."

"No." She snaps. "We're immigrants. Immigrants add value to the society they join. Colonizers don't *join* anything—they destroy it to build something of their own."

Hm. I mean, she's not wrong. I've always felt weird about those virtue-signaling "we are all immigrants" posts. 'Cause we sure as shit are not.

My relationship to whiteness is complicated. My dad's white, and my mom isn't. I'm white-presenting, in that *white* people think I'm one of them—but Natives clock me right away. Most other people of color can tell there's *something* about me, even if they can't put their finger on the thing itself. And then there's the "what is whiteness, anyway" conversation, a tangled mess.

At the end of the day, I benefit from the privilege of being my father's child, even when that privilege only benefits me within the same system that tried to destroy my mother's people. My blood is part of this land, and I am the one who spilled it. The duality of it all is enough to make my head hurt if I think about it for too long.

"So, you were white-passing? In Atlanta in the 1920s?" I raise my eyebrows, propping my arm against the center console. Our biceps brush when I do. I do not make a mental note of how warm she is. I do not think about how I can smell the wild-earth musk of her.

"Yep." The word is sharp, but her tone softens when she adds, "My family lived a lie in order to survive. But it was better than what happened to families who couldn't do the same."

I actually don't know that much about history. It's hard to tune into the lesson plan when I know I'm being lied to, and that's all history class is. At least in Gracie.

But I know enough for Willa Mae's words to make my stomach hurt.

I guess it makes sense *Billie Campbell* was white, if the godly gene flows down my father's bloodline. And I wonder what he would think of that. In his delusional state, would he be more or less likely to accept the truth of what I am? Not that it matters. It's not like I'm going to pick up the phone and call him.

"Was I also *rich*?" I smirk, crossing my legs at the knee and leaning back against the fuzzy seat. I pretend not to notice the way she glances at my almost-bare thighs. My heart totally doesn't thrum a beat in my throat. "Daddy owned a bank."

"Mhm. And then the Great Depression hit."

"Oh." Right. History.

"Of course, you made sure even *that* was a good thing for your family. People were desperate for help. With enough charm and magic, you used that desperation to make sure the Campbell fortune only grew."

"Oh." Well, that doesn't suck as much, but it does make me sound like a dick. No, not me—Billie. Whatever. "So, why the hell am I poor?"

"I don't know, Echols, maybe the same reason you're not white."

"Colonization?"

She rolls her eyes toward the Jeep's ceiling, but does not actually disagree with me.

"You know," I continue, because I really love the sound of my own voice, "for someone who's claiming to be my soulmate, you don't seem to like me all that much."

"Yeah, well, I've never known a version of you without your power." She glances down at me again. Her arm drags against mine, chicken skin against goose bumps. "It's like all of the bravado with zero ability to back it up. I'm underwhelmed."

"I—" Wow. Okay. Ouch. "I am not underwhelming."

And if I am, it is my worst fear come true, and I am going to grab the steering wheel and drive us straight into the water.

"If you knew what you were actually capable of, you'd feel differently." Willa Mae sighs. She tilts her head back, staring at the muddy road ahead, but with a glossy-eyed smile that tells me she's not really seeing it. "When you're in your element, you are . . . everything. You're the *god of gods*. There's no one like you."

"There's already no one like me," I mumble.

"You certainly have the energy of someone who thinks that." She just says this, like it isn't the meanest thing anyone has ever said to another person. "But don't worry, you'll get there."

We drive the rest of the way in silence, while I think about digging my own grave.

Willa Mae lives in an old log cabin with a bricked chimney and a red tin roof that's gone rusted with age. It's tucked off the main road, with acres and acres of wetland around it, and an ancient-looking sports car parked outside.

She stops the Jeep next to it, eyeing the house's wraparound porch. "All right. So, you remember me telling you my grandparents were record keepers?"

"Like, they know about all of"—I wave between us—"this?"

"Right. Well, so, by extension . . . they *know* about all of this."

I'm sure that's supposed to mean something to me.

I blink at her.

Willa Mae groans. "Like, they know you're a god. And they're going to treat you like one."

"Oh." *Oh.* "Um . . . okay? Cool."

"Yeah. Cool. Keep that energy."

I don't know why she's being so ominous. And it doesn't make any more sense when we get out of the car, and an adorable elderly couple steps onto the porch to greet us.

And I do mean *adorable.* Willa Mae's grandma walks with a curve to her spine, chubby body bent over a beautifully carved wooden walker, her long gray hair in a thick braid. She's dressed in layers and layers of different-colored fabrics, like she pulled out all her crafting scraps and wrapped them around herself until she was satisfied. Willa Mae's grandpa is whip-thin but *huge*—he has to be closing in on seven feet—with a gray and black beard that hangs down to the middle of his torso. He's wearing denim overalls and a camo jacket that hangs off his skinny, stretched-out shoulders.

"You're home early," her grandmother croons, in a tone that

doesn't indicate she might be upset about it. "And look who you brought. Oh, this must be them. It is, isn't it?"

"It is, Ellen."

Excuse me, "*Ellen*"? Damn. I only see my grandmother once or twice a year, but she'd slap the shit out of me if I ever called her "Norma."

I shoot Willa Mae a sidelong glance, trying to silently ask why she's so rude, but she's not looking at me. She crosses her arms, tilting her head up at them. "We're going out back to work. When we're done, I'm gonna take them home. We *don't* want you to bother us. Okay?"

"Of course, of course," Ellen agrees, too enthusiastic about being told to get lost. "Whatever you need."

"Great, thanks." She grabs my arm, fingers sinking into my skin as she tries to steer me away.

But her grandfather is hobbling his way down the steps toward us. And Willa Mae might be the rudest person on the planet, but I am not going to *shun* the cute old people. I jerk out of her grip and smile as he approaches.

"Great Magician," he wheezes, before falling to his knees in the mud at my feet. "We have waited for you for so long."

Oh. Oh no. I blink at him before shooting Willa Mae a desperate look for help. She's glaring at us like she hates me *and* her grandfather.

"Please," he continues, and the next thing I know he's reaching out to grab my calves. "I know I am unworthy, but might you grant me a blessing? Please, I—"

"Enough, Joseph." Willa Mae's tone rumbles from her chest, the warning growl before a bite. "You are humiliating yourself."

She grabs my arm again. This time, I don't fight her as she drags me away.

Out of earshot of her grandparents, as we make our way through the muck to the back side of the property, I demand, "What was that!"

"I told you—they know who you are." Her expression is grim, jaw tight, eyes shuttered. "They're hoping you'll grant them a miracle."

"What kind of miracle?"

She doesn't answer. A muscle in that locked jaw ticks.

"What kind of miracle, Willa Mae?"

Her fingers dig into my arm so tightly that a flash of pain follows. I suck in a breath, but refuse to give her the satisfaction of yanking away.

Finally, she answers. "They're trying to have a baby."

I—

"*Who* is trying to have a baby?" I do jerk out of her grip now, but only because my feet plant themselves where we're walking. "*Not* Father Time and Baba Yaga back there."

Willa Mae sighs the longest-suffering sigh, facing me. She crosses her arms. "They had three kids. One of my uncles died young; the other's a womanizer with a drinking problem who thankfully never reproduced. And my mom only had me before she got her tubes tied."

"Okay?" If that means something, it goes right over my head.

"If this line disappears, we don't know where I'll end up in my next life."

"Oh . . ." Okay. So, maybe less plain-bizarre and more sad-bizarre.

"Did your dad have any siblings?"

"Um. Yeah. A brother—I haven't seen him since I was little, but I think he has kids." I don't remember much about him. "So, you'll just . . . not be reborn if there's no one for you to be born as?"

She swallows—then rolls her eyes again. "I don't know. I'm not talking to you about this right now. Come on."

She turns and keeps marching farther and farther away from the house. I glance back, my stomach turning when I realize Joseph is still on his knees.

Should I go back and help him? The poor old guy's shoulders are drooped so low, his face is nearly in the mud.

After a long moment, I follow Willa Mae.

She's way back where the mud meets the riverbank, leaning against the low-hanging branch of a willow tree. It's actually annoying, the way she's perfected the Cool Masc Lean, all casually tough and hot with her ripped-off sleeves and mud-splattered combat boots. As I approach, she reaches up to take her curls down, tousling the dark waves through her fingers and letting her hair fall to her waist. Sunlight filtering through the moss reflects off the shiny locks and glints into dust flecks in the air.

I'm so distracted that I almost step onto the gator lying at her feet.

"*FUCK ME*," I yodel, falling ass-backward in an effort to get away from the beast.

The gator has the audacity not to even open its eyes. Willa Mae snorts.

"Calm down. He's not going to hurt you." She waves a hand at herself. "Land god, remember?"

It's not that I'm irrationally afraid of alligators, it's just that

I'm very rationally afraid of them, and I don't like this at all. I stand, keeping a totally reasonable distance. "You sure you have control? He's on land right now, but he's at least half water, right?"

For whatever reason, Willa Mae gives me a nasty glare in response to that question. She also doesn't answer it. Instead, she says, "Give me your shoes."

"What?"

"Your shoes. Give them to me." She holds out her hand.

"That's . . . not my thing."

"*Echols.*"

And, because I'm still trying to process the last ten minutes, I lean down and unlace them for her. Because why not?

Mud squelches between my toes as I toss the shoes in her general direction, shoving my balled-up socks in my pocket.

Willa Mae rolls her eyes, but snatches them up—and promptly drops them into the waiting mouth of the now-awake gator. He chomps down on my boots, before darting, creepy and too fast, into the water.

"I— You— What was that for!" Every time I think our time together cannot get weirder, she goes and does some *bullshit.*

"The purpose of your magic is balance. When you create something, something else has to be destroyed. Finding something means you lose something else." She flexes her arms, then grabs a low-hanging branch and yanks herself up, straddling it to sit in the tree. "A sacrifice is always required. Sometimes, the sacrifice is where it begins. Since you don't know how to *start* your magic, I thought this was a good first step."

"So, feeding my shoes to your pet alligator was step one of finding the god-killing knife." Wow, what a sentence.

"The god-killing knife and the god-killing knife's accompanying chain, which I'm told is the only thing that can destroy it." She shrugs. "And he's not my *pet*. He's a wild animal. Show some respect."

"He ate . . . my shoes."

"I will send you thirty dollars to buy them again on Shein."

"I—" I narrow my eyes, pointing a finger at her. "I don't like how you just *know* things."

She points right back at me, all mockery. "Then stop being predictable."

It's impossible this girl is my soulmate. After knowing her for twenty-four hours, I can say with confidence that she's the most annoying hot person I've ever met.

"What am I supposed to do here?" I ask-yell, throwing my arms out. "I don't know how to find the knife, and *shockingly* being barefoot isn't helping!"

Willa Mae shrugs, leaning too-nonchalant against the willow's trunk. "Figure it out."

"Is this your idea of helping?" I stomp to the base of the tree, glowering up at her. "You say we've spent lifetimes together, and you don't know anything about how my magic works? Some soulmate you are."

"Oh, boo-hoo." She grins. *Grins!*

Adrenaline pops and anger sizzles underneath my skin, flaring through my joints and into my muscles. I want my hands around her neck. I want to find this freaking knife just so I can make sure I never have to deal with *this* again.

"How do I know you're even telling the truth, huh? You could be lying about our history. About the Ouroboros, too. Maybe we're actually worst enemies, and you're hoping I'll lead you to it before I remember."

"Damn, you're right." She cocks her head and has the nerve to *wink*. "Guess you're gonna have to remember faster, then."

The wet-earth smell of the swamp, the mud beneath my feet, the distant sound of bugs and birds and snakes—it all falls away, disappearing into a blurred background, too distant to matter. Two things shift violently into sharp focus: my anger, bright and hot and rippling through my nerve endings, and Willa Mae's face, beautiful and irritating as she smirks at me through a curl. A single bead of sweat drips from her temple to her cheek.

I want to hurt her. This rage feels like something I can touch, like barbed wire snagging in my veins, like a living creature trying to claw its way free. I want to ball it up between my fists and force her to take it from me. I imagine doing that, and I swear my palms spark with anticipation.

"Come on," she whispers. That stupid pink tongue touches her tattooed lip. "Remember me. I *dare* you."

That fury bubbles over, amplified by my own sick frustration. I can't wring her neck, so I slam my hands into her tree, instead, as if she might feel an echo of pain through their connection. *I'm* the one it actually hurts, though. My hands crack against the wood so hard they burn. If I didn't know better, I'd think I even smelled smoke.

And suddenly, the world tilts back into place.

"Screw you, Willa Mae."

"Hm." She slings her leg over the side of the branch. "Hey, Echols? Look down."

I need to wipe that cocky smile off her face. I need her to be as offended as I was when she said I was underwhelming. Through clenched teeth, I repeat, "Screw—"

"I get it, you wanna screw me. Now, *look down*."

She's insufferable. I look down because I don't know what else to do.

On my feet are a pair of black Doc Martens.

"Wh—" Anything I might've said shrivels up as Willa Mae slides off the branch. She tugs a bleach-dyed bandana from the back pocket of her jeans before taking my chin between her thumb and finger. Her grip isn't gentle, but it isn't painful, and she tilts my head back to press the bandana against my nose.

Her mouth is too close to mine when she says, "Nosebleed. Guess the shoes weren't enough—new ones must be better quality."

Willa Mae's thumb strokes the length of my jaw while she holds my face. And I *did* wipe the cocky smile off her face. She's still smiling, but now there's something almost tender in the expression.

"You did it, honey."

I did it. I did *magic.* That feeling of being electrocuted from the inside out has faded, but there's still a quiet hum in my bones. It makes me want to bounce on the soles of my new boots. It makes me want to do something stupid, like kiss the girl in front of me.

The fog appears between us.

One second, I'm staring into Willa Mae's eyes. The next, there's a blanket of unreality between her face and mine. And another life unfolds.

"Do you ever wish things were different?" Rosalie asks Billie, her fingers running through their hair while they lie, face-to-face, chest-to-chest, in bed. "That we could stop running? That we could just be . . . human?"

Billie snares her fingers with their own and kisses her knuckles. "No."

I know they mean it because *I* mean it. I remember meaning it, anyway.

When Billie continues, I feel the weighty truth of every word like it's my own. "I wish I could give you peace, sugar. You've earned your rest, we both have. But to spend only *one* human life together? No. I'm too selfish for that. I'll face our enemies over and over, as long as the Earth turns, so long as I face them at your side."

Rosalie sighs, fond. "You *are* selfish. My greedy god."

"I am a vile and insatiable lech," Billie agrees. Their free hand finds her waist before dipping lower. "Now, kiss me."

She does without hesitation.

As quickly as they appeared, Billie and Rosalie are gone. Willa Mae is staring me down with those uncanny eyes, soft and searching. Her fingers tighten on my jaw.

Willa Mae. Rosalie. The Mountain.

My heart gets a head rush and has to lie down.

"What did you see?" When she whispers, I taste her breath.

I *remember* what it was like to kiss her.

This is so much scarier than the alligator.

And I can't do it. This thing with Willa Mae, with this girl I know and don't, I just . . . can't. Not now. Probably not ever.

I force myself to step back, using the sleeve of my black-and-white-striped shirt to wipe at my nose. The white stripes come back smeared with red. Oh well.

"Um." Not telling her. Can't tell her. *Change the subject. Think of anything else.* "If all magic requires a sacrifice, what did I sacrifice when I brought us to Earth? Seems like it would have taken a lot more than a pair of shoes and a nosebleed."

Somehow—and I really don't know how I did it, it must be another one of my magic talents—that was the exact wrong question to ask. Her eyes shutter instantly, the longing in them replaced by an emptiness that makes my skin crawl. She steps away, back straightening. "I don't know."

She's lying. I don't know how I know, but she is.

Willa Mae shoves her bloodied bandana back into her pocket. "Come on. That was a good start, but it was *only* a start."

"O-okay." I want to know what's going on inside her head. But I also want to feel that rush of power again. That crackling in my bloodstream. That *magic,* apparently. "What did you have in mind?"

"I have a feeling you're not going to like this, either." From her other pocket, she produces a pocketknife. And with her unapologetic eyes on mine, she flips the blade open.

8

SO LONG AS I'M WILLING
TO PAY THE PRICE

The next day is Saturday. I wake up past noon, disoriented and hungry and sore all over.

Willa Mae spent *hours* slicing me like deli meat, thinking eventually, somehow, the bloodletting would be enough to get my magic pumping. Apparently, my blood's not worth as much as a knockoff pair of boots, 'cause nothing happened. Maybe I felt a little fizzle here or there, an echo of spark, but it wasn't enough.

Finally, when she worried I might pass out or die, she'd taken me back to school. I don't remember getting myself home from there, though I guess I did.

The new trend of blackout driving isn't my favorite thing ever.

Hank is snoring like a chain saw at the foot of my bed. I can't even bring myself to be mad—at least it means he's still breathing. I can hear my mom opening and closing cabinets too-loudly-not-to-feel-passive-aggressive in the kitchen. And my phone is buzzing.

I snag it just as the ringing stops.

MISSED CALL
SPAM RISK

So glad I woke myself up for that. Maybe I should just go back to sleep. I'm not in the mood to deal with my mom's snide comments about sleeping in anyway, and the best way to avoid that is to just not get out of bed at all.

I roll onto my side, wincing at the pain that spikes along my ribs. There are at least a dozen shallow graves in my skin, and each one of them *burns.* I haven't felt this kind of burn in seven months.

Maybe I'm not going back to sleep.

I sit up, stretching my legs out and under Hank when I do. He grunts, startling awake, and flops over onto his stomach.

"Morning."

He growls and closes his eyes again.

Fair enough.

My notifications have exploded. I skim my TikTok inbox, double-tapping a few messages without actually watching any of the videos. There's a handful of people in my Insta DMs, some of the messages older than others, most of them replies to long-expired private stories. I'm in a Discord server with a group of Enzo's friends, and they're all losing their minds over some Broadway casting that means *absolutely nothing* to me.

I open my texts. There are a few from Enzo himself. Without opening the thread, I can make out the first bit of his last message.

Little Dumbass

Good morning. I checked your mom's Facebook and she's
sharing her little Millennial memes, and your . . .

My thumb hovers over the conversation; I'm not sure if I
want to open it to finish reading. Because I *do*, I would read an
entire book of Enzo's asinine little comments, and it would be
my *favorite* book. But what am I supposed to say? I disappeared
yesterday, after telling him I was going to Willa Mae's and she
might murder me. If I open our texts, he's going to know I'm
up and on my phone and I won't have any excuse to avoid texting him back and if I don't have a good story lined up . . .

I hate having to do this with him. The weight of this guilt
is seriously *wrong*.

In the end, I do open the conversation. He sent me six texts
the day before.

Little Dumbass

My, my, she truly does just live in the middle of a swamp. Tell
me, is she an ogre?

Well—am I to take it you did, in fact, have fun?

Darling, I know you are socially inept, but it is generally
considered bad form to ominously imply you may never be seen
or heard from again, and then stop responding to someone's
messages for hours on end.

Are you aware Willa Mae Hardy does not have a single scrap
of social media presence? Not that I've managed to find in

my lengthy searching, at least. Are you certain that's her real
name?

Gemothy. This isn't funny.
Okay, you win. I'm scared. Please just send me a fucking emoji
or something so I know you're still alive.

And the final one, sent a couple of hours ago:

Good morning. I checked your mom's Facebook and she's
sharing her little Millennial memes, and your location says
you're still at home. I'm going to assume she's not reposting
pro-vaccine quotes pasted over screenshots from Harry Potter
while you're lying on your deathbed. But I would appreciate
a text back and maybe an explanation when you . . . wake
up? And I'm not going to apologize for sounding like a crazy
boyfriend, either, because you invited this upon yourself.

He maybe only kind of sounds like a crazy boyfriend, but
he's right. I did invite it on myself. Enzo and I have lived up
each other's asses 24-7 since we became friends. And yesterday,
I told him I was worried about going to a stranger's house alone
before ghosting him for twenty-four hours. I don't think I've
gone twenty-four hours without talking to him since . . . well,
the very first time we spoke.

The shittiest part about this entire thing is that I *have* a
good excuse—it's just not one I can tell him. There's no scenario here where I come off looking like anything but a bad
friend.

After waffling for a minute on my wording, I finally reply.

i am SO sorry. while i was at willa mae's, i started feeling
really out of it, and she basically had to help me get home
while i was a zombie. i'm pretty sure i passed out and just
slept for sixteen hours straight. i still don't feel 100% but i
don't actively feel like i might be dying anymore? but like,
seriously, i'm so so so sorry. i didn't mean to freak you out.

I hit send . . . and then immediately turn off the notifications for our conversation. Because my anxiety cannot handle seeing his reply pop up right now.

What I *need* is to tell him everything. I need to call him up on FaceTime and start rambling about the dreams, and the flashbacks, and Willa Mae, and Poppy, until there isn't a single thing he doesn't know. I need to scoop out my insides with my bare hands and offer him the ugly, goopy parts of me that are normally hidden. The world's worst gift. And I need him, somehow, to want all of it when I do.

I don't know if that kind of wanting is possible. But it doesn't matter. I can't try in the first place.

And if I can't have what I need, I can't deal with this at all. If I can't have what I need, I'll have to settle for what can distract me—something that exists far away from the guilt of lying to Enzo, and the confusion of spending time with Willa Mae, and the gnawing fear of what Poppy might do next.

If I can't be wanted in the way I *need,* then I *need* to be wanted in the one way that's guaranteed.

With a couple clicks, I pull up my texts with Indigo Ramirez. Our last exchange was two days earlier, a swapping of curated selfies.

Maybe no one will ever want to love the ugliest parts of me. At least plenty of people want to fuck the prettiest ones.

hey. you busy tonight?

I've never hung out with Indy outside of school, so we plan to meet at the East Gracie Dollar General before he drives us to his place. I spot his truck in the parking lot immediately—an old red Ford, mud-splattered and rusted over, with a BLACK LIVES MATTER banner tucked into the back window. That's always a hard one to miss in the GHS parking lot.

Indy's leaning against the driver's-side door and looks up when I park. He smiles, sliding his phone into the front pocket of his pink Ouran High School Host Club hoodie.

Damn, he's pretty. He's a tiny guy, shorter and skinnier than I am, with sharp, petite features. Eyes the color of amber resin sit over a long nose and hollowed cheekbones. His skin, several shades darker and cooler than my own, is speckled by clusters of obsidian birthmarks across his cheeks and jaw. There's a hint of fading purple dye in his black twists.

"Was starting to think you got lost," he teases, stepping into my space until I can smell the charcoal and fresh paper scent of him.

"Sorry." I'm not all that sorry. It isn't my fault I'm late. My mother *did* stop me, as soon as I stepped out of my room, to start a fight about how late I slept. Because she's annoying. At least she still let me take the car. "I'll make it up to you."

"Hm." He smirks.

There's a chance I overdid today's look, considering our rendezvous spot. But if I'm throwing myself into this as a coping mechanism, distracting myself from any actual problems by embracing being Gracie's token pansexual slut, I intend to commit to the bit. Mesh and pleather and studs and all.

Inside, the dollar store is pointlessly ominous. There's too much peeling white linoleum, too many blinking fluorescent lights. The obviously broken AC is still on and cranking out the worst mechanical gurgling I've ever heard. The shelves are half bare, with handwritten notes tucked into the empty spots that say shit like, "DO NOT ASK."

I follow Indy as he moves toward the snack aisle. I just want condoms and candy and to get the hell out of here.

The migraine-inducing lighting bounces off the silver hoop in his cartilage. His long, slender fingers consider a bag of Doritos. And I do the stupid thing I always do at around this point. When I've decided to *hang out* with a Gracie local, but we're still fully dressed.

I start imagining a world where this was more than just hanging out. Where Indy and I might know more about each other than what the other's tongue tastes like by the end of the night. What that kind of life would look like, where someone like him wanted something *more* with me.

And I don't mean being his *significant other* or whatever. I have no desire to hold Indy's hand or send him a pink carnation on Valentine's Day or write him a poem or something. The idea makes me feel nothing.

No, what I'm fantasizing about is infinitely more humiliating. I start imagining a world where Indigo Ramirez might want to be my friend.

I imagine what my life would be like if I was the kind of person who could just *be friends* with people. Where we go back to his place and *actually* watch Netflix. Maybe he'd get me into anime and show me the drawings in his sketchbook no one else is allowed to see. I could make him listen to my unhappy indie-folk playlists and tell him I'm scared my dog is going to die soon. He might give me an ill-advised stick-and-poke tattoo in his bathroom and I'd convince him to let me pierce his ears with a sewing needle and an ice cube. When the river's low, we could go mudding on the bank, laughing on either side of his truck bench.

I've never been the sort of person who could just . . . make friends. I blame it on being in Gracie, on being surrounded by small-minded Bible-thumpers who don't understand me and who don't wanna try, but that's bullshit. It's not like I was winning any popularity contests back in Atlanta. And there are plenty of people here who are as far from the bigoted-hick stereotype as you can get, present company included.

No, the problem is me. That wall between me and the rest of the world, that bridge I can't make myself cross. Enzo's the first person who's ever really been my *friend,* the only person I've ever felt could see me and really wanted to, but . . . even with him, the wall is there. There are still secrets between us. And, as of two days ago, there are more piling up. If I don't get rid of Poppy and put an end to this whole battle-of-the-gods thing, I'm never going to have the kind of connection I'm desperate for, with Enzo or anyone else.

Unless. Well. There is one person who doesn't seem to think there's any bridge separating us, *despite* my protests.

As if he can read my mind, Indigo grabs a bag of salt-and-vinegar chips off the shelf and says, "I heard you and Willa Mae have been hanging out. What's her story?"

Yikes. Where to begin?

It doesn't matter anyway. Because I open my mouth to answer—and I can't breathe. The world tips beneath my feet, my stomach rolling. It's like I'm standing in the snack aisle, but I'm not tethered to the same gravity. Where are my feet? Why is my body sideways?

I want to ask for help, but I can't. I'm here, but I'm not.

The fog between me and the world returns, thicker than ever before. And a new scene begins to play.

In the Ether, the Caretaker's land is everything the Shade's is not. Her realm is a hub of life: ancient buildings clustered so close that they keep each other upright by leaning together, bodies bustling in crowds through the city's market-lined streets, skittering fauna and vining flora tangling their way through any crack they can breach. The laughter and shouting and music of her people push against the Shade and me even as we hide in the dankest, darkest underbelly of the city, the tunnels beneath their capitol.

This is where we have taken the Caretaker. This is where we have strapped the god of life to a stone slab so we can carve away the meat of her.

I've known for some time now that this could not be avoided. First was the Sun—she made herself the Shade's first victim because of her own prying eyes, always trying to *shed light* on his secrets. And she did, in the end. She shed enough light that her lover, the Moon, came running. He made himself the second to fall.

The Inferno, like the Moon, came to us of their own accord. The god of fire believed their rage alone might quell the shadow spreading across the Ether's surface. We put them down like mercy-killing a rabid dog.

Each time, the Shade has kept the powers we pull from the other gods' bodies. There is good reason for this, he reminds me—I don't *need* their power. I am the god of magic. I am untouchable. *He* is the one who needs the protection this new power provides. *He* is the one who has been abused for epochs by our pantheon.

When he says these things, I know he is attempting to manipulate me. Perhaps it even works. He does not know I would not keep their powers for myself, even if I wanted to. Because I *am* the god of magic—the keeper of the scales. There is nothing any of the others can do that I am not already capable of. While they operate in their limited realms with free rein, I can do anything, so long as I pay for it. This is balance. My existence is meant to offset theirs.

But were I to take one of their realms for myself? To open the floodgates for my magic *without* sacrifice? I do not know that the scales could ever be balanced again. . . .

No, he must be the one to inherit their gifts. Only when he holds dominion over all other realms will he be my equal—worthy of ruling this world at my side.

But first, the Caretaker must go. We will never control this world until life and death sit together in the palms of our hands.

I *know* this. Just as I know that what we are doing is true to my purpose—there is no justice in turning one of our kind into a scapegoat as the others have done to the Shade. His rise to power is the only way to balance the scales of history. This new era, *our era,* is what I was destined to bring forth. I am certain of it. I am certain of him.

And yet . . . somehow, I know all of this to be true, and my stomach still aches at the sight of the Caretaker on the slab.

I cannot seem to make myself move. My knife-wielding hand is frozen just above her chest, already carved open. I watch, disgusted and fascinated, as her exposed, bloody heart continues to pump without the armor of her ribs.

The Shade presses his hand to my lower back, stepping in against me. His horrible teeth brush the side of my face. "What ails you, creature?"

I try to speak, but my throat is tight with bile. I watch as tears spill from the corners of the Caretaker's eyes, streaking toward what used to be round cheeks. Now they're only empty craters of raw flesh and broken teeth in the center of what was once a beautiful face.

Finally, I find my voice. "Perhaps we could commence a moratorium. We have already taken a great deal of her power. I can feel it within the blade. And she will not seem . . . to die."

Why will she not just die? The agony she must be in is beyond comprehension. Her body is unrecognizable, a mutilated puddle of ivory and crimson and fleshy pink. It is unthinkable to me that she is clinging to consciousness, even now, no matter what I bring myself to do to her.

Life, I suppose, finds a way.

"You know we cannot stop," the Shade sighs. He kisses the top of my head, his fingers curling around my waist to pull me gently to his chest. A too-tender embrace in the midst of this carnage. "If she were to survive, and even a *fraction* of her power were to remain within her, it could be catastrophic. All of this, all that she has already suffered, would be for naught. We cannot risk that, can we?"

One of her green eyes begins to droop from its smashed socket.

"I suppose not. . . ."

Steeling my shoulders, I press the tip of the Ouroboros to the underside of her jaw. But just before I press the blade in to begin the process of removing her head from her spine, an *awful* moan begins to leak from her mouth. The creaking, popping, baritone crackle is low and broken as she struggles to form words, and nearly hidden beneath the noise on the heavy-trafficked street over our heads.

I lean forward, trying to make out something like language in the grotesque sound of her dying rattle. I don't know that I actually do. Perhaps I know what she means to say, somehow. Or perhaps I simply imagine I can make out something syllabic and project my own fear onto her tongue.

But I swear the Caretaker whispers, "May death evade you forever."

I shoot backward. How am I meant to take that?

Is she assuring me I will live for an eternity with the weight of what I've done?

Or begging a power higher than either of us that her twin sister, the Reaper, never falls beneath my knife?

My life has already been so long, and I have never feared death in all this time. Only now, in the wake of the sins brought forth tonight by my own hands, do I find myself nervous to meet death's eyes. I am afraid. I am very afraid.

Again, the world rocks beneath me, this time seeming to spin until everything is a blur. The Ether and the dollar store swirl in a mismatched jumble of color and sound, reality and unreality banging together like pots against pans. It makes me so dizzy that I would scream if I weren't worried about throwing up.

As quickly as it began, it stops. The swirling ends so abruptly that it knocks me off my feet, and I fall to the dirty floor. It takes me a moment to notice I really *am* screaming, out loud, in the dollar store. Another moment for me to stop. And a third for me to realize the lights in this place are flickering more wildly than they were before, like an electric pulse has just gone ricocheting off the walls.

Indy has dropped all the snacks in his hand to kneel next to me, one hand on my back as he rubs between my shoulder blades. His sharp eyes are bright with concern.

Somewhere else in the store, the clerk is yelling about a generator.

"Gem," Indy starts, but I cut him off.

"I gotta go." I grab the shelf to haul myself to my feet, groaning at the vertigo that hits me in the gut. I don't know how I'm going to drive home like this, but there's no way I'm staying here, no way I'm actually going to Indy's house. "I'm sorry— I'm—I'm sorry."

What else is there to say? I can't explain any of this.

The sight of the Caretaker's beating heart flashes through my mind. With every ticking of my own pulse, I hear hers winding down to its end. *Ba-boom . . . ba-boom . . . ba-boom . . .*

I feel Indy's eyes on me the whole time I stumble my way outside. I zigzag through the parking lot like I've had too many filched wine coolers. It takes me three tries to get the car door open, two to start the engine, and I'm pretty sure I tap someone's bumper on the way out of the lot.

Less than a mile down the road, I have to swerve into the ditch because I keep drifting into the wrong lane.

I don't even know what I'm doing until I'm already doing it. My phone's in my hand and I'm opening up my muted text thread with Enzo and seeing that he responded hours ago.

Little Dumbass

I'm glad you're okay.

I'm not okay. I'm so far from okay that I don't think I'm ever going to be okay again. How am I supposed to get through this? Even if I can somehow win against Poppy, I'm never going to be *me* again, am I?

Fuck. Poppy.

"May death evade you forever."

Death isn't evading me. She isn't even trying. She's coming right for my head, and of course she is—I killed her *twin sister*. And the way I did it . . .

How much longer did the god of life hold on? How many more bones did I dig out of her skin? How many of her organs did she watch spill to the floor with her one remaining eye? I'd been planning to behead her—how long can a god stay conscious while someone uses a dagger to saw off their head?

"Hello?"

Freeze.

Enzo's voice. Where is Enzo's voice coming from?

It's enough to shock my system into a restart. Like being splashed with cold water.

Phone. In my hand. I called him. I called Enzo. I don't remember doing that. I don't even remember thinking about doing it.

But there he is. In my hand. On the phone.

"Gem? Hello?"

I struggle for something to say—scramble for the ability to say anything at all, to push aside my panic and nausea and *panic* and pretend I'm okay and pretend I'm human and pretend everything isn't going to get worse, just so I can say, "Hi."

A single syllable. And it sounds pathetic, even to me.

"Gem, I—" On his end of the call, a door closes. Enzo's voice melts, like warm honey, tone softening when he speaks again. "Hey, what's going on? You don't sound good."

I'm not good. I'm not sure I ever have been.

Tears burn my eyes. I drop my phone into my lap to drag

my nails across my face, like I might be able to claw away the fit before it begins. And still, a sob slips its leash, breaking through the fence of my throat when I answer, "Things are getting bad."

And I can't tell you why.

"Oh. Oh, darling." More shuffling. He sighs. It's the weekend in Brooklyn. I wonder which cool queer apartment he's hanging out at. "What can I do?"

"I just—" I shove my hand in my mouth, biting down at my knuckles to stifle the scream that can't seem to stop itself from bubbling out of me. Everything is too big. My body isn't strong enough to hold it all in. Wrapping saliva-slicked fingers around the steering wheel, I choke out, "I just wish I was with you. I just want to be with you."

"You will be. You're going to be here so soon, and I'm gonna take care of you, and everything's going to be okay. You're going to be okay. I love you, and we'll be together soon."

He keeps repeating this, variations of the same oath over and over again, a whispered chant through my speaker.

And I can't say anything back, just sit in the driver's seat of my mom's car, in the ditch in the middle of nowhere, and cry until I think I might puke.

I cry because I'm tired and lonely and scared. I cry because I don't know that Enzo's right; I don't know that we *will* be together, ever, now.

I cry, mourning the life I once knew.

9

THERE ARE NO CIS GODS

The next time I see the Shade, he's pinning me down with his teeth at my throat. Sex, not murder.

It's Sunday night, and I'm dreaming. Beyond the fog, I can make out my open bedroom window and Hank snoring on my floor. I left on the light in my closet, and my laptop's open on my bedside table; I fell asleep watching *Euphoria* with the Discord group.

In front of the fog, though, is my shirtless demon, one hand curled around my back to lift my body toward his, the other tangled in my hair as he kisses across my jaw. It's a terrible thing, being kissed by someone with a mouth like this, knowing my flesh would tear so easily for him; a terrible thing that this monster could eat me alive. Somehow, I still tilt my head back to offer him my throat.

This night took place *before* we carved the Caretaker open. We haven't even killed the Inferno yet. We're riding on the high of taking out the Sun and the Moon. Their power's passed to my demon; now he controls both day and night.

And I control *him*. It's an intoxicating thing to have a monster this lethal pin me down—while knowing he's nothing without me.

His head dips lower, sweeping from my neck to my chest, the hint of his fangs brushing my sternum. When he tilts his eyes toward mine, they glitter an uncanny shade of silver laced with gold. A new development.

"Do you know why I love you, creature?" His voice is roughened. It's been a long day. I can still smell the coppery whisper of blood in the room.

"You don't." I chuckle, brushing my knuckles against his handsome face, curling my fingers beneath his jaw. "You love what I can make you."

"I do love our alliance," he smirks, wicked, leaning forward to nip my skin. A bloom of soft red appears between my stomach and his lips. He doesn't seem to notice my blood painting his mouth. "But I love you because you are the only one who has ever truly seen me. Do you know that? Do you know you are the only one who has ever tried?"

He hums, and I feel his breath against my navel. "The version of myself I am with you does not exist in the presence of any other—it cannot. I never wish to lose this feeling."

Now-me feels like my heart might burst. What a grotesquely soft admission from the worst person to ever live. What a humiliatingly *familiar* feeling.

Then-me is less moved, at least on the surface. I tangle my fingers in his hair, pressing down at the top of his head. He leaves a trail of scarlet kiss stains down my stomach as he moves lower, and lower . . .

It feels like someone grabs a rope behind my belly button and yanks on it. The me in my bed doesn't move, can't move, but the me in my memory is tossed away, disappearing like Alice going round and round down the rabbit hole. That same dizzying feeling from the dollar store hits me.

The vision blurs, spinning out, replaced by something else. As it does, the spinning begins to fade, settling until both versions of me can catch our breath. The Shade is gone.

I am Billie Campbell, once again. I'm sitting at a desk in the back of my father's bank, with my human older brother, Jack. And I'm holding the Ouroboros between us.

"I told Rosie I was taking it to the caves in Chickamauga. We agreed, with Wanda and Constance getting so close, it can't stay with us anymore. And it'd be well hidden there, until next time."

The name *Constance* makes my stomach churn. Wanda was the Reaper's last lifetime, but Constance was the Lionheart, the god of battle, her ominous other half. I still haven't recovered my memories of her. But my instincts fire off a warning shot. Not good.

Jack Campbell is a sweet boy with big blue eyes and black hair, pink-faced and openhearted and loyal enough to die for me without complaint. That's why I chose him for this task.

"Do you want me to take it? To the caves?" he asks, leaning forward.

"No." I place the dagger on top of the desk, pushing it toward him. "I *do* want you to take it. Not there."

My brother frowns, eyes darting between me and the knife, before he reaches forward and picks it up. "What do I do?"

"I need *you* to keep it hidden. No matter what happens, don't let it fall out of the hands of our family. We'll keep it tucked away in plain sight, the last place our enemies would think to look." I reach across the table and place my hand over his, curling our fists together over the sharp edge of the blade. "And, Jack? You don't tell a soul. As far as you know, this knife is long gone. This secret goes with you to your grave."

He trembles, eyes as wide as I've ever seen them. "Of course. Whatever you need, Magician. Anything to keep you safe."

"Good." I smile, knowing he means it. "That'll be all, then."

Jack rises from his seat and I, Gem Echols, shoot up in bed so fast that Hank barks without opening his eyes. My heart struggles to return to a normal speed while my eyes adjust to the semidarkness of the bedroom.

Okay. *Okay.*

Of three things, I'm feeling pretty certain.

One—no relationship has ever been more toxic or sexy than the one between original-me and the god of things forbidden.

Two—multiple versions of past-me *really* sucked.

And three—I think we have our first lead on the Ouroboros's location.

When I slide into Willa Mae's Jeep on Monday morning, she silently passes me a warm thermos that smells like chai. She's dressed in the most patch-covered denim jacket I've ever seen. There's a SHE/THEY pin on her shoulder.

"Of course you're trans," I mumble, as if this is some kind of inconvenience. Which it is, obviously. They continue to make themself more and more interesting to be around, and I really don't need that.

"There are no *cis* gods," they scoff. Willa Mae takes a sip from their own thermos—which smells like honey and mint and lavender—before asking, "All right, are you gonna tell me about this dream?"

I'd texted them when I woke up, telling them to meet me

here—with caffeine—so we could go over the things I saw the night before. Well. Some of the things I saw. Settling into the passenger seat, I launch into the details, starting from the moment the Ouroboros got involved, and leaving out everything about the Shade's half-naked body.

Their face grows increasingly more perturbed. By the time I finish, they're *glaring,* fingertips tapping against their drink in a rhythm that manages to sound hateful.

"*What?*" This was not the reaction I was expecting.

"You didn't tell me any of this."

"I—literally, I just did. What do you mean?"

"No." They roll their eyes. "You didn't tell me about any of this when it *happened.* You went back on our plan and you did it behind my back. Why?"

"Uh." This is so dramatically far away from the point. "Does that matter? Do you want to have a couple's spat in the school parking lot, or do you want to use this information to find the knife?"

Willa Mae narrows their eyes further and continues to stare at me like they're actually weighing their options.

"Oh, for fuck's sake."

"Okay, fine." They sigh. "So, you told your brother to keep it in the family. So, it's probably, what, with some distant cousin by now?"

I shake my head. "I don't know. I doubt it. My dad's family is pretty small. The Campbell line got filed down a lot, from what I can tell. You said my grandparents were record keepers. Maybe they had the knife."

"Which would mean . . . your dad has it?"

"If my dad *ever* had it, we're screwed. There's no way he still does." I don't want to get into this with them, have no desire to tell them my little sob story, so I just say, "He's not . . . well. He wouldn't have kept anything, especially if he had no idea it was supposed to be important."

They consider me like they're thinking about asking for more details. But they don't, and I'm grateful for small favors. "Well . . . shit."

"Yep."

Willa Mae slumps back in their seat, bringing their tea to their mouth and taking a sip. I try my own. When I asked for caffeine, I was imagining more along the lines of a can of Monster from the gas station. But it's good, actually. Warm and spicy and familiar, somehow, even though I can't remember ever trying chai before. I wonder how they knew I'd like it, but don't question it too much. There's no point.

Finally, they look at me again. "So, when you were talking to Jack. You said . . . he needed to keep the blade in the family. And he needed to take the secret of its location to his grave."

I replay the memory-dream from the night before. "Yeah."

"What if he . . . took that very literally?"

Immediately, I know what they're asking. I really wish I didn't, though. So, I play naïve. "Not following."

"What if he was buried with the Ouroboros? No one would go looking there."

"For good reason."

"Okay, well, the alternative is that your dad pawned it and we're never going to find it again. Is that what you're hoping for?" They raise their eyebrows, a double dog dare in their expression.

It takes everything in me not to say something awful just to hurt their feelings. "Okay. Fine. So, what, now we find where Jack's buried? Start looking at cemetery rosters in Atlanta?"

Willa Mae shakes their head. "He wouldn't be there. Our families fled Atlanta for further south—*after* convincing the Reaper and the Lionheart they were going west. I'm guessing that's why Poppy's family was out in Nebraska. And why Marian is still there."

"That's really cruel, condemning someone to be born in Nebraska."

They sigh like they hate me. Unfortunately for us both, I know they don't.

"All right, so, our families went south. My dad's family was living in the Florida panhandle when him and my mom met—is that where Jack would have gone?"

"Well . . . no. The Campbell family probably moved around a little bit, over the generations, to keep hidden. But when we left Atlanta, we came . . . here." They flick their wrist toward the parking lot around us, where students are still showing up and heading inside. "To Gracie."

"Oh." I guess that makes sense. Except, wait, "What do you mean, to keep hidden?"

They have that look like they need to tell me something they really don't want to tell me, which isn't great, because I'm not really in the mood to hear something else I don't want to hear. After running their hands along the steering wheel and visibly debating with themself, Willa Mae finally sighs out, "*O-kay.* So, uh. You remember how I warned you that things might get bad, if Poppy woke up some of the sleeping gods? The ones who don't remember who they are?"

"Yes. . . ." This is off to a horrible start.

"Well. Right. So. The reincarnation spell . . . something about it acts as almost a . . . beacon. We're pulled to each other, like magnets, even if we don't want to be."

"Can you please just spit out whatever point you're trying to make?"

"Fate has a way of bringing the sleeping gods back to us. And over the years, their families would have started showing up. One by one."

A long moment stretches out, the silence in the Jeep growing and growing until it starts to tear at the seams. I turn away from them and watch the students milling around outside. Some of them loitering by their cars, smoking or making out, checking Twitter before homeroom. Others darting off into the building to hurriedly do their forgotten homework before first period. Others are still showing up, last-minute bus arrivals and cars screeching into the parking lot.

I force myself to look back to Willa Mae. "You're telling me . . . there are other bloodlines living in Gracie? *Now?*"

"Yes."

"And that means . . ." I clench my teeth. I can't even make myself say it.

"The sleeping gods Poppy might try to wake up?" They nod. "Yeah. They're right here."

Somewhere, a clock ticks. It may just be the beating of my heart.

Willa Mae reaches over the center console and palms my knee. "Hey. Grave robbing doesn't sound so bad now, does it?"

10

WHAT A STRANGE AND CAPTIVATING COMMUNION

The Old Gracie Cemetery is little more than a cluster of tiny stones in the middle of a swamp, and its church is long gone, just rotting boards collected in a heap on the edge of the riverbank. I sneak out that night after Mom goes to bed and meet Willa Mae there.

There is something about the withering of consecrated ground that makes my skin crawl. I wonder what becomes of a god when their church falls to ruin and their congregants are nothing but bone. Is this place still holy? If we prayed to this god, would he hear us?

Would we want him to?

All around us, ancient cypress trees curl their limbs protectively around the graveyard. I know the hissing and chirping in the air is the sound of a thousand different bugs, but I could swear it feels like a warning whispered by the trees themselves—telling us to leave this place and let the buried stay that way.

Willa Mae tilts her head toward me and smiles, the kind of smile that crinkles the corners of her eyes. It feels at home here, in the wild and creepy underbelly of the world. "Would you believe me if I told you this isn't the weirdest date we've ever been on?"

At some point, I'm going to ask her to tell me more about that. But right now, she doesn't give me the chance. Instead, the god of land steps through the tree-lined boundary into the cemetery without fear or hesitation. I don't know if it's my brain playing tricks on me, but it almost looks like the swamp leans back to make room for her.

Jack's tomb is as small and unimpressive as the rest of them. It takes us a good twenty minutes to find him, shoved at the back, his grave marker overgrown with moss and rot.

HERE LIES THE BODY OF

JACK FRANKLIN CAMPBELL

FEBRUARY 23, 1910—DECEMBER 9, 1961

BEHOLD, HE IS COMING WITH THE CLOUDS,

AND EVERY EYE WILL SEE HIM, EVERY ONE WHO PIERCED HIM;

AND ALL TRIBES OF THE EARTH WILL WAIL ON

ACCOUNT OF HIM. EVEN SO. AMEN.

"1961," I mumble, crouching down to touch the cryptic verse etched on the tombstone's surface. "That feels so . . . recent."

The little brother from my last lifetime was still living in Gracie just twenty years before my this-life mom was born. Jack Franklin Campbell. And who is he to *me*? My great-grandfather, maybe? I don't know enough about my dad's side of the family to have any idea.

The whole thing makes me feel sick. I don't know why.

Willa Mae's hand curls around my shoulder, too heavy and too warm. A memory prods the back of my mind, threatening to make me relive it. I make a point not to lean in—to the touch *or* the flashback.

"Come on," she whispers, though I don't know why she bothers keeping her voice down. The dead probably don't care. "Let me do what I need to do."

I don't know what she means, but I have a feeling I'm gonna hate what happens next. Still, I shuffle out of her way, dropping onto my ass on top of the next grave over. (*Oh, hello, Beatrice Campbell. Do we know each other?*)

Willa Mae pulls the black hair tie off her wrist and gathers her mane of hair back as tight as possible. There's no light in the cemetery except for our phone flashlights, casting her in a collage of yellow and shadow. In this light, the tattooed lines along her chin seem longer, like fingers stretching down her throat.

When the glow catches her eyes, the red-brown of them looks almost like magma—and I'm reminded how uncontrollable nature really is. The hairs on the nape of my neck rise.

Not paying any attention to me, she kneels next to Jack's grave and presses the tips of her fingers into the earth. The soil here is soft and damp, and it makes way for her without resistance. She slides her hands into the earth until they disappear altogether, until mud collects at her wrists.

And then the world begins to shift under Willa Mae's command.

The wet dirt begins a slow crawl up her arms, the grave simply *digging itself up* and threatening to bury her alive, instead. Willa Mae doesn't look afraid; her expression burns with something akin to euphoria as her arms disappear beneath the muck.

As the plot beneath is uncovered, she isn't the only one the soil crawls toward. When a clump of soil drags itself onto my leg it feels *too* much like being grabbed by someone's hand. The horrible unreality of it all is enough to make me feel sick.

And yet . . . even as the mud unfurls, twining up around my own hands and arms, coating my clothes in debris, I don't feel afraid. Because something about this is familiar.

Maybe because I've been here before, with Willa Mae. Not this graveyard, not in this body. But *here,* where her power meets the earth and I'm an onlooker in awe of them both.

Or maybe because the land in Gracie's been trying to talk to me for years, and this is the closest I've ever come to understanding it.

Whatever the case, I have a feeling neither of them would ever hurt me.

I slide my fingers through the brown soil dragging itself over my lap. It moves as if to meet my palm, and my heart lodges itself like a stone in my throat. What a strange and captivating communion this is.

It isn't until the dirt shudders and falls lifeless into itself that I look back to Willa Mae. She's watching me, perched on the edge of Jack's grave—now overturned entirely, revealing the steel coffin inside. I can *feel* the weight of her stare as she considers me, my trembling hands coated in mud. She doesn't say anything. After a pause, she slides down to land on the coffin's lid with a thunk.

When she shuffles to the side and reaches for the latch, words bubble up and out of me without my permission. "Wait! Can we . . . can we just pause?"

She turns that stare on me again. I expect her to say something scathing, maybe—like, "*He's not going to get less dead the longer we wait*"—but it doesn't come. Instead, she drops onto her ass, on my dead brother's casket.

"Okay. We're paused."

"Okay." I sniff, searching the ground for something to talk about. I'm suddenly too aware of the screeching bugs, of the too-hot, too-damp air, of the tension like a knot in my chest. Sweat trickles over my temple and I swallow. "So, how was your day?"

"Echols, *really?*"

"I'm sorry! I just—" I wave a hand in her direction. "I'm doing my best here. But are you seriously not freaking out at all? This isn't like . . . the worst thing you've ever done?"

"I've been—"

"And I don't mean you, like the Mountain, okay, I mean *you*, like Willa Mae. Is there seriously no part of you that's still grossed out by the fact that we're about to *steal* from someone's *corpse?*"

She sighs and leans back against the hard-packed earth behind her. Roots buried deep in the ground crawl forward to play with the tresses of her hair. She doesn't seem to notice. "I'm not Willa Mae. Not really."

I want to argue with that, but she isn't done speaking. She adds, "But I get your point. Okay? I hear you. My day was fine. Did you hear Poppy is campaigning for prom queen?"

"Oh, *that*. Yes. I did." Considering she tried to gank me in the parking lot the first time we met, I expected Zombie

Barbie to be a much bigger problem in my day-to-day life. So far, she hasn't tried anything else. But she keeps looking at me, with this stupid evil-mastermind grin, and I know something's coming. Something very bad. I'm just hoping I'll be able to magically kick her ass by the time it does. "Is she this weird in every life?"

It's a joke, but Willa Mae answers honestly, "No. She gets worse every time. I think . . . We were all cut off from a lot of our power when we made the sacrifice to come here from the Ether. But no one lost quite as much as the Reaper did."

The sight of the Caretaker's heart, pumping blood directly onto the stone slab she was strapped to, burns in my mind's eye. I flinch. "I remembered—about her twin."

Willa Mae doesn't bother trying to hide her wince. "Yeah. That was . . ."

She trails off, maybe unable to find a word for what she actually wants to say, maybe just not wanting to say it to my face. I get it, though. I don't need her to tell me I was a monster. Finally, she continues, "If it makes you feel any better, that was your breaking point. You finally escaped the Shade's control after that. It wasn't much longer before you helped us get out."

I've noticed, when she talks about the Shade and me and the things we did, she talks like I was brainwashed. I don't feel brainwashed when I dream. But then, maybe no one ever *feels* brainwashed. Maybe that's why it works.

"But Poppy never forgave me." It's not a question, and it doesn't need an answer.

"The Reaper . . ." Willa Mae rubs her hands over her face. "Life and death are more than just twin sides of each other— they can't *exist* without the other. In the Ether, the Reaper and the Caretaker controlled the life and death cycles of all things. They nurtured souls on the other side, and sent them back, reincarnated, when they were ready. With the Caretaker's death, it wasn't just that Poppy lost her sister. It was that the whole of the *afterlife* fell into chaos—in the hands of the Shade. Maybe Poppy could have forgiven you if it was just about losing her twin. But she . . . she won't ever be whole again. Not unless she can use your magic to go back and take her sister's power from the god of things forbidden."

I don't know what's worse. The way Willa Mae says "just" when she talks about me slaughtering the god of life. Or the fact that Poppy is rotting from the inside out because of something *I* did. *Of course* she's getting worse in every lifetime. She doesn't have any life in her.

I don't know how to deal with the fact that Poppy's desire to see me dead is justified—and I still want to live. Maybe it would be *fair* if I died, but I don't *want to*. And why should I? Why should I take accountability for something I can barely remember doing, when accountability means I don't get to *exist* anymore?

"Why don't I just send her back, then?" I ask, throwing my arms out in frustration. "If I opened the door once, I can do it again, right? I can just kick her through and close it back up!"

"You've considered that." Willa Mae shrugs. "But it's not so much that there's a *door* you open and close. You tethered our souls to a new plane, dragging us through space to get here, leaving behind our true vessels and the world we came from. But you also tethered us to *each other*. Sending her back could mean sending everyone back." Her expression darkens, and she shakes her head. "The Shade has had one thousand years to warp the Ether, coercing the people there to indulge in every awful thought they have. And with no order in the reincarnation cycle? Souls coming at the wrong times, never meeting the ones they're supposed to, never fulfilling their purpose? Just returning again and again to more and more chaos? None of us should ever want to set foot in that world again."

And that's the world Poppy is going to drag Willa Mae, and everyone else, back to, if she gets her hands on the Ouroboros and manages to kill me.

I eye the coffin, but my nausea hasn't subsided. Not ready yet. Instead, I wipe the back of my hand over my forehead, smearing mud in an effort to clean off the sweat, and bring up a related anxiety. "So, these sleeping gods. The ones you say are in Gracie with us. How can we figure out who's who?"

"Oh, I already know." Willa Mae just says that like it's no big deal, shrugging her broad shoulders. "You'll start being able to soon. The more you remember, the more you'll be able to *feel* them for who they really are."

For crying out loud. "Okay. If you already can, you wanna clue me in?"

She considers the dirt under her fingernails. "Your friend, Zeke? He's one."

My heart slams on the brakes. "Absolutely not. No way. *Ezekiel King?*"

"Do you know another Zeke?"

I'm going to strangle her. "What could he possibly be the god of? Push-ups?"

"Sort of. Strength. We called him the Hammer."

The Hammer. I hate how ridiculous that title is, and I hate even more that, somehow, Zeke King being the god of strength makes complete sense.

But . . . still. "That is just—that's—"

"Look, I get it's weird. You think you know someone. But

it's like I told you before. We're *drawn* to each other. Fate might bring our families together, but *we* hunt each other down, even when we don't mean to. Maybe it's because of the magic tethering us. Maybe it's not. Look, honey, we're gods. We're not wired to make human connections. And we're the only ones who can really understand each other." She sighs. "I'm so sorry I have to be the one to tell you this, but anyone in Gracie you actually *like*? There's a solid chance they're a sleeper."

Which means they probably wouldn't like *me*, if they knew who I am—and who they are.

"Screw it." I stand up, spurred to action by the threat of being disliked. "Let's get this over with."

Willa Mae jumps up and shuffles to the edge of the grave, off the coffin's lid. She slides her fingers beneath the rim before shooting me a glance. "You don't have to look if you don't want to."

It's her way of calling me a coward.

And because I *am* a coward, I turn my head.

There's a sound of creaking metal, and then a too-long pause where the only things I can hear are the swamp bugs, and the distant laughter of coyotes, and my own off-beat heart. When the pause ends, there's a rustling of what sounds like leather, and a clinking-together I refuse to identify.

Then, "Goddammit!"

I turn back to Willa Mae just as she slams the lid closed, catching the briefest glimpse of my brother's bones, wrapped in his petrified skin like a moth inside a cocoon.

The earth begins to move again, dirt dragging itself back toward the grave. It threatens to carry me with it, rushing underneath my feet like flowing water, and I scramble to escape its tide. A wave of mud crests into the pit, burying the casket and disappearing beneath Willa Mae's shoes. It lifts her up, delivering her to the shore and setting her on her feet in front of me.

Her cheeks are a special shade of magenta-purple, fists clenched. She won't look at my face.

"Nothing?"

"*Nothing*," she snarls, and heads for the cars.

I turn back to Jack's grave. *Jack Franklin Campbell.* There is no logical explanation for the swell of grief threatening to drag me down—I shouldn't miss him. I can't miss him; *I* didn't know him.

And yet. My heart lurches at the idea of his dying at only fifty-one. What are fifty-one human years? That time passes in the blink of an eye. My beloved little brother barely lived at all.

That thought doesn't make any sense, either. *I'm* only seventeen. I remind myself of this like it might become true.

Without thought, I crouch down and press my hand to the top of his tombstone. Quietly, not knowing what I intend to say until it's leaving my mouth, I whisper, "You did good, Jackie. I'll take it from here. I'll figure it out."

The cypress tree at my back shakes like a warning. I stand and follow Willa Mae.

She's leaning against the bumper of her Jeep, head tilted back against the windshield, staring at the moon.

I join her, our shoulders pressing together as I look up at the Gracie night sky. I don't think about the way my knuckles brush hers. My head sits just above the slope of her shoulder. I don't think about the way it would fit perfectly against her neck.

"You know what this means," Willa Mae says after we've stood side by side beneath the stars for I don't know how long.

She turns her head toward me. Her curls graze my cheek. I shiver. I'm not cold. "Don't you?"

I do, but I wish I didn't. I swallow. "I have to find out if my dad has it."

She doesn't say yes out loud, but we both know I'm right—as much as I wish I weren't.

"Hey." Willa Mae takes my chin in her hand and tugs my face to hers. I pretend I'm still breathing. I pretend nothing about this girl feels familiar or safe. If I pretend hard enough, maybe I'll start to believe it. "Are you going to be okay?"

I don't know if she means after what happened here tonight, or because I have to go hunt down and confront the father I haven't seen in years, or because we aren't getting any closer to finding the knife and making sure Poppy can't use it against me. I don't know what my answer would be to any of those, even if I did.

So, I tell her the same thing I told my brother. "I'll figure it out."

11

YOU'RE ONLY HUMAN

It takes more concentration than it should *not* to dissociate behind the wheel. Memories keep rising to the surface. I see flashes of fire, and hands clasping hips, and wide eyes filled with fear or something worse—but I push them down every time.

Because I don't want to crash this car. I don't *want* to die. Maybe I've toyed with the idea before, dangling the fantasy in front of myself when the bad times got really bad. But that was always because I could never imagine things getting better. I couldn't look at me and look at the world and figure out how the hell I got to my happy ending.

But I *can* see it now. It's so close it's almost mine. Me and Enzo and an apartment in Brooklyn; changing my name and getting top surgery and tattoos and a cat; maybe finally figuring out what it is I actually want to do with my life, because I finally have one to do something with.

I'm not going to let anyone take that from me. Especially not *Poppy*. And that means I'm going to talk to my dad—if I can find him.

I turn the headlights off before I pull in the driveway. If Hank starts howling a warning and wakes up Mom, I'm screwed. I need to talk to her, but now isn't the time.

She's the only one who might know where my dad is, or how to get in touch with him. I assume she knows more than I do, anyway. Not that she'd ever bring it up unprompted. He's a forbidden subject.

Groaning, I grab my phone to send Enzo a text. It's just after one in the morning. He's probably still awake.

But when I look at the screen, my heart sounds an alarm.

3 MISSED CALLS
Mothership

My head snaps up—there's a light on inside, a yellow glow coming from our kitchen.

Fuck me.

I consider just . . . leaving. Turning the ignition back on, pulling out of the driveway. I could maybe find Willa Mae's house—and her grandparents definitely wouldn't care if I did. Hell, sleeping in the Piggly Wiggly parking lot sounds better than facing my mother.

But I can't avoid her forever, probably. And running away right now is only going to make things so much worse when I finally have to deal with this.

God, this is going to suck.

I slam the car door shut behind me, and Hank starts up his bullshit inside, eager to alert us all to a possible intruder. *Thanks, bud.* Mom snaps something I can't make out, and he gets quiet again.

Let's get this over with.

She's sitting at the table between the kitchen and the living room. The Weather Channel is playing on our ancient box TV, the muted screen warning of tornado watches in the next county over. The room smells like coffee and hazelnut creamer—she's got a mug between her hands.

At first, neither of us says anything. The front door swings closed at my back with a whoosh, and Hank shuffles over to sniff me with interest. My mother's eyes start at the top of my head and move down, taking in the sight of me streaked with mud. I can only stare back at her, knowing there's no defending this.

After an eternity, she asks, "Where did you go?"

It's unsettling, how quiet the question is. It would be better if she were yelling. At least then I could yell back.

"I went to see a friend. She's having a hard time."

My mother's eyes dart to my muddy hands and back to my face.

I swallow. "She lives out in the swamp."

It isn't even exactly a lie, which somehow makes it worse.

"Mm." Mom's hands tighten around her mug. She drags it toward her chest, like she's seeping warmth from the ceramic. "And how's she doin'?"

She doesn't care. She's trying to talk me into a corner, to get my words twisted around themselves so she can find the spot where the whole story unravels.

"She'll be okay." My hands close and open. When Hank sniffs at my fingers, I curl them under his chin and scratch. "I'm sorry I didn't answer your calls. I didn't see till just now."

"You could have woken me up before you left. I'm a nurse, Gem. If your friend is in crisis, I could help."

No, she couldn't. And not just because this isn't the right

kind of crisis. She doesn't have any interest in helping me. She says she's afraid for me, but I think she's always been afraid *of* me.

The more I remember, the more I think maybe she should be.

"Maybe you could give me her name. I could reach out to her parents."

"I— No." I shake my head, taking a step back, toward the hallway and my bedroom. "You don't need to do that."

"If a friend of yours is really goin' through something that gets you sneakin' out in the middle of the night to go and help her, it sounds like the kind of thing where an adult should be involved." Mom rises from her seat and places her coffee cup on the counter. "Who were you with tonight?"

"You don't need to know everything. This isn't about you." That much is true, anyway. This has nothing to do with her. "Just—I'm sorry for sneaking out. The end."

"Why do you look like you went crawling through the mud, Gem?" She crosses her arms, expression jagged.

"Because—" I don't have a good excuse for this. I didn't think I was going to need one. "We were outside. I told you—"

"It don't matter what you told me," she cuts me off. "I know you're lyin'. The school called me. You've been cuttin' class, yeah? I thought we were past this, but here we go again—right back to your bullshit."

"I—" I *have* been missing school again. But it's not what she thinks. None of this is the way she's making it out to seem, and I can't even explain it to her, and even if I could she'd just use it as an excuse to lock me up or something. "Whatever, fine, I'm back on my bullshit."

"What were you doin' tonight!" It's a question, but it's an accusation. She doesn't want to know what I was doing as much as she wants to make sure *I* know that *she* knows it was *wrong*. That *I'm* wrong. "Answer me!"

"It's none of your business!" I wave a hand at my chest. "I'm fine! Why do you need to know more than that?"

"Why—what do you mean, *why?*" She throws her hands up, a garbled sound escaping her. At my feet, Hank makes a disgruntled noise in response, before toddling away to collapse on the living room floor. "'Cause you're my kid! 'Cause you can't just disappear on me! 'Cause I was worried you might—that you—"

"Because you're worried I might be like my dad?"

She stiffens, jaw going tight, lips pursing into a thin line. Only after a long moment does she finally say, "You can't be angry at me for wantin' you to keep your problems under control, Gem. That ain't fair. Not when I'm doin' everything I can to help you."

"Yeah. The same way you did everything you could for him, right?"

I don't think I mean to say it. It just comes out of me, this awful, ugly thing. And then it's there, living in the room with us, and my mother looks like I've hit her. Her lips part in surprise, her arms going limp at her sides.

I know I should apologize. I can't seem to make myself.

When she speaks again, there's a quiet reverberation at the back of her throat. I get the impression she's barely holding her sentences together. "You will tell me where you were and what you were doin'. Or you won't be goin' *anywhere* for a very long time."

A sick kind of rage bubbles through my limbs, the sort of anger that makes me feel like I might puke and robs me of any ability to control my own body. I am me, but I am not me, and I don't have any hope of shutting up when I say, "We both know that's not true. You'd hate being stuck in this house with me, 'cause the only reason you want to prove I'm crazy is so you can ditch me like you did him."

My mother's backhand connects with my face so hard I see bright spots in my vision.

She's never hit me before. I think it takes us both by surprise. We stand there in a new, thicker kind of silence—her, wide-eyed, like she doesn't recognize either of us; me, pressing my fingers to my burning cheek and choking back the pathetic urge to cry.

"I know you never liked my methods," she finally whispers, "but I never thought you hated me till now."

"Really?" I shake my head, backing up toward the front door. I can't be here. Screw being afraid that things are going to get worse. Things are already as bad as they've ever been, and she doesn't even know the half of it. "Because I've only ever hated you as much as you *obviously* hate me."

"I don't hate you. I love you so much." She holds the hand that struck me in her other palm, massaging the memory of my skin from her fingertips. "I just hate what you are."

The door slams closed between us, and I flee to the dirt road on foot.

I just hate what you are. I just hate what you are. I just hate what you are. I just hate what you are. I just—

It plays over and over in my head, louder each time until I can't think anything else. How can she just *say that* to me? How can she not see that hating me and hating what I am are the same?

She loves me, but only if I'll pretend. She loves me, but only if I'll break my bones to twist myself into the version of me she wants? She loves me, but not for who I am, only for the mask she's desperately trying to tie around my eyes?

Well, I have awful news. The mask is slipping more than ever. And the me she already hates isn't nearly as bad as the me I actually *am*.

How would my mother feel if she met the Magician? How big would her hatred be then?

What would she do if I actually gave her a reason to be afraid?

A cow moos.

It's enough to shake me out of my head, to realize I'm standing in the middle of the road—between the Gracie Church of God and the edge of the Wheeler farm.

This late, the church is little more than a dark silhouette against the sky. I can barely make out the newest Bible verse fixed to their sign:

There is a way that appears to be right, but in the end it leads to death.

Great.

You know, even if I've never felt much pull toward this god, his influence has been inescapable my entire life. That's probably true everywhere in this country, but definitely here, in the South, where churches outnumber everything else. A neighbor, that's how I used to think of him. Maybe I was more right about that than I realized.

When his followers told me he'd hate me if he met me, I never took it very seriously. Why would I crave validation from someone who didn't exist? It's a lot more satisfying to get it from people who do.

But if *I* exist, what does that say about him? And I wonder, if he ever did meet me, what would he really think? And I wonder, does he ever wonder about meeting *me*?

I turn my head to the farm.

Beyond the pasture fencing, that same pretty tan cow with the heart-shaped mark on her face is watching me. She's lying in the grass, the moon lighting up her dark eyes.

Something about the moment feels surreal. Like being sucked out of my head and dropped into a daydream. The last time I was here, with this cow, was the morning everything changed.

Maybe that's why it feels significant. Like I'm waiting for the other shoe to drop. Like this cow is about to deliver an important message.

I move closer, until my hands are curling around the fence posts. When I do, I realize she's not alone. There's a tiny white calf curled up and asleep at her side. And on the other side of the calf is Buck Wheeler.

Dressed in his too-big plaid shirt and fraying overalls, he's spread out on his back and staring up at the sky. When our eyes meet, he smiles and waves me over. After a beat of hesitation, I hoist myself over the fence.

What am I doing here? This is ridiculous.

And still, I'm lying down next to him, looking up at the stars.

"I know none of it matters," I tell him. My body is moving ahead of my brain. I haven't consciously registered, yet, what a bigger part of me already knows to be true. "So why does it hurt so much?"

Buck giggles that absurd little giggle of his. He reaches over to pat the back of my hand. "You're only human."

"I'm not, though."

"No? Huh." His hand moves to my chest, knocking on it like rapping at a door. "Well, your heart is."

When I turn my head, it isn't Buck I see lying next to me. At least, it isn't *only* him.

Buck Wheeler is the Evergod. The god of time. The one who knows everything that's ever happened and everything that will ever come to pass. One of the most powerful gods in the Ether's pantheon, cursed to live in a human form that couldn't cope with its own limitless knowledge and driven mad by it.

And I have known this, somehow, all along. He has always been this, and I have always known him.

I just didn't *know* I knew until now.

"Could you tell me where the knife is?"

The Evergod has never been my ally. It's my fault he's like this. I saved him from the Shade by bringing him here, but I broke him in the process. Human bodies were not built to hold eternities. Even if he wanted to tell me, I don't know that he could sort through the maze of his own mind to get to it.

Buck sighs, dragging his hand off my chest, tugging his fingers through the grass stalks. "Yeah."

"Does my dad have it?"

"Daddy issues," he agrees with something I didn't say, nodding his head. "My parents think I'm Jesus."

"What?"

"Second coming." A frown tugs at his pink mouth, and then he giggles. I don't know what the joke is.

"If I hunt down my dad, will I find the knife?"

"A knife!" Another giggle. He taps the side of my head with one dirty, chewed-up fingernail. "Honey, you got a big storm comin'."

I know this conversation is useless. And still, because I am weak and pathetic and stupid, I can't help but ask one more thing. "Will anything ever get better? Do I get to be happy?"

Buck smiles, somehow both too-knowing and too-glossy, and touches his palm to my still-stinging cheek. "You will know pain like no one in any world has ever felt before you."

12

I HOPE YOU GET EVERYTHING YOU'RE LOOKING FOR

Look who's alive."

Enzo's words are teasing, but there's an edge in them I don't know either of us is ready to acknowledge when he shows up on my laptop screen the next afternoon. We haven't video-chatted in what feels like forever. Technically, it's been less than a week. Time works differently for us, though.

"Yeah, yeah. I like the green."

He hums, running his fingers through his newly dyed hair, a bright lime that isn't trying to look subtle. Of course, nothing about Enzo is.

It's pathetic, how much I've missed looking at him. He's not at his apartment now, instead sitting outside at some coffee shop, Brooklyn-looking people passing by on the sidewalk behind him. He's dressed in a Boy Scouts of America button-up that I'm certain he found in a thrift shop and bought as a joke, the worn blue fabric decorated with dozens of vintage-looking patches. He's leaning back far enough in his seat that I can see the shirt tucked into a pair of high-waisted plaid pants, the pattern an obnoxious blend of red and orange and blue. His nails are painted the same shade of shimmery, metallic silver as his oversized headphones and half of his costume-jewelry rings. The look is finished off with one of those gay little scarves around his neck.

I don't know how it's possible that I've missed him as badly as I have. He's been here, as much as he's ever been here, just a phone call or a text away. Always in my pocket. It's not like he's any farther away than he was a month ago, before I knew . . . any of the things I know now.

But it's *different*. For people like us, whatever "us" means. I know it's taken me longer to text him back than normal. I haven't been as present in our conversations, too much going on. And, maybe I'm imagining it, but it feels like he's pulled back, too, like maybe he's sensing the growing divide and compensating by retreating as much as I have.

I want to tell him everything. I don't think I'll ever stop wanting to tell him everything. And I know I can't, and I hope, one day, all of this will be a series of bad memories, and I won't have to because it won't matter anymore.

For the first time, though, thinking that doesn't actually make me feel better. I imagine a world where all of this is behind me, and all I can see is Willa Mae's face in my head. There are more than a thousand years stretched out between us. I've only just barely scratched the surface of my memories, and I'm already fighting to pretend I don't feel something more than I have any right to, for this girl who walked into my life five days ago.

Enzo is something *better;* Willa Mae is something *more.* And it isn't fair, and it makes no sense, but I'm homesick for both of them.

"I dunno, it's not my favorite," Enzo finally says, and it takes me a minute to realize he's talking about the hair. "I think next time I'll try pink."

"You'd look great with pink."

"Thanks, baby." He winks at me.

I'm a humiliating little weasel and get butterflies.

Maybe it doesn't have to be an either-or situation. Maybe I could have them both. Willa Mae and I could take care of the mess with Poppy (and her girlfriend, if she's ever going to show her face), and then, after graduation, we could move to Brooklyn *together*. I could introduce them and Enzo; they could be friends. I think they'd like each other, maybe. They're both plant gays who like animals. They both have an affinity for old shit, like Enzo's wardrobe and Willa Mae's car. They're both constantly and viciously telling me about myself.

Yeah, maybe we could do that. I could have my best friend, and I could have my . . . whatever Willa Mae is, and we could figure it out together. This weird little life of our own design. Like a queer commune.

Of course, I *do* know what the issue with that plan is. It's that Willa Mae and I might be soulmates—and I'm in love with Enzo. The only real friend I've ever had, and the only person I've ever wanted to be with, is the same person who lives a thousand miles away and can't know anything about this war between reincarnated gods.

But that's my problem, and no one else's. It's not like Enzo feels the same way. In the hypothetical future where I get everything I want, it wouldn't have to affect Willa Mae and me figuring our shit out.

"So . . ." Enzo says, and I realize I haven't said anything for a long moment, silence settling between us. I snap back into it, forcing myself to focus on nothing but him and the call. "Where'd you go last night? I thought you were sleeping, but I saw you were out."

Sharing my location with Enzo was supposed to be a gay little gesture and nothing more, making sure we always knew what the other one was up to—making us feel closer despite the distance. But it might be a problem now. Only there's no way I can unshare it without that being a *thing*. I guess I could start leaving my phone at home. The idea is terrifying.

"Oh, uh. You remember that girl I told you about?"

His eyes, kaleidoscopes in shades of brown, narrow. "Swamp Girl?"

"Willa Mae. Yeah." *Swamp Girl* isn't technically wrong, but I think he means it in a different way than I do. "They needed help. Their car got stuck in the mud. I was the only one who woke up when they called."

I wish I'd had that explanation ready when my mom confronted me. It's only after a day to think on it that I came up with a believable lie.

Maybe not *that* believable. Enzo doesn't look convinced.

"Uh-huh." He picks up his iced coffee—I don't know why it has a whole sprig of lavender in it—and takes a long sip. When he sets it back down, he asks, "So, what's going on there? Do you . . . like them?"

My instinct is to lie. I don't *want him* to know I might be developing (confusing, conflicting, too complicated to explain) feelings for Willa Mae. I don't want him to think it means something it doesn't about the way I feel about *him*, or the plans we've made.

But I'm already lying about so much—I shouldn't add something else just because I'm a coward. And if I'm really going to fight for this future where everyone gets everything they want, he has to know the truth. At least the slice of it I can offer him.

"Actually . . . I think so." I rub a hand over the back of my neck, shifting against the pillows on my bed. My laptop, balanced on my legs, jostles as I do, blurring the view of Enzo's face.

I can still see him looking at me like I've grown a second head, though.

"I know it's . . . you know. It's *Gracie*. And this is weird, for me." How am I supposed to explain being *demiromantic* and developing feelings for someone after less than a week—without telling him I've actually known them longer than I've known him? "But they're different. I actually think you'd like them a lot."

"Huh." It's difficult to parse what the look on Enzo's face might mean. He doesn't seem impressed. He takes another sip of that obnoxious drink. "So, let me meet them. Why don't the three of us have a little FaceTime rendezvous on Friday?"

"Oh! Um." Willa Mae is *not* going to like this. I still find myself saying, "Yeah, okay. Sounds good."

"Delightful." His tone doesn't indicate any delight. "Well, darling . . . any other life updates I've missed?"

"No—oh, um. Actually, one." There's a lot more than one more, but there's one I can talk to him about. At least partially. "I think I'm gonna try to find my dad."

I don't *think*, I just am. But those two words soften it, make it less big.

Enzo leans forward quickly, his face, twisted with concern, taking up half the screen. "What?"

"Yeah, no, I know." I tug my fingers into my hair. How to explain this without actually explaining it? "There's just a lot I don't know about him, and that whole side of my family. And my mom is so weird about talking about it, you know. I just thought—it might be good for me, to try and reconnect with him. And maybe he's better than he was, last time."

"Yeah, or maybe he's *worse*, Gem." Enzo isn't usually one for hard and fast disagreeing. He cloaks his disapproval in humor, rolls his eyes at my bad choices, and more or less lets me continue doing whatever I want. The seriousness in his tone takes me by surprise. "Have you thought about that? How's that gonna make you feel, if you find him and he can't be what you want?"

"I'm not looking for anything specific." A huge lie, but not in the way I mean it, so it doesn't count. "I'm not gonna get my feelings hurt."

That part is also maybe a lie. But my feelings have been hurt before, and they can take a hit. It'll be fine.

Enzo swallows. "Have you told your mom?"

"Not yet. I'm gonna have to; she's the only one who might know where I can start looking. But I know she's gonna be an asshole about it."

"Yeah . . . and maybe for good reason?" Enzo shakes his head, holding his palms out to the camera. "Gem . . . have you been taking your medication?"

Oh. Okay.

Maybe I shouldn't have told him about this.

The question, as deep as it hurts, isn't . . . unwarranted. I *have* missed a few doses. But I've been kind of *busy*.

And it turns out I might not even be depressed, or sick, or whatever. Maybe I've always just been bad at being human because I'm *not one*. Maybe I don't need the meds at all.

"Geez. You really hate the idea that much, huh?"

He doesn't evade the truth when he says, "Yeah, I really do."

"Um. Well, okay. Noted." I don't know what else to say. I'm not going to change my mind—I couldn't, even if I wanted to.

"You just—"

"I hear you, dude. But it really doesn't have anything to do with you, so I'd appreciate if you could just be supportive."

He blinks, then drops back in his chair.

"*Oh.*"

Fuck.

"I'm sorry, that was—"

"No, don't apologize." He waves a hand. The *actor* appears. I don't know what character he's playing, but I know Enzo's acting when I see it. "You're right. I hope you get everything you're looking for, *dude*, whatever that might be."

"Enzo—"

"I must run, though. I've a loaded schedule today. I trust we'll talk more later?" His smile is viciously polite. "Whenever is convenient for you, of course."

I could crawl in a hole and die. "Yeah. I'll text you soon."

"Lovely. Goodbye, then."

"Bye."

The screen goes dark. Not wanting to look at myself in its reflection, I slam the lid closed and shove it onto my bedside table.

In this hypothetical future where everyone gets everything they want, I wonder if I ever learn how to stop being *such* an asshole.

Hank announces Willa Mae's arrival an hour after my mom leaves for her night shift. I wasn't expecting them, but as soon as the decrepit dog starts waggling his whole backside and staring at the window, I know what's up.

Within seconds, a limb from the dogwood tree outside reaches over and uses the ends of its branch to push the window open. Willa Mae's hands curl around the ledge a moment later, and they hoist themself up into my room.

They chuckle as Hank starts snorting and chasing his tail in excitement. "All right, now, easy. Don't give yourself a heart attack."

I think he'd probably die happy if he did. Willa Mae crouches down, their oversized leather jacket falling off one shoulder as they rub their knuckles over the top of his skull.

And then I'm not here with them at all.

It's the turn of the eighteenth century in the Scottish isles. My name is Artis, theirs Ferelith. We tend to Highland cows and sheep and ponies; we grow potatoes and turnips and pear trees; we live in a cottage by the sea. Death and Battle have not stepped on our path for many years.

We are happy.

I'm rolling dough beneath my palms when Ferelith trots inside, whistling a familiar tune and carrying a basket of dried herbs. They smile when they see me.

Behind them, our bearded collie follows. The two are greeted by the deerhound, our loyal hunter, who'd slumbered before the fire until the moment they arrived. He bumps insistently into Ferelith's side until they acquiesce with head scratches. This, of course, only riles up the collie, who whines and whines until my wife can only laugh, setting down their basket so they have a hand for them both.

My hands pause in their kneading so I can watch them. Sunlight glows, soft and orange, through an open window, and bounces off the auburn of their curls. My heart is so full it could burst.

They look up when I wipe my hands on my apron and step toward them. I curl my finger beneath their chin and lift them to me without a word, pressing my mouth to theirs.

No matter how many lifetimes we share together, I know I will never get used to this.

Blink. It is not the 1700s. We are not in Scotland. And the only dog in the room is my mutt with arthritis.

"Echols?" Willa Mae grins. They're still crouched on the floor, still rubbing their knuckles against my old dog's head. "You okay in there?"

They are the most striking person I've ever looked at. Their full lips and tattoos, their broad shoulders and thick cords of muscle, their wild hair that won't be tamed. Those perfect, bizarre eyes; that single fleck of green in the brown like a flower bursting from soil. I think I could stare at them forever and not get bored.

I don't think I'd ever get used to it.

"Echols?"

If I don't touch them, I'm going to die. And then my feet are under me and I'm climbing off the bed. And my hand is curling under their chin and tilting their face up to mine. And they are warm, and soft, and their pulse is steady and strong against my fingertips. And everything else is going to hell, but they're here. They found me.

My thumb traces the slope of their cheek, brushing away one dark curl. My heart is too big for my body. "I've missed you."

Willa Mae's gasp is so quiet I might not've heard it at all if my hand weren't so close to their mouth. Our eyes meet; a question lingers in theirs. I don't know if they find the answer in mine.

I also don't know who moves forward first. Maybe we move at the same time. But then their fingers are snagging into my braid like they're grasping at chain links, and I'm clawing my nails behind their neck, and we're kissing. And any doubt I had left about them, or us, is gone as soon as their mouth touches mine.

Their plush lips are the softest I've ever kissed, and they part for me without hesitation when I give a greedy flick with my tongue. They taste like spearmint and pepper, burning hot and ice cold all at once. I run my tongue against their teeth before they drag their own against mine, almost lazy in their exploration of me.

As if they know we have all the time in the world. As if they know we have done this over and over again for a millennium, and we will do it over and over again still. Because we have—and we will.

I pull back only to catch my breath, my heart threatening to make a break for it. They dip their head forward to press their forehead to mine, sucking in a deep breath of their own.

"*Mountain.*" The word makes me rock forward on my toes, shaking something loose at the center of my body that I didn't know needed to be freed.

"*Magician.*" Their voice has gone thick with emotion. "I missed you, too. I swear, I won't leave you again."

Over and over again, for all of time, there will be them and me.

And Enzo.

The thought of him makes me jolt, like being splashed with cold water. Crashing back to reality, I pull my hands from Willa Mae's neck, and stumble back to bed. Hank comes to join me as I sink down, rubbing my hands over my face.

It's not fair, to have a kiss that good and start thinking about my best friend. Who might not even be my best friend at all anymore, soon, if I can't get my shit together.

Willa Mae kneels beside me, resting their arms over my thighs, tilting their head up to study my face. Their thick eyebrows crease over their nose. "Was that . . . too much? We can take it slower."

Yeah. We probably need to take it slower. It's only been six days. How has it only been six days?

No. I cannot take it any slower than this. I've been waiting for them my whole life. How have I let five whole days go by without kissing them?

"I don't know." I rub my knuckles into my eyes. Everything feels blurry around the edges. "I'm confused."

"I know. This is a confusing time. When I first started getting my memories back . . ." They trail off, and shake their head as if to reroute. "Look, it'll get easier. We'll figure it out together."

They move as if to touch my cheek and I wince without meaning to. Their hand falls before it ever touches my face.

"I'm sorry." I shake my head. "It's just—it's not just the memories. I mean, it is. I don't know how to sort through what I'm feeling and what I felt before? Or if there's even a difference? But it's also—I've never felt like this for anyone else. Except once."

Willa Mae drops to my floor, tugging their knees to their chest. "Brooklyn?"

I nod. "His name is Enzo."

"So, not just a friend."

"A friend—and something else." I shrug. "At least on my part."

They take a deep breath, looking down at a tear in the knee of their jeans. "But you're still messed up about it."

"I . . . guess." I swallow. "I know you've had longer to get used to this than I have. But I can't just . . . stop . . . caring about my human life. I don't know how to do that. And I don't know how to get them to . . . mix. I feel like I'm walking between worlds right now."

"Keeper of the scales," they murmur, shaking their head. "You've always had a problem with your heart pulling you in too many directions."

Keeper of the scales.

It reminds me of a conversation I had once with my demon—the dream I had the night before everything changed. Before I met Willa Mae and Poppy and started to remember.

"Do you think the Sun worried she'd gone too far as your scales tipped further and further out of balance?"

"Is that why the Shade was able to get me on his side?" I ask, studying their face with interest. "Because I've never been good at staying loyal?"

And then I turned around and betrayed him, too.

They give a sharp jerk of their head. "No. The Shade's scheme was about forcing people to do the worst things they'd ever imagined doing. He could convince anyone to be the wickedest version of themself. It was *not* your fault."

"You're the only one who seems to think that." From what they've told me, all the other gods would want me dead if they remembered. Or already do—except, apparently, Buck Wheeler.

"If you really wanted to do what you were doing, you would have kept their powers for yourself! You handed them all over to him, because he was *using* you."

I frown, thinking back to the memory of the Caretaker. "No, that's not right. I *couldn't* keep their powers. Someone else had to be the one to do it. It . . . it's like I was using him as much as he was using me."

The look Willa Mae gives me is as guarded as I've ever seen them. There's no telling what they know, or what they won't say.

"Please, I'm just trying to understand. How can you forgive me when no one else can?"

Willa Mae drags themself back to their feet. "Look, I just came to check on you. I know things are weird around here. I just wanted to make sure you were all right."

At lunch, I'd told them about things with my mom, and about meeting the Evergod the night before. It hadn't actually occurred to me that it was weird for them to come climbing in my window in the middle of the night, until just now.

"Clearly, you're fine. So, I should go."

When they move to the window again, I reach out to put a hand on the glass, stopping them. "Why are you trying to run away from this conversation?"

"I'm not." They glare at me. "I kissed you, and you told me you had feelings for someone else, and now I'm going home. Okay?"

And I know they're trying to make me feel guilty enough that I let it go, but it isn't going to work. Because, once again, I can *tell* they're lying. Somehow, I know there's part of this story I'm not getting.

"Do you need to believe he was controlling me, so you don't feel bad about wanting *us* to be together?" I ask, finally. "Would you be able to stomach me if you thought I'd actually wanted everything I did with him?"

"You've always had a problem with your heart pulling you in too many directions."

And not just between people—maybe between good and bad, too. If those things even exist.

I tilt my head at them. "Would you be able to stomach yourself?"

Willa Mae's red-green eyes meet mine. Voice like a knife about to slip its sheath, they whisper, "Get out of my way, Echols."

At our feet, Hank makes a sound I've never heard before. A terrible, garbled growl.

I backpedal away from them as quickly as I can. They disappear through the window, and I gather my whimpering dog in my arms.

13

FIGHTING AGAIN, I GUESS

For the next two days, Willa Mae doesn't speak to me. In her defense, I don't try to speak to her, either. I let the silence sit between us like an ice wall, knowing we're both too stubborn to climb it, and somehow knowing it'll melt on its own eventually. It seems unreal I had the best kiss of my life with this same girl, seconds before everything went to hell.

Poppy keeps making eyes at me any chance she gets. She hasn't actively tried to murder me again, which is nice, but the staring is making my skin crawl. I get the feeling she *knows* something, something I don't, something that's probably gonna kill me as soon as it gets the chance.

And she's been all over Zeke. Flirting with him in homeroom, sitting with him at lunch—I even saw him give her a ride home from school yesterday. Which was already annoying when I didn't know he was the god of strength, but is about a thousand times worse now. I can only hope Zeke likes me enough in this lifetime that the Hammer won't *also* try to kill me if he ever finds out who I used to be.

The *plan* is to let Poppy live unless she doesn't give me

another option. But maybe that's a shitty plan. We're just sitting around, waiting for her to do something awful, hoping we'll destroy the knife and she'll just—what? Say "oh well" and commit so much time to her prom-queen campaign that she forgets about me?

Besides, I may not have control over my power yet, but there are plenty of nonmagical ways to die. She might have advanced healing, but even the god of death probably wouldn't wake up from a bullet to the head, right?

Enzo's been talking to me, but he might as well not be. His responses come in single-sentence texts. Perfect punctuation. The occasional thumbs-up emoji. It's as close as he can get to telling me to go fuck myself while seeming totally polite.

By the time I get home Thursday afternoon, I'm ready to start a fight with the first person I see. It just happens to be my mother.

Which is great, since we have shit we need to deal with anyway.

Things have been awkward since she caught me sneaking in from my attempted grave robbing. She's been doing that thing where she pretends it didn't happen at all, because it's easier than actually unpacking it. But the tension in the house hasn't eased up. We can barely be in the same room together.

I don't think that's going to get any better now.

I fling my backpack onto the floor next to the front door, and she looks up from her cell phone. She's in her scrubs, dressed for her night shift, with coffee bubbling in the machine on the counter.

When she looks at me, I think she's going to say something. Ask me if I'm okay, maybe. I'm not, and I don't need her to pretend she cares, and I don't give her the chance.

"I need you to tell me how to get in touch with Dad."

Whatever she thought might be coming out of my mouth . . . I have a feeling it wasn't that. Catherine Echols blinks once. Then twice. Then presses the button to lock her phone screen, sliding her cell into her pocket.

"What in the world are you talkin' about?"

"My father? I want to talk to him. Do you know where he is?"

"I have no idea," she lies. "And even if I did, what good do you think that's gonna do you, huh?"

"He's my *dad*. I'm allowed to want a relationship with him." I curl my hands around the back of one of our kitchen chairs, fists clenching until my knuckles turn ivory. "You can't just pretend he doesn't exist because you don't wanna deal with him being sick."

Her eyebrows lift. She leans against the chair opposite me, folding her hands over the headrest. "I'm not pretending he don't exist. But what kinda relationship are you lookin' for? 'Cause I can guarantee you're gonna be disappointed."

Enzo would agree with you.

My teeth gnash the inside of my mouth, canines slicing at my inner lip until I taste copper. I swallow it back. "Just because you wrote him off, doesn't mean everyone *else* thinks he's worthless. Okay? And anyway, you're plenty disappointed in me; you still keep me around. For now."

"For crying out loud, Gem, do you even hear yourself?" She has the gall to roll her eyes, reaching up to rub a hand over her face. "He ain't right in the head. You act like you don't remember what it was like before he left. I mighta been the one to kick him out, but you didn't want anything to do with him, either.

And for good reason—he scared the shit outta both of us. You gonna tell me you blocked all that out? What, just to make me out to be the bad guy?"

"This has nothing to do with you!" That much is true. "Why do you think everything I do comes back to you? You're not the center of my fucking universe."

Her lip curls over her teeth. "Everything you do is about me. Whether you like it or not, you are my child. The whole world looks at you and decides for itself what kinda parent I am. And I sure as hell am not gonna be the kind who lets their kid get involved with people like James Echols—even if he is your dad."

James Echols. That might be the first time his name's been said between us since he left. James Echols, the oldest son of Morgan Echols and Diana, née Campbell. The maybe-grandson of Jack Campbell.

It takes me longer than it should to recover from the sound of his name. And when I do, I come back with more teeth, "Right. What you mean is, you sure as hell aren't gonna let the world *think* you're that kind of parent. 'Cause it doesn't actually matter who I am, or what I'm doing, as long as it doesn't blow back on you. Right?"

She sighs. "I don't have time for this."

"Make time for it." When she grabs her coffee cup, a metal to-go mug with a vacuum-sealed lid, and makes for the door, I block her way. "Tell me how to contact him. I *know* you know."

"Gem—you're outta line."

"No, you are!" I throw my hands up. Electric tremors rattle up and down my arms, shooting off fireworks of anxiety. I don't *want* to be having this conversation; I feel like I could puke.

"He's my dad! He doesn't stop being my dad just because you decide you're done with him, and you don't get to make that decision for both of us!"

Her eyes go huge. She takes a step back. I recognize the flicker in her eyes as fear.

Good. Maybe if she's more afraid, she'll be less awful. A different kind of spark, not anxiety this time, shoots through my chest.

"NOW GIVE ME HIS ADDRESS!"

In the aftermath of my blowup, the house is silent. She stares at me for a too-long moment, like she's trying to process what just happened. Her hand rises to fiddle with her silver necklace. Maybe she's thinking about hitting me again. My body tenses, waiting for it.

Only it doesn't come. Instead, when the moment passes, she steps around me and grabs her purse from the coatrack. Her hands shake as she gathers it in her arms, tugging out a pen and her tiny travel notepad.

"I don't know where he's living," she finally admits. "Not for certain. But you can try this number. As of a few months ago, it was still his."

A few months ago. Has she been in contact with him this whole time?

I want to wring her neck, but all I do is take the slip of paper when she hands it to me. My father's number scrawled in perfect handwriting.

She sniffs. "Can I go now?"

I'd like to keep yelling, actually. After the last few days, yelling feels great. But I got what I wanted. I step aside, and she darts out the door without another word.

As soon as it swings closed, my anxiety-nausea returns

tenfold. It hits me square in the back, and saliva floods my mouth seconds before I have to race for the bathroom. I only barely make it there in time, clutching the scrap of paper in my closed fist as I lose my cafeteria lunch to the toilet bowl.

Even when I've yarfed, the nervous stomach doesn't get any better. I groan, flat on my ass on the bathroom floor, leaning back against the tub and wiping my sleeve over my mouth. It feels 120 degrees in this room. I know our AC's temperamental, but it hasn't been *this* hot. Has it?

Hank shuffles into the room with me, and only when his blurry outline appears do I realize my vision's gone screwy. *What the hell is going on?* He collapses between my thighs, resting his head against my leg, and I slump forward to press my face into his fur.

I squeeze my eyes shut to fight off the pounding that's started up in my skull. And as soon as I do, memories begin rapid-cycling.

It's the mid-1800s in New York City and I use spell work to keep the basement apartment of our townhome magically protected—anti-abolitionist sentiment is vicious in the city, and our neighbors will see us dead if they find out Machque and I are helping enslaved people escape the South. The excessive use of magic keeps me bedridden more days than not.

It's the twelfth century and I'm on a Viking ship, using magic to calm the tides on a night when the thrashing waves threaten to take us all under. I sacrifice a fistful of *penningar* to the ocean floor, but the offering isn't deemed worthy—our next raid sees a battle so bloody our return home is delayed by weeks.

It's the Ether, long before the birth of the Ouroboros or my terrible union with the Shade, and I'm casting a spell to eclipse the Sun. She has been greedy, her reign stretching longer, the

Moon's growing shorter. Crops die in this long stretch of darkness, and my people starve—but only some. And balance is restored between day and night.

When I open my eyes, the yellow bathroom light makes my head hurt even worse. Hank is snoozing on my thigh. And I understand what happened here, though I wish I didn't.

Somehow, I used magic to get my dad's number from my mom.

And now I'm making my sacrifice.

By the next morning, I still feel like microwaved dog shit, so I don't even bother dragging myself out of bed for school. I'm not sure what's making me feel worse—the sickness itself, or the guilt of using *accidental mind control* against my own mother.

I mean, she sucks. But she's still my mom. Right now, when my body aches and my fever keeps spiking and I can't get out of bed without the room spinning, there's a part of me that just wants her to make us a big pot of sofkee and run a wet rag across my forehead and tell me everything's going to be okay. Even if she hasn't done anything like that in a long time.

What's worse is that I don't even know how I did this, really.

I send Willa Mae a text to explain my absence, breaking our no-contact streak.

> got into a fight with my mother.
> used psychic powers against her on accident.
> not doing good. won't be at school today.

Instead of a text back, she "reacts" to the message with a little thumbs-up emoji that makes me want to kill myself. I guess this isn't enough to melt the wall between us yet. Fine. Whatever. Let her continue to throw her fit.

I text Enzo, too.

> think i might have the flu. very sexy of me. i'm not going to school today.

Unlike my sensitive, bitchy soulmate, he texts back right away.

Little Dumbass
I'm sure your mother is delighted for the opportunity to put her skills to use.

> not exactly. we're still fighting.

> fighting again?

> i told her about wanting to talk to my dad.

I watch the way *delivered* changes to *read*. I barely stop myself from counting the seconds before he starts typing. There's no way to prove this, but I'm pretty sure it takes him longer than normal.

Little Dumbass
Oh? I would ask how it went, but I gather it was not particularly pleasant.

> not particularly, no.

Little Dumbass

I see. Well, darling, for what it's worth, I am sorry. Even if we disagreed on this subject, I know you were hopeful. I'm sure it's difficult, that hope being dashed.

oh. um. it wasn't, though. she gave me his number.

she wasn't happy about it. but she did it.

He definitely takes longer to start replying to that one. He types for what feels like forever, and the only thing that comes is:

Little Dumbass

Oh.

Oh, he *hates* me.

Somehow, I've gone and stomped on both of the most important relationships in my life. In my attempt to get everything, I'm going to end up with nothing at all.

Figures.

In a desperate bid for *anything* from Enzo, I send another message, changing the subject.

you still want to facetime today?

Little Dumbass

With you and Swamp Girl?

willa mae. yeah. tonight?

Little Dumbass

At this point, I don't see why not.

Instead of texting back like "what does that mean???" I text Willa Mae.

come over later?

She doesn't have her read receipts on, and I don't get a reply. So, I'll have to wait and see.

And because I'm a masochist—I guess—and I hate myself—I guess—I decide my day probably can't get any worse. I pull out the piece of paper my mom gave me and punch in the number.

I have no idea what I'm going to say. I don't even know what he's going to sound like when he answers. The version of my dad who existed through most of my childhood *stopped* existing when things got really bad. At this point, the person on the other end of the line is a complete stranger, and not just because we haven't spoken in years.

The line stops ringing. My breath hitches.

Voicemail.

I groan with relief. Dramatics aside, today probably *could* get worse, and I don't know that I'm actually ready for this.

When the automated voice finishes its spiel, I flounder for something to say. Ultimately, I spit out the eloquent "It's Gem. Call me back."

Click.

At this point, I don't know if it's magical sacrifices or my own stupidity that's making me sicker.

14

KICKING AND SCREAMING

.

You have got to stop breaking into my house every time my mom leaves."

Willa Mae doesn't bother with the window this time. She saunters through the front door while I'm curled in the corner of the couch rewatching the queer season of *Are You the One*. Hank leaps from the floor with the kind of agility I didn't know he still had in him, racing over to butt up against her legs.

"You invited me." She drops onto the coffee table and braces one of her combat boots on the edge of the couch; her long black skirt shifts, revealing an indecently high slit when it does. Apparently, she has another tattoo. A snake eating its own tail, wrapped around her thigh. The ouroboros itself.

She draws my attention back to her face with a pointed clearing of her throat. My cheeks burn; her eyes roll toward the ceiling.

"Uh, okay, yeah, I invited you, but you never texted me back." Not even with a degrading thumbs-up reaction.

"Yeah, well, I wasn't sure if I was going to show up or not." She shrugs. "But I decided you can't keep doing this."

"Doing what?" I bury myself deeper in the arm of the couch and pat the space next to me, trying to convince Hank to curl up at my side. He barely glances in my direction, continuing to sit next to her, chin balanced on her bare leg. Traitor. "I'm just sitting here."

"Exactly." Willa Mae points a finger at me. "You're just *sitting here.* You're not looking for the knife, you're not learning magic; you're not even making out with me, which is ridiculous. You're wallowing in self-pity."

"I am not *wallowing* in anything!" I might be wallowing a little. "I got sick! From *doing magic!*"

"Mhm. And are you still feeling sick?" She raises her dark eyebrows.

I sniff, turning my chin up at her. "My tummy hurts a little."

"This is the least attractive you've ever been. I hope you know that."

I'm going to crawl in a hole. My ego cannot take that kind of hit. "Okay, well, you're not exactly a beauty queen, either."

"Oh, okay, *sure.*" She laughs the sort of laugh she is only capable of because she must know I think she's the sexiest person I've ever seen in my pathetic little life.

"Why did you come here?" I throw my hands up and accidentally knock the TV remote to the floor in the process. "To make fun of me? Mission accomplished. Go away now."

"No, but I can make fun of you some more on the way." She swats at my knee. "Get up. Go get dressed. Make yourself look like *the* Gem Echols, everyone's favorite fuckboy."

"*Why?*" And also, *why* does my voice sound so *whiny?*

"Look." Willa Mae drops her boot to the ground, leaning forward until her face is too close to mine. "You want to pretend you're human? You want to fight your way out of this mess so you can live the rest of your life in peace with your not-boyfriend in Brooklyn? Fine. But that means you need to remember what's so damn great about being human in the first place. Because I think you've lost sight of what you're doing here."

So, she's taking me somewhere to remind me how cool it is to be human? "Oh shit, did you get tickets to the Ashnikko concert?"

The withering look she gives me is unimpressed. I give up, relinquishing any fantasy of winning—especially when I'm too curious now to *actually* not go—and get dressed.

Wardrobe choices for Everyone's Favorite Fuckboy include: demolished jeans with bleach stains, TomboyX boxers peeking above the hem; a comically oversized black hoodie, cropped high enough that the edge of my skin-toned binder is clearly visible; a pair of buckle-covered platform boots. I brush and re-braid my hair, twist all my gold piercings so they're facing in the right direction, and apply deodorant and a few drops of my favorite scent. (Some bizarre combination of verbena, patchouli, frankincense, and honey—a birthday gift from my grandmother to show her support for my *they/them stuff*.) And then we're out the door.

When we reach our destination, though, I realize I should have just come with swamp pits and a ratty T-shirt.

"Is this . . . Zeke's house?"

The King family has one of the nicer homes on Gracie's west side, a two-story farmhouse so far across the swamp that it's almost not in town at all. Off the house is an even bigger barn, maybe used for something real once, now just a place for Zeke's parties.

I've only ever been to one, my freshman year. It was fine, for the most part—but I did end up in an *interesting* position with two linebackers, an FFA junior officer, and someone's cell phone. I decided then that Zeke's barn parties weren't really for me. Yet here we are, pulling up in Willa Mae's Jeep, watching other cars full of Gracie townies arrive. Country-pop is already blaring inside.

"You brought me . . . to a hoedown."

Willa Mae cuts the ignition, twirling her key ring around her finger. "Yep."

I snag her hand before she can do something ridiculous like getting out of the car. "I'm *really* not sure this is going to reignite my spark for being human. Unless—oh, shit, was that your secret plan? Are you trying to get me to embrace my magic by reminding me young Republicans exist and I could hex them?"

She rolls her eyes—and doesn't answer. Just pulls her hand out of mine and climbs out of the cab.

I don't think about how warm and soft her fingers were when they were pressed beneath mine. I *do* wonder if I could use magic to hotwire the Jeep and get myself back home.

In the end, I shuffle after her.

The place is packed. People are gathered all along the throughway, sitting on stacks of hay, or leaning against wooden posts. Groups have clustered into the pointless stalls, where a few tables have been set up for games of Cups or Never Have I Ever. There's a whole second-story loft, and the party has spread up there, with people using the open space as a dance floor or a spot to make out or smoke. A giant folding table seems to be the focal point, and there are a mountain of plastic cups, cases of beer and wine coolers, and a keg set up.

It would already be kind of bad, but the music makes it

unbearable. Here I was, hoping we were on our way to an indie rock concert, and instead we're listening to . . . I don't actually know who the artist is. I *do* know that my parents, Johnny Cash and Dolly Parton, would be ashamed.

"Do we—" I groan, stumbling behind Willa Mae as she beelines for the table. "Come on, I know you don't—"

"Gem!"

Ah, shit.

"*Heeeeey.*" I turn slowly toward the sound of Zeke's voice, watching him approach through the crowd, a big, dopey smile on his face.

"Well, I'll be. Thought it was you, but then I thought, nah, Gem don't ever come around here. Oh, hey. Willa Mae, yeah?" He grins. "Y'all come here together? You drag their ass out here?"

"I did—kicking and screaming." She smiles, too tight to be friendly, and hands me a bottle of pink alcohol with peaches on the label.

I don't drink. There's always alcohol floating around at parties, and I've tried it here and there, but I learned the hard way it doesn't mix well with my meds.

I'm off my meds, though. So, why not.

"Sounds about right." He laughs, slapping my shoulder. The force is enough that it almost knocks my legs from under me. Willa Mae touches my lower back to keep me standing. "Gem's always been a little too good for the rest of us. But I'm glad you got 'em over it."

He winks at me, like we're in on some joke. "Knew this was why you wanted me to stay away from her."

"Uh." Jealousy isn't something I've had a lot of experience with. I wonder if Zeke hitting on Willa Mae would make me jealous. The idea is ridiculous enough that it's impossible to imagine, so I guess I won't know unless he tries. "Speaking of girls I told you to stay away from, is Poppy here?"

Zeke gives me a disappointed look. "Nah. Invited her, but she had other plans."

"Pity." Guess even a *god* can't keep up with a popularity contest for prom queen 24-7.

Though, I don't want to know what she had to do that took priority. Not with all those creepy smirks she's been giving me. Not with me no closer to having the knife than I was the day she showed up in Gracie.

Someone in the loft calls Zeke's name, and his attention gets pulled. With a last wave to Willa Mae and me, he dips into the crowd. He'd disappear if he weren't built like a tank. (Though, I notice homosexually, he *is* smaller than Willa Mae.)

"How long do I have to be here?" I spin toward her, and her hand drops from my back to my hip. It rests there for only a fraction of a second before she lets it fall, but I still feel her palm burning through my clothes like a brand.

"Just shut up." She rolls her eyes, takes a swig of my drink, and loops one of her fingers into my belt loop. I might try and stop her from tugging me into the crowd by it, except my entire lower half is suddenly on fire.

Three drinks and a joint into the party, and I have no idea why I ever protested being here.

Either the music has gotten better, or my taste has gotten worse. More people have showed up, making more noise, which *should* be overstimulating. But the more bodies there are, the less anyone gives a shit what mine is doing. Things have bled out from the barn and into the field. Someone started a bonfire, flames stretching toward the starry sky.

My head is swimming, but it doesn't hurt. My body feels all warm and tingly and off-kilter, but in a *good* way, not the unreal way I've gotten used to over the last couple of weeks. It feels like *my* body, and I feel grounded in it in a way that's too heavy and awkward and dizzying, but still, somehow, a relief.

Willa Mae laughs, and I already can't remember the joke I made. She stumbles out of the barn and toward the fire, her fingers twisting with mine to pull me into the grass. We land side by side, too hard, and our skulls crack together. She gasps, like she thinks she might've hurt me—and laughs harder when she realizes she didn't. And then I laugh, too, even though nothing is really funny, because I like the way she sounds, all loud and obnoxious and unreserved.

"I like you human," I tell her, leaning in like I'm sharing a secret, which I guess I am. Our cheeks sort of brush, our faces so close. She smells like flowers and smoke and green apple Smirnoff, and I want to kiss her so badly my legs hurt.

She chuckles, and presses her forehead against mine—softer, this time, less head-butting. The bridge of her nose lines up against mine. I can't look into her eyes without going all goofy and cross-eyed, but I can feel her breath against my lips, and I'm going to scream any minute now.

"I'm not human," she reminds me, but her tone is easy.

"Mm." I think about something Buck Wheeler said to me days ago, and tell her, "Your heart is."

The breathy sound of surprise she makes is enough to make my fingers curl into the grass, nails twisting around their roots in the soil. It makes me think of what it must feel like to grab fistfuls of her curls.

"And what do you know of my heart?" Willa Mae asks in a voice like hot tea with honey.

I don't think about it before raising one now-dirty hand and smoothing my fingers against the part of her chest visible through the unbuttoned clasps of her shirt. The strap of her sports bra brushes my fingertips. Her pulse races against my palm and my own heart quickens.

"Oh, come on. I'm finally learning the rules of our game," I whisper. "Don't walk away from the board now."

One of her hands curls around the back of my neck—strong and firm, warm and insistent—and I think, *This girl could do anything she wanted to me.* And there have been times when she has. And there will be times when she does again.

I don't know *how* we get there from where we are, and I don't know what exactly it's going to look like when we do, but I know we will. And every moment I spend with her, the more certain of it I become.

Whatever else is in my future, the Mountain is part of it.

Instead of kissing me again—I *really* wish she would kiss me again—Willa Mae releases me, letting go of my neck and pulling back so we aren't pressed together. I grumble in disappointment, but manage not to humiliate myself by chasing her face with my own.

"Are you happy I dragged you out here, then?" she asks, smirking at me as firelight dances in her dark eyes.

"Yeah, yeah." I rub my palms against the thighs of my jeans, smearing the grass stains and wet dirt onto them. "You were right. I *was* having a pity party."

"Mm. Well, in your defense, it hasn't been the easiest couple of weeks." Willa Mae sighs, sitting up straighter, her palms flattening on the dirt next to her hips. I watch, wondering if maybe I'm seeing things or if the grass is actually curling around her fingers. Like they're holding hands. "And I have this bad feeling . . ."

"That something's about to get worse?" When she shoots me a concerned nod, I groan and flop onto my back. The moon shines down on me, mockingly. "Yeah. Poppy keeps . . . *looking* at me."

"I've noticed."

If I didn't know better, and we were just two high schoolers talking about one of the girls who goes to our school, I'd think Willa Mae sounded *possessive*—like she didn't want Poppy staring at me because I'm *hers*. Of course, I do know better, and Willa Mae doesn't want Poppy staring at me because she doesn't want her to try to euthanize me again.

But it's enough to make me think again about how I'd feel if Zeke, or anyone else, flirted with Willa Mae. And I don't know if it's the alcohol or the weed or the fact that we almost-maybe could have kissed again just now, but this time something *ugly* gurgles in my chest at the thought.

Hm. I rub a hand over the shaved side of my head, blinking at the underside of Willa Mae's jaw. "Well, what do you think it is?"

"There are a few options, and none of them are good." Her eyes scan the crowd around us. "She's been spending a lot of time establishing herself here. I'm worried her plan is to wake the sleepers."

That gets me to shoot upright, following Willa Mae's eyes. I'm pretty sure the party has gotten bigger than just Gracie kids at this point, with students from the surrounding counties rolling up, and definitely a handful of guys who've already graduated. Most people around the fire are huddled together like we are, couples holding each other or swaying to the music, maybe a few people standing around talking. There are a group

of boys trying to catch a toad so they can lick it. No one jumps
out to me as particularly . . . godly.

"Do you see any of them? Here?"

Immediately, like she can't stop herself, Willa Mae's eyes
flick across the fire. I follow her gaze to another couple sitting
almost opposite us.

Dante Morales is one of Zeke's best friends, a football player
who's faster than he is muscled, who's always got a smile for
anyone. His girlfriend, Murphy Foster, is his perfect match—a
cheerleader with deep-set dimples and long box braids. Despite missing a *lot* of school because of chronic pain, she's at
the top of our class. They co-edit the high school newspaper.
Bathroom gossip likes to debate if Dante will go to the NFL
and Murphy will be the first Black woman president, the ulti-
mate power couple—*or* if they'll get married right out of high
school and end up stuck in Gracie forever.

For the first time, though, when I look at Murphy, I don't
just see Murphy. I see seaweed curled around my wrists like
iron cuffs, a tidal pool swirling beneath a ship of screaming
crewmates—and waves crashing against a burning shore. But
it isn't just about what I see. I look at her, and I feel water in my
lungs. I remember drowning.

I have to look away. "She's the Siren—the god of the sea."

Willa Mae isn't looking in Murphy's direction anymore,
and she won't look at me, either. "I don't think she's one we
really need to worry about."

Once again, I know there's something she isn't telling me.
I search my ancient memories for something, *anything*, about
the Mountain and the Siren. There are hurricanes destroying
entire forests, and sea creatures feasting on land animals who

wander too close to the water. And the creeping, bone-chilling feeling of a steadily rising tide, knowing that one day the ocean will consume us all.

But I don't get details.

"Who is she to you?" I demand. I don't mean to sound as annoyed as I do—but I *am* annoyed. It's starting to get old, the way Willa Mae keeps shit from me unless she thinks it's necessary.

She looks at me only to glare. "Drop it, Echols."

"Stop calling me 'Echols.' What is with that, anyway?" It's like she does it just to try and solidify this wedge between us. It's annoying.

"That's who you are, aren't you?" Willa Mae pushes herself to her feet, brushing dirt off her skirt. "That's who you want to be. Gem Echols. Perfectly, uninterestingly human."

I stand, too. I'm so *angry* all of a sudden. The increasingly familiar rush of electricity sparks through my arms. I wonder what I'd have to sacrifice just to put Willa Mae in her place— just once. "Trust me, *plenty* of people in this town have found me interesting. Hell, a lot of them are even at this party tonight."

Her eyes narrow, fists clenching. "Are you seriously proud of that? That this whole town sees you as an experimental *hole*? God, you really are pathetic."

"If *I'm* pathetic, what does that make you? As far as I can tell, your whole *life* revolves around me."

Willa Mae's hands shoot out and connect with my chest, hard. She shoves me with enough force that I fall back into the dirt. My head snaps so hard that my neck stings.

"Find another ride home, asshole."

By the time I stand, violent magic threatening to blow up inside me, she's gone.

And as soon as she is . . . I have no idea why I said *any* of that. I didn't even *mean* it! I just . . . I'd just wanted to hurt her. But why?

I've never been *great* at impulse control, but that was . . . bad. I yank out my cell phone, desperate to call her before she can get too far away, to apologize for whatever the hell just happened. But when the screen blinks to life, two texts from Enzo pop up, both sent over an hour ago.

Something sinks in my chest. I pull up that text thread instead.

The first message is a screenshot of an Instagram post. It's a series of pictures, posted by some random Gracie local, of Zeke's barn party. One of them, the one Enzo has open, features Willa Mae and me off to the side, drinks in hand, too busy staring at each other to notice we're being photographed. I'm tagged in it.

My heart seizes reading the second message.

Little Dumbass

Suppose I'll go out on a limb and wager you are not planning to show up tonight. No matter. I didn't have my heart set on it. I know when I'm not wanted.

No.

No, fuck, shit, no, he doesn't know. He doesn't know when he's not wanted—he's always wanted. I always want him.

How could I forget we were supposed to FaceTime? How could I hurt him like this?

The inexplicable rage I felt at Willa Mae gets pointed inward. I want to claw my own skin off. I want to walk straight into the fire. My fingers tighten around the phone so hard I think I could shatter it if I weren't so weak. So *pathetic*.

I have to get out of here.

But when I open up the phone app and press the button to dial Willa Mae's number . . . nothing happens. The phone refuses to dial out, or even recognize that it's trying. I go to our texts, try to send one off. It turns red, says "unable to deliver."

Well, that's weird. I must have service out here, if I got Enzo's message.

Whatever, I don't have time for this. I look up, wondering if there's someone I could ask for a ride, and—

Something . . . is not right.

Sometime between my recognizing the Siren and now, the mood of the party has shifted. Couples are no longer curled up and kissing. They're screaming in each other's faces. No one is dancing around the fire—all around me people are beating the hell out of each other, fists flying, while onlookers record and yell their encouragement. The group of boys trying to catch a toad are now wrestling in the mud.

They all look like they've lost control.

I can *feel it* when someone's eyes settle on me. My own stare rises, dragging away from one particularly brutal fight, to look past the fire and toward the barn. Through the smoke and flame, I can make out two figures headed in my direction.

The first one is eerily small and graceful, quick in a way she has no right being. Poppy's silhouette bleeds into color when she gets close enough, a sheet of gray skin draped in pastels.

The figure at her side is bigger—taller, broader, thicker. She walks more slowly than her counterpart; each step intentional as she crosses the field, not a single move wasted. When she gets close enough for me to make out her features, I see a fat butch with brown skin and a shaved head.

As soon as our eyes meet across the fire, I remember her.

The Lionheart. The god of battle.

And she's here to kill me.

She always is.

15

OUT OF TIME AND OUT
OF OPTIONS

The year is 1022, and we have arrived in this new world dropped in the bodies of a Viking crew—most of us, anyway. The Mountain has become the eldest daughter from a family of locals, the Native peoples of Vinland. These Natives recognize them for who they are and teach them the ways of this new world. But the rest of us must conceal our truth, playing the roles of those whose bodies we have stolen—or fleeing, as the Siren and the Stillness already have. Our powers are not as they once were, and I do not know that we could survive should our other crewmates deem us heretics.

After all, these Vikings have their own gods. I am not keen to meet them.

It is only because of this ruse that the Lionheart has not already slaughtered me. Every day, I feel her eyes fixed upon me, and I know she is only biding her time. Whatever she plans, there is a strategy in place, and I intend to be far away before she can see it through. Tonight, I will go to the Mountain, my only ally among them, and ask them to run with me. I know it is the coward's choice. But I no longer have the will to be brave.

Every day that passes, I miss my demon with an agony I did not think possible the day before. Even as my strength begins to return, my magic slowly rebuilding after the spell that brought us here, I know I will not be ready to face the Lionheart soon.

The year is 1305, and it should not take me by such surprise that Battle would hunt me down here, fighting a human war to keep the English out of Scotland. Truthfully, I should have *known* that the gallowglass Burunild O'Donnell, a merciless assassin and Norse-Gael shield-maiden leading her own vicious horde against King Edward's army, was the Lionheart.

Burunild and I circle one another in the aftermath of a battle where we fought on the same side. Our enemies and allies alike have been felled by the dozen, and any who held to their lives have fled this place by now. It is only us; two gods surrounded by human corpses.

She holds a double-headed ax in one hand and a longsword in the other, and when she finally stops circling, she raises the former to my throat. My own weapon of choice—a javelin— was snapped in the carnage, but that matters little. It is not any physical weapon that will aid me now.

I know, somewhere in the hills surrounding us, the Mountain lies in wait, ready to fire an arrow from their bow or send their pack of wolves to my defense. I know this, just as I know that, if the Lionheart is here, the Reaper is not far behind. Death is probably stalking the god of land even now.

Farther away, thunder booms across the Highland countryside.

"I've been looking for you," Burunild grates. "We need to talk."

"Ach. I don't have much to say." I hold my palms up in a mockery of surrender. "Sorry to keep you waiting for nothing."

"It's the Reaper." She snarls, showing me her teeth—stained with blood. "She cannot stay here any longer, Magician. She is—I believe it is killing her."

"Oh?" Interesting. "An odd concern for the god of death, no?"

"For fuck's sake." The sharp edge of her ax digs into my throat. "It's time we went home. You'll fight a war for these people, but not your own?"

"War is one thing—suicide is another." I step away from the steel. "If what you say is true, I am sorry about your Reaper. But I will not consign us all to the duill tree just for the *chance* to restore her power."

"The Shade cannot kill us without the knife!" Her bellow of rage echoes across the Highlands. In the distance, a wolf howls its response. "If you believe returning would result in our eternal deaths, you must believe it is because you are fool enough to fall for his guile once more."

I am no fool. And it is because I am not a fool that I will never give myself that chance.

I have found happiness here, with the Mountain. We are special in this world, unburdened by the weighty responsibility of godhood, yet powerful enough to be more than our human companions could hope to become. And they love me—*truly* love me, in a way I think only human hearts are capable of loving, without greed or hesitation. There is nothing that could convince me to give this up.

But I will tell none of this to the Lionheart. Instead, I say,

"There are worse things than eternal death. I'm not eager to learn what torture the Shade has developed in his years of solitude—are you?"

There is no fear on her face when she answers, "Aye."

I shake my head. "I am sorry. You've my answer already."

"Well, Magician, then I am sorry, too." Her fist tightens around the wood of her ax. "This won't kill you forever. But it will buy me some time to find the knife so I can."

Her ax swings through the air, poised to rend my head from my shoulders.

The year is 1717. The Mountain and I have spent lifetimes running from the Lionheart and the Reaper. We think we are finally safe. Years have passed since we last encountered our hunters. We settle into a home on the island, we get married, we raise our beloved livestock and working dogs.

When the evil of the transatlantic slave trade comes to our country, we fight to abolish it. I open the doors of my own church, a blasphemous congregation, and baptize as many enslaved people as I can reach. "*They are children of god,*" the Mountain and I tell the slavers. "*You cannot have them.*" When these slavers fight the legitimacy of my consecration, no one finds their bodies.

We hear rumors of a band to the west, a campaign of abolitionists and the previously enslaved they've set free, making their way through the country. In whispers, they stand taller than life—their leader in particular, a young woman born to an enslaved mother, who now uses the carved jawbone of her own rapist father as a knife. There is no doubt in my mind these whispers tell of the Lionheart.

The day our church is burned to the ground, we believe

slavers must be the ones behind it. We believe this until we return home and find our seaside cottage has been scorched to ash—with the dogs still locked inside.

The year is 1925 in Atlanta, and if I had any doubts that the Reaper was rotting with each lifetime, they are quelled. I have never seen her this decrepit; no matter how many layers of chiffon and makeup she hides beneath, she cannot conceal the truth that her skin is little more than a ghost's sheet covering her bones.

It seems fitting, then, that we bury her. The Mountain's dirt drags the Reaper down into its embrace as the vile god laughs.

And then rage as I have never known explodes within me.

All I can do is *howl*, clawing at my own body until my clothes are torn open and blood smears my fingers. My jaw aches with the urge to *bite*. It is as if an animal has come to life beneath the surface of my skin and I can do nothing but become one with it.

"Billie?" The Mountain whispers this body's name. Distracted by my episode, their control over the cemetery dirt wavers. The Reaper begins to claw herself free. I don't think the Mountain notices. "Are you—"

A baseball bat swings out and slams so hard into their head that I can suddenly see chunks of gray clumping their hair. Their eyes go wide, they mumble words that belong to no language, and their knees hit the ground.

I am helpless to do anything but scream. Everything becomes anger. My fear, my grief, my love for the Mountain—it is all rage. But at least now it has a target.

Standing over my fiancé's body, the Lionheart swings her now-bloody bat over one shoulder. She tilts her chin. "Think they were going to ask if you're doing all right, *Billie*."

The sound I make is primal as I run at her. Even as I *know* it is her power manipulating me, I have never needed anything the way I need to rip her apart.

So out of my mind with this rage, I don't notice when the Reaper's corpse-like hands reach for my neck.

Though I know nothing about the girl approaching me from the other side of the bonfire, I'm certain she's my undoing. That seems unfair. I've only *just* started to put myself together.

"I don't have the knife!" I call out before she can reach me, already backing away. If I start running, I wonder how far into the swamp I could get. Between being eaten by a gator and whatever this girl can do, I'd rather take my chance with the gator. "I already told your fucking girlfriend!"

Poppy—wearing a dress made of a dozen different sheer layers of tulle, with no shoes on—giggles. And then she moves with that sickening, broken speed; it looks like her skeleton is being thrown across the yard. I know, in that instant, I could never outrun her. Her hand, as delicate as an eggshell and as gnarled as barbed wire, shoots out and her nails sink into my throat.

And then that awful feeling of *death* begins to creep up into my muscles. I can still breathe this time, but it's difficult, labored, each inhale a slice of agony, and somehow that's worse. I can't do anything except stand there while Poppy holds me in place for the god of battle.

No one around us seems to notice. They're too busy giving in to their own bloodlust and beating each other senseless to realize I'm going to die, right here, outside Zeke King's barn.

As Marian gets within only a few feet of me, I can make out her features more clearly. She's a light-skinned Black girl with a wide jaw and heart-shaped lips. Her eyes are so dark brown they could be black. She's about my height, and as broad and powerful-looking as Willa Mae. Her hoodie and joggers don't match her girlfriend's dress.

And unlike Poppy's maniacal ass, Marian isn't smiling when she stops in front of me. In fact, I don't know that anyone has ever looked at me with this much *contempt*. If I were a bug, I would be squashed beneath her sneaker.

"I don't believe you." Her voice is twinged with just a hint of a Midwestern accent. "But this doesn't need to get uglier than it has to. I'm gonna kill you, Magician. But I'm giving you the choice to die quickly and with some dignity."

My voice warbles as I struggle to speak against the magic Poppy is flooding into my body. "Don't have . . . any dignity . . . *or* the knife."

The girls exchange a look. Poppy sighs, all drama. "Can't we just snap their neck? Maybe we'll find the knife once they're gone. We can harvest their power on the next go-around."

"I don't think you have another go-around *in you*," Marian snarls. I notice she's wearing brass knuckles on one hand, a golden strip of metal with spikes along each ring. "We have to get you home. We're out of time *and* options."

"Let me . . . help you . . ." I try to raise my hands, wanting to claw at the nails pressing into my throat, but I can't. My body is so heavy—it feels like I've been embalmed. "Don't have . . . the knife . . . but I can . . . magic . . . Can figure out . . . a way . . . to send you back."

The night Willa Mae and I dug up Jack Campbell's corpse, I asked why I couldn't send Poppy and Marian back on their own, if that's all they wanted. If that was all it would take to get them to stop hunting us and trying to kill me. Willa Mae said that it wasn't possible; that whatever spell brought us here tethered us all to each other and sending them back would mean my being forced back, too. And that's not what I want. I want to be here. I want to be human.

But maybe Willa Mae's wrong. And maybe past versions of me were too selfish and scared to try it, but I'm not them. If nothing else, I can *try*.

If nothing else, I can tell them I'll try just so I can escape tonight with my life.

Marian raises one eyebrow, a slit carved in the middle. Her eyes rake me up and down. If she agrees, I can get out of here. Go find Willa Mae. Tell her what's happening. We can throw ourselves into—

"You really must have forgotten who I am," Marian interrupts my thoughts. "If you think I'm stupid enough to take you at your word."

Her fist connects so hard with my face that I taste blood. It's knocks me off my feet, and I land on my side in the dirt, my cheek torn open from the spikes. I still can't move, can hardly breathe, can only quietly groan, watching the flames of the bonfire reach for the black sky.

Marian crouches into my field of vision. The fire behind her head looks uncannily like a crown.

"Let's imagine you're telling the truth." She rests her forearms on her thighs, as Poppy giggles and drapes her slender frame against her back. "You have no idea where the knife is. Okay. Well, we need you to find it. How are you gonna do that? Some kind of tracking spell, right? You need a sacrifice to make that happen."

She fishes in the front pocket of her hoodie and pulls out a piece of metal that flashes yellow in the glow of firelight. It takes a moment for my brain to catch up to what I'm seeing—but even when I make out what it is, a USB cable, I don't understand.

"So, this goes one of two ways. Either you're lying, and pretty soon I'm going to know the truth. Or you really are telling the truth—and I'm helping you with your sacrifice."

This horrible girl is going to kill me or worse, all to get her hands on a weapon I don't have, to save her girlfriend from a spell I don't remember casting. A spell *I* didn't even cast, but a version of me who doesn't exist and hasn't for a thousand years.

These twisted sadists are going to *murder me* for things that aren't my fault.

I am Gem Echols. Why should I pay for the Magician's mistakes?

Marian plucks my phone out of my hand, and plugs the cable into the bottom port. Over her shoulder, Poppy watches with wide-eyed delight.

"What . . . are you . . . doing?" I choke out.

She glances at me as she pulls her own phone from her pocket and attaches it to the cable's other end. "I'm downloading every piece of information there is to know about you, *Gem Echols*. Everywhere you've been, everything you've done, and everyone you love."

I'm going to throw up. If I could just get enough control over my body to actually do that.

She must see something on my face, because she asks, "What? Not what you imagined from the god of battle? It's the twenty-first century. Wars are fought on Twitter. I get to keep my sword at home—mostly."

I don't think she's joking, but Poppy lets out an unhinged laugh.

Like there's something funny about trying to hurt me.

But it's not even me they want to hurt. Not really. And if they want to hurt the god of magic so badly, maybe it's the god of magic they should have to face.

"Stop!" My voice doesn't sound anything like my own, forced out despite the impossible weight on my chest and the throbbing in my jaw. That electric wave of magic rolls under the surface of my skin, swelling up inside me so big that it nearly overshadows Poppy's influence.

Marian's hand wavers over my phone screen. Poppy frowns, glancing at her girlfriend's face.

I think of accidentally controlling my mom, forcing her to hand over my dad's number. The rest of the party slants away. The still-playing music in the barn, the roaring fire, the screams as people try to bury their friends. It all dips into a fog out of my reach.

Poppy and Marian come sharply into focus. For the first time, I notice the way Marian's lower body is turned, just slightly, as if she might need to run. I notice the subtle trembling in Poppy's curled fists.

And I say, even struggling to speak at all, "Leave . . . *now.*"

Marian's hand lowers again, but she doesn't hit me. Her arm falls across her thigh. Confusion and anger waver, at war, across her face.

"You will give me my phone back," I whisper. It's getting easier to breathe. Poppy's poisonous grasp is fading. I press my hands into the dirt and shove myself into a sitting position—though my chest wails in pain when I do. "And you will stay away from me!"

"Mare." Poppy's voice has no right to wobble. Her fingertips slide down one of Marian's arms, and she links their fingers. "Marian—"

"It's okay." Marian stands over me. The regret is clear in her voice—but there's something else, some warning beneath the surface. This isn't over. She tosses my phone into the dirt. "It's all right, baby. Let's get out of here."

They move like marionette dolls, an uncanny dissonance between their actions and their intentions. It's more subtle with Marian. She seems to have accepted her fate, turning and following the path out of Zeke's yard as if her walk has been choreographed. It's far more stark with Poppy; a puppet fighting her strings at every move, body jerking grotesquely as she's forced to follow her girlfriend.

When they disappear on the other side of the barn, everything shifts. All around me, the rest of the partygoers come back to themselves. The cacophony of screaming comes to a halt, instead warping into confused murmurs, apologies, even tears. No one understands what just happened here. I think I hear Zeke yell somewhere in the barn. I don't want to know what awful thing the Lionheart could have forced the *god of strength* to do in that berserker state.

I have no idea what my face must look like, but when I swipe my hand across it, it comes back bloody. I grab my phone and shove it into the front pocket of my hoodie.

"Gem!"

Willa Mae races across the Kings' lawn toward me.

They collapse to their knees at my side, hands hovering an inch from my skin. "I got all the way home—and then I realized—I got back as soon as I could—are you okay?"

"We need to get out of here. I don't think they'll stay gone." I reach for them, clasping their hand and letting them drag me to my feet. I stumble and Willa Mae curls an arm around me to keep me upright. Our eyes meet. "And I have no idea what I sacrificed to get them to leave."

16

I'M MAKING THIS UP
AS I GO

I spend the weekend at Willa Mae's, hiding out and waiting for the other shoe to drop.

It's as weird as the last time. Her grandparents hover, popping in constantly to see if they can get us anything. On Saturday, I catch Willa Mae and her grandfather arguing in the hallway. When they see me, the conversation ends abruptly.

Later, when I'm lying on her bedroom floor—too afraid to sleep in the guest room, equally afraid of sharing the bed with her—I ask about it.

She shrugs. "He wants us to have a baby."

"He—what now?"

"He's convinced if they can't have another, it'll have to be me."

It's bizarre enough that it briefly takes my mind off of everything else.

"It doesn't matter," she continues. "I told him to drop it."

She looks worried, though, her eyes distant. She twists her hands over her lap, not looking at me.

"Your relationship with them is . . . weird." An understatement. "Has it always been like this?"

"I didn't meet them until last year." She shrugs. "My mom cut them off before I was born. She thought they were crazy."

"What about now? Did she come around when she realized—"

"She doesn't know anything about this." Willa Mae rolls over, offering me her back. "I'm tired."

There's so much I want to ask, but I know she's not going to tell me. With a sigh, I roll over and grab my phone.

Over the last twenty-four hours or so, I've sent Enzo half a dozen texts.

you have no reason to believe me, and i have been the worst friend in the world the last few weeks. but there's an explanation for everything. if you just call me, i can tell you what happened.

enzo, please. this can't be how i lose you. you're the most important person in the world to me. there's stuff you don't know—but i'm going to tell you all of it. call me.

you say you know when you're not wanted, but do you have any idea when you ARE? i always want you. i want you so badly it scares me. on some level, you have to know that, right? you can't honestly believe i found someone new and just moved on.

you have to know i'm in love with you.

and if you're looking at my location and you see i'm in
the swamp again, there's a REASON for that. and you're
gonna have to CALL ME to find out what it is.

please.

So, there it is. In a frantic attempt at getting his attention, I've told Enzo how I feel. And if he ever calls, I'm going to tell him a lot more. Maybe he'll call my mother and she'll have me committed. Maybe he'll believe me and want nothing to do with it. Or maybe Poppy and Marian will kill me tomorrow and he won't ever know the truth. Either way, telling him is the only choice I have if I want to keep him—in whatever way he'll have me.

What it means for the future, I don't know. I'm making this up as I go.

Willa Mae isn't excited, but she's not going to stop me. She says we've told other humans before. It doesn't always end well. But there's precedent for it. And she knows how important he is to me.

Of course, I can only tell him if he *calls me.*

I open up Discord. There's nothing unusual going on. The last conversation was from a couple of hours ago, someone asking if three hundred dollars was too much to spend on a custom mushroom-cow plushie.

Navigating off the main thread, I pull up a private message with Ivy. The only child of an obnoxiously wealthy Manhattanite couple, and a transfem D&D DM in their first year of an anthropology degree at The New School, they're Enzo's best friend—besides me.

have you heard from enzo today?

They message back immediately.

No, but I heard from him last night.
Fuck off, Gem.

I lock my screen and toss my phone under the bed, like it can't hurt me there.

"What if . . . the thing I sacrificed to get rid of Poppy and Marian was my relationship with Enzo?" I sniff. "Like, what if he never talks to me again?"

It's probably not fair, and I know that. I'm asking Willa Mae to comfort me while I cry over someone else. And it's not like we're together, but it's also not like we aren't.

She sighs. I almost expect her to ignore me. I don't expect her to say, finally, "Just give him a few days. I'm sure it'll be fine."

I . . . can't deal with her being nice to me about this. It's worse than her getting mad. I press my face into the pillows.

We have bigger things to worry about. I *know* we do. And that's why I'm not making her answer questions like "*What are we?*" and "*How do you feel about ethical nonmonogamy?*" We can't avoid the conversation indefinitely. But now is not the time.

She emphasizes that by saying into the dark, "And anyway, Poppy and Marian will probably be back tomorrow trying to kill you—whatever you sacrificed couldn't have been enough to keep them away *forever.*"

But Poppy and Marian *aren't* back the next day. And I start to worry about that, too.

Because what if I did sacrifice enough to send them away forever? What if shit hasn't hit the fan *yet*, but it's only a matter of time before I realize something *really* awful happened?

I call my mom to check on her and Hank. They're both fine. She tells me to be home by nine, because tomorrow's a school day, and hangs up after a few minutes.

Enzo doesn't call me. I text him only once.

> i'm so sorry.

Indigo texts me, out of the blue.

> **Indy**
> Heard things got weird at Zeke's party. You okay?

I want to respond. I'd *still* like to be the sort of person who could be friends with him. But I'm not, so I don't. It's better this way. He shouldn't get attached to me.

Sitting on her front porch, pretending I can't feel her grand-parents watching us from the windows, I ask Willa Mae, "Do you really not know what I sacrificed to bring us all here?"

I asked her that the first time we worked on my magic to-gether. And today, just as it did then, her face becomes a mask. "I can't be certain."

"You have a guess, though?"

She shrugs.

I'm not getting anything out of this. "Well—what about the Ouroboros? What'd I have to do to make the knife?"

This time, when she says, "I have no idea," her eyes go soft with concern, lips turning down into a frown. "You've never told me. You said it was too hard to talk about. I don't know if anyone knew."

About this, I believe her. I don't know if it's because she *seems* to be telling the truth—or because her words brush the edges of my own buried memories. I try to remember the sacrifice, reaching desperately into another lifetime to grasp the piece of me I cut away to bring my blade to life, but all I get is goose bumps.

There's more I want to say—maybe now *is* the time to ask her how she feels about *us*—but I don't say any of it. When my phone buzzes, I scramble to yank it out. Maybe it's Enzo, maybe—

Dad (???)

I just listened to your voicemail. I am so happy you reached out!

I would love to see you. Do you think you could stop by tonight?

And then there's an address.

Just, casually, my dad's address. And him asking me if I want to come over.

Tonight.

My brain cannot be expected to process that. I read it over and over again. Eventually, Willa Mae takes the phone from my hand.

"Well . . . this is an *obvious* trap, right?" She slides it back against my palm. "Marian is usually better than this."

Of course. A trap.

"But we also have to go," she continues. "Because, if it's real . . . I mean, he still might have the knife."

Of course. We have to walk into the trap anyway.

17

YOU MUST HAVE BEEN
SO SCARED

My father lives in Sopchoppy, Florida—exactly an hour south of Gracie. I try not to spend the whole drive wondering how long he's been this close, but I don't think about anything else.

The address is tucked between a gas station and the Ochlockonee River, a washed-out patch of land surrounded by mossy oaks. The yard is bordered by a chain-link fence, gate decorated with two bright neon signs: DOG BITES. SO DOES OWNER. and THIS HOUSE IS PROTECTED BY GOD AND GUNS; TRESPASSERS WILL MEET BOTH. The bitey dogs—a pack of pit mixes from the looks of them—run to the fence, but don't bark. Willa Mae watches them through the windshield.

All that leaves me to worry about is the guns.

"You want me to come?" she asks, turning off the ignition. Her hand falls next to my thigh.

Without thinking, I squeeze her fingers. Her palm is so warm and so steady and so *familiar*. It helps stop my heart from pounding right out of my body.

"Yes?" I shake my head. "But don't. I think—this could be really bad. If it's even him, he was . . . you know, he wasn't great the last time I saw him."

The last night my mom and I ever lived under the same roof as my father, he'd started seeing things. According to him, they were like ghosts in our house. And they wanted us dead.

He was just trying to protect us, he said. He only wanted to hurt the monsters we couldn't see. He would never hurt *us*.

Not on purpose.

"Okay." Willa Mae's thumb brushes along mine. "And if it's not him?"

"I'll yell. Really loud."

The dogs don't seem to care when I open the gate and step inside, too focused on Willa Mae. Only one of them gives me any attention—a red pit bull that has to be mixed with something like mastiff. She's *huge*. She follows me to the door, tail wagging.

From the outside, the house is falling apart. It's a little white one-story with a raised porch to keep it from flooding when the river rises. The white paint is all peeling off, chunks of it missing to reveal rotting wood underneath. A whole section of the roof is missing, and a blue tarp has been stretched over it. Hurricane damage, probably. That time of year is gearing up again. The tarp has to have been there at least nine months, if that's the case.

One of the giant oak trees hangs over the porch, its branch extended in front of the roof like a parent's protective arm thrown in front of their kid. Moss hangs down in strands of soft gray, reaching for me. I push through them to get to the front door.

Sopchoppy is even closer to Seminole lands than Gracie. And I swear—it's so stupid, but I *swear*—when I push the moss out of my path, I hear a whisper in a language my mouth wants so *badly* to understand. A . . . warning?

I knock, and my stomach does a backflip. The dog licks my hand.

When the door opens, adrenaline hits me so hard I almost barf. Or maybe what *actually* almost makes me barf is the smell of old takeout, stale cigarette smoke, and dog piss in the living room. Someone clearly knows it's bad and has lit about two dozen different scented candles and incense sticks to try covering the stench, but that really doesn't help.

The man in front of me is not my dad. He's another forty-something white dude, this one with salt-and-pepper hair and tattoos. He isn't wearing anything but boxers. He makes a face at the dog next to me, burps, and asks, "What?"

"Um . . ." Good start. "Is James Echols here?"

"Nope."

"Oh, uh—"

"It's okay, Robby! That's my kid!" a voice calls from beyond the living room.

And a moment later, my father appears.

Where I get every feature from my mother and none of her personality, I've always worried I share a mirror of my dad's broken brain but none of his looks. I remember him as an almost generic white guy—blond, blue eyes, a narrow nose. A little short, a little scrawny, but not enough of either to be memorable. I remember the khaki cargo pants and thin cotton

T-shirts he'd wear to work, the way he always smelled like Polo cologne.

This guy is just close enough to being my dad that I guess he must be, under the circumstances. But he's nothing like I remember. He's gaunt thin, and his graying beard is long enough to braid. His shirt has a dragon on it.

He smiles up at me—I've got a couple of inches on him. "Wow. You look great, kiddo."

I don't know if that's true. I hadn't anticipated staying at Willa Mae's, so I'm wearing my ripped-up jeans from the party, and one of her vintage tees. I haven't brushed my hair or done my makeup or gotten a decent night's sleep in days.

"Ah, all right," the guy, Robby, chuckles. "Sorry 'bout that. Thought you might be the law."

"Do I *look* like a cop?" I sputter, but Robby is already leaving the room.

My dad claps. "Well, hey, come on in. Let's go back to my room, yeah? Let's talk. I wanna talk. I can't believe you're here. Gosh, you have no idea how much I've missed you."

Despite the smell, I step inside. The dog comes with me when I do, and I close the door behind us. When my dad heads down the hall, I follow after him, eyes scanning the place as we walk through.

It's . . . not great. The smell is the worst part of the living room, but the trash piled up everywhere is almost as concerning. When we walk past the kitchen, I notice the sink overflowing with food-encrusted dishes and surrounded by bugs. There are dead plants in every window, which means even more bugs. The rest of the house appears to be one long hallway, with doors on either side. All of them are closed.

My chest hurts. He seems okay, I guess. Weird, but not as bad as the last night I saw him. But clearly, whatever's going on in this house isn't exactly healthy. And I get it. Basic hygiene is one of the first things to go when someone's mental health starts to circle the drain. I've been there and have the cavities to show for it. It's just . . . I wonder how getting better could ever be possible in a situation like this.

Focus. There's a reason I'm here. It's not actually to play catch-up with my dad and hope he's gotten better. It's to try and find the knife. I need to keep my eyes peeled for a—

We step into my dad's bedroom, the room at the farthest end of the hall, and he has an entire wall of weapons hanging on display over his bed. Swords. Axes. Bows and arrows. Some of them are clearly plastic junk. Others look homemade. Some are pristine. My eyes get big, flicking from one to the next, taking it all in.

He laughs, probably at my expression, while the dog jumps onto his bed. "I started collecting a couple years ago. You like it?"

"Um . . ." The weapons aren't all he has. The shelves in his room are lined with crystals and little dragon statues and books with monsters on the covers. "Yeah, actually."

It's not a lie. It feels like a cross between a New Age shop and a TTRPG setup. I'm into it.

He paces around the room before grabbing some matches to light the incense on his dresser. "Yeah. Yeah. Of course you do. It calls to you. You know?"

I *don't* know. But sure.

"Yeah." I rub a hand over the back of my neck. "So, um, how've you been? You're a lot closer than I expected."

"Yeah! Yeah." He rolls his eyes, still pacing. He lights another candle, like he's looking for something to do with his hands. "Your mother—you know, she doesn't believe in me. She wouldn't. I tried, you know, to get her to let me see you. I needed to tell you, you know, but she—she doesn't understand. Should have just come and found you."

"You . . ." It's a little hard to keep up with what he's saying, but I think I'm following the track here. More or less. "You've been talking to Mom? Trying to get her to let you see me?"

"Yes!" He throws his hands up, then sighs, hard. "I needed to tell you. You know? But she wouldn't let me. She doesn't believe. But of course she doesn't. She's not one of us, you know? I should never have married an outsider. But you—you'll understand. You'll believe me. I know it."

I swallow. "You needed to tell me what?"

"Look—" He stops, a few feet in front of me. "I wish I didn't have to break it to you like this. You should have grown up knowing the truth. But you didn't, and now the time has come. And I have to tell you before it's too late and you get hurt."

Holy shit.

It hits me like another punch from the Lionheart.

He knows. There's no other explanation. All this time, my dad's crazy has covered up the fact that he *knows.*

"Okay. Tell me."

His hands are rough when they wrap around my elbows, his blue eyes wild as he looks up into mine. "*You* are not *you.*"

How is this possible?

My brain tumbles all over itself, trying to come up with any reason he might know. His mother was the record keeper. She died when he was a child, but maybe she'd told him stories about it before then. Maybe it was enough to plant a seed in his head, and when he got older, and his mental health started to decline, it . . . unlocked something? It sounds impossible. It is impossible.

But it's *true*. He's standing in front of me, telling me he knows. And . . . I owe it to him to do the same, right?

"Dad, I already know." I clasp my own hands around his elbows, so we're holding each other. "I found out a few weeks ago—that's why I'm here."

"Oh." His eyes go wet and shiny. He sniffles. "Oh, Gem, I'm so sorry you had to do that alone. You must have been so scared."

I feel my own eyes burn in response. Because he's right. I have been scared.

I'm scared *right fucking now*.

"My powers are so unpredictable." I take a shaky breath, a teardrop sliding down my cheek. "I don't know what I'm doing. I don't know how to protect myself, or the people that I care about."

"I know, oh, baby, I know." He gathers me in his arms, cradling me to his chest.

And I let him. I let him hold me, going limp in his embrace. I don't remember the last time my dad held me—I don't remember the last time *anyone* held me. And that thought is enough to break the dam. I crack open, pressing my face into his shoulder, my tears soaking his shirt.

"I've got you," he whispers, one hand rubbing up and down my spine. "You're going to be okay now."

And I actually believe him. Everything hurts and my world is on fire, but my dad is here, and he knows the truth. He loves me, and he wants to take care of me, and he isn't crazy, and he loves me, and it's going to be—

"Now that we're together, I can show you how to do it so it doesn't hurt."

I frown, tugging back so I can look at his face. "You know how to do that?"

Even Willa Mae doesn't know the ins and outs of my magic. She can press my buttons, pour gasoline on the fire, but she can't help me learn control.

He can?

"Of course I do." He chuckles, letting go of me to run one hand over my cheek. "I've been doing this for a long time now. Oh, sweetheart, I was so nervous to tell you. I thought you'd think I was crazy, just like everyone else. I hate that you had to start this off on your own, but I'm so glad you know I'm telling the truth."

His finger slides from my cheek to my nose, brushing the length of it. "You really are one of us. No matter how much you look like your mother."

Okay. Pause.

I take a big step back, reaching up to wipe the back of my hand over my eyes. "Dad, what do you mean you've been doing this for a long time? Doing what?"

He frowns. "Well . . . accessing our ancestral magic."

He knows. Of course he knows. Nothing else would make any sense. Everything he's saying to me, that's what it has to be.

"Right." I've gone through too many different emotions in the last few minutes. My body can't catch up. "Yeah, that's what I've been doing. I'm just wondering . . . what that looks like for you?"

"Oh, I see, okay." He chuckles. "You want to know what my other form looks like. I can show you. You'll have to come away with me, though. It isn't safe to transform here. You never know who might be watching. Where were you, the first time you shape-shifted?"

Blink.

I slide my hands into my pockets.

I take a deep breath.

"Shape-shifted?"

He takes his own step back, narrowing his eyes. "You said you knew—you said your powers had already come in."

"I can't shape-shift, Dad."

"But you are my child. You are of *my* bloodline, descended from the clan of the eternal serpent." He shakes his head, voice growing frantic. "We are the chosen people! We are the scales! We are the dragons concealed in human skin!"

Dragons.

My father is very sick.

He has no idea about the Magician.

"I think coming here was a bad idea," I whisper, backing toward the door. I need to get out of this house. I need to have a very big breakdown that I'm not safe enough to do here. Not the way I thought I was two minutes ago. "I should go."

He takes a step closer.

"But I'm going to keep in touch, okay? I'm going to tell Mom I want to keep talking to you." So that we can get him the help he needs.

"I don't understand," he whispers. "You said . . ."

And then I'm not entirely sure what happens. Because one moment he's standing there, looking as confused and sad as I feel. And the next, something furious has clouded his features.

"You are not my child."

"Dad—"

"DO NOT CALL ME THAT!" He raises a hand, waving

one finger. "Who sent you here? Who is after our magic? I will never betray my people!"

"Please." The whisper is so quiet, it's barely audible. It still manages to sound pitiful. "I just want—"

He grabs for his nightstand, wrenching open the drawer and yanking something free. When he slashes it toward my throat, it catches the light of the candle.

My heart drops into my stomach. A silver dagger with black crystals along the handle. A serpent circled around the blade until it consumes its own tail.

The Ouroboros knife.

"I WILL CARVE THE LIFE FROM YOUR BODY BEFORE I LET YOU TAKE WHAT IS MINE!"

He slashes with the knife again, and I wrench open the bedroom door, stumbling into the hall. The red pit bull leaps from his bed, snarling as she sinks her teeth into his calf and gives a violent shake of her blocky head. He screams, and the knife clatters to the ground between us.

As his roommates file out of their rooms to investigate, I leap for the blade. And I swear, as my fist tightens around it, a shock threads up my arm. *Power*. Power I have not known in a very, very long time.

But there isn't a moment to linger. I race from the house, pushing my way past the cluster of onlookers, escaping to the sounds of my father's screams as the dog threatens to eat him alive.

As I bound across the porch, the oak tree hisses its encouragement.

Willa Mae starts the car as I bolt across the yard. She doesn't ask questions, just peels out as soon as I'm in the passenger seat, doesn't even wait for me to close the door. I yank it shut before dragging on my seat belt with a shaky hand.

The Ouroboros sits across my lap.

"Gem—holy shit, I—" Whatever she's going to say dies in her mouth. "Oh, *honey*."

That's when I lose it. I crumple, torso dropping over my thighs, and the sobs overtake me. Willa Mae puts one hand on my back, rubbing slowly. She doesn't offer me any useless platitude about how it'll be okay. We both know it might not be.

Eventually, I don't know why I'm crying anymore. There are too many things my heart has broken over this week.

By the time we pull up at my house, it's a quarter to nine and my body doesn't have any tears left. I feel hollow and hot and I want to sleep for the next thousand years.

The knife in my lap is so heavy. I put my hand over its hilt.

"The chain?" Willa Mae asks quietly.

I shake my head without saying anything. It was only the knife. No chain, at least not that I saw. Which means we don't actually know *how* to go about destroying this thing. Or if we even can.

She sighs. Her thumb brushes the back of my neck. She hasn't stopped touching me this whole time. "We need to—"

When my phone starts buzzing too loud in my pocket, I almost ignore it. Until the buzzing doesn't stop, an incoming call and not a notification. I pull it out, even as my movements are slow and heavy, even as I don't want to deal with whatever's next.

INCOMING FACETIME CALL
Little Dumbass

"Okay, look, I know you—"

"I have to answer this." My voice doesn't sound convincing, not even to me. And at Willa Mae's horrified look, I shrug.

"I've been trying to get him to call me for days. I'm not going to ignore him now, not to keep what happened tonight a secret. I already told you. No more secrets. Not from Enzo."

She groans, pulling back her hand to jam her fingers into her hair, rubbing the heels of her palms into her eyes.

I know. Me too. But it is what it is.

I click the answer button, expecting to see Enzo sitting in his bedroom, looking beautiful and dour and ready to eviscerate me.

What I actually see is a dirty old wall with a faded, cracking sign that reads GRACIE COTTON MILL. Marian is leaning against it, arms crossed nonchalantly.

The camera pulls back just enough for me to see Enzo's crumpled body at her feet.

"You want us to stay away from you?" she asks. "Fine. But can you stay away from him?"

I didn't know a heart could beat this fast. It doesn't feel like something we should be able to survive. "How did you—"

"Clock's ticking, Magician. I wouldn't waste time asking questions."

Behind the camera, Poppy giggles before the call is disconnected.

18

LOOK WHO CAME TO SAVE YOU

Human bodies are only able to feel so many things at once. I think they're built with a safety switch, like computers programmed to shut off when they overheat.

Maybe that's what's happening. I put my phone down, balancing it on the thigh opposite from the knife. I fold my shaking hands over my stomach. I sit up straight.

I feel nothing except a stretching along my bones, like my skin has been pulled taut over the too-much inside my body. And there's a low-level buzzing in the front of my skull.

But there's an awful calm to this level of panic.

"They're at the Gracie Cotton Mill. It's an abandoned factory on the east side of town. Let's go." My hand curls around the Ouroboros's handle. "They can have the knife."

"What?" Willa Mae twists their upper body toward me. "No. I know you're scared, but there has to be another way. If they get the knife, they're just going to kill you—and probably him, too, to tie up loose ends."

Okay. They're right. Giving them the knife won't save Enzo.

"So, we go—and I kill them instead."

No more Poppy, and no more Marian. And my people and me will finally be safe.

"Yeah, great, except—" Willa Mae pinches the bridge of their nose, shaking their head. "Honey, I don't know if you're ready for that. You got them to leave you alone last time, but they'll be prepared for that now. And you still don't understand how your magic—"

"Then you tell me what I'm supposed to do." I swallow acid, tearing my eyes away from the fireflies in front of their headlights. "Give me something. Anything. Because if they kill him . . ."

I dry heave. My fingernails dig into my thighs. They sigh, reaching over to curl their hand around the back of my neck while I struggle to breathe.

When it subsides enough for me to speak, I meet their eyes again. "If they kill him, no one will be safe from what I do next."

Their thumb strokes the side of my throat. "You need your memories back. All of them. You need to *know* who you are, so you can *embrace* who you are. It's the only way to guarantee you'll be stronger than them."

For reasons I can't understand yet, they look wounded. "I should have pushed you harder. I wanted so badly to protect you from what I went through . . . and here we are anyway."

What I went through.

I can't bring myself to ask. Not right now. But we're circling back to that comment if we survive the night.

"I know I need my memories back, but what good does that do me now?" It feels like someone kicking gravel in my chest when I choke, "They have him *tied up*."

Some awful part of my brain remembers the way the Shade and I stood over the Sun's bound body. Maybe this is no worse than what *I* deserve. But Enzo shouldn't be punished for my crimes.

"There is one thing we could try," Willa Mae answers slowly. They shake their head. "But there's a reason I never suggested it before. A reason we've never tried this in *any* lifetime, no matter what happened. It's dangerous. I don't even know what kind of consequences—"

"Tell me what to do."

When someone knocks on the window, I jump out of my seat. I don't know what I'm expecting to find when I wrench around to face our company, but it isn't Buck Wheeler in flannel pajamas and a straw hat.

I use the hand crank to roll down the window. "Um?"

"You wanted to see me."

"I don't—"

"It's him, honey." Willa Mae sniffs. "He's the *god of time*. He's the one who can give you your memories back."

Without question, I jump out of the car. Buck chuckles and shuffles his bare feet to get out of the way, then puts his hands on my shoulders when I'm in front of him.

"Do it," I demand.

"Gem—" Willa Mae starts, getting out of the driver's seat to come around and join us.

"I don't care what the consequences are. Do it."

Buck grins. His hands are stronger than I expect when he squeezes my upper arms. "Your heart is human. And you would do anything to protect it. Even if it isn't whole."

"Okay." Not the time. "Give me my memories back. Now."

"Stop. Listen to me." Willa Mae comes around to step between us, eyeing the place where Buck is gripping my arm with concern. "We've never done this before because I don't know what'll happen when you do. Humans aren't built to handle the kind of memories we have. We lived for *eons* in the Ether before our lives here. Getting all of that information at once? It could break you."

Human bodies and their safety switches.

"I'll risk it."

"Oh? Okay. How do you plan to save Enzo if you're drooling on the ground?"

My teeth grind together so hard that it hurts. Fuck.

Buck doesn't seem concerned. He's sing-mumbling to himself—in a language I don't understand.

I clamp my hands down on his wrists, and he smiles. "Buck. What's going to happen if you give me my memories back?"

"There's a wall between you and you and you and you and you and—"

"*Buck.*"

"I can knock the wall down. Now *you* are *them.*"

Willa Mae and I exchange a glance. They clear their throat. "What will the consequences be for knocking down the wall?"

"*Ooooh.* Hmm." Buck clicks his tongue and nods. "The Magician will bring immeasurable pain to everyone who loves them. They will drown beneath the weight of their own cruelty. Ancient enemies will ally, united to bring the god of magic to their knees. Slumbering evils will at last awaken. And the scales will tip . . . tip . . . tip . . . until they fall from existence."

"Oh, is that all?" Willa Mae shakes their head. "No."

"He didn't say anything about it breaking my brain." My hands squeeze Buck's wrists harder. His grip on my arms tightens until I can imagine five bruises pressed into either side. "And what will the consequences be if you don't?"

Buck leans forward and presses his forehead against mine.

This close, I can make out each of the dozens and dozens of freckles on his face. He smells like gun oil and fertilizer and hay. "We will all be dead soon."

"Do it."

"Gem!"

"We're out of options and Enzo's running out of time. Whatever happens, we'll deal with it—together. Right?"

When they don't answer right away, I tear my eyes from Buck's face to look back at them. Their hands twist in front of their stomach, eyes wild and afraid.

"This is going to be bad," they whisper.

"I know. But it's going to be bad either way."

This whole time, I've been fighting for my happily-ever-after. This future where I get everything I want. Enzo and Willa Mae and the apartment in Brooklyn and the chance to figure out who I am and what I want.

But maybe a happy ending was never possible for me. Maybe some people don't deserve one, and maybe I'm one of them.

If that's the case, I'm still gonna fight like hell to get as close as I can. And I'll sure as fuck fight for Enzo's.

I turn back to Buck, the tip of my nose brushing his. "Do it. *Now.*"

And then the Evergod hums, tilts his head back, and presses the most absurdly tender kiss right between my eyebrows.

At first, I think that was just him being weird again. Because I don't feel anything. Nothing happens. Buck pulls back, rolling on the soles of his feet, and grins at me, flashing those dimples and his gapped teeth.

I'm going to ask him when he's going to get to it.

Only then the biggest surge of power I've felt in this life comes ripping through my body. I'm helpless to do anything but scream, gripping Buck's hands, Buck's hands gripping me, as an electrified tidal wave crashes against my nerve endings.

It's too much. I think it could rip me apart.

And it does.

The Gracie Cotton Mill is a thirty-minute drive from my house. Willa Mae gets us there in seventeen. I spend the entire time looking at my hands.

"*The wall is gone,*" Buck said when the pain of the power surge subsided. "*You have everything you need—if you can find it.*"

I no longer have to fight to find anything. I just *reach* for the memories, and they're on the surface, waiting.

I've faced the Lionheart on a dozen battlefields, the Reaper on almost as many. I know their strengths and weaknesses.

More importantly, I know my own.

I am the *Magician.* These two have something that belongs to me; I'm going to demonstrate why that is a very bad idea.

The mill hasn't been used in years, and there's nothing around it for miles. Outside, there's a pastel-pink sports car with Nebraska plates and a sunflower-speckled bumper sticker that reads IF MY DRIVING MAKES YOU MAD, CONSIDER GOING TO THERAPY.

I leave the Jeep in tandem with Willa Mae. They glance at the mill, then back to me. They look so afraid.

They shouldn't. They have nothing to fear. Not from me, and not from these people. Not so long as I'm living.

"Are you ready for this?" they ask, and I want to kiss away their nerves. If only there were more time. Maybe when this is over.

"We're going to be okay." Or we're not, if Buck's warning is to be believed. But we're going to live. That will have to be enough. "Do you want to wait here?"

The offense wipes the fear off their face. They scowl, moving toward the front door. I shrug and follow.

We enter a massive open room. The only light comes through a few dirty, splintered windows. Only piles of garbage litter the cement floor.

Well, garbage—and Enzo, with his wrists bound. Marian stands over him. She has the audacity to smirk when our eyes meet.

Rage hacks through my chest like a cleaver. I take a step forward. I could kill her with my bare hands, knife be damned—

No. *Fight it.* The bloodlust is her influence, and I know that. It won't do me any good here, not against her. There's no winning against the god of battle without a clear head.

I clench my jaw and force myself to stand still. Because of this pause, the very sacrifice it takes not to rush to Enzo's side, I can press my own magic into the open wound her anger made inside me, easing it. She does not control me. I am the one in control here.

"Well, look at that." Marian chuckles without humor, her onyx eyes fixed on my hand. "And here I was thinking you didn't know where the knife was."

From the rafters comes a mocking gasp. "Oh, my goodness. Gem—you *lied* to us?"

Poppy drops from the ceiling with the grace of a practiced ballerina and the appeal of an execution by hanging. I can *hear* her bones crack and pop out. Her limbs look crooked and *wrong* until she pulls herself back together into something resembling the living.

"Wow, that's so out of character for you." She flashes me a smile.

Marian slides her fingers through Enzo's hair. I think about breaking her hand. She pulls him up into a sitting position, tilting his head back. "Wake up, pretty boy. Look who came to save you."

Somehow, even with everything else going on, the fact that Enzo is *here* is enough to give me butterflies. I've always known he was small, but he looks tinier in person than I was expecting—fragile in a way that makes me nervous. But maybe that's because he's tied up. I notice his hair's gone pink.

He starts to blink, slowly, adjusting to the low light. He squints across the room at me. "Gem?"

The sound of his voice—his real voice, not corrupted by a computer or a phone or any of the other ways we've been forced to talk to each other—almost knocks my knees out from under me. How has it never occurred to me that I've never heard his real voice before?

How many nights have I spent fantasizing about being in the same space? How many times have I felt a bone-deep aching, because it was *so wrong* for him to be apart from me? And now he's here.

"Gem, how are you—what's—"

"It's okay." I hold my free hand toward him. "I'm going to get you out of here."

"Mmm, not exactly." Poppy spins, her oversized white jumpsuit swallowing her like a tent when she does. She spins all the way to Enzo's side before crouching next to him. "See, you *are* going to get out of here. But Gemmy's not going with you. They're gonna give us the knife, and we're gonna give you to the nice bitch with the tattoos. And then you two are going to leave while we stab your friend to death."

"Unless," Marian adds, "Gem doesn't love *either* of you the way they claim to."

I study Enzo's face. If this is the only time I'm ever going to see him in person, I want to make sure I soak it in. His big brown eyes are the widest I've ever seen, shiny with unshed tears. He's got smeared eyeliner, but no bruises—it looks like they didn't have to hurt him to get him here. The sweatpants and T-shirt tell me they must have snatched him from bed. One of the lenses in his glasses has a crack that's spiderwebbed out. And he's looking back at me with so much fear, and confusion, and maybe like he wants to memorize me just as badly.

Enzo is so soft, and so *good,* and loving him keeps me grounded to humanity with both feet planted. And when we live through this, I'm going to find a way to make it all up to him.

Even if he doesn't want anything to do with me anymore. Even if I couldn't blame him if he didn't.

Slowly, I look to Willa Mae. They're watching Enzo, too, their own expression somehow fierce and wounded in equal measure. When our eyes meet, they tilt their chin up.

When I look at them, I don't see *only* them. My Mountain is as their magic is—as vicious as the most dangerous predators, as gentle as wildflowers. Maybe because of the duality of their own nature, they can look directly at *every* part of me and love me. Not in spite of who I am, but because of it—all of it.

And when we live through this, I will prove just how well I remember them.

Finally, I turn my head back to Marian. And against all reason, I smile.

"I want to extend an offer."

Marian barks out a shocked laugh, exchanging a look with her girlfriend before turning back to me, raising her eyebrows. "You don't have anything I want but the knife."

"You probably want to live." I shrug. "See, I wasn't planning to kill you. Not unless I *had* to. But I think it'd be fun. Walk away now, and I'll do my best to move past this misstep of yours. And we can just stay the hell away from each other."

"Magician . . ." Marian narrows her eyes. "Has anyone ever told you not to let your mouth write a check your ass can't cash?"

I take it that's a no.

"Look, this was a fine plan, Battle. I would expect nothing less from the strategist of the pantheon. Except—you fucked up." I take a step forward, and raise the sharp blade of the Ouroboros into the air between us. "Loving them doesn't actually make me weak. It makes me ruthless."

In one quick slash, I slice open my own arm, a scarlet flood erupting. A sacrifice for the god who rules over bloodshed.

Magic pulses along my skin, so close and familiar I don't have to reach for it. It's *there*, ready and waiting to do what I ask of it. As blood pours down my arm and into my palm, I curl my fingers into the warm pool of it, making a fist. My magic responds in kind.

And across the room, Poppy's hands shoot to her neck as she chokes.

Marian roars, rushing toward me. But Willa Mae steps in her path. At first, panic seizes my chest. Any life in this building is long gone. What can the Mountain do here?

My worry is misplaced. When Marian is halfway across the room, she comes to a stop so suddenly that her upper body jerks forward, like it's trying to run without her legs. She looks down, bewilderment on her face. It quickly warps to horror as her legs begin *transforming into roots,* unsettling the concrete floor to dig their way into the earth beneath. Planting Marian where she stands.

"What power is this?" she screams, turning frantic eyes on Willa Mae.

I'd like to know that myself. This display of the land god's power is one I have no memory of.

The Mountain lifts one shoulder in nonanswer.

When Enzo lets out a horrible gurgle, my attention snaps back to him. Poppy, still gagging around her own tongue, has crawled over to him. Her hands are curled around his neck, and even in the darkness of the mill I can see his veins pulse black and ugly and wrong.

She's seeping death right into him. Into *Enzo*.

The sound I make is neither human nor godly, and I fly toward them. I tangle my fingers in her white hair and make a bloody fist, yanking her away from him as hard as I can. I think I hear her neck pop before her skull bounces off the concrete.

I straddle her whisp-thin waist—and press the Ouroboros to her throat.

Around us, the room goes still.

All I have to do is press a little harder and the god of death will never rise again. We'll be rid of the Reaper once and for all.

Poppy stares up without fear. She gasps around her words when she forces out, "Do it . . . *pussy* . . . I won't . . . beg . . . for life."

Marian's voice is nothing like I've ever heard it when she screams, "WELL, I WILL!"

Holding the knife in place, I turn my head toward the god of battle. The strange magic Willa Mae used has spread. From her knees down, Marian's body is *turning into a* tree, skin peeling back to make way for bark. Her expression holds the unfiltered fear her girlfriend can't spare.

But I don't care. The Reaper will not live past tonight.

I look down at Poppy. She smiles. The blade presses in deeper, and a thin ribbon of red appears along its sharpened edge.

"IF YOU KILL HER, YOU'LL ROT!" Marian screams.

A lot of big talk for someone being terraformed.

"Magician, that isn't a threat. It's a warning. *Look* at her." Marian's voice breaks. "She is the goddess of an afterlife she can't reach; a vessel of death with no chance of life. What used to be her gifts are now her curse—and if you kill her with the Ouroboros, you will inherit that curse for yourself."

Hm.

I lessen the pressure of the blade, just a fraction. Poppy lets out a quiet warble of a gasp.

It might all be the Lionheart's strategizing, but this is not the first time the issue of the Reaper's decay has come to my attention.

Even if it's a lie, I have my own hesitations. With my memories finally back to the forefront, my understanding of my own power is clearer than it's ever been.

I am the keeper of the scales. My magic is a balancing act. If I were to take another god's power for my own, *any* god's power, the scales would be thrown out of balance. And I don't know what might happen after.

Buck's eerie warning rings in my ears. "*And the scales will tip . . . tip . . . tip . . . until they fall from existence.*"

Previous versions of me might have worried about maintaining the balance for altruistic reasons—I don't. But my *purpose* as the god of magic is to keep the scales.

If they don't exist, I don't know if *I* will.

I glance at Willa Mae. They shrug when our eyes meet.

The only other option would be to let *them* have Poppy's power. And if it's true, about the death curse . . . no. I won't risk it.

Enzo is flush against the wall. He isn't looking at me. He's watching Marian's body shift from skin to wood. And he looks like he's going to break.

Okay.

What I need is to get him home. And *then* come up with a plan. He can't handle any more tonight, and he shouldn't have to. This isn't his fight. It's a mess he was forced into because he loves me.

"The Magician will bring immeasurable pain to everyone who loves them."

No kidding.

I rise, stepping away from Poppy's body. As my blood drips down my hand and splatters the floor, I release the magic holding her lungs hostage. Willa Mae must take the hint, because the bark on Marian's body quickly begins to strip away, like a vegetable peeler revealing the supple flesh underneath.

"Go. Both of you." I flick my bloody fingers toward the door. "But this isn't over."

"No," Marian snarls, kicking free of her roots and grabbing her girlfriend's arm. "It isn't."

I watch them leave, and ignore the ugly thing in my chest that wants to know what Poppy looks like with her torso carved open like her twin's.

"Gem?"

Enzo's quiet voice brings me back. I wheel toward him, dropping to my knees. The knife clatters on the floor next to us as I scramble to undo the ropes keeping his wrists behind his back.

As soon as they're freed, his hands raise to my face. After a brief hesitation, he touches my cheeks.

Fuck.

I could cry at how perfect this feels. How soft and tender he is. How, after all this time, after all the wanting, he's here. He's real.

"I don't—" He shakes his head. "How—"

"There is so much I have to tell you," I whisper, reaching up to push back his hair, careful not to use my bloody hand. "And I'm going to. I'm going to explain all of it. Let's get you to my house, and then—then no more secrets."

And if he wants to run back to Brooklyn and never speak to me again, I won't blame him. It will ruin some part of me, changing me forever. But I'll let him go. He deserves that.

He looks like he wants to ask his questions *now*, and I can see a thousand of them poised on his tongue. But, after another long moment, he nods. "O-okay. Yeah."

I grab the knife in one hand and shove it in my pocket. With my other hand, I grab his upper arm, helping him to his feet. He weighs nothing, built like a baby bird, and leans into my side as I walk him out.

Holding him like this would be life-changing if circumstances weren't what they are.

Maybe it still is.

I get Enzo in the backseat and climb in with him. He scoots into the middle and collapses into me. Like he didn't just see me try to kill the girl who kidnapped him, or the shit Willa Mae did. Like he could still want to touch me, even after all that.

I wrap my arms around him and bury my face in his hair. For years, I've wondered what he smells like, and now I have my answer. Cardamom and oat milk, leather and smoke; soft and strange and the exact sort of genteel eccentricity I would expect.

Nervous, but knowing I won't forgive myself if I don't, I press a kiss to his temple. It's meant to comfort, to ground him—and, selfishly, to get me as close to actually kissing him as I ever might.

Enzo tilts his head back to blink at me. I can't piece together the look on his face. He makes a quiet sound and turns away, neither accepting or rejecting the affection. He seems lost in thought. I can't blame him.

Willa Mae watches us in the rearview, though when I catch them looking they turn their eyes to the road. There's so much I want to say to them, too. How this doesn't change the way I feel about them—and I want to tell them *how* I feel now that I know. And I do know.

I am so in love with them.

Both of them.

Whatever that means.

At my house, I plan to ask Willa Mae to stay the night. But I don't get the chance. They park, and turn to frown at us over their shoulder.

"What's Zeke King doing on your porch?"

I . . . don't know.

This is not what I want to be doing right now. But *okay*.

My night can't get any worse.

"I'll make this quick," I promise, opening the door and jumping out. My mom's car is gone—she must've left for her night shift. She would've realized I wasn't home when she did. It'll be a whole thing later.

Can't believe I'm thinking about my curfew right now.

Raising my voice as I move toward the porch, I call out, "Hey, Zeke—"

"I have been waiting *five hundred years* to kick your ass."

Oh.

Wait, what?

Zeke stomps down the porch steps and makes his way toward me, face red and twisted. I've never seen my golden retriever this angry.

"What do you . . ."

Buck's voice whispers in my mind. "*Slumbering evils will at last awaken.*"

We couldn't send Poppy back to the Ether on her own, because the magic keeping us here tethered us all to each other. *All* the gods are connected.

And when Buck knocked down the wall between me and my past lives . . .

This isn't Zeke. This is the Hammer.

"Wait—wait, no, listen to me—"

He doesn't seem interested in listening. He gives a roar, charging at me. Even as I rapidly back up, trying to scramble away from his fists, I *know* I can't outrun him.

I survived the gods of death and battle just to get punched to death by the god of strength.

He's right on top of me now. He pulls back his arm—

Enzo slides between us. I didn't hear him get out of the car—and I certainly didn't feel him pull the Ouroboros from my pocket, but there it is in his hand.

"Enzo, no!" He's going to get himself killed! He's going to—

Zeke's furious roar dies as the rest of him does. When Enzo shoves the god-killing blade into his chest.

The quarterback crumples. Behind us, Willa Mae yells out a string of profanities.

Very slowly, Enzo turns to face me. And he smiles.

No.

No, no, no.

This isn't possible.

"Hello, creature." The Shade, wearing Enzo's skin, steps forward and slides the bloody tip of my own knife beneath my chin. "We've a lot of catching up to do."

19

WITH EACH HALF BENT TOWARD THE OTHER'S DAMNATION

Tonight is the last time I will ever see the Shade. This is what I think as I watch him sleep, beautiful and peaceful in ways he never can be when he's awake. My beloved monster does not know I have betrayed him—by the time he learns, it will be too late. At dawn, the pantheon will gather, and I will cast the spell to take us away from here.

How badly I ache with want, that another solution might be possible. It is as if my heart has been cleaved in two. When I have left this world behind, half of me will remain here, with him, forever.

But there is no other way. The others have formed an alliance against us, setting aside ancient disputes to form an army that might take both of our heads. It is not them I fear, though. It is true they plan to come for us—but should that plan ever see its end, we would kill them one by one.

I know this because I have the Ouroboros. The god-killing knife is the only way this war concludes. They could attack all they liked, and they may even make headway—though I have seen the Shade's new power firsthand, and do not doubt he could take on an army alone—but it would not matter, in the end. So long as we hold the blade, we will come out as victors.

This means my options for staying in the Ether are three-fold:

In the first, I could help the Shade see our plans through to the end, ridding this world of the rest of the pantheon and inheriting dominion over all. This was, after all, our intention. And it was not so long ago that I remained on the path to do just this.

Carving the Caretaker's heart from her chest was when I began to realize the gravity of my mistakes. This is not balance; in an attempt to right an ancient wrong, I have created something worse. It is my hand now, tilting the scales out of balance. And it is my *duty* to right them.

In the second, I could turn the blade against the Shade himself. I could carve the power I've given him out of his body, distributing it among the rest of the pantheon to garner their forgiveness for my role in his crimes. It is even possible that he could live through this, that I could allow him a life without the gifts of a god, but a life nonetheless.

But this is *still* not balance. The Shade has earned a right to the power long denied him. Where is the justice in putting down a dog who bites back, when that dog has spent his entire life chained and starved?

To say nothing of the shameful truth that I do not believe I am strong enough to raise the knife against him. Even if I were to overpower him, I would fall victim to my own treacherous heart.

There is, of course, the third scenario—I could destroy the knife. This has always been part of my plan. The Ouroboros is incomplete without its chain, a delicate thread forged of the same silver, intended to curl around the blade and render it useless, should I ever decide that time has come. One could argue that time has long since arrived.

A part of me wishes I had never forged this knife to begin with. If I had only listened to the warnings of what would come . . .

No, I cannot think of that. If I allow myself to think of all I lost to bring this knife to power, I will lose myself to grief.

Without the Ouroboros, the Shade could not take more power. The pantheon could not take our heads. We would be forced to find a way to live in harmony, as we have been forced to do since our world began, with the playing field between the Shade and the others finally leveled.

That would be balance. I know this to be true.

And I know it to be true even as I know I cannot go through with it. My wretched heart is too twisted, so torn between its lust for power and its need for equipoise, with each half bent toward the other's damnation. For this reason, I will *never* be able to do the only thing I should—to destroy the weapon that has made me the god-killer.

Though I have known this to be true for some time now, I've been frozen over my indecision, caught in a series of impossible choices. I sense the Shade has felt my mind at war with itself, but instead of using that to strike with accusations of looming betrayal, he's done the opposite. My monster has pulled me closer, tangling me deeper into his web, tying my hands with the seductive rope of his guile.

Knowing my own bleak heart as well as I do, I think I would have stayed at his side no matter what were to come next. That is, if *she* had not found me.

It was not the Mountain's shadow I expected to darken my doorstep, but it was her shadow I found, slinking to me in secret only nights earlier.

She is afraid. They are all afraid, I know they must be, but she is the only one who has sought me out. Her fear began in earnest the day the Shade took the Inferno's power, flooding his monstrous veins with fire. The Inferno was her ally, bound to her because he was wed to her cherished sister. It was only because of that bond that the gods of land and fire were able to live in harmony. Without that alliance, she knows how vulnerable her territory is—one spark, and he could turn the land to ash.

But she has presented to me a fourth scenario, an option I never would have considered on my own. Let the Shade have this world—we will stake claim to a new one.

The spell is ready, all the components in place. Even now, as I spend my last night in the Shade's stronghold, the Mountain is gathering the others, compelling them to meet me at dawn.

We've elected not to tell them the plan. We know there are those who would say no. But the more of our number in this new world, the greater our collective power. We will not leave them here for the Shade to torment when they could be of use to us moving forward.

But even this plan is not without consequence. It requires magic stronger than any I have attempted before it, and demands a sacrifice just as powerful.

As I sit before the fireplace in the Shade's chamber, watching him sleep and hoping he does not wake, I've no doubt what that sacrifice is. I get to live—but I lose *him*. And with him, I lose a part of myself never to be recovered; I condemn myself to walk this new world like an open wound, for all of eternity, as half my heart rots in the Ether.

I know this, and I know it is fair, but I still cannot bring myself to accept it. The memory of a warning whispers, but I push it away.

I do not care that my heart is never satisfied. I do not care that it is hungry and ugly and raw. I do not want to find peace. There is even a secret, awful of part of me that does not care about the balance.

What I want is a world where I get *everything*.

And so here I am, with my secret shame and my cracked-open chest, giving life to one last spell before I flee this place. In the morning, my beloved monster will find it. And he will rage, and he will ache, and he will not forgive me for this. Not soon.

But maybe someday, he will. And I will be ready for him.

Shaking, I finish my letter and cross to his bedside. I set the parchment on his table, along with a small glass vial, stoppered with a cork and filled with a dark gray liquid that glints in the light of the fire. I allow myself one last look at him, this malevolent god-king of my own creation and the most beautiful man in this world or any other.

Please come and find me, I want to whisper. *Please find the will to forgive this so I do not have to walk this new world without you forever.*

As quiet as the shadows from which my lover was born, I slip from his room and set on my journey to break both our hearts.

Willa Mae's fist connects so hard with Enzo's face that something shatters. The knife slips from under my chin, grazing it, and I stumble until my ass hits the bumper of the Jeep. She sweeps down to snatch the blade from the ground, raising it over his body—

"No!" I snap back to myself in time to grab her forearm with both of my hands. I'm not strong enough to win a physical fight against her, but all of my weight hanging from her arm is enough to give her pause. "Don't hurt him!"

"HAVE YOU LOST YOUR MIND?" I've never seen her like this. Her uncanny eyes are massive, stark fear on her face, even as *she* wields the one weapon that can kill any of us. "He's *here*—how is he here?"

The answer to that question is going to hurt her so badly I'm not sure we'll recover.

I've had *lifetimes* to tell the Mountain about the spell I left behind, a one-way ticket to Earth if the Shade ever decided to use it. I made excuses, convinced myself it made sense not to open the can of worms. He was never *actually* going to come for me—even without knowing the safety net I'd added to his spell, that he would arrive here as a *newborn*, with *none* of his memories, he would never give up the power he'd accumulated in the Ether just so we might reunite. He'd loved me. But he'd loved power more.

He wasn't like *her*. With her, I'd found a sort of love that I did not think possible and that I did not deserve. Her love didn't glue the pieces of my heart back together, but it nursed the half that was left until it was strong enough to beat on its own. Why would I risk losing that to submerge her in an entirely hypothetical fear? He was *never* coming.

Enzo straightens, wiping the back of his hand across his bloody mouth, leaving a slash of red across his cheek and jaw. His eyes dart between the knife, suspended in the air as I dig my fingers into Willa Mae's arm, and my face. "Yes, creature. Why don't you tell the Mountain how I got here?"

Suspended in silence, and all I can think is that the way Enzo Truly's mouth forms the word "creature" makes goose bumps crawl up my neck.

When I don't answer, Willa Mae yanks her arm out of my grip and takes a step back, twisting so she can face us both, the three of us making a triangle in the front yard. The oak tree outside my bedroom window bristles. One spindly branch curls against her throat, nuzzling like an obedient pet.

"Gem?"

"I left a spell behind." It feels as if my voice is coming from somewhere beyond my body. The loss of control is disturbingly familiar, like I'm just a puppet on a string once more. "It would grant him access to this world, limiting his power the same as ours—but I never believed he would use it."

"Then why," she whispers, voice hoarse, "do it at all?"

I can't bring myself to answer, not when we both *know*. Because I hoped he would. Because I loved him enough to let my own world fall, and I hoped he would love me enough to walk away from the empire he'd made in its wreckage. Because, despite Willa Mae's insistence that the Shade had manipulated me, I loved him with half of my horrible heart, as deeply as I've ever loved her.

His being here means she can't pretend anymore that I was the Shade's first victim. The bogeyman has come to call, and with him comes proof that I crawled willingly beneath the bed.

"Would you be able to stomach me if you thought I'd actually wanted everything I did with him? Would you be able to stomach yourself?"

She does not cry, though her eyes water. She stares as if seeing me in the light for the first time.

Enzo clears his throat. Though it takes effort to drag my eyes from Willa Mae's face, I look to him. He smiles. "You know, it's remarkably lucky that your little friends came and grabbed me from my bed. It must have knocked something loose. I feel like I've woken up for the first time in years."

It had nothing to do with Poppy and Marian and everything to do with Buck Wheeler. The Shade wasn't tethered by the original spell the way the rest of us are, but somehow, the Evergod's magic must have pulled him in.

He flicks his wrist in the same way I've seen Enzo do a thousand times, motioning between Willa Mae and me. "Swamp Girl is the god of land, hm? Interesting. How long has *this* been going on?"

There's so much I want to say, and even more I want to *ask*. But every word gets caught in my throat, like they're all trying to break free at once and the doorway is jammed.

Willa Mae finds her voice before I do. "You can't really plan to let him live."

My head snaps back to her. "I won't let you hurt him. And he won't hurt you."

"Your *friend* is dead." The words drag themselves from between her teeth like zombies from the grave. "The boy you loved is gone."

"No. *This* life matters, and Enzo doesn't deserve to die." I don't say out loud that I don't want either version of him to die—that I love them both. She knows. There's no point pouring salt in the cut.

"*Enzo* isn't real! We're not human, Gem!"

My eyes glide across the tattoos on her chin, the tribal markings given to her by her *human* people. How can she wear those and not realize her own hypocrisy? How can she pretend her humanity doesn't matter when it's her humanity that connects her to the very land she governs here? "You don't believe that."

"If it would make you feel better, kitten, you're welcome to *try* to kill me," Enzo drawls, studying his hands. "I'm a little rusty, but I'd like to see what this body can do."

Kitten? He must have a death wish.

She's looking at him like she's thinking the same thing. Finally, that disgusted stare turns back to me. "It won't be long before the others realize he's here. And once people know, they're not going to listen to any sad excuse you have about who he is now. The entire *newly woken pantheon* is going to fight their way through you to rip him apart. And that's before they find out he killed Zeke!"

Her arm sweeps toward the football player's body.

"Right." Almost forgot. "What are we gonna do about . . . that?"

I motion vaguely at his corpse. Willa Mae groans and snatches her cell phone from her pocket, typing furiously.

"The others can try whatever they want. *I'm not letting anyone hurt him.*" Not Enzo or the Shade. Not when I finally have him here, right in front of me. Not when I've been waiting so long to touch him—longer than I even knew. "And I just—I need you to get on board with that."

She flashes me a wounded look. "You ask too much from me."

"I know. But your options are to stand with me or walk away. I don't want to lose you, but I need you to understand what it looks like if you stay." I shake my head. "He's *our* problem. Not their martyr, or their salvation, or their prey."

I think Enzo gives an indignant scoff. I don't look at him.

Willa Mae stares at me unblinking for too long before she groans and rubs her hands over her eyes. "He's *evil.*"

I can't tell her he isn't. I throw my hands up. "He's a twink!"

"As delightful as this is for *me*," Enzo cuts in, "I would like the chance to spend a moment *alone* with Gem, before I have to leave your charming little town. Perhaps, Swamp Girl, you could come back in the morning."

"Absolutely fucking not." Willa Mae shakes her head. "Gem? No. Even if I weren't still thinking about shoving this knife up his ass, there's no way I'd leave you alone with him. Not gonna happen."

"He won't hurt me." Even as I say it, I know I can't be sure. *Enzo* would never hurt me. And the Shade being here means he *must* have forgiven me—I hope.

She raises her eyebrows. The tree branch looks like a middle finger when it flicks the air.

"I suppose you can sleep on the couch," Enzo offers. "If you're really so eager to eavesdrop on our . . . reunion."

The way he says the word makes my face heat. It doesn't get any better when he reaches over and brushes his fingers against the side of my neck. Our eyes meet and he smiles. It isn't Enzo's charming grin or the awful baring of the Shade's sharp fangs, but some combination of the two.

"I'll be in bed, waiting for you." His thumb etches the notch in my jaw before his hand falls. And I watch as the Shade steps over the Hammer's body and walks into my house.

When I manage to drag my eyes back to Willa Mae, she's already watching me. The look on her face is not one I've seen before.

And is one I'd like to never see again.

"Babe—"

"No." She holds up a flattened palm. "I'm not ready to hear it."

I swallow, fighting the urge to keep talking anyway.

"My grandparents are coming to deal with the body. When they're gone, I'll crash out here."

Of course she will. The tree branch is tangling itself in her curls already.

"Okay." I suck in a breath. "Wi—"

"I said *no*." Her breath shakes. "You know, Echols, you've never been kind. Not in any lifetime, not really. Maybe you've never even been *good*. But you've never been cruel—not to me. Not until now."

"The Magician will bring immeasurable pain to everyone who loves them. They will drown beneath the weight of their own cruelty."

Even though her words feel like knives of their own digging pinpricks into my skin, there is an ugly truth beneath them that I need her to hear out loud. I meet her eyes when I say, "I've never been good—and you chose me anyway. I think that says as much about you as it does me."

I leave her with that, standing in my front yard with Zeke's corpse and the trees, as I turn to follow Enzo inside.

20

WHAT IS A THOUSAND YEARS TO A GOD?

Hank's on the couch when I walk inside. He's wide awake and staring at my bedroom door with his ears flush against the sides of his skull. When he sees me, he growls.

"Yeah, I get it," I mumble, and head to my room anyway.

Enzo's not actually waiting in bed. He's standing in front of my open closet, rifling through my stuff. He looks up when I join him, a smirk in the corner of his mouth.

"Your dog's not nice."

"He loves Willa Mae."

"Hm." He spins, turning toward a wall of posters and printed photos. "Your house is so much bigger than I thought it would be. It's *way* bigger than mine."

Not what I was expecting him to say. I want to touch him. I stay where I am, and shove my hands in my pockets. "Oh— your apartment always looked so nice on FaceTime."

"Well, I said *bigger*." His eyes dart toward the window, the outline of the tree visible through the closed blinds. "Bigger doesn't mean better."

Okay. For the sake of everything else, I will pretend the rotten little shit didn't just insult me.

"How are you here?" I watch him study my photos. I think about running my fingers through his pink hair.

"You'd know that better than I would, wouldn't you?"

"I don't mean—" I take a deep breath. "*Why* are you here? You chose to come and find me—why now?"

"You assume this is the first life I've lived on Earth? That I haven't been wandering this world in different bodies for hundreds of years, unable to find you because *I didn't even remember I was looking?*"

Oh. Oh, no. My lips part, and I suck in breath, explanations and apologies each poised on my tongue—

"Well, it is, and I haven't." Enzo snickers. "It would seem I found you on my first try."

My chest deflates like a popped balloon. I want to strangle him.

"Nearly unbelievable, isn't it? Billions of people on this grotesque planet, thousands of miles separating us, and I hunted you down." He turns his head over his shoulder to meet my eyes, the brown stained glass of his stare lit with delight. "Feels fated, hm?"

It does. But because I'm still irritated with him, I answer, "Willa Mae says we're all drawn to each other. It's how the magic works."

Enzo's eyes are just as pretty when they're trying to roll out of his head. "*Willa Mae,*" he mocks. "I do not like that name."

I'm not sure what he'd like me to do about that.

"And really, Gem, the god of land? Tell me this is a fling."

"Is this why you wanted to be alone? To complain about her? Because I've had a long day, and if that's all you want, I'd rather—"

Enzo shuts me up with his bloody mouth on mine.

I've kissed a lot of people. But for all the years I've wanted *this* to happen, I've never let myself imagine what it would be like. Maybe because I wanted it *too* much, and letting myself fantasize would make it harder to know I was never going to have it. Or maybe because it felt wrong, like betrayal, picturing him like that without consent. Especially if thinking about kissing led to something more.

Which is nothing like the way I've thought of the Shade. Since the demon began appearing in my dreams, I've wanted him unapologetically and viscerally. More than once, I've woken with my legs tangled in the bedsheets, hand desperately seeking the waistband of my underwear, needing fast relief for an ache I could never soothe on my own.

And now I'm kissing them both.

One of his hands finds my waist, the other curls around my neck, and he uses both to guide me into him. Sparks fly along my skin, more electric than any magic I've ever felt. His lips are impossibly soft, but his teeth are sharp when he bites, demanding entrance—though we both know I wouldn't deny him. He explores the roof of my mouth, tongue snaking against the ridges.

I remember who I am, and my hands grip his slim waist. It takes no effort to drag him off his feet, and soon we're both toppling into bed, him underneath me, his legs spread so I can kneel between his thighs. My palms move to his waist, pushing his shirt with me until my fingertips brush the raised lines of his top surgery scars. I twist my hands in the fabric of his shirt, yanking it over his head before my mouth descends on his chest, sucking a mark into the center where the scars don't meet.

When he unties my braid and makes a fist in the hair at the base of my head, he uses it to tug my face back.

Both panting, we stare at each other for a long moment. His eyes are as wild as I've ever seen them. Finally, he brushes the fingertips of his free hand against my cheek and growls, "I want to make you come undone."

Oh.

Despite my body's immediate reaction to that—another pulse of electricity in a more concentrated area—I know we should pause. As on-board as my body is with having sex with Enzo, I'll be the one undoing him when that happens. And I'm . . . exhausted.

As badly as I want to be with him, I also don't. Not now.

But I don't know how to tell him that. Because he's here, and he's touching me, and he wants me, and what if I ruin everything by pulling back? What if I hurt his feelings? He came all this way. He went through so much. He wants this, and he deserves it.

And I want it, too. I *do.*

His hand slips down to my waistband, fingertips pushing past the hem of my jeans. When he presses against the elastic band of my underwear, my stomach rolls with anxiety even as I feel myself getting more turned on. How bad would it be, really, to give him what he deserves? It would feel so good . . .

And then *Enzo* stops. And slowly pulls his hand out of my pants.

I meet his eye, frowning. "What's wrong?"

His fingers slide free of my hair. He settles back against the pillows, tucking his hands behind his head. And he takes me off guard when he says, "I'm sorry. I got carried away."

"Huh?" I'm not sure if an apology from the Shade is more shocking, or an apology in this situation at all. Because it isn't warranted. "No— What? You don't have to stop."

"Darling . . . is that really what you want?"

Why do I feel like I'm going to cry?

I swallow. "Yes. Just—"

Not after the day I've had. Not when I just found out who you are. Not when there are so many unanswered questions between us.

Not before I talk to Willa Mae. Not before I figure out what this means for all three of us.

"Not tonight," I emphasize.

He considers me for a moment before nodding. "You're right. There are more important things."

I need to do something else so I don't cry. I sit on the edge of the bed and yank my shoes off, then my socks and jeans. When I settle back, Enzo pulls one hand out from under his head and curls it around my back, tugging my chest against his side.

I do not think about how I'm still wearing Willa Mae's shirt.

When I speak, I start with the most important question. "Does this mean you aren't mad at me?"

"For not sleeping with me? Or for abandoning me in the Ether?"

I groan.

He chuckles. "No. I'm not mad at you. Oh, I certainly was. For a very long time, alone in our world, perhaps I even hated you. But no. No, creature, I'm not mad at you anymore. I understand why you made your choice."

My palm rests over his chest, the even beating of his heart under my hand. "Why now?"

The strangest frown crosses his face, eyebrows tightening. It's almost like he doesn't know the answer. "I've mourned you all this time. The grief of the loss never lessened, only became easier to carry—until it wasn't. I realized I'd been living in denial, for so long, only pretending to have moved on. And once I recognized that, I *felt* the gap in my life where you should have been. With every step, I became more and more keenly aware of your absence. It did not matter what else I had if I did not have you. Eventually, it became unbearable. I was left with no other choice. I had to find you."

My toes curl of their own accord. "So, it's not like . . . the Ether was invaded by aliens and you had to leave. Right? You *wanted* me. You gave it up for *me*."

His eyes flick to my face. He tugs his other hand from behind his head and brushes his thumb against my cheek. "Why do you sound so surprised?"

"We don't have time to unpack my baggage." I brush his question off. "If it isn't alien-infested, what is our home like? How much has changed since you took over?"

The others live in dread over the kind of hellhole the Shade could have designed. But a sick kind of excitement bubbles in me.

"In many ways, things are the same as they are here. Many on Earth are inclined to give in to their most depraved nature without my influence. . . ." He smirks. "We've seen similar advances in medicine and technology and the arts. We have our own Hollywood—we even have an Ether version of Tom Hanks."

"Wait, really?"

"He's evil, though."

"Oh."

"You could see it for yourself."

I suppose that's true. I used scrying to find my way to Earth all those lifetimes ago. I could do the same thing, just to open a window in the Ether. I never have before, worried about what I might find. But now . . .

Enzo drags me out of my head when he continues, "I want us to go back together."

"What?"

He rolls so we're chest-to-chest, his hand sliding from my face to my neck. "We had so many plans. I know a millennium is stretched between us, but what is a thousand years to a god?"

It's true. My memories are still downloading, and the farther back I reach, the harder they are to access, even with the wall down. A thousand years we've been on Earth, but that's nothing compared to the thousands upon thousands we ruled in our world.

Still. There's a flaw in his plan. "I can't go back. The spell I cast to bring us here, it tethered the gods to each other. We would *all* go back."

He shrugs. "Then we'll deal with them as we intended to."

I roll my eyes in response.

"It was worth a shot." Enzo sighs. "Look, you are the most powerful of us all. Your magic has no limitations. If that's the way the spell is written—rewrite it."

Hm. Something to consider. "If I went back, I wouldn't go without her."

Enzo hums, trailing his fingertips over my shoulder. "Not a fling, then."

"No. Not a fling."

I can't tell how he feels about that. Maybe he can't, either.

"We could stay here," I hedge, twisting our free hands together.

"In Gracie, Georgia?" His tone indicates he'd rather die.

"God, no. No. Not for a second longer than I have to. I mean—*here*. Earth. We have lives. You have friends and family who love you. We don't have to . . . rule anything."

He makes a face.

Okay, I get it. Trading in unlimited power and dominion over an entire world versus a happy human life in New York?

It's a lot to think about.

"Why are the war lord and the plague nurse on your ass?" He changes the subject. "Enough to kidnap innocent little *me*. For shame."

"I'm going to hurt them for that." Even if Enzo is about as far from innocent as . . . well, as I am. "They want the Ouroboros—so they can kill me, and take my power, and go back to the Ether. So they can kill you."

"Naturally." He chuckles.

"We didn't even *have* the knife. It got lost, and they showed up trying to kill me for it, and I had no idea where it was, and—" I suck in my breath between my teeth, the weight of everything that's happened finally starting to sink in. "And then I went and saw my dad, and *he* used it to try to kill me."

How was that only a few hours ago?

"What?" The smug god has disappeared from Enzo's expression, and the familiar softness of my best friend bleeds through. "Oh, darling . . ."

He wraps his arms around my shoulders, and holds me to him. My own arms curl around his waist, locking over his middle, like I could keep him there forever.

And maybe I can. Maybe I will.

I don't know how long it takes me to fall asleep in his arms. But when I do, I sleep without dreams.

When I wake up, it's still dark and Enzo is wearing my clothes.

I don't tell him I'm awake at first. I lie there, curled in the still-warm blankets, eyes lidded, watching as he shuffles around in my black leggings and a mauve sweater that swallows him whole. Like this, with his still-cracked glasses, he looks so . . . young.

Only when I realize he's using my cell phone do I actually sit up.

He jumps, like he's been caught doing something awful, but immediately grins. "Good morning."

"Morning. Nice outfit." I yawn, pressing the back of my hand over my mouth so he isn't killed by morning breath. "Sneaking out?"

"I was going to wake you up before I left. I called a car. Do you know how expensive it is to have a driver come all the way out here to bumfuck nowhere?" He rolls his eyes, looking down at the screen again. "It's almost here. Don't even *ask me* what I'm going to have to do to get on a plane without my wallet."

"You're going back to Brooklyn?"

I don't know why I didn't expect that. He's a person. His parents would care if he was stolen from his bed and just never came back.

"Loose ends," he mumbles, before tossing me my phone. "Walk me out? Your mother is finally sleeping."

My mother. Shit. I'm going to have to deal with her sooner or later.

Hoping for later—and not bothering to put on pants—I

crawl out of bed and sluggishly trail after Enzo through my hallway and onto the porch. The sun is just beginning to rise, black and navy meeting with a swirl of pinks and oranges between them. I swat a bug that dives for my face when the light flickers on.

Enzo laughs, quietly, as he runs his fingers through my hair. "I'll text you as soon as I can. All right?"

"Okay." This sucks.

When I hear tires approaching, I blink my still-sleep-addled vision clear, watching as a little red car appears down the driveway. I *hate* this little red car.

"Kiss me goodbye." Enzo curls his fingers in my shirt, tilting his head back to look into my face.

He'll never need to ask twice. I lean down, pressing my mouth to his. It's exactly as terrible and perfect as our first kiss. But furiously short-lived, with Enzo pulling back almost as soon as it's started. One could even call that chaste.

"As soon as I can," he repeats, bounding off the steps and toward the car. With his fingers on the handle, he turns to look at me again, and grins. "Oh, and Gem? I'm in love with you, too."

My last texts to him flash in my mind, and my stomach drops, and Enzo climbs in the backseat of a stranger's car and disappears before I can even be dramatic about it.

In fact, I'm *still* trying to process what he said when I look up and realize Willa Mae's Jeep is still outside.

And she's here. In the driver's seat. It's too dark to make out her face, but I swear I feel her eyes on me.

I open my mouth and take a step forward.

I don't know what I would have said, but it doesn't matter. Her ignition roars to life, and she leaves the same way Enzo did.

21

WANTING TO LIVE DOESN'T MAKE SOMEONE A VILLAIN

We are beyond heartbroken to inform you all of the loss of one of our beloved students, Ezekiel King, who passed this weekend in a tragic accident. His parents have asked we respect their privacy. Youth counselors from First Church of Gracie have volunteered their time, and they'll be here all week."

A frantic whisper sweeps across the room as the Monday-morning announcements roll out news of Zeke's death. One of the football players starts to cry, body shaking with a horrible, high-pitched wheeze. Someone else gasp-screams "*NO!*"

From her place at the front of the room, Poppy's head snaps back to me. Our eyes meet for only an instant before I look away, unable to handle the silent accusation.

I didn't kill him. This isn't my fault.

Over the speaker, the front-desk clerk clears her throat. "All right, now, we have our list of final candidates for prom court.

For queen—Madison Blackwell, Savannah Riley, and Poppy White. For king . . ."

She continues on, but I tune her out, my thoughts a thousand miles away.

I look down at my lap, tugging my phone out of my hoodie pocket to check the screen under the edge of my desk. Still nothing, not from Enzo *or* Willa Mae. After they'd left, I'd tried calling Willa Mae an annoying number of times, and sent way too many texts to seem even vaguely cool or normal.

> i know we have a lot to talk about but we cannot do that if
> you run away from me again.

> sometimes people have to have hard conversations,
> willa mae!

> okay, that was rude. but i want to work through this.

> can you pick me up? we can talk on the way to school.

> you knew i loved him, even before we knew who he was.
> and yeah, it changes things, but it doesn't. it doesn't
> change the way i feel about him, and it doesn't change the
> way i feel about you. and none of us can figure out what
> that means for our future if you're never willing to talk to
> me about it.

> i still want us to have a future. do you?

> i didn't sleep with him.

in case you were wondering.

okay. i take it you're not coming to get me.

that's fine. we'll talk at lunch.

We don't talk at lunch, though, because they're not here. I scan the cafeteria and find nothing but somber cheerleaders and crying jocks and grief counselors in cargo shorts wandering from table to table. Maybe they didn't even come to school. I don't know why *I* came. It's not like I should still be worrying about getting into a good college, right? I can use magic to do whatever I want.

If Willa Mae didn't skip, maybe they took one look at the situation here and decided to eat in the library. When a puppy-dog-eyed twenty-something with a hemp cross necklace starts approaching me, I turn and leave.

I don't have any idea what I'm doing, but that's nothing new. It feels like the harder I fight for the life I want, the further out of reach it slips. And at every turn, I end up hurting someone. Maybe I could live with that—but not when the people I keep hurting are Willa Mae and Enzo.

"The Magician will bring immeasurable pain to everyone who loves them."

Well, fuck that and fuck the Evergod for saying it, too. I'm gonna fix this. I'm gonna make this right. Because I *deserve* everything I want.

And even if I don't, I don't care.

I just need Willa Mae to talk to me. Me and them and Enzo, we *all* need to get our shit together and start acting like a team—quickly. Before the rest of the gods can.

That is, ironically, what I'm thinking when a hand shoots out from behind a closed door, grabs me by the scruff of my hoodie, and tosses me, unceremoniously, into the auditorium.

"We have thirty minutes before debate team uses this space for practice."

I scramble to my feet, stars in my eyes from the blow my head took on the floor. Maybe it's that, or maybe it's the dim stage lights in the background, the only lighting in the room, but it takes me a moment of squinting before I realize who's here with me.

When I do, I know I'm screwed.

Poppy's the one who grabbed me. She crosses her arms over her fluffy tie-dyed fur coat, tapping the toes on her Frankenstein-themed stilettos as she looks me up and down with contempt.

Marian sits on the edge of the stage, hands curled around the rim, shoulders pulled in so she can lean forward—like she might attack at any second. The shoulder strap of her binder is barely visible under the collar of her gray University of Nebraska crewneck. The basketball shorts and Air Jordans make the whole look.

God, why is she even here? Why is she at my *school* now? Was it not enough for her to torture me at parties, now she has to stalk me in the hallways, too?

So much has happened over the last seventy-two hours that Zeke's barn party feels like it was years ago. But my jaw's still wearing the puncture wounds from her brass knuckles. And it gives a throb when I look at her.

Willa Mae is leaning against the far wall, hands tucked in the front pockets of their skintight black cargo joggers, one combat boot lifted and propped against the wall behind them. And they don't even have the decency to spare a look in my direction.

While that might normally be soul-crushing, I can't take it too personally this time. Because instead of looking at me, they're staring at the last two people in the room.

Murphy Foster is the Siren, the god of water. I first recognized her at Zeke's party. But now, with the wall knocked down, when I look at her—braids pulled into a high pony, perfectly put-together in her plaid skirt and cropped blazer, staring at me like she's going to pull my organs out one by one through my nostrils—I remember something else.

The Siren is the Mountain's sister.

The memories flood, no pun intended. The god of water loved no one more than she loved the god of land—except for maybe her husband, the Inferno. The husband whose power I carved out and gave to Enzo a long, long time ago.

When we came to Earth, the Siren would not even entertain the idea of forgiveness. When she realized the truth of her sister's alliance with me, she turned against *them* in her grief. The loss of her husband and her sister and her *world* was too much for the Siren to handle. She turned her back on the pantheon, choosing not to leave a legacy for her family line to keep records of, choosing to forget us all. To walk this world as human, lifetime after lifetime, rather than face the pain of her own losses ever again.

And now the Evergod's gone and ripped that bandage off, on my orders.

And she isn't even the one I'm most worried about.

The boy at her side is known, in this life, as Rhett Clancy— though more people in Gracie might know him as just *Red.*

He has thick, coppery waves that fall to the midpoint of his shoulder blades, and a big red beard to match. The beard's been around since puberty, fitting his six-foot-three dad-bod-at-seventeen frame, and his mud-coated work boots and coveralls. Like he's leaving biology class to go to his construction job.

He's also the Librarian, the god of knowledge. And the last time I saw him, the Mountain and I were ruining his lives.

The year is 1613 and the Mountain and I have been running from Death and Battle for more years of this lifetime than not. They would be formidable enough on their own, but it is their alliance with the Librarian that continues to entrap us at our every turn.

They've made it clear they intend to return to the Ether by any means necessary. We've dedicated ourselves to keeping the Ouroboros hidden, but *nothing* can remain secret from the Librarian for long. His power is insurmountable in this way. A single touch of his skin against ours, and suddenly we are laid bare to him, every thought we've ever had revealing itself to his hungry mind.

There is only one option. We must destroy him—not only destroy in this lifetime, but destroy any chance he has of returning in the next. His records, the history of his family, must be wiped clean. If they are willing to see their ends met by any means necessary, we must be willing to do the same.

I tell myself this as I slip like a ghost through the halls of his home, poisonous spores drifting from the magic in my palm, taking his bloodline in their sleep. I tell myself at least they have been spared violent deaths. Elsewhere, the Mountain feeds herself the same placations as she takes his records—immaculately detailed accounts of our generations on this Earth—and turns them each to ash.

Back in the auditorium. Back in my body.

These people are going to kill me.

"Okay, look—"

Rhett Clancy's fist connects with the side of my head.

Even though I'm the one getting my shit rocked, he lets out an awful cry as I fall. When I manage to grab a seat and drag myself to my knees, blinking at him to clear my vision, the big ginger has his own head in his hands, palms squeezing his temples. And I realize the Librarian is *downloading* every horrible thought I've ever had; my every secret, my every wicked want, they're all up for grabs in his mind.

This is so, so much worse than Marian hacking into my fucking phone.

Behind him, the Lionheart's eyes darken with delight. "That's my boy."

A hand curls into the neck of my shirt again, and this time, instead of being tossed around like a dog toy, I'm pulled to my feet. Willa Mae brushes a hand down my back, though their sour expression is focused on Rhett. "*Your boy* now knows everything I've told you is true. Tell them."

Tell them what? What have they already told these people? Panic and anger misfire in my chest. I jerk away from their touch, shooting them a sidelong glance.

Their shoulders stiffen. But they're still not looking at me.

Everyone's watching Rhett. After what feels like forever, he lowers his hands and nods. "They ain't lyin'. They ain't had the knife till yesterday. They're still tryin' to take it outta the equation, but don't know how. And yeah—yeah, the Shade's back. He's the one that killed Zeke. Took his power, too."

Willa Mae *told them* about Enzo?

They still can't bring themself to spare me a glance. But they must feel my eyes on them, because they say, "I told you—they were going to find out no matter what. And now they know we have nothing to hide."

"This . . ." Poppy's voice rolls thick over her tongue as she sashays around me and moves toward the stage. "Changes everything."

"It changes nothing." I snap my teeth on the edge of the words. "We're getting rid of the knife. And you're going to keep your hands off Enzo—or did you not learn your lesson last night?"

Poppy tilts her head, like she's imagining what I'd look like without skin.

Marian puts her palm over the smaller girl's shoulder. "But you have no idea how to destroy the knife. Isn't that right, Magician?"

"It has a chain—"

Rhett cuts me off. "Chain's lost. You ain't have shit."

My fists curl and uncurl. I remind myself it would be ill-advised to murder anyone in the school auditorium on a weekday afternoon. "Rhett, I know we've never exactly been friends, but—"

Again, Rhett cuts me off. "My mama's got four fuckin' jobs. Hair's fallin' out, knees 'bout to give up on her. My daddy ate a bullet 'cause he couldn't get his truck fixed to get to work—ain't know we wouldn't ever see the insurance if he done himself in. And me?"

He raises his left hand—the one missing his index and middle fingers. "This is what under-the-table crew work got me when I's barely big enough to hold a saw. Now only place that'll hire me is the fuckin' Piggly Wiggly, breakin' my back for seven fuckin' dollars an hour."

I swallow.

"You know, my whole life, people been tellin' me how fuckin' smart I am. How I don't live up to my potential or some shit, like how I got all these brains in my head but I'm still failin' classes. How I'm never gonna get to college 'cause I don't apply myself." He snorts. "You know, it's real easy to *apply yourself* when you ain't gotta worry about makin' sure your family eats."

He growls, "Y'all took everything from me. I coulda set 'em up right. I was s'pose to take care of 'em, and take care of *my future* when I did. And then y'all came around . . . and you made sure we'd never be able to claw our way outta the shit ever again."

It's awful. And he's not wrong. If we hadn't destroyed his records, his family might not be where they are.

But he can't seriously blame us for all of it, right? At a certain point, he can't pin every bad thing that's happened to him on one night from four hundred years ago.

"With all due respect," I finally manage to say, "and my sincere condolences, I didn't make your dad kill himself."

"Jesus Christ," Murphy whispers, turning away to pace toward the other side of the room, waving an exasperated hand over her head.

For a moment, Rhett looks like he's going to hit me again. Instead, he says, "Aight, then. Guess I'd rather have a dead dad than an abusive psycho livin' in a slum house."

I take a step forward, and Willa Mae curls their arm around my chest. The world tries to slant away, magic pummeling through my system as it aches to narrow in on the Librarian, imagining all the other limbs he still has left to lose. Imagining all the ways I could still make his family's life worse.

But Willa Mae whispers against my ear, "We are outnumbered and in public. Do you want your happy ending, you selfish bastard? Try to be a little more charming."

I know they're right. I don't *want* to want to kill anyone. I just want to live. Me, and them, and Enzo. And if there's a way to do that . . .

I focus on their hand against my chest, strong and solid, and their soft body along my spine. I focus on the dirt-and-honey smell of them, and how impossibly warm they feel. I've missed them. I was with them all day for the last two days, apart for less than twelve hours, and I've missed them so much that all I want to do is make a nest in their bones.

Finally, I look to Marian. "Why are we here?"

She runs her tongue along her lower lip, and glances at Poppy. Some silent communication passes between them before they both look back to me. "If the Shade is here, we don't have to go back to the Ether. If we don't have to go back to the Ether, you don't have to die."

I raise an eyebrow, skeptical. "Oh?"

"Only he does."

Right, there it is. "If you want him, you'll have to go through me, anyway."

"You cannot be serious!" Murphy wheels around. "I knew you were a liar—we all knew. When the Mountain came to us, claiming you'd broken out from under his spell, the rest of us knew it was bullshit. But I didn't think you'd ever be so blatant about it. You won't even pretend? Won't even try to go along with the ruse that you aren't just as awful as he is?"

I don't have anything to offer her except the truth. And even as I say it, I know it won't be good enough. Even as I say it, I know it isn't entirely true anyway. "I'm not the person I once was. I'm Gem Echols, not the Magician you remember. Just like *he's* not the same anymore, either."

She shakes her head, as disappointed with my answer as I expected. "Why even bring us here? Why not just let him kill us *all* the way you planned? At least then our bodies would be buried in their own world."

"Is that what you would have preferred?"

Willa Mae's arm tightens around my chest. I don't know if it's meant to be comforting or punishing.

Instead of Murphy answering me, it's Rhett who answers *her*. "Please. They brought us here 'cause they knew was only a matter of time 'fore they lost their use. They were the last name on the Shade's list, and they started to see it comin'."

"That isn't true," I snap. "I brought you here to restore the balance."

And he never would have turned against me. He wouldn't have. He loved me. He loved me so much that he traveled across worlds to come and find me . . . one thousand years later.

I wasn't on his list. I wasn't.

Rhett snorts, shaking his head. He leans in close to Murphy's back—though I note he's careful not to actually touch her. "Why don'cha ask the *Mountain* why they drug us all here, huh? Was their idea, after all. They went crawlin' to 'em, beggin' for a new world to take over. Not the other way round."

"What?" Marian's eyes go wide. She jumps from the stage. "A thousand years you've let me go after the Magician, and never once owned up to this being *your* plan from the beginning?"

Oh. I guess none of them knew that.

But none of them look quite as upset about it as Murphy does.

For the first time since I got yanked into this room, she's looking *directly* at Willa Mae. Her black eyes are huge, and I watch them fill with tears, like sloshing buckets being dragged to the surface of a well. She gives the smallest shake of her head and stomps up the path toward the doors.

Willa Mae lets me go to face her. "Sister—"

"Don't you dare!" Murphy snarls. "A millennium ago, I thought you were just an idiot. I was so sure they'd tricked you somehow, and I blamed *them* for my loss—but now I realize I didn't lose you at all. You *left* me. You went crawling on your knees to the Inferno's *murderer* to save your own hide."

No, that isn't . . . Well, yes, that's what happened, but . . . Look, the Mountain came to me for help to save their own life, sure, but they saved everyone else in the process, too.

And wanting to live doesn't make someone a villain.

"And now what? You're *with* them? Tell me, is it just the Magician, or are you giving it up for the Shade, too? Now that he's back, how long do you *really* think they'll let you live before they decide they want your power more than a girlfriend—especially when they already have each other?"

"I would never do anything to hurt them." I take a warning step in Murphy's direction. "You have no idea what you're talking about."

"I wish I didn't. So do me a favor. The next time I forget you people exist—don't remind me."

The auditorium door swings closed behind her. Willa Mae remains silent at my side. I would almost believe they weren't breaking, if not for the subtle shaking of their entire body.

When I lace my fingers with theirs, they don't squeeze back, but they don't pull away.

"Damn." Poppy tsks. "Everyone here is just riddled with

family drama, huh? Well, except me. Aww, and I have *you* to thank for that, Magician."

She giggles in her special fucked-up way, and the bell blares, signaling a class change.

Rhett gives me one last death stare before grabbing his backpack from one of the seats and heading out the same way Murphy left.

"Okay." I run my thumb against Willa Mae's and turn my attention to Marian. "The debate team's gonna be here any minute. You know where I stand. I don't *want* to hurt you"—*not entirely true*—"but I'm not going to let you hurt my people."

Marian shrugs. "And you know where I stand. I never wanted to *have* to kill you"—*arguable at best*—"but I'll do anything to anyone who stands in the way of getting my girl what she needs."

There's no nonviolent solution here. Not unless—

"Guess you better hurry up and find a way to destroy that knife." Marian levels me with a hard look. "Because it's only a matter of time before one of us gets our hands on it. And not *everyone* would only kill you as a last resort."

Poppy giggles and makes an explosion with her fingers. "He's gonna bring the thunder!"

Whatever that means.

As people start filing into the room behind us, Poppy grins, greeting a few of them. I overhear someone ask her about being nominated for prom queen and my eyes nearly roll out of my head at her excited hand flapping.

Willa Mae turns to leave and I move with them. They pause, dropping my hand. With a shake of their head, they say, "I need a minute."

"Oh. Yeah. Okay."

When Willa Mae disappears, I realize Poppy's no longer midconversation. And she's watching me. She grins. "Your boyfriend's arrival causing marital problems?"

I really hate that she's not *wrong*.

She slinks past me, headed for the door, and asks, "You know, if Willa Mae's *your* lapdog, and you were always the *Shade's*, that would make them his . . . ?"

The question hangs in the air after she's gone.

I turn to Marian, even as the debate team starts unpacking. Even knowing we're both going to be late for our own classes.

I can't seem to make myself move. I know I should start walking, even if it's just to get the hell out of this spot. Maybe school and grades and planning for my future don't mean anything anymore, but there's still a roomful of students who can see me. Standing where I'm not supposed to be. Staring at Marian like I'm frozen in place.

She's not moving either, though. For whatever reason, she stands right there with me.

Are her thoughts as scrambled as mine?

Is she as afraid as I am?

Our stare-off ends abruptly when a voice from the other side of the room decides it's the perfect moment to *loudly* make a transmisogynistic joke. With Poppy as the punch line.

There are a couple of uncomfortable chuckles. Someone mumbles, "Hey, that's not cool."

Marian and I both turn in unison toward the culprit. Of course it's an ugly white boy in a THIN BLUE LINE T-shirt.

I glance at Marian. She glances back at me. Neither of us is frozen anymore.

"Fifteen-minute truce?" she asks.

Electric pulses fire into my palms and toward my chest. And now they have a target.

"Make it thirty."

22

AS BAD AS THERAPY

I leave school an hour later with blood on my knuckles and a text from Enzo.

Little Demon
Safe and sound and back in Brooklyn. I have some things to take care of. You may not hear from me as much this week. But don't fret—I'm the big bad. No one's going to hurt me. More soon, darling creature.

My big bad monster and my insufferable little shit. I'm glad *one of us* isn't afraid of him getting hurt.

I don't go home right away. Mom'll be awake by now. She knows I was out last night, and I can't explain why. I don't need to add skipping school to that conversation. And I want to talk to her about my dad, but I don't.

I don't go to Willa Mae's, even though she's where I want to be. I told her I'd give her space. When she's ready, she'll find me.

Somehow, I end up parked on the side of the road, half a mile away from my house, outside the Wheeler farm.

The engine rolls into silence as I pull out the keys, slamming the driver's-side door shut. There's no cow waiting for me in the field this time.

I don't know what I'm doing. Or maybe I do? I don't know anything, *including* whether I know anything.

Regardless, I don't have any conscious plan as I grab the top of the fence and haul myself over it. If there's any part of my brain that knows what's going to happen, it's not the part in charge as I make my way down the long dirt driveway.

Buck is waiting for me, though—and he isn't alone. I jerk to a stop at the edge of the front yard.

The Wheeler house is bigger and nicer than I expected. I'm not sure what I expected at all, but it's not this sprawling red-brick farmhouse. It looks old, but has clearly been kept up over the years. There's a sign on the front door that reads SORRY, Y'ALL! WE ARE TOO POOR TO BUY ANYTHING, WE KNOW WHO WE ARE VOTING FOR, AND WE HAVE ALREADY FOUND JESUS. The yard has a few scattered yard toys—a red wagon, some kind of slip-and-slide, a giant dart gun—but it's tidied up, for the most part. There are three cars parked in the covered bay between the house and barn: a luxury SUV and a huge, lifted truck. And another, smaller, familiar truck.

Buck is half naked again, in nothing but a pair of overalls, the straps of which are undone and drooping around his waist. He's sitting on the porch railing, swinging his legs back and forth.

And Indigo Ramirez, in his baby-blue crop top and color-block white and pink sweatpants, is leaning against the railing next to him.

Of course, Indy isn't *only* Indy. And it makes sense as soon as I lay eyes on him.

Like the Evergod, the Muse is not my ally *or* my enemy. The god of art is an observer, a storyteller to document our histories when they've unfolded, not a fighter for any side. Not that his powers would make him useful against Death and Battle, anyway.

Art is meant to work as a mirror—it shows us ourselves and the world around us. That's what the Muse does, too. While the Librarian knows what we know, the Muse's power is more subjective—he *sees* people, sees them for exactly who they are. And he can reflect that sight inward, amplifying our strengths and weaknesses, forcing us to reckon with ourselves.

I've always hated dealing with this guy. It's as bad as therapy. He's always been there, every lifetime, sitting on the outskirts. I've avoided him wherever I could, and he's let me, for the most part.

Of course, he's never tried to *sleep with me* before.

But . . . wait. Wait just one McFucking minute.

If Indy is the Muse, and the Muse sees people for who they are—

"You knew." I throw a hand up, motioning between us. "You knew who I was this whole time."

Indigo rests his elbow on the railing and props his sharp chin in his hand. "I did."

"And you were *sexting me?*" I can't believe this. "When you *knew* I had more important things to do!"

And was really only using him to hurt myself. How embarrassing for us both.

"It's what you wanted." His eyes flick me up and down. He smiles a smile that makes no sense. "At the time. It's not my job to make sure you're making healthy choices, Gem."

I don't think there's enough money in the world to pay

someone a fair wage for *that* job. Buck giggles, and I scowl at him.

"This is fucked. Is there not a single part of my life that's safe from godly bullshit?"

"Hank!" Buck offers excitedly. Then he frowns, looking down at his hands. "Oh, wait. No, never mind . . ."

"WHAT THE HELL IS GONNA HAPPEN TO MY DOG?"

Buck sighs all dreamy and falls off the railing, landing with a thump on the porch. Indy offers him a hand and helps him to his feet as Buck says, "Okay, okay, okay, okay, come on."

He grabs my hand, twisting our fingers together to lead me inside. Indy follows behind us.

Inside, the Wheeler home is . . . closer to what I was imagining. The walls are covered in guns and crosses and stuffed deer heads, staring down at me with their glossy eyes. It smells like soup and corn bread and pine-scented floor cleaner. There's gospel music playing on the TV, and homeschool books are open on the dining room table.

"Where is everyone?"

Buck frowns, looking around the room. Indy reaches up and puts a hand on his shoulder. The two exchange a look before Buck says, "I told them to hide. They think I'm Jesus."

Right. He's mentioned that. "Why?"

"I started putting up Bible verses on the church sign across the street." He blinks. "I wasn't big enough to talk yet."

Oh. That'd do it.

It doesn't escape my notice that Buck seems more *lucid* than he usually does. But that's Indy's doing, I realize. The Muse reflects us back to ourselves. The Evergod's human body struggles under the weight of everything he knows, but Indy can help him focus on being *Buck,* the boy.

We continue down a long hallway. I swear I hear shuffling behind one door—maybe a quiet whimper. I don't linger on it, just stepping into what I guess is Buck's bedroom.

It's terrifying. The walls and windows are covered in newspaper clippings and printouts from online articles and frantic, nonsensical scribbles on white paper. The only furniture is his bed, a mattress on the floor with a quilt on top.

You'd think the Wheelers would want Jesus to have better accommodations, but okay. I guess it's not far off from a manger.

Buck finally drops my hand so he can go rifling through the clippings on the walls, hunting for something specific. Indy plops right onto the mattress, leaning back on his palms to watch him. I get the feeling this isn't the first time he's been here. How often have they hung out before all this? How many times did I drive past this house with no clue two ancient gods were inside?

"You're dressed like the trans flag."

Indy winks at me.

"Aha!" Buck rips a page off the wall, and hands it to him.

The god of art considers it for a moment before reaching into his pocket and producing his phone. I try to lean in while he types, to check out the paper, but Buck steps in front of me. He touches his fingertips to my cheeks.

I let him, because maybe he's going to tell me something important, and because I think I might actually like Buck, no matter how weird he is. In fact, the little unashamed displays of tenderness with no sexual underpinnings are nice.

Except then he says, "You will still be pretty after they cut out your eyes," and I don't want to do this anymore.

My phone buzzes. Indy is looking at me expectantly, so I tug it out.

Indy
Dead: The Sun, The Moon, The Inferno, The Caretaker, and The Hammer.

The Evergod, god of time, Buck Wheeler, in Gracie

Can see all events, past and future. (And pays the price for it.) Can also slow and speed time. Maybe more?

The Magician, god of magic, you

Can cast any spell as long as it doesn't offset the balance.

The Shade, god of things forbidden, ???, in Brooklyn (???)

Can manipulate people to do the awful things they think about but would never actually act on. Now has the powers of Sun/ Moon/Inferno/Caretaker/Hammer, too. Not sure how these will manifest for him.

The Mountain, god of land, "Willa Mae Hardy," in Gracie

Can control earth and animals.

The Muse, god of art, me

Can see things and people for what they really are, and reveal them to others.

The Librarian, god of knowledge, Rhett Clancy, in Gracie

Can learn a person's thoughts from touch. (Power limited by being in a human body—too many thoughts can hurt him, like with Buck.)

The Reaper, god of death, Poppy White, in Gracie

Can necrotize. Controlled afterlife in the Ether. (With the Caretaker.)

The Lionheart, god of battle, Marian Colquitt, in Gracie

Can cause battle-rages and possesses inhuman strategy and skill with weapons.

The Siren, god of sea, Murphy Foster, in Gracie

Can control water and water animals/plants.

The Stillness, god of peace, name unknown, location unknown

Can cause catatonic-like "peace" states in others.

The Cyclone, god of air, name unknown, location unknown

Can control the weather.

The Heartkeeper, god of love, name unknown, location
unknown

Can sense and manipulate any bonds of love between people.

I know most of these people firsthand, except the last three
names on the list.

The last time I saw the Stillness was in the 1800s, in New
York. They were a pacifist, and wanted to get their hands on
the Ouroboros for the same reason I do now—to destroy it. We
lost track of each other in the chaos of the American Civil War.
I have no idea what happened after that.

The Cyclone's been gone even longer. He fought in the
same war that saw the Lionheart and me defending Scottish
sovereignty—though, he fought for the British. I have no desire
to ever see that one again.

And the Heartkeeper . . . huh.

Even with the wall down between this life and the others, my
head's not big enough for *everything* I know, too human to work
the way it's supposed to. Without the other names to trigger the
memories, I don't know how long it would've taken to remember
the Stillness or the Cyclone.

Still, there's always *something*. A flash, or a whisper, or even
just a *feeling*. But when I think of the Heartkeeper, this supposed god of love, it's like . . . static. Like there's an empty, gaping void where a memory should be.

The only time I've felt something similar was with my dad's
brother. We used to spend a lot of time together when I was a
little kid. Now I can't remember him at all.

Strange. Oh well.

I look up to find that Buck has climbed into the bed with Indy, his head in the other boy's lap. Indy scrubs his knuckles back and forth across the top of Buck's shaved head.

"Why give this to me?"

"The future is long," Buck sighs. "I see, and see, and see, and see, and see, and see, and see, and see—"

Indy taps his thumb to Buck's cheek, like hitting a reset button. When the other boy falls silent, he looks to me. "You're different in this life, you know. It's the only one where I've ever liked you."

"Indigo, do you know what a backhanded compliment is?"

"But you're changing," he continues. "I'm watching it happen. I don't know if it can be stopped, but . . . you can't make the right choices if you don't even have all the information."

I sniff. "Thought it wasn't your job to help me make good choices."

Indy chuckles, looking back at Buck. "Oh, it's not. This is a gift."

"Enjoy it while it lasts, Magician," Buck whispers, his eyes closing. "Because one day you will wake up and realize you have disappointed everyone who ever tried to save you. And the only gift *they'll* want is your blood on the altar floor. Oh!"

He sits up very quickly and grabs Indy's shoulders. "Piggly Wiggly."

Indy looks . . . resigned? He asks, "Today?"

"That is a funny joke." Buck turns to look at me again and balks, as if surprised to see me. "Gem! Why are you still here?"

Oh. *Okay.*

23

NO MORE AVOIDING HARD CONVERSATIONS

Willa Mae's Jeep is parked in the ditch in front of my car, and she's rifling through my backseat. She doesn't see me at first, so I stop to watch her. Only when I spot the look of panic do I clear my throat.

"Hi?"

She jumps, yanking her broad shoulders out of my car door, and looks at me over the roof. "Oh. Um."

A beat passes. I step out of the driveway as Indy's truck comes crawling past, heading in the direction of town.

Willa Mae clears her throat. "I was on my way to see you, and I saw the car, and I thought—I don't know. That someone had taken you or something."

I nod, moving closer, leaning against my trunk. "I'm okay."

She sniffs, looking over my head, after Indy's truck. "What's going on?"

"Oh, uh." I laugh, though it's uncomfortable. "Just having a chat with *the Evergod and the Muse*."

"Oh?" Willa Mae's eyebrows shoot up. "About . . . what?"

I'm not ready to go home. Especially not when my mom would send Willa Mae away, and all I want is to spend time with her. It's pathetic, this ache in my side where she's been missing today.

So, instead, I cock my head toward the cemetery across the street, and we head there. We pass the church sign on our way.

Love does not delight in evil but rejoices with the truth. It always protects, always trusts, always hopes, always perseveres.

I wonder if Buck Wheeler is still choosing the verses.

At the back edge of the cemetery is a cluster of older tombstones, weathered by time. They're gathered beneath a blooming dogwood tree, its branches stretching out like a mother's arms. We settle beneath one limb, on a pile of fallen pink petals.

Can't believe this is our second graveyard date.

I pull up the list Indy texted me, and pass my phone over to her without an explanation.

Her eyes scan the details. After a long moment, she hands it back to me. "Huh."

"Yeah." I read it again, like maybe I'll find something hidden in his word choices. "They said—I don't know. They wanted me to have all the information so I could make the right decision."

Whatever that means.

Willa Mae has that *look* again. That look that tells me she's about to lie. Like we're veering dangerously close to a conversation she doesn't want to have, and will escape by any means necessary.

I hate when she gets that look. "Something to add?"

"Um." She sniffs. "They seem to know a lot."

"But?"

I can *see* the moment she decides she's going to tell me the truth. Her stiffened shoulders sink, and her expression shifts from guarded to . . . guilty?

"You can cross off the Stillness. They're dead."

"The . . . how do you know that?" I look between her face and the list. "The last time we saw them was . . . what, Virginia? 1860-something?"

"That was certainly the last time you saw them." She sniffs. Petals from the dogwood tree start crawling up her legs like little ants in a row, clustering after each other to snuggle protectively up her torso and chest.

"Mountain."

"When you died in the war, you left me with the Ouroboros. They found me. They wanted to get their hands on it." She bites her bottom lip. "I'd promised you I would keep it safe."

"You—" Something I'd been wondering in the back of my mind suddenly clicks into place. "Oh my god, that thing you did to Marian. Turning her into a tree. That was—"

"Yeah." Willa Mae nods, her eyes flicking over my face. "When I took the Stillness's power, it sort of . . . blended with mine. That's what it looks like, when I make someone, uh. *Peaceful.*"

"Holy shit. But—that was the lifetime before last. You had the whole time we were in Atlanta to tell me about this."

"I know, and I'm sorry. I just—"

"You got mad at me for sending the Ouroboros with my brother instead of the hiding spot we agreed on! But you *love* secrets."

"Look, I *know*. But it's—it's different?"

She doesn't sound sure, and she shouldn't. Because it isn't different at all. Still, I ask, "Okay, how? Make me understand."

"You not telling me Jack had the knife feels like you keeping a secret because you didn't trust me with the truth. I didn't tell you about this because—because I didn't want to disappoint you." Willa Mae groans, rubbing her hands over her face. It disturbs some of the little petals, knocking them to the ground. But they start climbing again as soon as they hit the grass. "You've always been so adamant about not taking any of their lives. I just didn't want you to think I was . . . a bad person, I guess."

I consider her, and that, for a long moment. The breeze makes her curls dance, but she doesn't bother trying to snatch them up into a bun like she usually might. Sunlight glints through the dogwood flowers, catching strands of her flowing hair and setting them aglow. There is a kind of softness that moves with her, wherever she goes, that is somehow not at odds with her strength.

I'll never get used to this.

"What makes someone a bad person? Doing what it takes to survive?" I shrug. "I'm *adamant* about not using the knife because I can't. Scales? Balance? It'd be apocalyptic or . . . something. But think about it. We had the chain all those years. And we never once even thought of getting rid of the knife, even though we swore we were never going to use it. Why not? If we *really* didn't ever want to take anyone else's power . . . why not?"

She shivers, running her fingers through the grass blades like I'm imagining running my hands through her hair. I don't think the breeze is making her cold.

"I'm not disappointed in you. Not for doing what you had to

do to take care of yourself." I point at her. "You should've told me, though. That's fucked up."

"Yeah. Okay. You're right."

"No more avoiding hard conversations."

She visibly winces, but repeats, "No more avoiding hard conversations."

"Good girl." I look back down at Indy's list. After a moment, I ask, "That's weird. Why do you think he put your name in quotes like that?"

"Uh, probably because it isn't actually my name."

I throw my phone down. "What the hell does that mean?!"

"Oh!" Her face scrunches up and she rubs a hand over the back of her neck. "I mean, this wasn't a secret—I wasn't avoiding telling you. I don't know. I mean. You know, my grandparents took me away so they could make me remember. They couldn't exactly enroll me under the name of an active missing person."

"And you . . ." This is setting off every red-alert warning in my body. "You keep saying they made you remember. How'd they do that?"

That *look* starts creeping back onto her face.

"Hey. You agreed no more avoiding hard conversations," I remind her. "Like, thirty seconds ago."

She lets out a slow breath. "My grandfather locked me in their basement, tied me to an old worktable, and wouldn't let me eat or sleep until my mind broke. When it did, I was me again."

I'm going to rip her grandparents' skin from their bodies and *eat it*.

"Hey." She touches my arm. "It's okay. I lived. He did what had to be done."

My brain turns over and over, every time she's ever mentioned wanting me to remember but not wanting to *hurt me*. Not like she was hurt. Like her grandfather hurt her.

When are people going to learn not to touch what belongs to me?

I fight to rein it in, to drag the rage back into my wicked heart. This is a problem for another time. Instead of telling her my gruesome thoughts, I ask, "Do you miss your parents?"

She considers me a moment longer, like she wants to ask what I'm not saying. But, after a pause, she admits, "Sometimes I miss them a lot. But . . . I think it would just scare them if they knew. It's better this way—to not involve them."

I reach out and put a hand over her thigh, brushing my thumb against her knee. She takes my hand and squeezes.

"It's just one lifetime, anyway. It doesn't matter, in the big picture."

"We both know that's crap." I swallow. "Everybody keeps saying I'm supposed to be all about balance, but I don't feel *balanced* at all. I feel like there are two of me, Gem and the Magician, and they're fighting to see who's stronger."

She brushes her other hand against my face, dusting the top of my ear. "Maybe that *is* keeping the balance. The push-and-pull."

"Yeah, well. If that's true, you know you're not just the Mountain, either. You're also—my god, what's your *name*?"

Willa Mae, or whoever she is, hesitates. I can see the shadow of my least favorite look, and the moment when she decides to say, "Aurora. I went by Rory."

Rory.

"Do you want me to call you that?"

"I— It doesn't matter. It's just a name, we get a different name every lifetime, and—"

"Stop." I get on my knees and shuffle over until I'm right in front of her. My hands curl around her shoulders, pressing down on flower petals as they do. "We are not just gods walking around steering human bodies. We are also humans housing the souls of gods. Okay? And if it really matters that the Mountain is never a colonizer"—I brush my thumb against the tattoos on her chin—"that must mean you couldn't just be colonizing a Native body. And if it really matters that we've fallen in love over and over again across lifetimes, that must mean those lifetimes mattered."

And every second of pain her grandfather caused her mattered.

"This life matters. Now—what name do you want me to call you?"

She presses her forehead to mine. "Rory."

"Rory," I repeat. It already feels so much more . . . her. "Nice to meet you."

She laughs, and her fingers curl in the front of my shirt, and then she's dragging me into a bed of petals with her. And I don't know who moves to kiss who first, but it doesn't matter because then we're *kissing*. And her mouth is warm, and soft, and firm, and her hands are holding me to her chest, and I think I could die here, and that would be fitting, dying in this cemetery.

And then she bites my lip, and my knees are on either side of her waist, and I wonder how many sins we'd be committing if I went down on her right now.

I don't, though. She tugs her face away, sucking in a deep breath. Now's not the time. There's always our third date, which I assume will also be in a graveyard.

Rolling off of her, I settle into the crook of her elbow, curling against her side.

Rory's quiet for a moment, looking at the petals on the tree. Finally, she says, "Enzo matters as much as the Shade does."

Ah. Okay. Definitely not the time for cunnilingus.

"I don't know anything about Enzo except that you love him," she continues. "And the Shade . . ."

The pause stretches out, heavy between us. I tilt my head, considerately. So many eons we spent on the other side, the paths of the gods crossing and uncrossing over and over again through time immemorial. We all have history. I realize I'm not sure what theirs looks like.

Finally, she continues, "I still think he manipulated you, and you just don't want to see it. But if he didn't . . . if I'm wrong, and you went into it with your eyes wide open . . . I would still forgive you. Because, apparently, I'm *that* messed up. So, I guess I can . . . tolerate him."

It's something.

"We need to set some ground rules, though. For what we're doing here."

"Oh." I prop myself up on my elbow. "Okay, definitely. Um. What are we doing here?"

Rory rolls her eyes. "Well, we're dating. And I think you're also dating Enzo. Right?"

"Uh. Maybe. We're dating?"

She raises her eyebrows.

"I mean, yes. We're dating. Good." I know I have the stupidest grin on my face. But I can't bring myself to care. "What are the ground rules?"

"You cannot do any*thing* else with any*one* else." When I open my mouth, she cuts me off: "I'm not even going to *pretend* I could stop you from flirting with the entire population of Gracie. But no more hooking up with anyone else. And I swear, if you find a third you didn't know about, just—ugh, *tell me*, I guess."

"Yes. Absolutely. Is that all?"

"That's all I've got right now. I'll let you know if that changes. You think you can handle it?"

"I'll have to talk to Enzo, but . . . what? Of course I can. Why are you looking at me like that?"

Rory shrugs. "People in Gracie never shut up. I *know* how you are. If this life matters just as much as all our other lives, that *includes* you being a player."

"I am not a player!"

"What would you call it?"

The words leave my mouth before I can actually think to stop them. "I just don't know how to say no!"

The admission hangs there. Rory watches me with her eyebrows creased. I frown and pull out of her grip, sitting up straight.

This is the part where I should make a self-deprecating joke and change the subject. This is the part where I would add an "lol" if we were texting.

But I said no more avoiding hard conversations. And if I'm holding her to that, I should hold myself to it, too.

"I just, um. I don't really know who I am, a lot of the time, outside of the way people see me. And people . . . usually see me in one way." I sniff. "And it's not like I don't like it, you know, most of the time. I just. It's like if I say yes, I'm this androgynous sex god and everybody wants me. And if I said no, they might get upset or—think I was boring, or rude, or . . ."

Rory's fingers find my arm. She runs her knuckles from my elbow to my wrist, then back again.

Now that I've started, I can't stop. "I'd rather be wanted.

Sometimes, I want to be wanted so bad, it's like I can't say no. Even when maybe I should. Like, I went to this party once, and there were these guys—I'd never—not with more than one person, you know, but—and then—my mom sent me to this therapist. He was like, thirty. Married. He—and I said yes, you know? Because I can't . . . not."

Her fingers curl around my arm, thumb pressing into my pulse. "Gem, that . . . that wasn't on you, that was—"

"No, I know, I just. If I hadn't been in therapy to begin with, I wouldn't have been in that position. And, like, okay, I can't say no when someone wants me. Or sometimes I can't brush my teeth for weeks. And sometimes I get so angry, I just say . . . whatever the worst thing I can think of is, whatever I know would hurt someone the most, I just say it, and then five minutes later I'm not even angry anymore. And I've spent my whole life walking around feeling like I was an alien, like everyone else knows how to exist except me."

She brings my hand to her mouth and kisses my knuckles.

"And when my dad . . . I thought maybe I was like him. I was so scared I was going to end up like him. But then you came along, and I thought—hey, there's nothing wrong with me. I'm a god. That's why I'm like *this*." I take a deep breath, my hand curling into a fist against her mouth. "But it's not because I'm a god, is it?"

"No, honey," she whispers against my skin. "No, I don't think so."

Gem Echols matters as much as the Magician. And Gem Echols is . . . sick.

I lie back down, pressing my face into her shoulder, letting myself disappear into her hair.

She wraps her arm around my waist, and kisses my head.

"When you feel up to talking about it, you're going to give me the name of that therapist."

"When you feel up to it, you're going to let me deal with your grandfather."

Neither of us agrees, but neither of us argues. And we hold each other, my girlfriend and me, in the Gracie Church of God cemetery, our secrets carried on the Southern breeze all around us.

24

WORRY ABOUT YOURSELF

Almost a week goes by without fanfare or murder.

My mother and I don't see each other. She works nights, then comes home and disappears. I go to school, then to Rory's, and if I'm home I disappear, too. We need to talk—about my dad, about Rory and Enzo, about as much as I *can* talk to her about. But even when we're both there, with nothing but bedroom doors between us, I can't seem to make myself knock.

I exchange a few texts with Enzo. I tell him about Rory (*Aurora, hm? Well, that's better than Willa Mae*) and the boundaries we talked about (*Oh, darling. If this is what you want, far be it from me to put up a protest. I may not understand your affection for the swamp girl, but who am I to discourage anyone from indulging in what brings them pleasure? Besides, the whole world could put their hands on you, and it wouldn't make you any less mine—I've left you stained deeper than they could dream of getting*) immediately followed up by (*So long as we're in agreement that, if she hurts you, I will string her arteries together to make us friendship bracelets.* <3), but he follows through on his warning of limited contact.

Murphy and Rhett stop showing up to school. I can't blame them—I don't know why *I* bother going anymore—but it makes me nervous. Whatever they're doing, it can't bode well for me.

And every day, Rory and I work on destroying the Ouroboros. Even with my memories back, with my magic more or less in my own control, it isn't *working*. I try, but it feels like fumbling in the dark, my hand running against a wall and searching for the light switch, only to realize there isn't a switch at all. And every failed attempt comes with some small sacrifice—another bloody nose or a spiked fever or a nail on the road popping my tire on the way to school.

Yesterday, I demanded we stop after Hank—lounging in the grass outside with us—almost got bitten by a rattler. Rory swears he would have been fine, she had a handle on the snake, but Buck's ominous mention of my dog still pings in my head.

And these are sacrifices for doing *nothing*. These small problems—a rip in my favorite shirt, a spambot calling me fifty times in one day, my Twitter getting suspended because I called someone a TERF—are the price to pay for magic that isn't accomplishing anything. What would happen if I managed to actually destroy the knife?

Rory and I are coming to the same conclusion. We need the chain. There's no destroying the knife without it. But finding the chain might mean going back to my dad's house and rifling through his shit, which . . . I don't know if I'm ever gonna be ready for.

Life, of course, doesn't actually care what I'm ready for.

Neither does Death. Poppy and Marian are both being

weird. Poppy's going right along campaigning for prom queen, acting like that's completely normal and she has nothing better to do. Marian has been helping the administration apply for grants the school didn't know existed, getting iPads and laptops for students. And they both just keep *watching me*. Everywhere I go at school, it's like I can feel their eyes. Indy's, too. It's like everyone's waiting to see what I'm going to do next—like they're waiting for *me* to attack, when it is so obviously going to be the other way around.

Or maybe we're just all tired and afraid and no one wants to have to be the one to spin this even more out of control than it is. Maybe it's nice, dressing up and playing prom queen, instead of having to plot a murder. Maybe we're all just backed into corners, standing at a crossroads, and hoping like hell someone else blinks first.

I say as much to Rory on Friday afternoon, the two of us making our way through the crowded school hallway, planning to go back to her house for the weekend.

"Poppy is demented and feral and would probably eat you if left alone in a room with you for too long" is what she has to say about that. "But she's easily distracted by shiny things. Marian, though—she worries me. She's *never* distracted. If Lionheart is holding still, it's because she's plotting her next move—or she's already plotted it, and now she's waiting for the best time to execute."

"*Where* are Murphy and Rhett?" I groan.

"I've been wondering the same thing." She sighs, rubbing a hand over the back of her neck. "The Siren doesn't want anything to do with this, but Rhett . . . he's had a lot of time to sit with your thoughts in his head."

I open my mouth to tell her just how much I hate *that*, but the words don't make it out. Instead, as we pass through the front of the school toward the exit, a too-familiar voice yanks my attention toward the office.

"Your behavior is absurd. I have all the necessary paperwork. I have been a straight-A student my entire high school career. What is so complicated about this?"

"First of all, sweet pea, I don't know who you think you're talkin' to, but I'm gon' need you to watch that tongue. Second of all, you come in here on a Friday afternoon, six weeks 'fore the end of the school year, tellin' me you wanna start on Monday and graduate right after? Now, if you did think you were talkin' to a miracle worker, lemme just tell ya, you ain't. And third of all? I mean, for heaven's sake, you mighta been a senior at your old school, but you barely got the credits to call yourself a sophomore here. What are some of these classes?"

I grab Rory's hand and drag her with me, beelining for the office.

He's here.

Enzo's standing there, leaning against the front desk, so wrapped up in his argument with the clerk that he doesn't notice us. He's dressed in a billowy white tunic tucked into red velvet pants, and black boots with a heel. There's a ring on each of his ten fingers, and he's swiped out his glasses for contacts. His hair's faded to peach, with a hint of black peeking in at the root. Guess he's been too busy for upkeep.

The clerk is reading his transcript to him. "Hand Modelin'? Clown? Crew Are People Too: Empathy for Actors?"

Rather than acknowledge that a single one of those classes is as ridiculous as it is, Enzo snaps, "I don't see why I should be punished for your Podunk school refusing to invest in the arts."

"What are you doing here?" Rory and I demand at the same time.

Enzo glances over his shoulder and grins, a wicked slash of a smile that makes my knees shake. But he doesn't respond, just goes back to his argument.

Rory, I realize, wasn't even talking to him. Of all people, *Poppy* is sitting in an office chair, utter delight on her gaunt face—and she's got her sparkly cell phone out, recording the interaction.

"I was dress-coded." She flicks her free hand at her white T-shirt, which reads DEATH TO RACISTS (: across the chest. "Told them I didn't own any other clothes, so they made me sit in here all day. Was just about to leave when *this* happened. Wow. You weren't kidding, huh? He's . . . bizarre."

She giggles. She's calling *him* bizarre?

"Now," the clerk scoffs, shuffling Enzo's papers behind the desk. "You can go ahead and start on Monday, I'll getcha squared away. But you ain't graduatin' in May. You can get that li'l idea outta your head, or you can haul your skinny ass back to New York."

He grinds his teeth. I can *see* him weighing the option of just leaning over and immolating this woman.

In the end, he turns back to me. "Darling, can we please get out of here? The fluorescent lighting is giving me a migraine."

I let him take my hand and twist my fingers with his, dragging me out of the office. I'm still holding Rory's hand, pulling her along behind me. And it's nice, in its own special fucked-up way, being with both of them.

We make it all the way to the parking lot before I realize Poppy followed us, still recording.

Enzo looks her up and down. "Corpse. Nice to see you again."

"Oh my god, imagine if we had killed you last weekend," she giggles. "Without even knowing who you were. Wouldn't that have been crazy? Oh my god! *This* is camp!"

"Is it?" Rory asks, deadpan.

"I do appreciate you not murdering me." Enzo is entirely too smiley about that. "I hope you'll give me the chance to return the favor sometime."

"Oooh. I can think of one way." She clicks her phone closed and slides it into the back pocket of her purple suede pants. "You can lie very still, and be very quiet, and let me show the Magician what their boyfriend looks like with his organs on the outside."

"Are you flirting, Reaper?"

Poppy laughs and laughs and laughs, and the three of us walk away from her, headed toward the far side of the parking lot.

I expect we'll get off of school property, head back to my place, and then Enzo can explain what the hell is going on. But when we pass Rory's Jeep, she lets go of my hand—and grabs his shoulders. With enough force that he'll bruise, she slams him against the back of her car.

I groan. "Hey—"

She doesn't let me finish, focused on him. "How long have you been in town?"

"*Relax*, kitten." Enzo tilts his chin up to glare at her. "I got back this afternoon. I wasn't aware you missed me so badly."

She bares her teeth, fingers digging into his shoulders. It must hurt—but Enzo could fight back if he wanted to. So, I don't get between them, even if part of me is screaming I should.

"Really? And you didn't give Gem a heads-up? Why?"

"I was a bit preoccupied. It took a lot, you know, getting my parents to agree to come here. Convincing them what they secretly wanted was to uproot their lives and move to a *farm* in South Georgia. It was *exhausting*."

"Wait, really?" I move over to the Jeep, leaning my shoulder against it so the three of us form our triangle. "How did you do that?"

"I told you," Rory growls. "He *manipulates people.* He can make anyone do anything."

"Oh, we both know that's not true." He smiles, something too-knowing in his eyes. "Don't we, kitten?"

"Call me 'kitten' one more time—"

"There has to be at least some sliver that already wants what I'm offering."

His wicked stare meets mine. I wonder if he's thinking of guiding my hand as I made the first slice into the Sun's body.

To Rory, he continues, "You saw me with the clerk in there—she was determined I wasn't going to get my way, so I didn't. My parents have been daydreaming about getting back to their humble roots for years now. I helped them along."

She doesn't look placated. "Where is Murphy?"

"Who?"

"*My sister.* The Siren." Rory snarls the words. "She's been gone for days. And now you stroll in here. What did you do to her?"

He sighs. "Darling, can you call her off?"

"Rory—"

"Gem. This is not about you."

I take a deep breath. "Enzo, did you kill her sister?"

"Not that I recall."

"Babe, I don't think he killed her."

She's unconvinced.

When Rory doesn't move, I throw my hands up. "Okay. Fine. Let him prove it. Let's go find her."

There's no good reason I should know where the Foster home is, except I was in Murphy's eighth-grade English class. Back then, it was rude not to invite everyone in all your classes to your birthday parties, and I went over just the one time for pizza and ice cream and a short-lived game of spin the bottle in her basement. She lives north of downtown Gracie, in the suburban, white-picket-fence zone that isn't quite *rich*, but still has more money than most of the town.

I was thirteen the last time I was here, so it's not like I know exactly where I'm going. But Gracie's not that big, and it doesn't take us long to spot Murphy's powder-blue Subaru in one of the driveways.

And Indy's truck alongside it.

"What the hell is with this guy?" I mumble as Rory parks on the curb. "Is he the god of art or the god of being up my ass all the time?"

Enzo, relegated to the backseat, leans over the center console. His shoulder brushes mine—and his other shoulder brushes hers—when he does, and then his neck is right there, only an inch from my mouth.

He smells so good. Not exactly like he did last time, like an oat milk latte that got lost in a vintage store. There's a sharpness that wasn't there before. Now he smells like an oat milk latte that got lost in a vintage store . . . and started wielding a knife.

I want to press my teeth to his jumping pulse, the patch of

skin under his jaw where I can see his heartbeat. Now's not the time. But it is deeply aggravating to me that, every time Enzo and I are reunited, we have to *wait* for the right time.

The obvious solution is never being separated again.

"The Siren *and* the Muse?" he asks, eyes skirting like he might catch a glimpse of someone through a window. "How *annoying*."

Rory growls and jumps out of the car, heading up the driveway. Even I roll my eyes at him before following.

He's not wrong. Still—read the room.

Rory heads toward the side gate to the backyard. I trail along after her, with Enzo begrudgingly falling into last place. As Rory lifts the metal lock and pushes our way into the yard, I start to hear the sound of . . . splashing? And voices. Definitely voices. And then there's the smell of chlorine.

While the house itself is so unremarkable it's basically invisible, the Foster backyard is something special. There are plants *everywhere*, like an urban garden of flowers and herbs and perfectly manicured little trees. And they're all clustered around a massive pool in the center, deep and crystal-clear and made of natural stone.

I remember hearing about the pool. I guess Murphy's parents built it because water therapy was the only thing they found to help her fibromyalgia symptoms. She has her back to us when we approach. She's in the water, in a white one-piece with her hair tucked under a matching swim cap.

And it's not only Indy she's talking to—Rhett's here.

The two of them are sitting on the stone pavers next to the pool, neither dressed for the water. Rhett looks like shit. The bags under his eyes are practically black, like he hasn't slept since I last saw him, and his red hair is pulled up in a greasy ponytail. And he's wearing . . . gloves? Not sexy leather gloves, not latex gloves, but big-ass brown work gloves.

Indy's hands are on Rhett's bare skin. He's got the big red-head's forearm stretched over his lap, and he's just brushing his fingertips up and down a line of freckles.

So, that's *interesting.*

Their conversation dies as we approach, Rhett and Indy taking in the sight of Rory, then me. Murphy must notice the change in their expressions and spins to face us.

For a too-long moment, it's silent.

And then the Siren lays eyes on the Shade.

"You . . . brought . . . him . . . here?" Her voice is *wrong.* Or maybe not. Maybe it's right, for the first time. Her usual soft Southern lilt has been replaced by something hoarse, and layered, and deep. Like the sound of waves building and building just before they crash.

"I—I was worried about you," Rory begins, but it doesn't matter.

The water is rising. It gurgles over the edge of the pool like a beast waking. Long tendrils of water shift and twist, morphing into something like arms, and I watch in fascination and a little horror as it drags itself up and over the ledge.

Indy and Rhett scramble away, but Murphy is carried along with it. Her body rises to the top of the surge, water wrapping around her legs from the knees down, holding her steady as it makes a wet, sloshing path toward us.

Murphy opens her mouth, and water pours out of her. From her lips, her nose, her ears, her *eyes.* But she doesn't seem to notice. In a voice like a whirlpool, she screams, "WORRY ABOUT YOURSELF!"

"Gem!" Indy calls from across the yard. I can barely make

him out around the mass of water between us. "She hasn't used this power in a thousand years—she's not in control."

What the hell does he want me to do about that?

Rory must have an idea. The earth begins to shift beneath us, the perfect lawn splitting open, creating a massive trench between our bodies and Murphy's water.

When she tries to edge closer, the trench drags her down a few feet, and she screams again.

"Sister, please! I don't want to hurt you." Rory's voice may as well be a whisper. I don't even know how Murphy could hear her.

Except she must. Because she says, mouth like a faucet, leaking eyes locked on us, "Then get out of my way."

Behind me, Enzo chokes.

I wheel around, watching as he hits his knees, that same water pouring from *him*. He gasps, only drowning himself faster.

The world melts away. The only thing left is this—me, and Enzo, and the water. I'm not thinking when I curl my hands around his face, demanding my magic *take this away from him*, by any means necessary. I will not lose him. Not like this. Not at all.

He finally manages to suck in a breath, slumping into my hands as the pouring slows and then stops. Enzo's chest heaves, and he tilts his face to mine—he looks so afraid.

And then I begin to choke.

Sacrifice. Balance. The air in my lungs in exchange for his.

Even as my chest begins to burn, even as my vision is sucked underwater, I know I'd make the same choice.

My knees hit grass. I think I hear screaming above the waves. My magic pulses, looking for an outlet, looking for me to guide it, but I can only drown.

And then, as quickly as it started, it's over. I cough, hacking water, blinking to clear my eyes.

Murphy is at the bottom of the now-empty swimming pool. There are gusts of *steam* rising off of her as she sobs, head in her hands.

Enzo is still on his knees, now at the edge of the pool. His hands are curled around the ledge—and there are scorch marks on either side of him, black lines running below, a trail of burnt grass on the lawn.

Rory stands behind him with the Ouroboros to the back of his neck.

Panic. I force myself to stand, stumbling toward them. When I reach for the knife, she doesn't stop me from taking it.

She does say, "You will not hurt her again."

Enzo lifts his chin, baring his throat. There is no humor in his eyes now. "I am not a hound you can bring to heel."

"We'll see."

As Indy jumps into the pool and wraps a towel around Murphy's shoulders, Rhett says, "Y'all need to leave."

Enzo stands, dusting off his stupid velvet pants. "It was nice seeing you all again. Librarian—let's talk soon."

He leaves the way we came, with Rhett Clancy staring at his back like the poor kid's gonna have an aneurysm.

Rory watches Murphy for a second too long before she follows him.

And I stand there, with the Ouroboros in my hand and three gods with unthinkable power in front of me. And I am suddenly, shamefully aware of how easy it would be to uncomplicate my life. All it took was one strike to bring down the Hammer.

I'm not going to. I couldn't, even if I wanted to. Which I

don't. I just sort of wish I did. It would be so much easier, being everyone's villain, if I got to actually play the part.

Indy tilts his head to meet my eye. I'm not sure what he sees when he looks at me. But I turn and leave before he can examine it closer.

25

NIGHT AND DAY HAVE CRASHED INTO EACH OTHER

Rory drives us to their grandparents' house, but I'm too tired and frayed at the edges to deal with that right now. I open my mouth to protest when I realize where we're going, but the look they give me shuts that down.

When we crawl to a stop in front of the swamp house, they're the first one out, slamming the driver's door behind them. They move in front of the car, crossing their arms, staring through the windshield—directly at Enzo in the backseat.

He sighs, leaning forward so his chin is against my shoulder. "I am being *attacked*."

"You are such a shit." I kiss his cheek. I know I can't keep him in here forever. I probably can't keep him in here another thirty seconds. But I still say, "I missed you. I'm glad you're here—all things considered."

"I'm going to *show you* how happy I am to be here. As soon as I'm done with your girlfriend."

He snags a quick, sharp kiss, and then we're both climbing out of the Jeep.

"Look," he starts. That's all he manages to get out.

"You used her *dead husband's power* against her." Rory's vibrating. "You can't expect anyone to think you've changed when you're pulling shit like that."

"Who says I've changed?" Enzo asks, all nonchalant, and leans against the hood of their car.

Rory looks to me accusingly.

I clear my throat, putting my hand on Enzo's arm. "You ruled that world alone for a thousand years. You've lived a human life for eighteen more. Of course you're different."

He holds out a hand, wiggling it slightly as if to say *Eh*. "Be that as it may, I'm still me. I'm not going to beg for forgiveness. If you're waiting for my redemption arc, you've set yourself up to be disappointed."

"Gem," Rory bites out. "Are you hearing this?"

I open my mouth, but Enzo cuts me off. "What were you expecting? That I came all this way to make things *right*? My death is the only thing that could satisfy the pantheon. And I've no intention of being a martyr."

"I hardly expected you to offer yourself up as a sacrificial lamb." Rory rolls their eyes. "I'm not naïve enough to think there's a selfless bone in your body. But I *did* think you'd at least pretend not to be such a monster. For Gem's sake."

An awful smile curls Enzo's lips around his teeth. And even though this body is human, I swear I see the Shade's terrible fangs. "Why? When my being a monster is the very thing that pulled them to me?"

Rory looks at me and I look at my hands.

"You want me to be different, so you can pretend they are. So you can pretend *you* are. Because like calls to like, and if I'm the villain," he sneers, "you are, too."

Rory growls, "You don't know anything about—"

"But was I the villain when the rest of the pantheon stole my kingdom, piece by piece, until I had nothing but a shadowy corner of our world for my own? Was I the villain when I was refused kinship of any kind because my power made the others *uncomfortable*? Or was I only the villain when I'd finally had enough abuse?"

Where is the justice in putting down a dog who bites back, when that dog has spent his entire life chained and starved?

Rory is quiet, watching him with a scowl. But her eyes are thoughtful.

And he's not done. "Was the Magician the villain when they crafted the only weapon in our world that could kill a god? Were they the villain when they used it to carve open four of our kind, so that their own influence over the Ether might grow? Or was I the villain then, too? Because I'd forced them, somehow? Tell me, how do you explain that they'd made the knife long before our alliance began?"

He steps forward until he has to tilt his head back to look into her face. "How about you, kitten? Were you the villain when you made your bargain with the Inferno's killer? When, instead of staying to defend your *own* land, you abandoned it to stake a claim over someone else's?"

Rory swallows when Enzo's tongue swipes at his lower lip. "If not a villain, a coward. Does the Magician know why you truly fled? Do they know you came to *me* first?"

"What?" I must've heard him wrong.

"Enough," Rory hisses, eyes flashing.

Suddenly, Enzo spins away from her and toward me. I don't know what's happening until he's already grabbed the knife from my pocket again. This time, there is no Hammer. This time, the blade points to me.

His eyes meet mine as he slides the dull edge of the Ouroboros against my throat. My stomach drops, pulse racing as cool metal glides against my skin. It's mocking, the softness of it.

"What are you doing?" I swallow, and the blade bites into my neck.

"Were you the villain, creature, when you abandoned me? Were you the villain when you took my heart and ate your fill, only to leave me behind like a carcass? Should I cling to resentment that you upended every plan we made and exiled me to an existence even more lonely than the one that came before it?" Something breaks in his voice, and something snaps in my chest in response. "Should I demand you beg me for mercy now? Convince me you've *changed*?"

I am pathetic and weak and I can't help that my eyes flood with tears. "I *was* the villain. But I thought you'd forgiven me. I thought you understood—isn't that why you came here?"

Enzo blinks. He looks down at the knife in his hand . . . as if confused to find it there. Frowning, he slowly hands it back to me.

The weight feels blasphemous in my palm.

"Yes. Of course I have. That's my whole point." He turns back to Rory. "I understand why Gem did what they did. No matter how much we care for someone, sometimes our needs conflict with theirs. And I will not try to convince a bunch of feral children that I've become a better person because they're too infantile to grasp that simple concept. If that makes me their villain?" He shrugs. "I'll dress the part and make the most of it."

Rory shakes their head, disgust clear on their face. "You really are a nasty little thing."

"Hey, Gem, do you know why Aurora is so fucking boring?" He smirks. Even though he's addressing me, he's still looking at them. "Because they're just as nasty as I am, only they spend all their time pretending they're not. It must be exhausting."

They grab him by the collar of his tunic and throw him down on the hood of their car. With their body covering Enzo's, their soft curves stretched over his elegant sharpness, Rory growls, "Do you want to see nasty?"

"Yes," he hisses. The excitement in his eyes is wild, bordering on arousal.

"You might be the most powerful god on Earth—"

"Besides me," I mumble.

"Besides Gem. But you're still a twig. And I could break you in half without a warm-up stretch. So, why don't you learn when to shut the fuck up?"

Enzo's smile grows. And that terrible excitement in his eyes gets brighter and brighter . . . until it isn't excitement at all.

I can only sway forward in fascination as his eyes begin to *glow*. They've always had the strangest pattern of browns and reds, like fallen leaves. But now those broken shards of color become even more contrasted—browns turn to bright gray and silver and blue, reds turn to violent oranges and yellows. They illuminate the air between his face and Rory's, like twin lighthouses.

Something catches my attention in my periphery, but I don't want to look away from his face. When I finally manage to drag my eyes toward the sky, my heart stops. The sky overhead is *mirroring* Enzo's eyes. Night and day have crashed into each other, streaks of black and blue, gray moonlight and orange sunlight, all battling for dominance.

When I hear another hiss, this one less human, I look back to them.

A massive black snake has slithered from the grass at their feet. It makes its way up Rory's body, curling around her shoulders, resting its head on top of hers. When it hisses again, it flashes massive fangs, dripping with venom.

I don't know if it's Gem Echols or the Magician who hears the trees around us whispering a warning. And I really don't know if these two are about to kiss or kill each other. Either way, it's time to intervene.

"Enough." Sparks light up my hand when I wave it toward the sky, feeling a surge of magic as I do. Day submits to night, black overtaking blue, the moon hanging low and bright above us. I reach for the snake, wrapping my fist around it and pulling it free from Rory's skin, putting it on the ground and watching it slip away. "The dick-measuring contest can come to an end. You both lose."

After a beat, Rory straightens up and steps back, letting Enzo's feet fall to the ground underneath him. They dust off the front of their T-shirt, like it might have cooties, and he rolls his eyes.

"Actually," I amend, "you both win, because you get me. Now, what was that about you going to the Shade before me? Back in the Ether?"

Rory winces. "I wanted to know . . . if he could be convinced to let me live."

"I could not," Enzo purrs. "Though the offer was . . . enticing."

"Why not tell me this? After all this time?"

Rory struggles for an answer, so Enzo provides one. "For all they'd like you to believe otherwise, nature is neither good nor evil. It just *is*. And it finds a way to survive."

Right.

"Anyway." Enzo clears his throat, leaning back against the Jeep's hood, the irritating picture of nonchalance. "*My* plan is for us to go back. But we have all the time in the world to make that happen—or for you to convince me to stay. I mean, I did have the thought, if I can manipulate rich people into giving me all their money, I might actually be able to afford to pursue acting now."

That's the most human-Enzo thing I've heard him say in a while. I grin. "Yeah, dude, always steal from the rich."

"You want us to go *back*?" Rory raises their eyebrows skeptically. "To what, exactly?"

"Well." Enzo licks his teeth and shrugs. "The Heartkeeper's had, oh, eighteen years to take over? I can't say for sure what she might've done."

"The Heartkeeper is *there*?" Rory sounds shocked.

"You didn't know?"

"No—I mean, we knew it was possible." They shake their head, looking to me and then back to Enzo. "She was supposed to be part of the spell that brought us here, but she didn't show up. We weren't sure what happened. If she was dead, if she made it here but kept hidden, if *you* had her."

"Oh, I *tried*. That bitch has been running guerrilla warfare against me for a thousand years. Honestly, never dealing with her little cult again might be reason enough to stay put."

"I'm sorry—who's the Heartkeeper?" When they both look at me like I've just asked who the Beatles are, or something, I add, "I mean. She's the god of love. But I don't . . . remember her."

Even still, when I reach for a memory, I come back with nothing but static.

Enzo and Rory exchange a *look*.

"Weird. Anyway." Enzo claps his hands together. I think I could probably kill him. It wouldn't be too hard. "If we're not using the knife for its intended purpose, what *are* we doing?"

"We're going to destroy it." Rory crosses their arms, glaring at him again like they're ready for a fight.

"Okay." Enzo raises one eyebrow. "So why haven't you?"

"Well . . ."

"We don't have the chain," I explain. "And I'm pretty sure it can't be destroyed any other way."

"Why destroy it at all?" He holds up his palms when Rory opens their mouth, clearly about to yell. "Seriously. Why not keep it hidden, but usable? Just in case?"

"We tried that already. It's too risky." Rory takes a deep breath. "Too many people want it. As long as it exists, we'll never be safe."

"Not unless you killed everyone who wants it," Enzo offers.

Rory looks unimpressed—but it's true.

And that's one more reason we need to get rid of it. Because there is an ugly part of me that knows how easy it would be to use it. Too easy.

Best not to let the temptation exist. Especially not when I'm pretty sure my taking another god's power would be some harbinger of total doom or . . . something.

"Fine." He shrugs. "So, we'll destroy it."

"You're going to help us?" I try not to sound so surprised. "You love that knife. Why help us get rid of it?"

"Because I love you more." He turns to me and smiles. And just when my heart is about to go all soft over that, he adds, "Besides, when the others come for me—and they will—I won't *need* the knife."

26

ANYWHERE THAT ISN'T HERE

Do you know what it sounds like when a grieving parent screams?

There's no other sound like it, not across worlds, and you won't understand it until you've heard it for yourself. It is a heart carved from one's own chest and offered at the altar of a god who does not want it—a violent sacrifice without reprieve. It is the closest to godhood a human can ever get, their bodies suddenly conduits for a cataclysm they were never meant to hold.

Zeke's funeral is held at the First Church of Gracie the next day. When Rory and I step inside, shuffled through in a throng of ashen-faced adults and teenagers trying to hide their Saturday-morning hangovers and little kids clinging to their caretakers' pant legs, I know immediately that I shouldn't be here.

Mrs. King, with her honey-blond hair in a frantic nest on top of her head and two different heels on her feet, lets out the most terrible scream as she falls over Zeke's closed casket. Her oldest son, Zeke's brother, hurries to gather her in his arms and pull her back to the front pew, where her husband—Zeke's spitting image, thirty years in the future . . . a future his son will never see—offers only a thousand-yard stare.

This is wrong. My being here is *wrong*. I don't know what I was thinking. I did this to them. This family is broken because of *me*. Maybe I wasn't the one holding the knife—this time—but I was the one the Hammer was attacking. And I was the one who had Buck give him his memories. In doing so, I'd already killed my favorite golden retriever before Enzo ever had the chance to use the Ouroboros.

Rory squeezes my hand, and I look up to find her watching me with raised eyebrows. We should go. We should just go.

But before I can tell her as much, an usher puts a hand on my back and steers us toward our seats. We're swept into a pew at the back, and I hope I can at least disappear without anyone realizing I'm here.

No such luck. I feel the stare on me before I realize where it's coming from—and it doesn't feel any better when I do.

Marian and Poppy are in the second row from the front, right behind Zeke's weeping mother. Marian's the one with her eyes on me, dressed in her understated black suit. If Battle's glare could kill, I'd be deader than the quarterback. Poppy, in a black lace Edwardian dress and matching veil, either hasn't noticed me or doesn't care. She's leaned over to whisper something in Mrs. King's ear. I can only begin to imagine what she might be saying. None of it seems promising.

It takes me a moment to realize the family in their row must be Poppy's. Record keepers, the Reaper's family has taken their role seriously in every incarnation—too seriously. They unironically refer to themselves as the House of Death. And these people *look* like they'd call themselves that.

There are four other girls, each younger than Poppy, the oldest probably at the edge of high school while the youngest can't be older than kindergarten. Each of them has Poppy's white-blond hair and porcelain skin—though they look more alive than their older sister. They've been dressed up like matching haunted dolls, with braided hair and black collared dresses.

Poppy's father is an unbearably ordinary man—in fact, with him seated next to his wife, my eyes only dart over him to get to her, not bothering to retain any details. The matriarch of the House of Death is a willowy woman with the sharpest cheekbones I've ever seen, eyes the color of a robin's egg, and a dramatic white pixie cut. Her lips are painted black, and her black turtleneck rests just beneath her strong jaw.

It makes me wonder, looking back to Marian, who's stopped glaring at me so she can turn her attention to her girlfriend—where is the Lionheart's family? They're record keepers, too. Shouldn't they be with her? They have been in every other life. I remember seeing the traces of that family across time and continents, in every war, every humanitarian crisis. But not here, now, with their daughter?

"Gem," Rory whispers at my shoulder, tugging my attention back to her. "You okay?"

No. I don't know.

Zeke is dead. The Hammer is dead, sure, but I didn't know the Hammer. Not in this lifetime, anyway. I knew Zeke.

The big, sweet, stupid, gentle jock. The most heterosexual boy in the world, who would have (peacefully) put a stop to anyone in Gracie ever giving me shit for existing as I am. My friend. My friend, *Zeke*.

He's dead. He's not coming back. Because of choices I made.

What right do I have to be here? Why the hell do I deserve to mourn in the same church as his mother?

I groan, tilting my head to stare at the ceiling.

There is also, of course, the fact that I'm not sure I should be in this church to begin with. Of all the churches in Gracie, this is my least favorite. It reeks of *megachurch*, of Evangelical TV channels and conversion camps backed by family-friendly corporations.

It's huge. The exterior looks out of place on Gracie's modest Main Street, a giant white circle of a building with stained-glass windows arching up into a single point at the top, which turns into a cross that overlooks the entire downtown. Inside, the pews are curved to fit inside the circle, all of them facing the pulpit—which, in this case, is a stage with a seventy-inch flat screen behind it. It might feel like being in a movie theater, if not for the depictions of crucifixion and hellfire on the windows all around us.

There's a weird, over-the-top clashing of old-school crusades aesthetic with an attempt to be ultramodern and minimalist, and it doesn't work well. Maybe that's why my skin is crawling. Or maybe it's because I'm in a church for the first time in my life.

Just as the preacher steps up to the microphone and starts his spiel, someone slides into the pew next to me. "Apologies for being late."

Rory and I turn to Enzo in unison. He left her place late the night before, after many failed attempts at using his own magic to destroy the Ouroboros, picked up by his mother in the middle of the night. (Something Rory is never going to let him live down, probably.) He'd have heard us mention the funeral, of course, but in no world did I expect him to *show up*.

On the one hand, I'm glad he's here, because I always want him where I am. The sight of him—dressed in a suit so dark it looks black at first but is actually the deepest shade of purple, with his hair slicked back and a new pair of dramatic skinny cat-eye glasses—immediately sets me at ease. I slide my hand against his thigh, and he twists his fingers with mine, and my heart feels tethered.

On the other hand, he really should not be here.

Maybe no one will notice.

I cling to that hope for about four minutes, before the preacher asks if anyone would like to speak. Dante Morales is the first out of his seat, moving to the stage. He stumbles over his words, trying to tell a story about what a great teammate and friend Zeke was, but he's too choked up to get them out.

Of course, Murphy comes to his rescue. As she ascends the stairs and wraps an arm around her boyfriend's waist, whispering something in his ear and guiding him toward the stairs, I sink lower in my seat.

Don't look back here, don't look back here, don't look—

Her eyes find mine.

Shit. What are we supposed to do if she loses control again, in front of all these people?

A look flickers across her face and then it's gone. She turns away, helping Dante to his seat, keeping her arms around him. Pretending she didn't just see his friend's murderers in the crowd.

Dante is only the first of many people who have nice things to say about Zeke. The whole team and all the coaches get up to talk, some of them getting through more than Dante managed to, some of them even less. At least half the cheerleading squad, a handful of the band, some of the teachers, they all have nothing but good to say about Zeke King.

At anyone else's funeral, this would be overkill. For anyone else, I might think, *Okay, now. Pack it up. Let's not put the dead on a pedestal.*

But everything they're saying is true.

When Poppy stands, leaning down to say something to his mother before she breezes to the mic, I want to crawl inside my own bone marrow and see if I can drown there. She pinches the hem of her veil, pulling it dramatically off her face, and leans forward.

"I didn't have the chance to know Ezekiel for very long," she begins, and her eyes find Enzo immediately. My fingers tighten around his hand, like I might save him from whatever she says next, but Poppy looks away before she continues, "But every moment I spent with him was a gift. All my life, people have taken one look at me and wondered what's *wrong with me*. Why I look so *sick*. And I'm sure Zeke had those questions. But to him, that wasn't the important thing. The important thing, to him, was making sure I knew he saw me for more than just being the sick girl."

She sniffs, looking down at her hands for a moment too long.

It's disconcerting. I don't think I've ever seen her quite so . . . lucid. One could actually believe she's being genuine.

If I didn't know better.

Finally, she continues, "I think that was especially important to him, because some people may have looked at him and only seen the surface, too. But I was lucky enough to learn the kind of person Zeke really was, even in our short time together. And it sounds like many of the people in this room were, too. I believe he left us all with an invaluable lesson. To take the time to see people for who they really are." Her eyes find Enzo's face again. "And to judge them accordingly."

A sick chill creeps through my insides as Poppy makes her way back to her seat. I exchange a look with Enzo, then Rory.

That can't mean anything good.

The preacher returns to the stage and launches into his sermon, and after a few Bible passages, I tune out. It drags on for longer than it should, and even the grief of Zeke's loss isn't enough to keep my eyelids from trying to close. It's still before noon on a weekend, after all.

Eventually, the service ends. People file over to say their goodbyes and offer condolences to the King family. I grab Enzo's and Rory's hands and tug them toward the church doors. If I don't have any right to be here, I really don't have the right to speak to his family. Even if a part of me would like to tell them how much I loved their son—how good he always was to me—how much it meant to have someone like him in my corner.

But I can't bring myself to do it. And instead, the three of us step onto the sidewalk. With the sun high in the clear blue sky, I suck in my first real deep breath all morning.

"That was interesting," Enzo comments, eyes running along the church windows like he's checking out the art.

"*Interesting*." Rory scoffs. "It was awful."

"The two aren't mutually exclusive."

"You had no reason to show up here."

"I wanted to be here for Gem. He was a friend of theirs."

"A friend you *stabbed.*"

"Why don't you try saying that just a little louder, kitten? I'm not sure the Gracie PD heard you from all the way down the block."

"How'd you even get inside? Shouldn't you have burst into flame the moment you crossed the threshold?"

"Hilarious—but fair. In Christian myth, Lucifer *was* cast to Hell for demanding equality in Heaven. . . ."

I take a step away, leaving them to their bitching. I need a minute. Rory's right. That was awful.

The corner where the church sits looks like most other corners in downtown Gracie. Diagonal from it is a gas station that's probably been around since the invention of the automobile. Across the road in one direction is a tiny mom-and-pop grocer that's kept in business only by the friends and family of the people who own it, because there's no way they're actually competing with the Piggly Wiggly for sales. Across it in the other direction is an offensively boring-looking apartment building, slapped together in the last few years to try and convince people they shouldn't move to Atlanta, or Tallahassee, or literally anywhere that isn't here.

The curtains in one of the apartments shift. I tilt my head, eyes narrowing.

Behind me, Rory and Enzo are still going.

"Where's your mommy? Is she giving you another ride home?"

"I'm sorry, are you mocking me because this town doesn't have Uber?"

"No, I'm mocking you because you're eighteen and you can't drive."

"Forgive me for growing up in the most exciting city in the

world, with twenty-four-seven public transportation at my finger-tips, and not, what? The bayou?"

"I was born in *Alaska*."

"Oh, my mistake. An igloo, then."

"Hey, shut up." I wave my hand at them, without tearing my eyes from the apartment window. "Are you two seeing this? Is someone . . . watching me?"

Rory immediately steps behind me, the warmth of her at my back, and the sharp line of Enzo's smaller frame slots next to mine.

"I don't see anyone." He shrugs. "Don't get paranoid. There's enough real threats to worry about."

"No, they're right." Rory frowns, leaning forward so her chest presses against my shoulders. "Someone's behind the curtain."

"Probably just some creep trying to voyeur on a dead kid's funeral."

I tilt my head. "Maybe."

But I swear I can *feel* someone's eyes on me. I've felt it since Poppy White dragged her ass through the graveyard to get to me. I know it when I feel it now.

"Well," Rory sighs. "What can you do about it? It's not like—"

I hold up my hand, make a fist, and jerk. Right in front of us, the curtain in the window comes crashing down, rod and all. And I see the boy behind it.

On the surface, there isn't anything interesting about him. A skinny white boy with a mop of brown hair and a collared shirt. The only notable thing is his expression—a grimace of *rage*.

Of course, it isn't only the surface I see. And even as I'm looking at this boy, I'm looking at who he used to be. The Cy-clone. The god of air.

The last time we saw each other, it was 1306 and he was using a small tornado to rip my body to shreds from the inside out, hunks of me flying around the Scottish countryside while he laughed and laughed.

The Mountain and I decided to keep far away from him after that. In my next life, I made sure his records were destroyed—and that the child who should've *grown up* to be the god of air never made it to puberty.

As we stare at each other like this, me in front of the church, him behind a window across the street, the funeralgoers slowly make their way onto the sidewalk around us. And at the same time, the eerily blue sky opens up as if from nothing—and it begins to rain.

Through the pounding of water, Enzo says, "I know him."

"We *all* know him," Rory growls, taking off her leather jacket and draping it over my head.

"No, you insufferable hag, I mean I know *him*. The boy." Enzo glances at me, though I only see him in my periphery. I can't seem to look away from the window. "His name is Zephyr Beauregard."

"*Zephyr Beauregard?*" Rory practically shrieks.

"Believe me, *I know*. He moved to Manhattan from Cambridge a few years ago—we volunteered at the refugee center last summer. Well, I volunteered. He was given fifteen hours of community service for beating the shit out of his girlfriend."

"Huh." Rory's tone is incredulous when she asks, "You do *volunteer work*? Of your own free will?"

I step out from under the protection of her jacket just as a boom of thunder rattles the ground so hard a car alarm goes off. Zephyr's lip curls over his teeth, and he turns away from the window and out of my sight.

Behind us, someone giggles.

On the other side of Rory, Poppy and Marian have left the church and are standing under the rain on the sidewalk. Maybe it's just the rain that's got Poppy's mascara melting down her cheeks. I tell myself this so I don't have to acknowledge her puffy, bloodshot eyes.

It's her laughing, though. As her creepy little family stands behind her, stoic and dry beneath their matching black umbrellas, the ninety-pounds-soaking-wet Reaper just laughs and laughs. She makes that explosion with her hands again. "Boom."

Murphy steps out of the church and tilts her head toward the sky. The rain seems to fall *away* from her, drops pelting the ground in a perfect circle around her feet but leaving her dry.

At Poppy's side, hood pulled up on her black denim jacket to protect her from the rain, Marian meets my eye. "Tell me, Magician—did you find a way to destroy your knife?"

Everyone's eyes turn to me, including Murphy's. But I don't look away from Marian.

As we stare each other down, the weight of the question she *isn't* asking makes my gut churn. Because I know what happens next. We've all been standing still for too long. We've *all* been staring, waiting, hoping . . .

But that ends with the Cyclone's arrival.

It's time for someone to blink.

27

ONE WAS NEVER MEANT TO EXIST WITHOUT THE OTHER

As soon as the passenger-side door of Rory's Jeep slams closed behind me, I announce, "We have to destroy the knife—today."

Rory slides into the driver's seat while Enzo hauls himself into the back, then leans onto the console between us. He puts a hand on top of mine, thumb brushing over my knuckles. I think I almost feel a spark there, like flame licking at my palm, but that's probably my imagination.

"Gem . . . we aren't going to do that." He sighs, as if informing me of this is a heavy burden. "We're going to kill Zephyr."

"What?" Maybe it shouldn't be as shocking to hear as it is, but it takes me off guard. I jerk my hand away from his conniving petting, shaking my head. "No. No, look, if we get rid of the knife, we get rid of the one thing the other gods want. If they can't use it to take my power—or yours—they'll just . . . they'll leave us alone."

Maybe. It's the best shot we have, though, isn't it? Hasn't

that been why we've planned on doing exactly this, this entire time?

Enzo voices my thoughts. "Perhaps. It's *possible* Death and Battle will let you live out the rest of this life in peace. But what about in the next? What if the Reaper truly does not have another lifetime left, and the Lionheart is forced to return to this world alone? Do you think she would let you know a single moment without pain?"

"What are you suggesting? That we kill *all* of them?" The knife burns like a brand against my side, hidden in my waistband.

"Not all of them. Zephyr, because he's an insufferable cretin who enjoys pain for pain's sake and he doesn't deserve to live. And Poppy and Marian—because they won't give you another choice, creature. And I think a part of you has known that for a long time." He touches his hand to the side of my face. "Why do you fight so hard to choose clemency, when they will cast you as their monster no matter what you do?"

"He's right."

Rory's words are so soft I almost think I don't hear them. Enzo's head practically snaps off his neck as his attention shoots to her.

Her hands tighten around the steering wheel until her knuckles go white. She swallows, looking out the front windshield, refusing to look at either of us. "Not about Poppy and Marian— not yet. They at least operate with purpose. And I think—I don't think Marian was lying when she said she wanted a solution that didn't require anyone dying. Maybe there is one. Maybe we can find a compromise. And if we can't . . . we'll deal with it."

My stomach twists at the idea. And still, I ask, "But Zephyr?"

Her eyes flick to mine. Her shoulders droop. "Gem, we have to kill him. Look, Enzo's right. Sometimes evil is just a person whose needs are at odds with yours, but *sometimes* evil is a person who sets the world on fire because they like the smell of smoke. The Cyclone doesn't *care* about the knife. He doesn't care about going back to the Ether, or making things right, and he never has. The only thing he wants is for you to suffer. And so, he'll come after you no matter what we do. He isn't going to stop unless we stop him."

I've known about this kid for five minutes. It feels wrong to sit here plotting the death of a stranger—and even more than that, I'm grossly aware of how *normal* it feels.

Maybe Enzo is right. Why am I trying so hard not to be the monster when no one else seems to care?

"Besides," Rory continues, when I've been silent for too long to be comfortable. "If we *could* destroy the knife, I think we *would have* by now."

Maybe she means over the last week. Or maybe she means in all the other lives before this one. When we swore we wouldn't use it, but kept our hands on it anyway—for the *what if.*

Either way, she's right.

"I can't use the knife," I remind them. "I can't take his power."

In the Ether, in the bodies of gods, pulling magic from someone was a much longer process. I could wield the knife only because they didn't die right away. There, I could perform the rite of executioner without worrying about upsetting the balance, slowly carving out the power I sought with my own magic serving as a bridge between hosts. And that worked for me, because I didn't trust the Shade to hold the knife on his own.

But in these human bodies, it's over more quickly. There is no carving, only killing. And whoever's holding the blade will be the one who takes the power.

"That's all right," Enzo purrs. "I can do it."

"*Or*," Rory bites out, "I could."

"It's a lot of responsibility, kitten." He smirks. "I'm not sure you could handle it."

Her face is perfectly neutral as she tells him, "I wasn't worried about that when I gutted the Stillness and took Peace for my own."

A vicious interest sparks in Enzo's eyes.

I put my palm flat against his face and shove him into the backseat. To Rory, I ask, "Do you know how to get in touch with Poppy and Marian?"

She shrugs. "I could figure it out."

"Do it. Tell them we need to meet tonight." My hand presses against the knife at my side, feeling the outline of it through my clothes. "If we're gonna start killing gods again, I need to know how many have to die."

Two thoughts occur simultaneously when we drive up to the House of Death a few hours later—that this place is not at all what I was expecting, and *why the fuck is Indy Ramirez's truck outside?*

The house itself is a massive Southern colonial, with white siding and dozens of windows. There's a wraparound porch on the first and second floors, and a rooftop balcony. Backlit by the setting sun, it's almost idyllic in its promise of good old-fashioned racist Americana.

That's not really why it's interesting, though. The entire property—at least ten acres—is covered in plants. Not the oak trees swathed in Spanish moss or the fields of sunflowers we'd usually find around here. There are . . . palm trees? Giant ferns?

Rows upon rows of vibrant flowers planted all along the front yard? The entire thing looks like some kind of secret garden, straight off a magazine cover. Not at all where I'd picture Death's cohorts doing their scheming.

But it also looks *wrong*. And I don't realize why until the car parks and Rory, Enzo, and I climb out. Only then does Rory say, "You've got to be shitting me."

"What?" I ask, as Enzo tilts his head.

"It's all plastic." She stomps her boot against the ground, eyes narrowed. "Even the *grass* is fucking Astroturf."

She sounds disgusted, which is fair. I can't help but also think it's brilliant. Credit where credit's due, that's a begrudging point to the Reaper.

As if summoned, the front door swings open and Poppy sweeps onto the porch in a dramatic swish of a feathery neon-green dress, as if summoned. She looks like a sick chicken. Her hands claw her waist as she smiles, lips pulled back from her teeth as if manipulated by a dentist's tools.

Marian steps out with her. She hasn't dressed up in a costume, I'm grateful to discover, and is still wearing the black funeral attire I saw her in earlier. She looks tired, though. There's a slope to her shoulders that's new, a ticking tension in her jaw I hadn't noticed before. There are dark rings around her eyes.

Indy flanks Poppy from the other side. There's always been something inherently dichromatic about him, with his brown skin decorated in dark birthmarks like puddles of spilled ink on parchment. It's underscored by the sweater he's wearing, black and white fabrics stitched together in the center, oversized enough that it falls to his knees. He offers me a weak wave.

I can't explain why it makes me as angry as it does.

"What's your endgame?" I demand, narrowing my eyes as I take a step closer to the house. "Just playing every corner so you've got your bases covered no matter what happens?"

He's cruel enough to look bored by my accusation. He doesn't even bother offering a response, just stares at me, disappointed.

"Oh my god, awkward, *anyway,*" Poppy singsongs in a rush. "Mountain. Hi, bestie. You said you wanted to chat. What's up?"

Rory's eye twitches. I don't know which part she's struggling to process—the fake plants, Poppy's green feather dress, or the fact that she just called her "bestie." She tilts her tattooed chin up and meets Death's eye with her shoulders back. "We want to walk away from this without anyone here having to lose their life."

"Wouldn't that be convenient for you," Marian drawls. "Now that you're the ones afraid to die."

I take a step closer, eyes on Poppy now. "Did you mean what you said at the funeral? That you think you should see people for who they really are and judge them accordingly?"

She smirks, though her head tilts—"falls" would be a more accurate word, like her neck simply fails at holding it up any longer—with interest.

"Enzo and the Shade might be living in the same body, but they aren't one and the same. Not entirely. And you can't kill one of them without killing the other. How is that judging him for who he *really* is? How is that fair?"

"Fairness." The word curls like smoke out of Poppy's lips. She huffs, looking to Marian with a sweep of her arm as if to say *Can you believe this idiot?*

Marian exchanges that look with her girlfriend before facing me again. "I don't care about fairness. I care about *justice.*"

Confusion tugs my lips into a frown. "Aren't they the same thing?"

Poppy bursts into laughter. Indy shakes his head—more disappointment.

Marian sighs. "I guess that's what I'd expect you to say, *keeper of the scales.*"

"This is asinine." Enzo steps forward, brushing past Rory's shoulder and then my own to stand at the base of the steps. He holds his hands out at his sides, palms up, as if to mimic submission. Though it looks more like a challenge. "Tell us how we can compromise, or decide which one of you would like to be filleted first."

"Oh-ho-ho, Prince Charming." Poppy snickers.

"For someone who's not used to using their powers in a human body, you certainly have a lot of nerve." Marian raises her slit eyebrow. "Challenging the god of battle? Really?"

Enzo shrugs, unfazed. "What's a warlord without an army?"

That tick in her jaw picks up speed.

"And where's your army, Lionheart?" Though I can't see his face from behind him, I swear I can hear the ugly smile in his voice when he says, "Ah, that's right. They fell to my command when you abandoned them a millennium ago."

It's Poppy, not Marian, who takes a step down the porch stairs. But Marian's hand shoots out, her muscular arm curling around her girlfriend's waist, her fingers gripping a fistful of green.

"Easy," she tells her. "It's exactly what the little shit wants."

"If you don't want the *little shit* to have his way"—I grind the words out, reaching forward to grab Enzo's shoulder and yank him backward. My eyes meet Marian's—"then tell us how we find a compromise."

"Fuck a compromise—" Poppy snarls, but Marian steers her back, tugging her from the steps. The frail girl scowls, twirling around and stomping to one far corner of the porch for a breather.

Marian looks back to me. "Understand, we *want* to go home. A thousand years we've spent waiting for the day you might open the rift and send us back where we belong. But—" She must sense my oncoming argument, because she holds up a hand to cut me off. "I do understand you do not want to return. I can't even blame you. If I'd helped destroy a world I was meant to protect, I, too, would hesitate to reckon with the gravity of that crime."

Okay, well . . . that wasn't nice.

"We can stay here. We've had this long to adapt. I realize as long as there are humans, there will be battles to fight. It may not be *my* army," she sneers. "But there are no shortage of armies in need of a leader."

"Get to the point, Battle," Rory snaps.

Marian takes a deep breath, letting it out through her nose. "*She* cannot continue like this. You see it for yourself. Death cannot be sustained for an eternity without *life*. One was never meant to exist without the other."

I shake my head, knowing where this is going. "We said a plan where no one here has to lose their life. That includes Enzo. I won't let you kill him to give Poppy the Caretaker's power."

"Then you will carve it out of him!" Poppy shrieks from the corner of the porch, *jumping* as if stomping her feet wouldn't be enough to convey her anger. She wheels toward us, standing just behind Marian to glare from around her girlfriend's shoulder. "Let him keep the other powers. Let him keep his pathetic life. I want my sister's magic back."

"She *needs* it back," Marian amends. "You want a solution where we all live. This is it, Magician."

I frown, looking over my shoulder at Rory and Enzo. Rory is frowning. Enzo has the gall to smirk. Am I meant to take that as encouragement?

It doesn't matter. I know my answer.

I turn back to Death and Battle. "No."

Indy sighs.

Marian's fists curl. I can practically *see* the struggle for control in her face. "*Why?*"

"It's too dangerous." I shrug. "Removing power like that? Bit by bit? It requires carving someone open."

I would know.

"You're asking me to vivisect his *human body*, and expecting me to say yes? To put him through unbelievable pain and risk his life for *her*?" Even if I were willing to put him through that, *I'd* be the only one I trusted to hold the knife. And one wrong slip of the blade, one millisecond lapse in judgment, would mean a dead Enzo, and me suddenly inheriting a whole slew of powers I'm not supposed to. The balance and my boyfriend, both gone with one nicked artery. "Absolutely not."

"With the powers of life and death together, she could heal him!" Marian throws her hands up, frustration in every line of her body. "The only pain he would experience would be during the act itself—"

"And it would be far less than he deserves," Poppy hisses, her fingernails digging into Marian's shoulder, stringy hair falling over her face.

"Gem," Rory begins, and I know what she's going to say.

But I don't need to hear it. I already know why this is a good compromise. I understand it's as fair as fair could get, in this situation.

Just like I understand I'm *never* going to do it.

"My answer is no," I repeat, squaring my shoulders.

Indy shakes his head, turning away from the porch railing to sit down in a rocking chair by the front door. He tilts his head back and closes his eyes, pushing himself back and forth with the toes of his shoes. He looks as tired as any ancient god has the right to be.

Poppy looks like she's about to pop a blood vessel. Her human-mask is slipping, and each passing second has her looking more and more like a demented, animated skeleton. She smiles a smile that is not a smile, and takes a step back, toward her front door. Yeah. Maybe she should go inside and lie down.

Marian's eyes move to Enzo. "And you're on the same page, then?"

My head snaps back. I *dare him* to try and martyr himself.

He's watching her with the strangest smile. When he speaks, there's a peculiar calm to his voice that doesn't belong. "Have you ever considered, Marian, how much easier your lives would be if you just let her go?"

Poppy's eyes widen. Marian's expression is blank.

Enzo takes a step forward. "Your power is unfathomable. You can do so much good for this world. Yet you waste your potential, all to protect a corpse."

A moment of silence passes. The whole yard seems to hold its breath.

Finally, Marian glowers. "You know that isn't going to work, dumbass. There is no part of me that wants to hurt her."

There never has been. Lionheart and the Reaper have

always been immune to the Shade's manipulation—the one alliance he can't sever.

"Bitch," Poppy adds from the corner.

Enzo chuckles. "Fine. In that case, my answer is the same as theirs. This is the Magician's world, after all. I'm only living in it."

Marian . . . nods.

I think it's time we left. I turn my back to her, putting one hand on Enzo's arm, the other on Rory's, steering them toward the Jeep.

"You wanted to know where my army was, Shade?" Marian calls at our backs.

All of us freeze, all in a row together, as if we'd practiced it. Slowly, I turn around to face the house again. On either side of me, Rory and Enzo do the same.

"Well, a good soldier knows how to lie low and wait for orders."

Almost in sync, six windows along the front of the house all slide open at once.

Poppy giggles. "What's that saying, baby?"

Marian cracks her neck and begins to descend the porch steps. "Don't bring a knife to a gunfight."

And the House of Death opens fire on their lawn.

28

KILL ME OR WALK AWAY

Bullets plug the Jeep's tires and ricochet off the exterior. Rory shoves me *hard*, sending me spinning behind the car—and Enzo along with me. I grab his shirt, dragging him down into a crouch behind the tire, and reach up to latch on to Rory's sleeve and yank her with us.

With the three of us on the ground, Enzo yells, "*GUNS?* THIS IS THE MOST REDNECK BULLSHIT—"

"Gem," Rory presses over the sound of shots ringing.

When I look at her, she's got her fingers tangled in the fake grass, expression hysterical. Our eyes meet.

"This is sitting on concrete. They set this place up to make sure I couldn't—that I wouldn't be able to— Look, there's no life here. There's nothing for me to— Even to make them *still*, I need to make them take root, I—" She fumbles over her words, eyes huge. "I don't think I can do *anything*."

I nod. "Okay. Go."

"I can't leave—"

"Yes, you can." I curl a hand around the side of her neck, bringing my forehead to hers. "There is nothing wrong with doing what you have to, to survive. And I need you alive—now *go*. We'll cover you."

It's been a long time since I've seen fear like this in the Mountain's eyes. But she nods.

I face Enzo, heart thundering. "Are you ready?"

He smiles. "You and me against the world? This brings back fond memories, creature."

I don't know what to say to that. But I know what I need to do next. With shaking fingers, I reach into the waistband of my jeans and produce the Ouroboros. There's no time to unpack the vile look of lust on Enzo's face when I press it into his hand. We're out of options.

"Olly-olly-oxen-free, motherfuckers!" Poppy's voice croons, closer than it should be. "Come out, come out, wherever you are!"

Crouched low, Rory makes her break for it.

"If you say so!" I shout back. I shove my hands against the side of the Jeep that *hasn't* been destroyed, magic pulsing through my arms, shooting electricity into my palms as I *pick up the car and throw it at the house.*

With a horrible crash, the Jeep collides with the home, knocking out part of the upper floor, and at least some of the shooters inside.

But it doesn't come without a price. A bullet zings through the air and grazes my arm, blood erupting from my shoulder and pain bursting along the side of my body.

The gunfire ends, though, presumably so the family members left can go check on the ones I might've killed.

"Child soldiers, Lionheart? Really?" Enzo asks as he makes his way toward the house.

"We do what we have to," she answers, and lunges for the knife in his hand.

I don't get to see what happens next.

"Boo," comes a whisper at my side, and only when I wheel toward it do I realize the Reaper is lurking inches away. She grins. "I always *did* want to be the one to do this."

One hand shoots out with unnatural speed to claw into the bullet wound on my shoulder. It would be painful enough without the added venom of her deathly touch seeping under the surface of my skin.

That feeling of necrotic tissue worming its way through my body starts to spread, starting at my shoulder but moving across my chest, and down my torso. My lungs freeze, breathing slowing, and slowing.

We've been here before. And before, I had Rory to save me.

But before, I *needed* Rory to save me.

I don't need to be able to move. I reach for something *inside* myself, gripping my magic like grabbing at the edge of a blanket. I imagine lifting it up and shaking the blanket out and knocking loose Poppy's curse in the process.

As soon as I do, a gust of black spores shoot from my skin, the deathly magic forced out and into the air. Poppy, only inches away, sucks one in—and starts to choke on her own venom. She stumbles, gasping for air, hands gripping her throat.

"NO!" Marian roars. But instead of abandoning her struggle for the knife, she doubles her efforts. She manages to grab a fistful of Enzo's hair and slams his head against the bottom porch step. There's a *crack* and a spurt of blood and then the knife is in her fist.

My own hand shoots up, and it's as if a magnet pulses in

my palm. The Ouroboros flies through the air and returns to me.

Marian races in my direction, though she moves past me and leaps for Poppy. The other girl has hit her knees, gray face turning blue. Behind her girlfriend, I watch as Battle shoves two fingers down her throat—trying to get her to throw up her own inhaled toxin?

Interesting.

Enzo stumbles to his feet, and we meet each other halfway, bloody hands reaching for one another while our eyes stay fixed on the girls across the yard.

Poppy never looks good, but she *really* doesn't look good now. When her body seems to sputter out and go limp, Marian rolls her onto her back and starts CPR.

I might've just killed her. And I didn't even have to take on Death's curse to do it.

But there is no magic without sacrifice. Not for me.

I hear the car five seconds before it comes peeling into the front lawn, a black convertible with the top down.

Zephyr fucking Beauregard. The slimy god of air, with his perfectly mundane face and his unremarkable rich-boy clothes, climbs out of the driver's seat and makes his way toward us. His eyes zero in on me as he stalks across the fake grass, boring face made ugly by the twisted look of hatred.

He isn't alone. Rhett Clancy, that asshole, slams the passenger door and follows him.

"Red, what are you doing here?!" The demand comes from Indy—the first time he's spoken since the gunfire started. When I look over, he's risen from his rocking chair, staring at Rhett with real fear on his face.

Rhett glances to him, then back to me. He doesn't answer.

Zephyr, though, finally opens his mouth. In his *egregiously* posh accent, he says, "Now, you didn't really think I'd let you get through the whole party without me, did you?"

All around us, cyclones of dust begin to swirl from the ground, rising like the corpses of old tornadoes. They spin themselves wider and faster and louder, the wind picking up, and I squeeze Enzo's hand until my own hurts, afraid we might both be blown away. My braid is forced undone, hair whipping viciously around my face and screwing up my vision.

Behind us, Poppy heaves a choking breath as she comes back online. Not dead.

Just pissed.

The Cyclone takes a step closer, and his impossible tornadoes swirl nearer. The once-beautiful house gives a terrible groan as the attic begins to tear away, pieces of roof and siding flying into the night. "Lovely to see you again, Magician. And I see you've brought the Shade this time. It'll be my pleasure to send you both back to the hell you crawled from."

"*Hell*, weather boy? Really?" Enzo sighs. "I've grown tired of this. Let's be done."

And then his eyes begin to glow their jagged, mismatched shades of silver and gold. He tilts his head back to the sky, and I follow his vision—as does everyone else, helpless to stop themselves from watching what the Shade can do.

As we watch, the stars begin to . . . move. All across the dark expanse of night, they start to *drop*. Closer and closer they fall to Earth, until each of them hurtles, a ball of fire, behind the horizon. In every direction we can see, all around us, they simply *fall*.

Except for one. One ball of flame soars, as if tossed by an invisible hand, directly at Zephyr's body. When it gets close,

I can *feel* the heat radiating from it, *smell* the burnt sugar and gunpowder scent.

Enzo's fingers curl in the collar of my shirt and he pulls me out of the way seconds before the space rock comes crashing into Zephyr's body.

Or it would have, I assume, if one of those ungodly tornadoes hadn't swept in and yanked it out of the air at the last second. Still, the two forces hitting each other is enough to rock the ground beneath us, and Zephyr screams as his body is lifted right off the dirt and dragged through the air with his own cyclone—now ablaze with star fire.

As Zephyr and the rock and the tornado spin together, a tendril of flame licks out and connects with the white siding of the house. A vicious fire bursts to life, sneaking in through the upstairs window.

A little girl screams.

"NO!" Poppy throws herself toward the burning building, using that unnatural grace and speed to all but fly up the steps and inside.

Marian doesn't follow, though she does race toward the porch. I watch as she skids to a stop in front of one of the fake palm trees. When she reaches for its branches and yanks them open, I realize the palm tree isn't just a *plastic plant* at all—it's camouflage. And when she pulls it away, she reveals the computer beneath it, all neon and chrome and out of place.

Her fingers fly across a screen, numbers appearing and disappearing too quickly for my brain to keep up, especially at a distance. When she's satisfied—I don't know with what—she runs after her girlfriend, into the house.

The ground starts to move under my feet.

"Wars are fought on Twitter," she'd told me once. *"I get to keep my sword at home."*

My eyes widen as a patch of square grass *slides away*, and a long black cylinder rises from the ground. It tilts forward, and the top pops open like a lid.

I have the brief thought that I don't know how smart Marian really is, or how much money Poppy's family has, but it may not have been the best idea to meet them on their turf.

And then a *rocket* blasts its way out of the cylinder, shooting across the lawn and connecting with Enzo's meteor. The explosion is loud enough to knock me off my feet, ears ringing. Through smoke, I watch as Zephyr and the blazing deathtrap of his own creation are pushed away from the house, spinning out of control and out of sight.

I'm not the only one knocked over. Enzo stumbles next to me, only stopping himself from getting a mouthful of fake grass by grabbing my shoulder at the last minute.

But he loses the knife. Within seconds, Rhett Clancy snatches the Ouroboros into one gloved hand. And then he has it against Enzo's chest.

Magic crackles in my arms again and I rise to my feet, the world narrowing down to Rhett and the knife. What will I have to sacrifice if I use magic to rip his heart right out?

But Enzo doesn't need my help. Before Rhett can do anything, Enzo calmly rises to his feet and asks, "Do you really want all my power for yourself, when you can barely handle your own?"

Rhett wavers, a frown pulling at his bushy red beard.

"You're already crumbling. Just look at you." Enzo reaches out and puts a hand on Rhett's shoulder. The much taller, much *stronger* boy visibly shakes beneath the touch, until he hits his knees in front of us.

Is this the Hammer's magic, warped by the Shade? Is he robbing the strength of others instead of building his own?

Even knowing there's a fiery tornado somewhere nearby, even with the fire spreading through the house in front of us, somehow, right now, the yard feels quiet. The impossible ease of the Shade's influence settles over us like a weighted blanket.

Standing over Rhett's body, Enzo touches a too-gentle palm to his cheek. "You have known so much pain. You're so tired, aren't you? I can help you. You don't have to keep fighting. You can just . . . give in."

His thumb brushes Rhett's cheekbone, catching a tear as it falls. "Shh. We both know you can't carry this burden. You aren't strong enough. But you can hand it to someone who is. Someone like me."

And I stand there at Enzo's back, watching as Rhett very, very slowly begins to turn the Ouroboros around until it's poised at his own throat. I stand there, watching, as more tears spill, and this broken boy gazes up at the god of things forbidden like he might be the answer to his prayers.

"That's it," the Shade whispers. "You've earned your rest."

"Shut the fuck up." Indy slams a hand over Enzo's mouth.

Whatever spell Enzo cast on Rhett is broken. The Ouroboros clatters to the ground, and I dive for it, snatching it up and stumbling away from the others. But the redhead doesn't seem to notice or care. He stays there, on his knees, shaking.

And Enzo screams.

As Indy lowers him to the ground, Enzo's eyes squeeze shut, his hands shooting up to grab at the sides of his head, and he screams, and screams, the most terrible sound. His chest rips out a sob.

I don't have time to reach for my magic. I shove Indy away from him, forcing him against the side of Zephyr's car, the Ouroboros at his throat. "What did you do to him!?"

Indy eyes the knife, and then my face. He doesn't look afraid. I wish he did. "I made him look at himself. Don't blame me if he can't handle what he sees."

Inside, all at once, the house fire is extinguished.

"Kill me or walk away, Gem," Indy snaps. "Or do you prefer Magician?"

Slowly, I lower the knife.

From the front porch, marred with soot but still standing, the House of Death stumbles outside. Marian holds a fire extinguisher in one hand and a fire ax in the other, while Poppy's shaking hands corral her parents and sisters. I'm surprised they all still look *alive*. Poppy's mother and father huddle their daughters at the edge of the yard, casting wide-eyed looks toward the rest of us.

I know that look. I've seen it before. Like they aren't sure if we're gods or monsters.

"I AM GOING TO SHRED YOU INTO PIECES, SHADE," comes a scream from the other side of the property. Lightning bolts strike, as plentiful as bullets, as Zephyr—clothes burnt, face bloodied—comes racing at us.

At the same moment, Poppy wheels away from her family to face us. "YOU COULD HAVE KILLED MY SISTERS. *AGAIN!*"

Enzo does not rise from his knees. He tilts his head toward her, gaze wide-shot and vacant, and whispers, "I didn't mean for this to happen."

I'm not even sure he knows what he's responding to.

I shove the knife back into my waistband, clapping my hands together over Enzo's head. The magic reverberates around us both, an invisible shudder of power that creates a bubble of protection. When one of Zephyr's bolts comes directly toward Enzo's chest, the shield knocks it away, sending it back into the sky where it came from.

Within seconds, the Reaper and the Cyclone converge in the center of the lawn. I expect them to join forces, to focus all of their combined energy on attacking Enzo and me.

Instead, Poppy screams at the air god, "And you! You're just as much to blame!"

Zephyr cocks his head at her. "Do you think I give a fuck about your family, Reaper? EVERY LAST ONE OF YOU CAN FRY!"

As if to enunciate his point, lightning begins to *rain* like I've never seen it before. I throw my body over Enzo's, praying to my own magic that the wall holds.

Letting out a battle cry, Marian throws her ax across the yard. It spins and spins, turning over and over itself, before landing in Zephyr's side with a wet thunk.

He throws his head back and screams, and a boom of thunder follows. With both hands, he wrenches the ax-head free. It's only a flesh wound, not lethal, but blood pours from his hip, soaking his polo and oozing onto his khakis.

From the other side of the yard, another shot rings out. A bullet whizzes past Zephyr's cheek.

All heads turn to look at Poppy's father, standing there with his gun raised, a petrified look on his forgettable face.

Zephyr tilts his head. He raises one hand. And, as if bored, he sends a single bolt of lightning directly into the man's chest.

His burnt and blackened torso cracks open. I think he dies before his knees hit the ground.

So many people are screaming.

Holy shit.

Rory's words play back in my head. *"Sometimes evil is just a person whose needs are at odds with yours, but* sometimes *evil is a person who sets the world on fire because they like the smell of smoke."* The charred remains of the house make the property reek of it.

I think maybe I understand what Marian meant when she told me she wasn't interested in fairness but justice. The god of battle is not an imperialist warlord, seeking out violence for violence's sake. Her power is in leading people into revolution against things that are hurting them—channeling their anger and their skill so they can fight *back.*

And from where she stands now, *I* am the thing hurting the House of Death. We may never agree on a compromise between my need to balance the scales and hers to see righteousness win, but at least I understand how we got here. At least she works from a moral compass, even if it isn't the same as mine.

I don't think Poppy has a moral compass. Death is fickle and unkind, but it doesn't go out of its way to be cruel. Death, for some, can even be relief. And it moves in tandem with life— most of the time.

And then there's Zephyr.

I know as well as anyone there's no reasoning with a hurricane. There's no stopping it once it begins, no knowing if you've over- or underprepared for it, no understanding why it does what it does. Even when you start to pick up the patterns, mapping the way tornadoes move around it, it's too late to do anything but get in your bathtub and pray.

The god of air is going to rip us all apart just because he can. Just because we're in his path.

The magical bubble protecting Enzo and me disappears when I leap to my feet and grab Poppy as she loses her footing. The Reaper screeches with such force that blood puddles at the back of her throat and slicks up her tongue, over the corners of her chapped mouth.

Marian takes her from my arms when she reaches us, and our eyes meet for the briefest moment. I wonder if we're thinking the same thing.

I don't have time to dwell on it. When I look back to Zephyr, my breath screeches to a halt in my cold lungs.

He's got his bloody hands wrapped around the handle of the ax. And he's raised it over Enzo's head.

And Enzo isn't moving to protect himself.

I reach for my magic, even knowing it's too late, knowing I cannot stop this.

Zephyr lets the blade swing—and the earth rips open underneath him, fake grass and concrete and deep-buried weapons and even deeper-buried roots tearing apart to drag him down.

"If anyone's going to kill that bastard, it's going to be me."

Rory makes her way up the driveway and into the front yard, arms spread wide at her sides for the row of owls perched on her frame.

My people have long believed owls to be a sign of dark magic and death. I've always been taught that association is a bad thing. Looking at her now, I'll have to rethink that.

Trailing at her feet are a menagerie of other animals—coyotes and opossums, deer and gators, rabbits and skunks. The grass shifts with the ones we can't see—snakes and lizards and bugs. More bugs swirl in the air over her head, along with a slew of screeching bats.

Her grandfather follows behind them all in his ancient sports car.

The animals converge on Zephyr's body where he's fallen into the ditch, greeting him with a frenzy of snarls and hisses. He screams, and lightning strikes again as he digs his fingers into the dirt and drags himself up. Pushed forward by the snapping at his heels, he clambers into his car.

Rhett finally gets up off his ass and climbs in with him, shouting, "Indy, let's go!"

But Indy gives the black convertible a dark look and steps back.

Zephyr doesn't wait. He peels off and away from this place as quickly as he can, kicking up dirt behind him and leaving the rest of us in the dust.

A runaway hurricane—and at his side is a library of every thought I've ever had.

Rory curls her hands around either side of my neck. "Are you okay?"

I only just remember I have a bullet wound in my arm. I'm not okay, not at all, and for plenty more reasons than that. But none of it's important right now. What's important is us getting the hell out of here.

"Help him," I mutter, tilting my head toward Enzo.

She looks at him kneeling on the ground and nods, grabbing him beneath the armpits and steering him toward Joseph's car.

"Indy," I start, watching him walk toward his truck.

But he shoots me a look so full of hurt, I don't think there's anything I could say to counter it.

Behind me, the girls of the House of Death scream their

grief without end. I can't bring myself to look directly at them, but I find Marian. She stands to the side, face broken open with a helplessness that does not feel like it belongs on the god of battle.

As if she senses me looking, she turns her head away from her makeshift army and stand-in family and finds my eyes.

A moment ago, when our eyes locked, I'd wondered if she was thinking the same thing I was. Looking at her now, I know she is.

One of us is going to kill the other. Maybe that was always true. Maybe all these attempts at waiting, or hoping, or compromising were just delaying the inevitable. Advocating for justice versus fairness; seeking victory through struggle versus miracle; loving Death versus loving the gods of stolen Life and all things living. Even when we've fought for the same cause, our methods have always been at odds. This was never ending any other way. And the time is coming, sooner rather than later, for one of us to finally put an end to the other.

But before it does, we're going to fight on the same side once more—to kill the god of air.

29

WE RISE TO HUNT OUR PREY

I f it's just the same to y'all, I'm gonna take first shower," I say quietly, after Enzo and I follow Rory into their bedroom.

I've spent enough time here that it's starting to feel like a second home—but only now, seeing Enzo in the room for the first time, do I realize how little this space actually seems to reflect Rory at all. Their room is sparse, just the bed and a dresser, no photos or posters on the wall. There are hanging plants, and a few more plants on the windowsill, but they don't even have a dog, their own Hank to curl up and snore at the foot of the bed. In every other lifetime, Rory's had a dog.

That's weird, right?

Enzo glances up at me when I speak, frowning as if only just realizing I'm there. It makes my heart jerk with worry, and I reach over to brush my fingertips through his dirty, faded hair. He tilts his skull into the touch, but still waves me off with a flick of his wrist, a silent encouragement to go ahead.

Rory sits on top of their dresser, leaning back against the mirror. When our eyes meet, they sigh, heavy and long and sad and about to burst open with all the same things my chest is trying so hard to carry right now. "Yeah. I'll get the first-aid kit from the kitchen."

With both of us giving Enzo a last, lingering look, we slip together from the room. When we part ways at the end of the hall, Rory's knuckles brush a line down my back, pressing firm over each notch of my spine as if to silently say *I've got you.*

I step into the bathroom alone, but I'm not. I need a minute by myself, to stand beneath burning-hot water and dissociate and cry and maybe have a panic attack. I don't need to find Joseph standing next to the toilet, the trash can in one hand, and a *used tampon* in the other.

He jumps when I catch him, his entire body jerking like he's just been hit. He drops the bloody wand into the basket, then shoves the garbage can back into the corner, under the toilet, where it belongs.

"What . . . are you doing?" If I weren't so tired, I might have it in me to sound angrier about this. I'd already decided I would kill Joseph someday, and somewhere, deep down, I know *this* is really, really wrong. But my brain is swimming through concrete. I can't seem to remember *why* this is as bad as it is.

"Hi!" That isn't an answer. He smiles. "I was just leaving."

"Okay."

"Is the Mountain in their bedroom?"

"Rory is in the kitchen, getting first aid."

Something wild flashes over his face. "They told you— You should not call them that, you know. That is not who they are. It is only who they thought they were once."

"Joseph." I shake my head. "Are you telling one god how to address another?"

Panic replaces his wild-eyed look. He shakes his head, frenzied as he starts to back away, inching along the wall to get to the bathroom door. He holds up the palms of his hands. "Of course not. No, Magician, I would not dream of it. I only want to protect them. Everything I do, I do to protect them. Please—please remember that."

The bathroom door swings shut behind him, and I stare at it for a long moment. This needs to be dealt with. Just not tonight.

I strip out of my mud-splattered, blood-soaked funeral clothes and turn the shower faucet on as hot as it'll go. The water burns when I step underneath it, but it's a good kind of burning. It forces me to remember I'm alive, and I'm right here in this body. I tilt my head back, the heavy weight of my hair falling down to the tops of my thighs as water soaks into it. More dirt, more blood. All of it washing off me and down the drain.

The only shampoo in the shower is Rory's. It smells like coconut and is meant for curls I don't have, but I lather a glob of it into my hair anyway. Then the matching conditioner.

I take my time with the washcloth. First the tear on my shoulder. It doesn't look like a gunshot wound, but I guess I didn't actually know what a gunshot wound looked like before now. I'm careful to wash the dried blood away, to clean out the dirt lodged under the strips of torn flesh. It hurts, too—worse than the burn of the water, but just as grounding. I don't let myself flinch away from it.

I'm just as thorough with the rest of me. The sweat and grime on my chest and belly and between my legs. My legs themselves, sore and trembling like they don't want to keep holding me up, covered in fresh bruises and old scars. The bottoms of my aching feet.

Only when the water starts to feel less hot do I realize I've overstayed my turn. I yank the faucet off, climbing out onto the bath mat and grabbing a towel off the rack over the toilet. I don't bother getting dressed, or even gathering up my dirty clothes. Let Joseph come in here and smell them, and then he can do my laundry.

With a towel around my chest, I shuffle back to the bedroom. I don't know what I'm expecting when I get there, but it isn't what I find.

Rory's sitting at the end of their bed, in front of Enzo, with the first-aid kit open and spread out on the other side of them. They've got his chin in one hand, forcing his head up, and they're using the other to smooth out a bandage over the gash on his forehead. And he's staring up at them, brown eyes round and soft and awed. Like he can't believe they would touch him with this much tenderness, because he knows he doesn't deserve it.

I know that look. I'm pretty sure it's the same one I wear any time Rory touches *me*.

And suddenly, for a moment, I'm not in this room at all anymore. Not entirely. My body feels unhooked from my brain—a feeling I've never liked, but especially don't like right now, when I just worked so hard to get myself back in my own skin. The fog of a flashback rolls in, clouding my vision, as another time and another world and another version of us begins to unfold.

I haven't had a flashback since Buck knocked the wall down. I think it's probably because my memories have all been closer to the surface, and instead of needing to relive these moments, I've only had to *think* about them. This one is different, maybe, because it's *so far away*. In fact, I don't know that I've *ever* had a memory this long-buried come to the forefront.

I'm back in the Ether. And our world is so new.

Much like our world, we are also terribly young, at least

by the standards of eternity. I cannot be sure how long we've been here, not when time moves so strangely, not when the time *before* time feels as close as yesterday and as distant as another life.

We are like children at play, and this world is whatever we imagine it to be. We chase one another across a swath of nothing, and in our footsteps rise kingdoms and cathedrals, oceans and forests, good and evil. We make-believe our world into existence, and the Ether is shaped by the precocious whims of its child gods.

The Mountain giggles, practically flying as they race away from the Shade, and flowers bloom at their feet as they do. His own laughter bounces off the walls of the world, and I watch from a close distance as he finally descends upon them. His arms curl around their waist and the two go tumbling to the ground.

The young god of land grins, reaching one tender hand into the air over his head, and pulls a new animal into existence. A snake curls around their wrist, with scales as dark as the Shade's pitch eyes, that glitter when they catch the Sun's light overhead.

He grins, flashing his fantastical teeth, and reaches out to pull the serpent into his own grip. It hisses a warning when he does, and flashes its long, dripping fangs. I watch as the touch of the god of things forbidden changes this new animal, giving it a kind of venom that did not exist in this world until they made it so. When he sets it in the grass, it hurries away, beautiful and lethal.

I leap from my hiding place, making my way toward them. Both heads face me when I do, and my childhood companions grin and giggle at the arrival of another playmate.

When I'm close enough to grab, the Shade rolls his

body off the Mountain's, reaching for my hand to tug me closer.

My knees hit the dirt next to them, and I seed my fingers into the earth, grasping for the roots of the very wildflowers that bloomed beneath their game. Magic coils from my touch, and I imagine an antidote, turning these flowers into a cure for the venom of the same snake that just slithered away from them. Balancing their union's creation with one of my own.

Delighted, the Mountain leans forward to press a chaste kiss to my cheek before declaring, "You're it!" They leap to their feet and take off again.

The Shade meets my eye. We smile the conspiratorial smiles of childish scheming. And, like hounds on a scent, we rise to hunt our prey.

As quickly as it arrived, the fog evaporates, leaving me standing there in my towel, staring at Enzo and Rory. They're both watching me, still and waiting.

If human minds are not meant to hold the burden of our memories, how is my human heart expected to carry the weight of the eternal devotion with which I've loved these two?

Legs still shaking, I ease onto the bed, pushing the first-aid kit out of the way with my foot so I can lie down. My wet hair soaks the pillow underneath me, but I can't bring myself to care.

To Enzo, Rory says, "Okay. You're good. You can take the next one."

I watch the ceiling fan in the center of their room whirr. The air feels nice on my damp skin, cooling me down after I tried to boil myself alive. Enzo must hesitate, because it takes him longer than it should to leave. But I don't look at him, only watch the spinning blades.

When I start to see Marian's ax spinning through the air instead, I finally turn my head away.

Rory is watching me from where they still sit. When our eyes meet, they offer a sad smile. "I . . ."

A long moment passes before I finally push myself up on my elbows, wincing at the pain in my shoulder. "You what?"

"I'm sorry I left you."

"No."

"Honey—"

"Listen to me." With effort, I lean forward and wrap one hand around their wrist. "If you *ever* have to choose between maybe saving my ass and definitely saving yourself—get the fuck away from me."

"That's not—"

"I don't want to be in a world you're not part of." I shake my head, falling back onto the pillow, closing my eyes. "I already did that. For seventeen years. It sucked."

Rory doesn't say anything else. They're quiet for a long moment, and I think they're probably *considering* arguing. I don't know why they don't. Maybe because they agree with me, or maybe because we're both too tired to do this tonight.

Either way, when the moment passes, they shuffle up the bed to sit next to me. Their hands are warm and strong when they tug my arm, just slightly, so they can examine the spot the bullet grazed.

"*Guns,*" they mumble with disdain, mirroring Enzo's earlier disbelief. "That was so . . ."

"Human?" I ask, opening my eyes again to consider the underside of their chin.

Rory meets my eye. "Clever. I was going to say—Marian's

annoyingly clever. With the fake plants, too. I know she had a hand in that."

I note the begrudging respect in their voice. After a moment, I nod.

"Okay, this is going to sting."

They tell me with only enough warning for me to grit my teeth and snag my fingers in a fistful of the bedsheets when pain shoots through my shoulder. My back arches, the towel falling away, and I groan when the flare finally subsides.

Rory unpackages a bandage and presses the adhesive to my skin, covering the grisly wound from sight. Good. I don't want to look at it anymore. When they lean forward and press a kiss over the beige dressing, my stomach tightens.

Their eyes flick to my chest—not on purpose, I don't think. Maybe because they can't help it. When they raise their hand and brush their knuckles over my sternum, I'm still not sure they're in control of what they're doing. When their knuckles graze lower, over my belly, then lower, ghosting at the hair between my thighs, my body clenches. Finally, their eyes meet mine. Their palm flattens over my skin, and for one wild moment I wonder if they're actually going to slide their fingers even lower—

"The keeper of the scales apparently doesn't know how to balance the hot and cold water," Enzo announces as he steps back in the room, hair wet, with a towel around his waist. "Shower was—*oh*."

I jump, like I've been caught doing something wrong. It doesn't matter if I know I haven't.

Rory, though, just looks over their shoulder and shrugs. "It's fine. I can deal with a cold shower."

Yes, I think, *that might be for the best. Maybe I should join you.*

Enzo's eyebrows rise, but he doesn't say anything, even as Rory stands and moves out of the room. Leaving me lying there, naked, in their bed.

I sit up and clear my throat. "Sorry about that."

"No big deal." He shrugs. "It was actually still warm when I got in. Technically, I'm the one who used up the hot water."

I roll my eyes. "You seem to be feeling better."

More himself, at least.

"It's amazing what soap can accomplish," he answers, before dropping his own towel and kneeing his way onto the bed with me.

"*Oh,*" I say, because I don't actually know what else to say, watching him crawl toward me on his knees. I've seen *pieces* of Enzo before. I've seen thirst-trap selfies posted to his private story and even thirstier ones he'd send me privately, not wanting to share them with anyone else, but wanting someone to tell him he looked good. But neither of us has ever actually crossed the line of *nudes.* That would've required admitting we wanted each other, something we weren't ready to do until he got kidnapped and turned into a demon.

So, here we are, from zero to him completely naked and wet from the shower and on his knees in front of me in Rory's bed.

"Darling?" he asks.

I drag my eyes up and up until they find his. They glitter when he smiles.

"Huh?"

"Do you have clothes here I can sleep in?"

My first instinct is to say *Clothes? Why would you need clothes?* because I am terrible and horny—not related to each other, just equally true. Instead, I struggle to find my own tongue and then say, "Uh. Maybe, yeah."

I have a whole bag I brought for my weekend at Rory's. I lean forward, intending to stand up and climb off the bed, to go get the bag, to put some clothes on myself.

Only, when I do, Enzo's hand finds my hip. His fingertips dig into my flesh, stilling me in place. Our bare chests and bare stomachs and bare hips mere inches apart. Our mouths so close I can feel his breath on mine.

"Do you know how many times I thought about you when I was naked in bed in Brooklyn?" His whispered words send a spike of heat shooting right down the center of me.

I raise one hand to curl around the back of his neck, dragging his face closer until our noses and foreheads touch. "Oh? And what were you doing while you were thinking about me?"

"Someday"—his tongue flicks out to touch my lower lip—"I'll put on an encore performance, and you can see for yourself."

The mental picture is almost enough to make me black out.

Enzo tugs away from me, leaning back and waving me off to continue on my path to my overnight bag. It takes my legs a minute to remember how to walk, and even when I do stand, I almost eat shit on Rory's dresser.

He chuckles. Though, when I reach my bag and bend at the waist to rifle through it, his laughter turns to a choked cough. Good.

After digging around, I toss him a pair of my boxers.

"Ugh. What is this, polyblend?" He groans.

I'm not sure what my face looks like when I stare back at him, but he holds his hands up in surrender. While he drags my *cheap*, probably *poorly made* boxers up his legs, lifting his hips to yank them over his ass, I pull on a pair of black underwear.

Instead of grabbing one of my own shirts, I help myself to Rory's T-shirt drawer, dragging one of theirs out and pulling it on. Their collection is huge, a bunch of thrifted tees with obscure old bands or bizarre sayings removed from their original context.

Back in bed, I curl an arm around Enzo's waist and tuck him against my side. He's fished his phone out from wherever it was hiding, and a glance at the screen tells me he's opened up our Discord server.

"Everything okay?"

"Mm." He shrugs. "I'm sending Ivy a message. They're . . . worried."

Ivy, his best friend back in Brooklyn. Who probably really, *really* does not understand why he up and disappeared for Gracie, Georgia.

How are we meant to balance these lives? Is it really supposed to be this hard?

I don't have time to dwell, because the door opens again. Rory considers us, kicking their door closed. And then, seeming to come to a decision—though I couldn't begin to guess what—they toss their own towel onto the dresser, sauntering over to open up their underwear drawer.

There was a point tonight when I'd thought I was going to die, but I didn't realize it would be because these two teamed up and killed me.

Rory's dramatic curves are even more noticeable with nothing to conceal them. My eyes travel up the backs of their thighs and backside, the latter almost concealed by their wet curls. I imagine my fingers tangled in those curls and my throat goes dry.

When they turn around and lift one foot into the leg of their underwear, my tongue dips out to wet my lips without me meaning it to. I watch them slide the cotton up their legs, over the endless stretch of warm brown skin streaked with stretch marks and toned with muscle. When elastic snaps into place over their hips, my eyes dart up again, wanting a look at their bare chest—after all, it's already a lot to take in fully clothed.

Instead of making it to my pervert's destination, I land on a fourth and final tattoo. A single wave, in simple black ink, etched into their rib cage.

My heart lurches.

It's enough to make me slightly less bound to the whims of my crotch, and I manage to tear my eyes away from Rory's body to look at Enzo. Wondering if he's okay with what's happening, if everyone's comfort level is still good or if maybe we need to—

Oh, he's ogling them. My boyfriend is lying in my arms, phone forgotten, lips parted, staring at my girlfriend's chest like he's thinking about writing it a poem.

Because I'm *me*, I feel a flare of jealousy. Of course, that flare is met head-on with another wave of horny. Imagining the three of us together is probably crossing some kind of unspoken boundary, but I can't help the image that jolts through my head.

Rory turns off the light before they climb in on the other side of me. I roll to bury my face in their—now clothed—chest, my back tight to Enzo. He wraps an arm around my waist, pressing his hand over my stomach, his arm tucked between Rory's body and mine when he does. Rory curls their own around me, their palm between my shoulder blades, the back of their hand at the base of Enzo's throat.

This is the first time I've been this close to both of them. Beneath the bar soap and shampoo and memory of blood, the bed smells like heady spices and sweet smoke and wet, packed dirt, like a freshly dug grave.

I close my eyes and breathe them in. And I know, whatever happens next, whatever I have to sacrifice, it will be worth it.

The next morning, I wake up alone and pitiful about it.

I find Enzo and Rory on the front porch, him drinking a glass of iced coffee and them drinking a mug of tea, both of which smell like lavender. Rory hands me a thermos of chai. I kiss their knuckles, and the top of Enzo's head, and we take Joseph's car when we leave. The Jeep is never getting fixed.

"I'll call Marian and ask for a cease-fire," Rory says, as we turn onto my dirt road, the sports car shaking as we approach my house. "We can all get together and come up with a game plan for finding Zephyr."

Because I'm beginning to understand Marian, I know she'll say yes.

We pass by the Wheeler farm and the First Church of Gracie. The field of cows and the letterboard sign both disappear in a blur. I only just barely make out the verse:

The Lord will never be willing to forgive them; his wrath and zeal will burn against them. All the curses written in this book will fall on them, and the Lord will blot out their names from under heaven.

When we park in front of my house, the first thing I notice is the open door. Not just open, I realize, climbing out and walking toward the front steps—off its hinges.

Enzo steps around me, taking my arm and steering me to the side so he can enter the house first. Rory, too, sweeps past me to get inside.

But whoever was here is already gone. And they've done what it was they came here to do.

I know what I'm going to find when I make my way to my mother's room. I still struggle to get a breath in when I see it with my own eyes. Her sheets, bloody. Her, nowhere to be found.

"Hank—oh my god, hey, buddy," Rory's voice floats in from down the hall.

I turn from my mom's room to walk toward the sound. Rory is kneeling in front of the hall closet—that reeks like dog shit—and petting Hank's side. The old dog is slumped over across their shins, a miserable, low whine coming from his chest as he pants so hard he struggles to breathe.

Rory meets my eye. "He was locked in here."

"Is he okay?"

"Y-yeah, he's fine. Just scared."

I sit on the floor with them, pulling my mutt into my lap. He whimpers as he licks my face, old body shaking. My fingers tug at the fur behind his ears.

Enzo circles back from my bedroom, carrying a slip of paper. He crouches next to me, and hands it over. When he does, I notice he has his phone against his ear, and it's ringing.

"Pick up," he whispers.

I turn the paper over. In frantic but elegant handwriting, someone's written:

*What will the three of you do when
you lose everything?*

*Let's find out. Come and find God.
Hopefully before I get bored.*

"Fuck," Enzo snaps when the phone goes to voicemail, slamming his finger against the end call button. "My parents aren't answering."

"Why would Zephyr do this?" Rory demands. "This isn't like Marian and Poppy taking Enzo—he doesn't even *want* anything. Why go through the trouble of taking your parents?"

I press a kiss to the top of Hank's head, standing up with him still in my arms. When I've let him outside to run off into the yard, I turn back to the others.

"What he wants is pain. And Rhett Clancy has given him a road map." I swear the Ouroboros burns a little against my side when I say, "So now we get to kill them both."

30

DON'T MAKE
THE WRONG MOVE

We meet Poppy and Marian outside of Zephyr's apartment building, across the street from the church where my mother and Enzo's parents are being held hostage by two very different gods on a power trip.

Poppy greets us in a floor-length white cloak, cinched at the waist with gold chain. A matching gold band has been wrapped around her head, over the white hood—and she's glued googly eyes all over it. When she lifts her arms, there are giant gold and white wings draping from the sleeves of her cloak, and they're *also* covered in googly eyes. When she raises her head to look at us as we approach, I almost choke at the sight of her face—painted, yes, with a bunch of fucking eyes.

There are almost no words. I force out, "I . . . Why?"

"I'm a biblically accurate angel!" She points at her head-band, as if to say *Duh!*

"You know what, Poppy?" Rory sighs. "*This* is camp."

The smaller girl *glows*.

"Have you ever considered theater?" Enzo asks.

"Maybe we could do this later," Marian suggests.

"How's your family doing?" The question is directed at both of them, my eyes flicking between their faces.

Marian glares. One of Poppy's eyes twitches. "Homeless and despondent. But still better than yours."

"Right," Rory agrees, turning to face the megachurch. "So, are we sure they're . . . in *there*?"

It's a fair question. There are enough churches in Gracie that searching them all would take us an entire day. But I'm certain this is where Zephyr took them.

The problem—it's a Sunday morning. And service is in session.

"Unfortunately." Marian nods, tilting her head to consider the stained-glass windows. "There are half a dozen offices in the back, behind the stage. And an entire attic space we can only access through a stairwell in the back alley. I'm going to *assume* that's where they all are. Most privacy. Easiest to hide the noise."

"So, what's our plan, then?" Enzo demands, antsy, bouncing on the soles of his shoes.

Marian and I look at each other. There's expectation in her eyes.

I sigh. "I'm going to give these two the Ouroboros."

Enzo chokes. "You're going to what?"

"I'm sorry," Rory snaps. "Did that not seem like something that should be a group decision?"

Marian tilts her head forward. "Finally, the Magician makes a decent choice. If we could keep this going, I might actually start to believe all of Indy's blathering about how much you've changed."

To Rory and Enzo, I explain, "We all know Zephyr and Rhett have to die. But Death and Battle could just send us in there on our own, to take care of our people or die trying. These two have no dog in this fight."

"Except," Marian presses, "that we can use their power."

"No. I don't get it." Rory shrugs.

Poppy laughs, then presses a hand to her own chest. To Rory, she explains, "I'm? Rotting."

I take a deep breath and exhale through my teeth.

Rory glares, but Enzo says, slowly, "Continue. . . ."

"Rotting?" Poppy frowns. "Oh. Right. Um—so. What we know *now* is that when one god steals another's power, it doesn't just transfer over all clean and pretty. They get smashed together and gross."

"So . . ." Rory takes a deep breath of her own. "You're hoping taking another god's power will cancel out some of your symptoms. That you'll be able to survive—because you won't just be *Death* anymore."

"I mean, what is a defibrillator," Poppy says, with such profound thoughtfulness I can only hope it's mockery, "if not lightning persevering?"

"And the Librarian?" Enzo asks, looking to me.

"You've seen Rhett." If we're being fair, Enzo did a lot more than just *see* Rhett last night. He almost made him kill himself. "I don't want you *or* Rory going anywhere near that power."

"But if anyone's mind can handle that kind of knowledge, it's mine." From someone else, it would be undeserved arrogance. From Marian, it's just true. "And if the Cyclone's gifts don't save Poppy, I can use the Librarian's to find something that will."

"So, Poppy lives. Zephyr and Rhett die. Your families get

rescued. And everyone gets to go home after." Rory looks between Enzo and me. "That's what we're saying?"

"It's not a solution without flaws," I admit, turning my head to Marian. "For starters, I'm not convinced you won't go after my boyfriend."

"He's not my *tyyyype*," Poppy whines.

Marian puts a hand on her shoulder. "Oh, if this doesn't work, I have every intention of going after your boyfriend. But it's still worth a shot, isn't it?"

It is.

"Okay." I look to Enzo and Rory, glancing from his face to hers. "Are we ready to do this?"

No, probably not. Their faces tell me the same thing I'm thinking. But they both nod. And I turn back to Marian and offer her the Ouroboros anyway.

When she curls her fingers around the black gemstones encrusting the handle, I feel like I'm going to throw up.

"Don't make the wrong move here, Lionheart."

She tests the weight of it in her hand, calculating and calm. "Don't make me, Magician."

From the alley stairwell, I can hear music blaring from inside. Look, plenty of gospel music is great. All you have to do is sub out the image of the Christian god for someone you're in love with or your abusive father, depending on the lyrics. But *this*? Sucks. This is not some "it is easier for a camel to go through the eye of a needle than for someone who is rich to enter the kingdom of God" group with long hair and tattoos. And if it's not that, what's the point?

As we climb closer to the attic access door, my ears twitch at a sound beneath the music. Shouting?

The closer we get, the clearer it becomes. There are *definitely* people arguing in the attic. I stop just outside the door, fingers hovering over the handle. Over my shoulder, I glance at Marian, and the others lined up on the steps behind her.

"Can anyone hear what they're saying?"

"I know how we can find out." Poppy smiles. "Open the damn door."

And even though I roll my eyes, I turn around and do just that.

The attic walls are made almost entirely of stained-glass windows, which all up and come together at the dramatic point in the center of the ceiling. The massive cross perched on top of the church casts its long shadow across the windows. When the sunlight hits, it reflects the shadow onto the attic floor, illuminated by the glimmers of red from the windows' art that glint in the air, sparkling off dust motes and making them look like floating flecks of blood. There's almost nothing up here except for a few boxes, holiday storage based on labels like CHRISTMAS and EASTER scrawled across the cardboard in messy Sharpie. Most of the boxes have been pushed toward the walls.

Zephyr stands at the center of the room, directly beneath the cross. His face is screwed up into a knot, beet red, and he wheels toward us when the door opens. Our presence doesn't seem to make him happier.

Rhett stands at the back of the room, opposite the door we entered from, with his still-gloved hands outstretched. Like he's trying to talk Zephyr down? His head shoots up and his eyes widen when he looks at us.

But they aren't alone.

At this point, it doesn't even surprise me to see Indy. The god of art may as well be omnipresent. He's right in front of me when I step inside, and even though he must see me and the others from his periphery, he doesn't turn his head. He's staring across the room at Rhett, his own hands outstretched as if to mirror the larger boy's. Only Indy's are trembling.

No, I'm not surprised to see Indy. I do, however, pull up short a little at the sight of *Murphy*—with her wrists bound in front of her, a neck scarf knotted around her mouth, sitting on the ground at Zephyr's feet. There are tearstained mascara tracks down her cheeks.

Oh, dear.

The others come in behind me, and I can *feel* the way the air shifts when the Mountain sees her sister tied up like the Cyclone's prisoner.

Whatever he sees on Rory's face, Rhett folds like a cheap lawn chair. "I ain't know he was gon' grab her. I told him who she was—that's all. Look, I jus' wanted the knife—he said we could get it this way. But I ain't have no part in her bein' brought here, and I'm tryin' to get him to let her go!"

Murphy looks up and whimpers. She meets my eye and then, over my shoulder, Rory's. The long-separated sisters stare into each other's eyes. I can't be sure what either of them sees.

We knew Rory's grandparents were safe because we spent the night at their place. Zephyr didn't have the *chance* to hurt them. But I wish he had—it would've been better than this. The Siren keeps getting dragged into this fight she doesn't want to be part of. Her power might be terrifying, but she has no control. Without a body of water around, she would've been helpless to defend herself against Zephyr.

She might not be my favorite person in the world. But she doesn't deserve this. Neither does Rory.

"Reaper . . ." Rory whispers from beside me, voice twisted with the promise of an ass beating. Marian takes Poppy's elbow and steers her away from the Mountain. Enzo whistles, low and steps off in the other direction. I watch Rory's face as she tilts her chin up and meets Zephyr's eyes, though it's still Poppy she's addressing. "Don't worry. I'll make sure whatever's left of him is still breathing when I'm done."

Poppy giggles. Zephyr's thin upper lip curls over his teeth, and he opens his mouth as if to sneer some snide insult—

Birds circle the church roof. Crows and sparrows, hummingbirds and hawks, cardinals and bluebirds. A single eagle joins the swarm. They swirl around the stained glass, predators and prey moving as one, and their red-black shadow on the attic floor looks like a single vicious creature overhead. Like one of Zephyr's own cyclones.

Fascinated and horrified, I watch as the first bird bashes its skull against the top of the glass. Its bloody body falls, but it's quickly replaced by another. Another slam of wings and beak and fragile bones. Another dead bird, and another to take its place right after.

"Oh, *yuck*," Poppy whispers, just as a thin vein of cracked glass appears, stretching from the base of the rooftop cross down to Jesus's crown of thorns.

Indy has the presence of mind to duck behind a stack of boxes, crouching low and covering his head, just before the glass explodes and the swarm makes its way inside.

The vicious, mismatched flock screams as it descends on Zephyr. The larger birds grab at his shoulders, yanking him off his feet and throwing him to the ground, while the smaller ones use their beaks and talons to rip at his clothes, desperately trying to get to his flesh beneath. The air god screams; lightning flashes, streaked red by the tinted glass, and thunder booms so loud it rattles the church's foundation, knocking more glass loose from overhead.

Enzo kneels in front of Murphy, picking up one piece of the window glass. When he leans toward her with it between his fingers, she winces, teary-eyed, and shifts away. He pauses, only for a moment, before carefully using the broken shard to cut away her bindings, then undoing the scarf around her mouth. He helps her to her feet, and she stumbles away from him. When she loses her footing, Marian catches her and helps her stay upright.

Enzo, still on the floor, looks up at me. Is that humiliation, from the god of things forbidden?

When one bird tears a long strip of flesh from Zephyr's throat, revealing muscle and tissue and blood beneath it, the god of air gives an *awful* cry. Outside, torrential rain begins to descend, the sky opening up as if to offer a scream of its own. The water spills through the broken window at the top of the attic, soaking into the thick green carpet at our feet, beginning to flood the room.

The water and wind are enough to slow down some of the birds, throwing smaller ones against the wall and cracking their bodies like the eggshells they hatched from, pummeling the larger ones so they can't move as quickly.

But it doesn't matter. I know this, because I know Zephyr has already made his fatal mistake.

I turn to Murphy. The god of water stares down at her feet, watching the wet carpet squelch under her, and slowly lifts her head. The tears in her eyes are not tears anymore. Water begins to pour from her, as angrily as it did that day in the pool. From her eyes, her ears, mouth, and nose. And when she moves toward Zephyr and Rory, I realize she isn't walking. The wet ground is carrying her, delivering her to them.

She comes to a stop at her sister's side, gazing down into Zephyr's face. Her own expression is impossible to read past the curtain of water, but I don't need to. I can imagine what she must be thinking when she lifts her hand—and the water soaked into the floor underneath the Cyclone begins to crawl its way up, sloshing over his body and dragging itself into his mouth and nose. Choking him. Drowning him.

Whatever happens next, I don't have time to pay attention to, because Rhett Clancy has the audacity to try and sneak past me and out the door. I step in front of him, magic crackling in my palms, tilting my head to the side.

"Where do you think you're going, Librarian?"

"I told you, I ain't want—"

"Where's my mother?"

He winces. "Look—"

Rhett is cut off by Enzo, who's pulled himself to his feet and come up behind him, pressing his hands into the bigger god's shoulders. Sapping his strength, Enzo forces Rhett to his knees once again. He twists his fingers in the Librarian's red hair and tilts his head back, forcing him to bare his throat.

Marian steps against my side, the knife perfectly still in her clenched hand. She stares down at Rhett with contempt.

"You betrayed me." She shakes her head. "I don't like turn-coats, Red."

When she presses the tip of the knife to his chest, Rhett cries out, "Y'all are teamin' up with the *Shade* now? With the Mountain and the Magician? And you callin' me a turncoat?"

"Is this your best attempt at pleading for your life?" I ask, cocking my head. "It's not very effective."

He doesn't look at me, his eyes staying on Marian and my weapon in her hand. "Look—we both know how this ends. She's gotta kill 'em. Right? Only way she can get her hands on Life. He's gotta die for her. Pretendin' y'all don't know that is only pushin' back the inevitable. But you got the knife in your hand right now—why waste it on me? Take your shot. Save your girl."

Marian's eyes flick from Rhett's face to Poppy's. Then to Enzo's.

I turn toward her, just slightly, eyes narrowed.

"Even if that were true," she tells Rhett, "we have time to figure it out. And you're still going to pay for the role you played in her father's death."

She presses the blade in tighter. Rhett winces, trying to jerk back, but Enzo holds him in place.

"Aight! How 'bout this!" The redhead looks up at Enzo, expression wild. "Death ain't supposed to go forever without Life—but you're human now. And you ain't supposed to be all Life and no Death, either. You're fine for now, but so was she first time she walked on Earth. What's gon' happen in another few lifetimes? You're gon' be just as fucked up as she is, in a different way—unless *you* kill *her*."

Enzo's fingers stroke too gently through Rhett's hair. "Hm."

"Shade," Marian says slowly, reaching into the front pocket of her hoodie with her free hand. What is she reaching for? "Do you really want the distinction of being the only god who couldn't make it past a single human lifetime?"

"No," he agrees, looking up to meet my eye.

"It could be a trap," I suggest. "A way to get rid of Poppy *and* force you to take on Death's curse."

"True," he agrees, glancing back down at Rhett with narrowed eyes. "Is this a trap, Librarian?"

"Or," I admit, not giving Rhett a chance to answer, "it could be that your only option is to gut the Reaper. Either way, Marian's right. We have time."

At my side, the god of battle sighs. Something flashes in her hand.

"All right," Poppy snarls, her twisted body spinning toward us with that impossible speed, making her look like more of a ghost than a girl. "Everyone *shut up*. The Cyclone's at my doorstep."

She wrenches the knife from Marian and soars across the room. Zephyr has gone limp, skin turning a sickly grayish blue, eyes rolled back in his head. With the Ouroboros clenched between her palms, Poppy slips between Rory and Murphy and slams her knee, twisted grotesquely at the wrong angle, into his chest, raising the blade over his body, and—

Everything stops.

31

COME BACK

*E*verything stops.

Poppy freezes in place, but so do all the others. The rain stops pouring, droplets hanging in the air, suspended all around us. Birds stop moving in midflight, where they surround Zephyr's dying body. Downstairs, the faint sound of bad church music has gone silent. Outside, cars park in the middle of the street.

Everything is quiet, and time stands still.

Only I seem to be immune to whatever's happening—at least, that's what I think, before Indy sits up from where he was crouched behind the boxes. He looks around the room, studying it the same way I did, before he turns to me.

"What's happening?" I ask.

Another box, shoved far against the wall, suddenly starts to move. It falls over, wise men costumes spilling onto the carpet as *Buck* sits up from where he was tucked away, taking a nap. He blinks, looks around, and yawns. "Oh! It's time."

"When did you . . ." I let the question trail off without finishing it. There is no point in asking Buck Wheeler *when* anything. I look back to Indy. "What is this? What the hell did you two cook up?"

"I am not allowed to use the stove," Buck says very seriously.

Indy moves toward me, slowly, hands outstretched, like he's approaching a wild animal. "Something very bad is about to happen. But you have a chance to stop it. And, Gem, I need you to want to stop it."

He must be talking about Zephyr's death. I glance at the boy on the floor, then back to Indy. "He deserves to die."

"I'm not going to argue about that with you—but do you really care about people getting what they deserve?" Indy moves slowly toward me. The closer he gets, the more I can make out the panic and pleading in his eyes. "He is the worst possible version of himself. But even the worst of us can change. You should know that better than anyone in this room."

I frown, watching as Buck stands up and starts tracing the art on the stained-glass windows, mumbling something to himself while he does. After a moment, my eyes flick back to Indy. "I don't understand. Why go through all this just to save Zephyr's life? He's not important. And he's a bad person."

"He's a scared, sad, angry little rich boy whose parents never loved him and who spent his entire life feeling like he wasn't quite human and not understanding why." Indy shakes his head. "And you're right. He's a bad person. But this isn't about him—it's about you."

"You said something bad was about to happen. . . ." I glance around the room, nerves crawling. "You meant to me."

Indy doesn't deny it. "You are the most powerful person in this room and you have always had the choice to make things right—I'm asking you to make that choice. You told me I was a coward, that I was playing every corner, just waiting to see who came out on top in the end. But I've picked a side. It's yours, Gem. I'm on *your* side, but I need you to be on your side, too."

I look to Poppy, her face twisted in a snarl, my knife over Zephyr's chest. To Murphy, face coated in wet mascara, eyes swimming in puddles of her own tears. To Rory, her own beautiful face as deadly as I've ever seen it, cold and cruel as she watches the boy who hurt her sister die. To Enzo, his fingers twisted in Rhett's hair, expression calculating as he considers Marian. And Marian, looking where I stood—disappointed and resigned.

To Indy, I ask, "What do you want me to do?"

"We both know this knife shouldn't exist. A weapon like this can only ever lead to an endless cycle of pain. You knew that when you created it, but you did it anyway. The *Magician* did. But *Gem Echols* decided to destroy it. For the first time in all of your lives, you are someone who can make that impossible decision, because you know it's what's right." He swallows. "But you're faltering. You're getting further and further away from that, because you're losing *you*. Come back, Gem. Destroy the knife."

"I don't know how." Is that me, whimpering? "And even if I did—what if Rhett's right? What if Enzo's only going to die anyway, unless he takes Poppy's power? What if we—what if we need the knife to protect ourselves? People hate me. They hate us. They're not going to stop just because the knife disappears."

Indy takes a deep breath, and lets it out slowly. "No. They're not. But you shouldn't get to wield a weapon of mass destruction just because you're too scared to put in the hard work to fix the things you've broken."

"Ouch, Indigo."

He presses on, "The Reaper and the Caretaker were never one and the same; Life and Death didn't have to live in the same body. They just had to *work together*. Killing Poppy might sound a hell of a lot easier than teaching Enzo how to get along with her, but that doesn't make it right. Killing everyone who comes after you because of ancient grudges might be easier than being held accountable, but that doesn't make it *right*."

"Why do you care so much? Why fight so hard to get me to be the good guy?"

Something inscrutable crosses his face, like he's thinking of saying something but changes his mind and offers a different answer instead. "Art is an act of *love*. And I have known and loved all of you for a very long time—even when I hated you."

My brain hurts. Buck and Rory warned me that human brains weren't supposed to hold all of our lifetimes, but this is the first time I've really felt like my skull might crack from the pressure.

Speaking of Buck. The Evergod pops up around Marian's shoulder, smiling that gap-toothed smile at me. "When I can't stop screaming, sometimes I lock myself in the closet."

". . . Oh?"

"Do you want to take a minute in the closet?"

"I'm not screaming."

"Oh. I guess it hasn't started yet."

He blinks at me. I blink back at him.

"Oookay." At this point, in my relationship with Buck, there is an element of just giving up and seeing what happens.

I exchange one last look with Indy as Buck takes my elbow and steers me from the attic. He whistles as we make our way down the outdoor staircase, winding around to the lower-level back door of the church. He pops it open with ease, and I step into the back room, where the offices are. We must be behind the stage. If the world weren't completely silent, that music would be a lot louder from here.

There are half a dozen different doors, each of them as sterile and plain as the last, blending into each other. Buck walks up to one and presses his ear against it. He lifts his hand and taps his knuckles against the wood, and smiles.

From inside, I hear someone start moving around. *Not frozen?*

"Take all the time you need," Buck says, and giggles and giggles and giggles as he walks away, back outside, leaving me alone with this door.

I don't know what else to do but step through it.

Enzo's parents are in the corner. His mother has her face buried in her husband's chest, shoulders shaking. His father, eyes glossed over, only seems to wake up when he hears the door open, turning his eyes to me.

"Gem?"

"Hi, Mr. Truly." Not the way I'd always imagined meeting my boyfriend's parents for the first time.

"Gem!"

My eyes slide across the room to my own mother. Her usually put-together appearance has been mangled, hair in knotted disarray, matching pajama set torn. Her hands and feet are bound, and I notice blood pooling around her long but broken fingernails, where she tried to claw her way out of her restraints.

And she's sitting right next to . . . my father.

The Librarian and the Cyclone went to Sopchoppy and kidnapped my severely ill dad.

I'm not entirely sure he *knows* he's been kidnapped, though. He's staring up at the fluorescent strip lights on the ceiling, lips parted, body still. If it weren't for the rise and fall of his chest, I might think he was dead.

Human brains are only meant to handle so much. And his has been under attack for so long already, since he was a little boy who lost his parents. What if this is the thing that finally breaks him beyond repair?

I move over to my mother, kneel in front of her, and grab her wrists to untie them.

"Gem, what is going on?" Her voice breaks. "Baby, what happened to you?"

Oh. I guess I probably don't look my best, either. I got my ass kicked last night. She can't see the gunshot wound on my shoulder, but I've no doubt there are bruises and cuts on my face still.

"Do you know who did this?" Enzo's father demands.

I glance over at him but look back at my mom when I answer. "It's a long story. And I'm gonna tell you everything. But for right now, I just need you all to stay here, and stay quiet. Someone will come and get you when it's over."

"When what is over?" Mr. Truly's voice breaks. "Where is my son?"

"Enzo is safe. I won't let anything happen to him."

When her hands are untied, my mother grabs for the binds on her ankles and starts ripping at them. But she's shaking too badly to make much headway. After a moment, I push her hands away to take care of it myself.

Voice as weak as I've ever heard it, she says, "He warned me about this. Your father—he said you were in danger. He said there were things happening I would never understand, he wanted to save you, I—I thought he was crazy, I—"

I pause to look up at her. Her face is turned so she can watch my dad's.

"I loved him so much—I wanted him to get help—I begged and I pleaded and I watched as he got worse and he—and there was nothing I could do, I had to protect you—when he hurt you, I couldn't—I couldn't let you get hurt again—but I abandoned him, even when I knew he needed me, and this whole time he was right—*what have I done?*"

"Mom—"

Her face jerks toward mine, tears spilling from her familiar dark eyes. She reaches out one shaking hand to touch my bruised cheek. "And then I saw it happening to you—it was like looking at him a decade ago—and I loved you so much, even more than I loved him—and all I wanted was to help, I couldn't help him, I thought I could help you, but you weren't sick, I was wrong, I wasn't helping, you were in pain and I was just hurting, I was hurting you more." She chokes, snot and tears bubbling over. "I'm so sorry, I'm so sorry."

"Mom." I tug her hand from my face and squeeze. "He *is* sick. And so am I."

She whimpers, sucking in a breath over the jagged edges of her own cries, and reaches up to twist her fingers through her silver necklace. A nervous habit.

"You did what you thought was right." As I say it to her, I realize the truth of it for maybe the first time. My mother has caused me unbelievable pain—and every time, she thought she was helping. "Even when it was the wrong thing, it was for the right reasons."

We are trapped in a cycle of harm. My father hurt us, and we took those wounds and we hurt each other with them. And how did my father become what he is? And how many more people could *I* hurt if the cycle is left to continue?

I should get back on my meds.

"I have to finish this," I tell her, pulling away the binds that held her ankles. "Can you—"

When I motion to Enzo's parents, still tied up on the other side of the room, she nods. Her hand falls away from the silver chain as she stands and—

And I get my first good look at my mother's necklace, for the first time since getting my memories back. We've been avoiding each other so hard, I haven't seen her since that night.

Around her neck, she wears the Ouroboros chain. The one thing that can destroy the god-killing knife.

"Where did you get that necklace?" I ask, rising slowly to my feet.

She frowns, looking down at it. "It was a gift from your dad. He gave it to me when we first started dating. Even when we divorced, I . . ."

She never stopped loving him. And she never stopped wearing it.

Every day, for as long as I've known her, my mother has worn this necklace. It's been right there, in my house, this whole time.

"Can I—do you think I could borrow that?"

Her frown deepens, her fingertips brushing the metal. After a moment, she unclasps it and passes it into my palm. "Sure. It was your grandmother's, after all. I suppose it should have ended up with you."

The chain feels as electric as magic in my palm. My fingers close around it.

Outside, the world is still frozen and Buck is nowhere to be seen. I lift my hand to pass through the rain suspended in midair all around me. The uncanniness of it all makes my stomach ache.

Without understanding why, I move over to a patch of dirt behind the church. A stretch amid the concrete where they've attempted to make this place look less sterile by planting a tiny little flower bed. One of the raindrops has landed on a petal and splashed, frozen in time at the moment of impact so it looks like one of those fake flowers with little plastic beads of water on them.

I wonder if that's why I don't feel anything when I reach down and press my fingers into the earth. But another part of me knows that probably isn't it.

For so long, I've felt like the land in Gracie was trying to talk to me. It was always whispering in a language I desperately wanted to understand, the language some long-buried part of me *does* understand even if my mouth can't translate it.

But it hasn't spoken to me in a while. I don't think the land has tried to talk to me since the night Buck knocked down the wall between Gem Echols and the Magician.

Gem belongs here. Gem is *part* of this land. The Magician is a trespasser. And at some point, I chose to lean in to the trespasser.

Slowly, I rise to my feet and back away from the garden, turning toward the stairs to the attic. I know what I have to do.

If my parents and I are stuck in a cycle of harm, what kind of cycle am I caught in with the rest of these gods? How far back does it go, this spinning wheel of hurting each other again and again until we are shaped entirely by the worst things we have ever done? How much farther can it continue? In the end, will any of us recognize ourselves?

When I slip into the attic, Indy looks up from where he's perched on a box. I don't know what he sees when he looks at me, but relief spreads across his face.

I move toward Poppy's still-frozen body and gently take the knife from her raised hand.

The dagger feels as perfect in my palm as it always does. The beautiful silver metal, the black stones that shimmer in the light, the snake curled in a perfect circle, eating its own tail.

We are trapped in this loop, consuming each other, unable to break free because we are all just doing what we have to in order to survive.

But I am the most powerful one in this room. I can change that. *I* can break the cycle.

I curl the chain around the blade, my heart pounding so hard my pulse ripples in my jaw. It *feels* wrong, even though I know I'm making the right choice. I swallow past an uncomfortable lump in my throat.

All I have to do is make the choice. And all of this is over.

"I'm proud of you," Indy says, and I don't know why that makes me want to cry.

I look up at him. The colorful windows surrounding us cast a strange, jagged light along his skin, illuminating him like *he* is made of stained glass.

The water droplets and flecks of dust, all hanging in the air, are caught in that same reflection, the whole room tinged red, like we're standing in the middle of a bloodbath. Slowly, I spin around one more time, taking in the way the red light paints everything.

Red light. Blink. I tilt my head, staring at the door I just walked back through, at a tiny dot of red against it.

That isn't a speck of dust or a drop of rain illuminated by the glass. What is that?

"Gem?" Indy whispers from behind me.

I don't look at him. I step forward, the chain around the knife, both curled in one of my hands, as I examine the tiny, innocuous red dot on the door. I press my finger against it, and the light jumps onto my nail.

Light. A laser?

I turn around. The laser is pointed directly at the spot where I was standing when time froze, the spot right next to Marian. What's across from me? I make my way to the other side of the room, pushing past boxes to get to the window-covered wall, looking out into the world.

Directly across the street is the unremarkable apartment building where Zephyr has been staying. My eyes find his window.

The curtain, rehung since our last encounter, is pushed back just slightly. Just enough that I can make out the barrel of a gun through the window, its precision sight locked directly on the spot where I'm supposed to be.

"Gem . . ." Indy's tone is low and warning.

I turn back around and storm toward Marian. Just before Poppy took the knife, I'd watched her reach into her pocket, something flashing in her hand.

Her phone. I look at the screen to see she's already sent her message. It reads only:

Now.

Did the Lionheart ever intend to let me leave this place?

Something horrible has been rooted in me for a long time. And when I look into Marian's face, now, it begins to bloom.

Why is it *my* responsibility to end the cycle?

"Gem!" Indy is screaming now, but I'm not listening.

Why am I the one who has to choose fairness? Why should

I crawl back to them, begging for forgiveness, when it is not only *my* actions that have gotten us here? Why do they never have to beg *me*?

Why am I expected to be the only god in our pantheon who cares about the balance?

They look at me, and they see a monster. But they refuse to look that closely at themselves. Art may be a mirror, but so is magic. They get out what they put in, and it's not my fault none of them has ever wanted to face the consequences of their actions.

They look at me, and they see a monster. So, they think they'll put me down—shoot me like a rabid dog?

I tilt my head to look at Marian's face, frozen in all her stoic acceptance. She knows what's coming, and she thinks it's what I deserve. What about what she deserves? What about what her girlfriend deserves?

Here I am, trying to keep the balance. And here they are, lifetime after miserable lifetime, stacking the scales against me.

Have they forgotten I am the most powerful god in existence?

Have they somehow forgotten there is no limit to what I can do?

Fuck the balance.

I stand in the exact spot I was in when time froze, the red laser pointed directly at my chest. Magic pulses through me, ripping across my muscles until I can feel it in every frayed nerve. In my hand, the *chain,* not the knife, begins to turn to ash, melting away and away and out of existence.

"No, no, no, Gem, please, don't do this, please." Indy scrambles toward me, but my choice is made.

When I meet Buck's eyes, I say, "Now."

"Buck, NO! Do not let them do this!"

But the Evergod laughs and laughs and laughs. And time begins to move again.

And as it does, I use my magic to switch my body's position with Poppy's.

Zephyr does not have a moment to register what's happened before I plunge my knife into his chest. Lightning strikes the stained glass at the same moment a bullet does, and the windows explode all around us.

The shot connects with the Reaper's skull.

And I take the Cyclone's power for myself.

If they will never see anything but a monster when they look at me, then it's a monster I'm going to give them.

LIST OF CHARACTERS

The Pantheon, as described by the god of art

Already dead: The Sun, The Moon, The Inferno, The Caretaker, and The Hammer.[1]

The Evergod, god of time, Buck Wheeler, in Gracie

Can see all events, past and future. (And pays the price for it.) Can also slow and speed time. Maybe more?

The Magician, god of magic, you[2]

Can cast any spell as long as it doesn't off-set the balance.[3]

The Shade, god of things forbidden, ??,[4] in Brooklyn[5] (??)

Can manipulate people to do the awful things they think about but would never actually act on.[6] Now has the

---

1 RIP Zeke King.

2 That's me! Gem Echols.

3 Um . . . to be determined.

4 Enzo Truly.

5 Not anymore . . .

6 Listen . . . this makes it sound worse than it is. (Kind of.)

powers of Sun/Moon/Inferno/Caretaker/Hammer, too. Not sure how these will manifest for him.

The Mountain, god of land, "Willa Mae Hardy,"[7] in Gracie

Can control earth and animals.[8]

The Muse, god of art, me[9]

Can see things and people for what they really are and reveal them to others.

The Librarian, god of knowledge, Rhett Clancy, in Gracie

Can learn a person's thoughts from touch. (Power limited by being in a human body—too many thoughts can hurt him, like with Buck.)

The Reaper, god of death, Poppy White, in Gracie[10]

Can necrotize. Controlled afterlife in the Ether. (With the Caretaker.)

The Lionheart, god of battle, Marian Colquitt, in Gracie

Can cause battle-rages and possesses inhuman strategy and skill with weapons.

The Siren, god of sea, Murphy Foster, in Gracie

Can control water and water animals/plants.

~~**The Stillness,** god of peace, name unknown, location unknown~~

~~Can cause catatonic-like "peace" states in others.~~[11]

~~**The Cyclone,** god of air, name unknown, location unknown~~

~~Can control the weather.~~[12]

---

7 Rory.

8 Also has the powers of the Stillness. And is just so hot.

9 Indigo "Indy" Ramirez.

10 Or in hell—RIP Poppy?

11 RIP. :/

12 RIP. (:

The Heartkeeper, god of love, name unknown, location
  unknown
Can sense and manipulate any bonds of love between
  people.

ACKNOWLEDGMENTS

Although this book is a work of fiction, much of my experience growing up in the rural South can be found within its pages—and that's messy. The South is full of many good people who have been systematically disenfranchised, fed a steady diet of propaganda, and used as a distraction by those we should *actually* be angry at. And it would've threatened my life to stay there. In some ways, this story is both a love letter to and an exposé of the small town I once lived in. I miss you. I'm so glad I never have to go back.

I am extraordinarily grateful to the whole team at Wednesday (especially Tiffany, my editor) for seeing the potential in my story and helping shape what this book has become.

As always, I owe everything to my agents, Lee and Victoria, who saved my life once and haven't slowed down since.

My life would be nothing like it is—and I never would've become the person I needed to be in order to write this book—if it weren't for the support of my chosen family. Y'all know who you are. Thank you for letting me love you. Thank you for loving me in return.

For Fin. You changed everything. In turn, everything I do is yours. This was no exception.

And thank you to me. Thank you to the younger versions of myself who kept us alive however they had to when we were backed into a corner. You've earned your rest. I've got it from here.

The conclusion to the
**"ABSOLUTELY UNHINGED
AND UTTERLY UNFORGETTABLE"***
tale that begins in *Godly Heathens*

**"SHARP AS A BLADE, TWICE AS VICIOUS,
AND AN OUTSTRETCHED HAND ALL AT ONCE;**
a reminder to messy, angry kids that they can find their power
no matter what they must do to survive."
—ANDREW JOSEPH WHITE, *New York Times* bestselling author
of *Hell Followed with Us* on *Godly Heathens*

WEDNESDAY BOOKS